Crocotta's Hackles

Katharine E. Wibell

Phaesporia Press

i

Crocotta's Hackles

Printed in the United States of America.

First Edition November 2018

Visit us on the Web! KatharineWibellBooks.com

Phaesporia Press

ISBN-13: 978-0-9983779-4-0

DEDICATION

To the brave women of history and myth who expanded societal boundaries,
established new ways of thought, and were not afraid
to display the raw power of the feminine.

CONTENTS

SPECIAL THANKS

To April Wells-Hayes, my editor; to Karen Wibell, who served as reader and preserved my sanity; to the Madison Writers Group, who encouraged and supported me during this process; and OliviaProDesign for the cover.

And I tip my hat to all those who told the stories that became the myths and legends that I read while growing up—and still do.

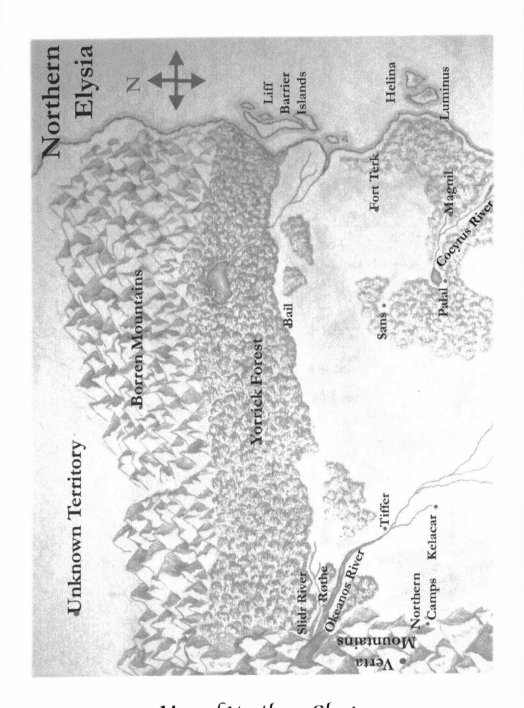

Map of Northern Elysia

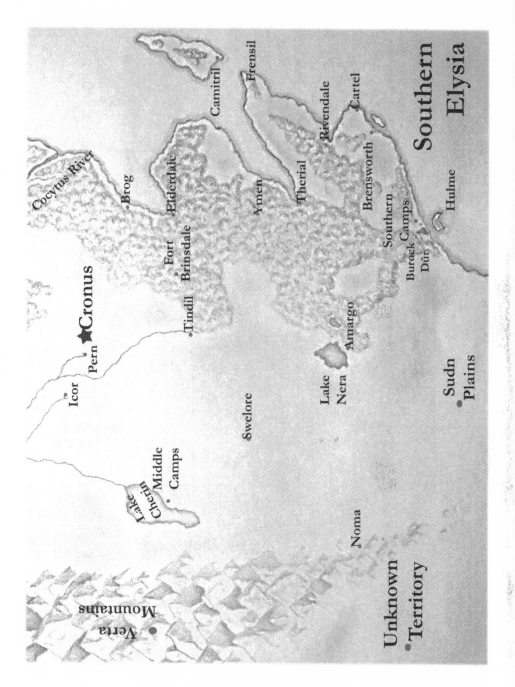

Map of Southern Elysia

CROCOTTA'S HACKLES

PART 1

Prologue

The translucent beam of moonlight slipped through the perfectly circular opening at the peak of the dome. The sanctuary's sole source of illumination traversed the chamber to its preordained destination. A pair of unblinking eyes, glinting silver, observed the slow procession in silence.

As the light crept up the ancient pedestal, a low hum began to reverberate. Heavy, throaty, almost a purr, the sounds resembled a melody that rose and fell in practiced rhythm.

When the beam breached the lip of the basin, the incantation ended. The vocalist approached and gazed upon the liquid in the hollow. Uttering the scripted words under her breath, she dipped her forefinger into a liquid so dark it seemed to suck all light into its depths. As she lifted her hand high, onyx droplets ran down skin the color of black pearls. As each drop fell, ripples raced across the gently undulating surface of the hollow.

"Crocotta, O magnanimous Queen of the Gods and all that lives, Prophetess, Matriarch of the Blessed. I have come to learn your will."

The moonglow reached the basin's quivering contents.

"Bestow upon me, your servant, keeper of your word, the knowledge you wish to instill."

The small pool calmed and, as the moonbeam hit its heart, an image manifested in the murky darkness of its surface. Two figures trudged in a field of ivory. Torrents of white pelted them from above. Bent low, they clutched at their wind-torn cloaks. A fur-wrapped form blended into the pristine landscape. Tall though not as tall as the other, this one was female.

The vision faded. The light had passed its peak.

In the chamber's deepening gloom, the woman smiled; a pleasant thought crossed her mind.

"They are almost here."

She cast her eyes upward and completed the appropriate rites. Lowering her head, she contemplated the basin for a moment, then briefly closed her eyes.

"It is time to send an invitation."

The woman receded into the shadows until only the silvery reflection of her eyes could be seen.

"It is *time* to bring Ullr and Issaura home."

As she vanished in the blackness, her unhindered laughter bounded upward to meet the observant moonlight.

1

Chapter 1

Tundra

White.

Mile after mile, white was the only color she could see. Ice and snow, flat and barren. The cold was even worse. Could anything survive this inhospitable climate? She hated the cold, the ice, the snow, the *white*.

It wasn't just the white nothingness that lay ahead. It was the platinum-blond hair blowing in her face. It was the white fur cloak, a gift from Apex and her only viable source of warmth, in that nothingness color. Even the ever-shrinking mountain range was capped in the horrible, unadulterated hue.

At one point, she wondered if she had become color blind, yet those thoughts were cast aside when she glimpsed her own olive-hued skin or spied her travel companion and his mongrel.

Looking back at the Borren Mountains, she silently cursed them for blocking her view of Elysia, her homeland—the kingdom she had left in order to save it. Somewhere in Elysia's heartland resided her military partner, the man she loved.

Closing her eyes, she tried to picture every minuscule detail, from the soft curls of his dark hair to the gentle blue of his eyes and the wonderful smile that always made her feel warm inside. If she concentrated long enough on his image, she could almost convince herself that she wasn't slowly freezing to death.

"Varren," she uttered.

The crown prince's name was swallowed by the wind.

By now, he would have been crowned king. How long had they been traveling? She had lost count of the days. Weeks, certainly. Maybe a month.

Every day was the same. She awoke to the white and walked northward, searching for any clue of life in the frigid wilderness. At least she wasn't alone. Well, at least today she wasn't. Recently her temperament toward her companion had grown as volatile as the blizzards that hit without warning. She was grateful he had come, true; yet to be with only one other person, day after day, in a land as unforgiving as this, was so very trying.

"Lluava." A voice rudely cut into her thoughts. Why did she hate the sound of it so?

"What now, Apex?" she growled. The huntsman had put up with her complaints, caught food until no more could be found, dealt with her bouts of anger, and refrained from judging her tears. Although Lluava rarely cried, the tears freezing on her skin always felt like ribbons of fire burning her face.

She hoped that Varren was more successful in his endeavor. As King of Elysia, he would be able to keep Head Councilman Themis in check. Although she doubted it, Themis might be willing to give up some of his power if Varren was in the capital.

Lluava was glad Varren wasn't alone. Talos, Byron, Yamir, and Rosalyn were with him. All her friends were together. All but her. She was forced to travel with Apex, a man she barely tolerated. Her relationship with him was tentative at best.

Apex pointed ahead. His strong back and shoulders were slumped from the cold. He looked nothing like the fierce warrior god that he had so personified during the battle for the North. In the unforgiving sunlight, his hair took on a bronze hue. At least it wasn't white.

"Look," he said, as tiny clouds materialized from his breath. "Tracks."

At first, Lluava didn't see them. The wolf-mix, Sköll, began sniffing about, and Lluava followed Apex's pet with her eyes. Watching him, she found she missed her own animal. Even though Onyx was a ratty, half-blind raven, she had grown fond of the black bird. He had disappeared after the siege of Alcazar Castle. Had he abandoned her during the battle? She couldn't blame the poor creature. More than once, she had thought she was going to meet her end. The Berserker Legion could have killed them all. Yet they hadn't. Someone had called them back—someone more powerful than Ambassador Alcove. Lluava would not refer to that man as the Raiders' leader anymore. He clearly wasn't.

And now, here she was, searching a desolate landscape for others like herself and Apex. Why? Because she and Apex were special. At least that was what they had been told. Apex still believed it. Good for him.

Lluava had begun to question her decision. Were they really special? True, they were Theriomorphs. The ability to change into an animal form distinguished them from humans such as Varren. Yet there were many Theriomorphs in Elysia.

Then again, she and Apex each had a dual form identical to the form of a god: hers a white tiger; his, the Yorrick wolverine. This was rare but not impossible, right? To be sure, they had both received weapons that mirrored the ones the gods possessed, weapons that changed form with them, but that was all coincidence. That was the only logical explanation: coincidence.

Sköll paused above slight imprints in the snow. Apex was right. An animal had trudged through not long ago. Lluava had never been good at tracking. Outside of the heightened senses typical of her race, she was not much help in these situations. Apex had grown up a huntsman in the north, well south of here. Hunting was an art, and he had the gift, one he had tried to share with her on their journey.

Many days had passed since they last crossed the path of any living creature. No wonder these tracks excited both the wolf-mutt and Apex. Lluava bent over the cloven imprints. It was a deer—but a different sort from the whitetails that frequented the Yorrick Forest, and vastly larger than the mountain goats that scaled the Borren Mountains.

Lluava was glad this wasn't a goat. Dried strips of that meat had lasted the bulk of their trek, and she had grown weary of the stringy flesh. Fresh meat of any kind would be welcome right now.

"This bull is heading off to the west," noted Apex. "With its slow gait, there is a chance we can catch up."

Her curiosity never fully waning, Lluava said, "Let me guess: it's a male by its size. But why a bull, not a buck?"

"Because," Apex said excitedly as he started walking in the direction the animal had taken. "It's not just a deer. It's a caribou."

There had been a Theriomorph in the southern training camps whose dual form was a caribou. He was never in her troop, so Lluava had seldom thought of him. All she remembered was that this animal form was shaggier than Talos's stag. A caribou was a big animal, which meant lots of meat. Her stomach growled. They needed food, or they would perish in this wasteland.

By evening, Lluava wasn't sure whether they had gained on the caribou. Pulling out the last bit of frozen goat meat, she gnawed on it in hope of alleviating her hunger.

She pitched her tent. The moss-green structure's thin material did not keep her warm, nor would it prevent an attack from a predator if any actually existed. Yet it provided privacy from Apex when she needed it and offered some protection from the blowing snow and wind.

As she struggled to shove the stakes into the icy ground, Lluava asked, "Why would other Theriomorphs live here? Nothing else does. Maybe they are hiding in the Yorrick Forest."

These sentiments weren't new. Lluava had voiced them many times before, always hoping for a different answer.

"I am familiar with everyone who travels in those woods," commented Apex. "If an Incarn existed there, I would have known."

Incarn. The word made Lluava want to vomit. That's what she was supposed to be, wasn't it? That's what she had been told before she left. Some toy the gods created when they wanted to play on the earth. Lluava's lip curled. She refused to believe it.

She had a family, one that loved her. Lluava could not imagine that her siblings and her mother were not real, not hers. Apex never doubted these lies because he had never had a family. He needed to believe that there was a reason for his childhood struggles. But Lluava had grown up a happy child in Rivendale. Despite the unwarranted prejudice directed toward her as a Theriomorph, she missed that small village.

"The best chance of finding other Incarn," Apex continued, "is far outside Elysia's borders in these unexplored lands. We need to keep looking."

Lluava did not want to find the other Incarn anymore. How could they help fend off Elysia's enemy? She had seen what the Berserker Legion, those unnaturally large Raiders, were capable of. Though already horribly strong and adept fighters, once they smoked their drug, they became something else, something inhuman. They lost all sense of pain, all emotion except rage, and they would continue to attack until they bled to death. It took several men together to take down a single Berserker.

Elysia was not prepared for an enemy like that. The kingdom needed help, that was certain; but finding and uniting all Incarn into one force could hardly be a workable solution. Lluava was skilled at fighting because she had trained in the camps, not because she was the Incarn for Theri, Goddess of War, who was also called Issaura. Apex's wild demeanor and brute strength were needed to survive in the Outlands, not because he was the Incarn for Ullr, God of War, also known as Tyr.

If Lluava and Apex did find other Incarn, how could they help? Would they know how to fight? Doubtful. Would their skills be deemed worthy? Probably not. If two war gods could not defend the kingdom, how could the Incarn for Slypher, Goddess of Air, or Hendren, God of Virtue and Knowledge, be of service?

This quest was madness. They were wasting their time, Lluava was almost certain. Almost. But what if there was some truth to this? What if a small group of Theriomorphs, each with the dual form of a god, could actually be the key to defeating the Raiders and forcing them to return to their empire across the sea? What if….

Lluava growled. This time it didn't come from her stomach. As she crawled into her tent to lie down, she hoped her volatile nightmares would subside and allow her to sleep through the night. She was tired of waking up screaming. The nightmares never ceased. They even seemed to be getting worse. Lluava's only hope was that on the day the Raiders' ships disappeared over the horizon, so would the bad dreams.

From Apex's tent, she heard his nightly chant. Before sleeping, he would repeat all twelve gods' names and their animal forms. She knew he wanted to make sure he would recognize the other Incarn in their dual forms. He repeated the names and animals as if he might somehow forget.

The humans were lucky. They only had one god, some omnipotent being who was supposedly powerful enough to have created everything. Lluava had always struggled with the idea that a single god could watch over the entire human race; maybe that's why Elysia had been overlooked.

Lluava didn't care one way or another. Her father had raised her in the old beliefs, and to her mother's dismay she had never converted to the human religion after he died. Lluava had already lost faith. The gods, whatever they were, had let her father die. What good were they?

Now, with this new bloodshed Lluava was even more certain that all religion was unwarranted. She still had questions. Something must have started everything, but the idea that some powerful god cared anything about them yet allowed this violence—this destruction, this death—made no sense. Whatever the creative entity, it surely held no love for them, nor did she feel any connection to that elusive higher power.

Let her friends and family pray if that made them feel better. Lluava refused to accept such false beliefs. They were alone in this world and must fend for themselves. They must make their own destinies. Lluava would make sure hers did not end here. She had promised Varren that she would return, and she would keep that promise.

"Three more days," she muttered. "I will give him three more days before we go home."

That night, Lluava's dreams took a new direction. The white that had suffused all her thoughts now took on vibrant, lush colors. Everything around her was green. Was she in a forest? If so, it was different from any she had seen before.

Trees sent filtered light through their canopy, but they were a strange, unknown variety. The underbrush was thick and full of broad leaves longer than her arm. Tangled vines cascaded from above, and flowers reminiscent of those in the capital's garden bloomed in profusion.

One flower caught her eye, the only one she recognized: a black-and-white striped beauty known in Elysia as the Theri iris. The first time Varren gave her one, he said it reminded him of her dual form. Afterward, he had given her one every night in a fresh bouquet.

Lluava moved closer. As she approached, the flower began to wither and dropped off the plant before she could reach it. Almost tripping over a root, she realized that her clothes were stuck to her body and a film of sweat was building. How hot was it? She couldn't tell. The plant's leaves begin to brown and wither.

What was happening? As Lluava reached toward the plant, tendrils sprang out at her like serpents striking at prey. Suddenly a vine wrapped itself around her arm. She tried to untwist the thick botanical rope as it looped around her ankle.

Vines don't do this, she thought. They can't grow that fast. Was she hallucinating? All at once, she realized what it was: an anaconda! Immobilized by the snake's ever-tightening grip, she heard a sound reverberate through the forest. It was the pealing of laughter, rising and falling in waves.

"Issaura!" the voice called out, "Fight! Kill or die!" The laughter returned as the coils of the giant snake contracted about her waist.

Lluava couldn't breathe, much less defend herself. The air in her lungs was being squeezed out. She was suffocating. Her gasps for air were drowned out by the unending laughter. Could she have spoken, she would have screamed, "Stop laughing! Help me!"

Without air, Lluava's thoughts were beginning to fog. Was this her end?

A hand grabbed her shoulder and ripped her free of the anaconda's coils and the frightening dream.

"Lluava, wake up!" Apex was shouting. He pulled her partially out of her tent, which had collapsed during the night. "You're okay."

"I can't sleep anymore." She was exhausted. "I can't take the dreams."

"You'll rest better once you have eaten," Apex told her. "Look, our friend has returned."

There on the ground were the lone caribou's hoof prints. It must have decided to explore their camp during the night. This meant it was nearby.

"Let's go hunting!" said Apex.

Energized, Lluava sprang to her feet and reached for Issaura's Claws, her weapons. "Way ahead of you."

She slipped each golden Claw over her knuckles, smiling at her distorted reflection in the three slightly curved blades. Lluava tested each, relaxing her hands so the claws retracted, then balling her hands into fists around the grip, which caused the blades to spring erect. They felt so right, like razor-sharp extensions of herself.

Ever since she had broken the arm-brace attachments Holly had made for her, Lluava had been more cautious when she used the Claws. She was able to use them, but her old shoulder injury could be aggravated by the strain of impact. Nonetheless, if her shoulder became dislocated again, she could reset it. A good breakfast would be worth the pain.

Nearby, Apex pulled out Ullr's Fangs. The twin Gladius swords looked as fierce as the determination on the huntsman's face. By his feet, Sköll stretched and yawned. It seemed that everyone would take part in the hunt.

Several hours later, Apex spotted a brown shape treading off into the distance: their prey. Food would be coming soon. Lluava salivated at the thought of fresh venison. They couldn't let this animal escape.

Following Apex's command, the trio moved downwind and began to inch their way closer to the unsuspecting creature. Though not heavy, it was surprisingly well fed, which meant it had a food source nearby. More good news, Lluava thought happily. Maybe their luck was turning.

Lluava tested the air as the huntsman gave an unspoken command to Sköll. The wolf-mix bolted toward the caribou. Suddenly, the young woman's senses exploded.

"Stop him!" she shouted, but it was too late. Apex whistled, but the mongrel was solely focused on its prey.

Exasperated, Lluava sank to the ground. "He's chasing a Theriomorph."

Chapter 2

Splitting Apart

A second sharp whistle sounded.

Lluava recognized the small silver device. About the length of a finger, it was the same instrument she had used to summon the huntsmen on her first journey through the Yorrick Forest. Its pitch was beyond the range of human ears, but Theriomorphs could barely endure the shrill incessant trill.

Was the sound meant to call off Sköll? The wolf-dog seemed to falter and slow down. At the same time, the caribou Theriomorph caught sight of the charging wolf-mix and bounded off at a remarkable pace.

"Damn it," snapped Apex as he watched their only lead disappear.

Lluava felt sorry for her companion. "You're a huntsman; track him. Come on."

"No. We should return to camp," sighed Apex in his gruff voice. "Pack up our supplies."

"Or," Lluava countered, "we follow the caribou now and not risk losing him. He is still within our reach if we don't let him get too far ahead of us."

Shaking his head, Apex said, "We are getting our supplies."

"Do you expect our supplies to wander off while we are gone?" asked Lluava. "The only other Theriomorph in this cursed frozen land is escaping; our camp is stationary. We need to go after the man we have been searching for this whole wretched time. If we lose him, we have failed. Or are you afraid you will lose the camp?"

"You're such a…child," Apex said. Lluava knew he had wanted to use a different word. This riled her even more.

"I'll turn eighteen this month. And what of my age?" demanded Lluava.

"You're a quarter century old—you can't comprehend what is at risk if we lose that Theriomorph. I'm going after him. Follow or not, that's up to you."

Turning on her heel, Lluava strode off in the direction of the caribou. At first, she didn't care if Apex followed her or not, but as soon as she heard his footfalls, a sigh of relief passed her lips.

Lluava would never allow Apex to see her fear of heading into the wilderness with no clue where to go or how to survive. But now there was a chance to communicate with another Theriomorph, one who lived in the Outlands and who might lead them to other Incarn. This was their mission. They had to succeed. Failure meant wasted time—time that Elysia could not afford to lose.

Sköll, who had trotted ahead, stopped and looked warily about. Lluava noticed that the wind had grown appreciably stronger. She realized what was about to occur even without Apex's warning: "A blizzard's coming!"

Her stomach flipped; she knew what that meant,

"Back to our camp! Hurry!" she shouted as she turned to run. "Or else it will get buried."

Apex reached out and grabbed her. "Too late."

"No!" Lluava balked. Their remaining food, shelter, and supplies, were all at camp. Leaving it meant losing everything.

"It's already gone. We need to dig down. Help me."

Apex began to hack at the frozen ground with one of Ullr's Fangs. Lluava followed suit with the Claws. Once chunks of icy snow broke apart, they tossed them aside to carve out a trench.

The winds began to tear by. Lluava could see snowfall rapidly approaching. The wall of white would be upon them in no time. As fast as they could, the pair ripped out the final slabs of ice and then lowered themselves into the trench. At some unheard command, Sköll crept in beside Apex, who stretched his heavy fur cloak over all three of them.

Clutching the edges of the cloak, Lluava pushed her body against Apex's in a desperate attempt to stay warm, just as the roaring gales of snow began to blow over them. At first, she worried that the cloak would be ripped from their grip, but as the weight of massing snow increased, she began to fear suffocation.

Lluava sensed Apex's heartbeat quickening. Was he scared? Was that possible? She could not envision Apex afraid. He was far too resilient. If he was afraid, it had to be bad.

The winds rampaged above them for several hours, and the weight of snow on their backs continued to increase. Strangely, even though they were encapsulated in ice and snow, warmth could still be found. While Apex may have been happy with this fact, his companion was not. She was trapped, entombed, unable to break free.

Lluava began to panic. The thought of being imprisoned under the snow revived her fear of dying in a situation she could not escape. Was the air decreasing? Why else was it so hard to breathe?

Next to her, Apex must have sensed her growing terror. Before she could attempt to break out of their underground shelter, he maneuvered his arm over her. With light pressure, he made sure she made no move to escape. Though the teen could have easily resisted, his presence reminded her that she was not alone. Concentrating all her attention, Lluava focused on Varren and her desire to return to his side.

"It's over," Apex finally whispered.

Listening, Lluava realized the winds had stopped. The blizzard had passed. Everything was dark. Her fear returned; they were buried alive. The layer of snow felt heavy on her back. How much had fallen during the storm? Her breathing became faster again. She had to escape.

Suddenly Lluava was forced away from Apex and shoved into the hard wall of ice. What was going on?

There was a muffled crackle and then a beam of light from above. Lluava gulped the cold, fresh air as strong arms pulled her from the frozen tunnel. When she spotted the paw prints surrounding the hole, she realized what had happened.

Apex had shifted into his large dual form and broken through the snow. Why hadn't she thought of that? Then again, she and her dual form had been at odds for a while. Recently, when she shifted into tigress form she would lose control, lose herself in her animal side, and black out. When she came to, she would be confronted by bloodshed—blood *she* had shed. But, inexplicably, she would retain no memory of what she had done. So, no. She must not shift. To learn she had killed an innocent person—or even worse, a friend—would be unbearable.

"Thanks," she said as Sköll slipped by her legs and almost knocked her back down.

The three of them had survived, but for how much longer? Because of her, they had lost everything. Even if they double back to try to find their campsite, the likelihood was minuscule that they would see any sign of it that wasn't buried by snow.

"What are we going to do now?" Lluava asked aloud.

"Survive," answered Apex abruptly. He had never been much of a talker. Sometimes Lluava was grateful for this; at other times, she yearned to hear another voice even if it was her own.

"Well, where do you want to go?" Lluava hoped the answer would be in her favor.

"Not back to Elysia."

This was not the answer she had hoped for.

"Why not?" she griped. "There's nothing left here for us. We've wasted too much time already."

"Because," Apex began as he pointed beyond her, "he is waiting for us."

Standing like a dark smudge against the vast expanse of white was the caribou. The Theriomorph was watching them, waiting for them to take some sort of action. Why? Did he expect them to follow? Did he want to talk with them? Was he intending to help?

Lluava shook off the remaining snow that clung to her white fur cloak.

"Let's see what he wants."

Sköll kept his ears perked and alert as he eyed the caribou. Although he did not charge after the animal, he kept turning to look at Apex as if waiting for a signal.

The reindeer calmly observed their approach but began walking away before they could get too close. At first Lluava was confused, but then she realized the Theriomorph was not only watching them but also making sure he was still in their sights.

"He's leading us somewhere." She stated the obvious. "Do you think he's a friend?"

"I'm reserving judgment," Apex replied, his right hand resting lightly on the carved pommel of one of Ullr's Fangs.

The trio followed the caribou throughout the evening and into the night. Even with the aid of starlight, the lack of lunar presence made it hard to see. Lluava was dumbfounded that, despite her heightened night vision, the reindeer continued to slip in and out of sight, preferring to remain on the cusp of darkness. They had to focus on the tracks left in the snow, which were easier to follow than the Theriomorph.

The excitement of the unusual situation kept Lluava moving. This was worth a sleepless night. Her high spirits returning, she happily led the way.

There was a rushing noise up ahead. Water! The caribou was leading them to fresh water! He was helping them.

"Come on!" Lluava summoned her lagging companions as she moved rapidly toward the sound.

"Lluava," Apex called out behind her. "Slow down. Stop!"

"But there's water up ahead," she countered, not slowing her speed.

"Stay where you are!" growled Apex.

What was his problem? Lluava glared back at the huntsman to see him tentatively approaching her. Far behind him, Sköll paced in the snow but did not follow Apex. What was going on?

Then Lluava heard it—the crack. First came the sound, then a line appeared in the snow. Crouching, she brushed away the fresh white fluff and exposed fractured ice. Eyes growing wide, the teen looked about her.

She was walking on top of a frozen river. Unfortunately, the ice beneath was not thick enough to bear her weight; several more cracks appeared.

"Apex," she croaked out.

"I'm coming," he replied. "Stand still."

Every muscle tensing, Lluava focused on the numerous lines in the ice at her feet.

"Lluava, listen to me," Apex began. "Lie down on your stomach and stretch your arms and legs out on the ice like a log. You need to distribute your weight as much as possible."

By the sound of the huntsman's voice, he was not coming closer. Clearly he was not going to risk breaking the ice with his own weight. Following his orders, Lluava cautiously lay down on her stomach. She felt the ice shift under her in minute but horrifying ways.

"Okay," Apex breathed out.

Lluava heard the concern in his tone.

"Now, start rolling slowly toward me."

Bringing her arms together on the icy surface, she slowly rolled onto her back and paused. The ice cracked but held. She repeated the movement, this time rolling onto her stomach, and began to make slow progress. Apex carefully lowered himself and motioned for her to keep moving.

"Don't stop. Steady, now."

Lluava's heart was pounding so hard she feared its beating might break the ice. She reached out. Apex grabbed her hand and pulled her toward him. Slowly the pair inched backward until they reached thicker ice. Only then did they stand up.

"Okay. Okay," Lluava huffed as she tested her footing and found it sound. A form moving in the darkness caught her attention. She stared into the night until she could make out the caribou moving toward them.

The Theriomorph's eyes sparkled in the dark. Did this Theriomorph not realize that it could talk in its animal form? Lluava hadn't known how to do that for years. Was this why he remained? Nodding in the direction of the animal, Apex now took note of their observer.

The caribou took several steps forward and then reared, sending its forelegs flailing in the air. As the large animal landed, a resounding crack was heard, and a web of fractures spread across the icy plane. Looking directly at them, the reindeer reared again.

"Stop!" yelled Lluava as Apex pulled her back. "Watch it!"

The deer's second impact caused a ripple effect of breaking ice. Large islands of white liberated themselves from the grip of the mainland. Those nearest the river's central current were carried rapidly downstream. The caribou had lured them onto the frozen river. Now he was trying to send them to a watery death.

"We have to get to shore," snarled Apex as he jumped over a widening fissure. Lluava followed, but the gaps between the drifting ice chunks were increasing rapidly, and the block nearest the bank was already floating farther into the river.

Without warning, Apex skidded to a halt. Lluava passed him and jumped, barely landing on the center of a large ice floe. When she did not hear him follow her, she turned. His icy sheet, now caught by the tug of the river, was floating away.

She felt hers pick up speed. With nothing to grab hold of, Lluava slid about as the shattered sheets of ice collided with each other on their aquatic journey. A large floe rammed into the side of her natural raft. She slipped. With a last quick gasp of breath, the teen fell into the frozen water.

Beneath the surface, the water was almost pitch black. The current dragged her down, beneath an icy ceiling. There were few gaps among the drift ice, but Lluava struggled to swim toward one.

Her white fur cloak, now waterlogged, was pulling her down. She would not reach the surface with its extra weight. Shrugging it off, she kicked her way to the top. As she gasped for breath, she heard Apex shouting. He had to be nearby, but with water in her eyes and sections of ice bashing into her Lluava could not orient herself.

Forced to dive under the ice again lest she be smashed to bits, Lluava searched for another gap among the floes of surface ice. Her body was growing numb. She would not survive the cold much longer. Using her last resort, Lluava shifted.

She felt the instant sensation of burning in her core, which then extended to her extremities. She did not have to see in the blackness to sense fur emerging over her body; she felt her bones and muscles shifting, cracking, and reforming. The piercing sensation of her tail erupting from the base of her vertebrae offered hope that in this form she might have a chance.

Her weapons, forged from an ancient, forgotten Theriomorph material, also remolded themselves. Melting down but not floating away, the golden material coated Lluava's front claws. In mere moments, the white tigress resurfaced, clawing her way up onto any section of ice that could hold her large body.

Another shape similar in size paddled nearby in the maze of ice. The gigantic wolverine's enormous head bobbed past her. The creature was headed toward the largest frozen island, and Lluava followed in the dark.

If the ice floe was large enough and strong enough, there was a chance they could escape the freezing water and rest. Had either Apex or Lluava remained in human form, they would have died of hypothermia. Thanks to their thick coats of fur, they would survive a bit longer.

Once the tigress reached the ice, she dug her gilded claws into the surface. Using her remaining strength, she pulled herself up. Rolling onto her back, she heaved a sigh. Nearby she heard Apex moan.

They were alive—at least for now.

Chapter 3

Blind Suspicion

Darkness still held sway when Lluava woke. Her white-and-black fur was losing the battle to maintain warmth. How long had she been in her dual form? As far as she could tell, she was still fully in control of herself.

Recently, whatever caused her to black out seemed to correlate with shifting into her white tigress form. Lluava looked quickly about to see if Apex was all right. He was asleep, still lying on his side and breathing heavily. She had not hurt him, at least not yet.

Lluava watched the rise and fall of the Yorrick wolverine's chest. The enormous beast was an amazing animal to behold. Actual wolverines were either extinct or wandering the remote forest for which they were named. Matching the white tigress's size, the bronze-furred creature's violent temperament was comparable to that of a honey badger but considerably more dangerous. At least in that form, Apex might be able to defend himself against her. But why take the chance?

Shifting into human form, Lluava curled up in a ball. She would rather risk the cold than the possibility of harming her companion. She had gotten Apex into this whole mess, hadn't she? There was no way she would make it worse.

Her clothes—made of Endun, a rare material woven in olden days by Theriomorphs—shifted with her. Although the cloth was light and resilient enough to wear, it was not warm. Cupping her hands in front of her face, Lluava blew on her fingers to prevent them from growing numb. Were the tips of her fingers turning blue? She could not tell in the dark. She kept Issaura's Claws on her hands even though the metal chilled her skin faster.

She could not risk them sliding off their icy island.

"What do you think you're doing?"

Apex's tone of voice was not pleasant. What was he angry about now?

The wolverine was standing up. Lluava could see the metallic bronze encasing his muzzle. Ullr's Fangs shifted differently from her Claws. Once, she had wondered how their weapons could be capable of such strange transformations. But she was used to them now. What did it matter, anyway? The weapons helped protect them.

Apex growled out, "What in the names of the gods possessed you to shift back? You'll freeze!"

"I don't care," Lluava said. "I will not lose myself to the darkness again."

The wolverine remained silent for a long while. Was he angry that she had lost the cloak he'd made? She doubted it. It must be something else. Lluava had already told him about her loss of control when she shifted, and the carnage she left behind. Apex had never seemed to judge her. Yet now his eyes gleamed in a different way.

"I don't like shifting into my dual form either."

"Why not?" Lluava asked, surprised.

"I was around your age—eighteen I think—when my own blackouts began to occur. The things that happen when you lose control are… there are no words."

"Why didn't you tell me this before?" She had no idea this happened to him, too. It comforted her to know that she was not the only one, that someone understood. She should have expected as much.

"You will come to terms with this darker side in your own time."

"So…," Lluava began. Wanting to confirm her other suspicions, she asked, "Does this mean that you believe in the Incarn and the Guardians who protect their secrets? Do you believe the blackouts occur when one of the gods takes over?"

"I believe we must do what we must in order to survive. Now, shift into your dual form."

Lluava was not happy with Apex's blatant deflection of her questions. Originally, she had not considered him religious, but after Councilman Hyrax explained their alleged purpose in life, the huntsman had seemed to change.

Apex stared her down. She knew he was right. To fend off the cold, she needed to be in her dual form. Her winter coat was thick enough to insulate her, but still she balked at his order. She hated to give him the satisfaction of being right. He didn't need anything else to boost his ego.

"What do you think will happen to Sköll?" Lluava questioned as she thought about the poor wolf-mutt pacing longingly on the snow bank.

"He'll survive."

"Do you really think he will be all right on his own?"

"He's gone, Lluava. What does it matter?" was all the reply the huntsman clearly cared to give.

Lluava couldn't feel the tips of her fingers. How long could she last?

She watched several smaller sections of ice collide and shatter into bits.

"We need to get off this," she said suddenly.

"Unless you feel comfortable 'step-stoning' it across, I think we have to wait until the current slows."

"Do you think we could do that? Step-stone, I mean."

"That was not an actual suggestion. The ice will turn, sink, move under you. It may even break apart from your weight. Don't even—"

She cut him off. "Do you want to wait until we freeze? How long before our island smashes apart like the others?"

A small section of ice rammed into theirs and rocked it slightly.

"See what I mean?" she asked testily.

"Don't even think about it."

"There's a large section approaching." Lluava pointed to the gray form moving toward them on the current.

"You won't make it."

"On the count of three."

Apex took a step closer, and their raft swayed.

"One."

"Lluava," Apex growled as he carefully moved toward her.

"Two."

"Stop."

"Three!"

The entire block of ice rocked so violently that the pair was almost hurled off. Lluava dug Issaura's Claws into the surface to keep from slipping as Apex skidded down beside her. Once they had righted themselves, Apex pointed at the far end of their piece of ice and asked, "Is that—?"

"A grappling hook!" Lluava exclaimed. A five-barbed device had punctured the end of the ice farthest from them.

"Watch it!" Apex bellowed as a second and then a third hooked tool bit into their raft, causing it to undulate in the water. Without a break in the frenetic movement, the cords attached to the hooks tautened, and the little island of ice moved toward shore. At least, that is what they assumed, for the entire river was enveloped in a thickening mist.

"We need to get off this immediately," agreed Apex.

This time, Lluava did not argue. He was right. Whoever was pulling the ice to shore might not have good intentions. Based on their recent encounter with the Theriomorph from the Outlands, caution was the safest bet.

Shifting, Lluava slid into the water and began to paddle downstream toward dry land. They were not far from shore, but their swim was harrowing, with numerous close calls among the floating boulders of ice. Navigating the river took them much longer as their limbs grew numb in the frigid water.

Once Lluava's feet touched ground, she hoisted herself onto the bank with a sigh. Nearby, Apex clawed at slippery footholds until he, too, had hauled himself out.

They were safe, but there was no time to rest. Someone had thrown the grappling hooks; therefore, somewhere upriver was an unknown group of people. Lluava and Apex had to find out who they were. They both shook themselves off and began to stalk this new prey.

As they followed the riverbank, they could hear the murmur of voices. Lluava shifted into human form, and Apex did the same; their smaller, human forms would be easier to hide.

Cloaked in the waning darkness, they peered around a snowdrift. Several dozen warmly dressed men were hauling in the large section of ice upon which Apex and Lluava had taken refuge. Another group was cutting ice into blocks and loading them onto sleighs.

Giving her companion a sideways glance, Lluava saw him shrug; whatever these men were doing, it was foreign to him, too. Keeping silent, the pair lay in wait until the men finished their work. Once the sleighs were loaded and ready, the men lined up to leave.

"Where are their work animals?" Lluava asked in a whisper. Suddenly, several men transformed into oxen and horses.

"Theriomorphs!" Lluava gasped out. Yet why was she so surprised?

"Come on," Apex said as he began to slink after them. When Lluava hesitated, he motioned her to follow. "This is why we are here, isn't it?"

For several miles, they trailed the Theriomorphs. As the sun rose, Lluava and Apex dropped farther back to avoid being seen. The land was no longer flat; large shapes loomed up in the dim light. Were they in a mountain range? That was impossible. The Borren Mountains were behind them. How long had they been adrift on the river? How far had they traveled?

Keeping silent, Lluava could not be sure what Apex was thinking. Regardless of where they were now, what would they do when they found the men's camp? Walk up and talk with them? Stay hidden and observe them for a while?

She did not have long to ponder their options, as she felt a pair of sharp objects press against her back. From the corner of her eye, she saw Apex reluctantly move his hands away from the hilts of Ullr's Fangs. She, on the other hand, had balled her hands into fists, causing the Claws to remain erect.

Pivoting, Lluava sliced at the spearheads, splintering one while the other slashed at the side of her arm. Backing away, she concentrated on the weapons that drove toward her again and again.

Hearing a muffled sound, she turned to see Apex forced to his knees by a half-dozen spearmen, with more headed their way. Too many to fight alone.

In a strange accent, a small man with slicked-back white hair commanded, "Drop your weapons!"

Lluava took one more step back.

"Or we'll kill your friend."

Could she really relinquish Issaura's Claws to these men? One had already collected Ullr's Fangs and was admiring their wolverine-headed pommels. Could they even comprehend what these weapons could do? And in the wrong hands, what harm could occur?

The Claws were an extension of herself. If she surrendered them, she would feel broken. Once, they had disappeared for several days, and it had been horrible. But these men had Apex. They certainly looked as if they would kill him if she tried anything.

As soon as Lluava slid Issaura's Claws off her hands, she was thrown to the ground, blindfolded, and tied up. Jerked to her feet, she was half dragged, half shoved onto one of the sleighs. Apex was thrown alongside her. With a lurch, the sleigh moved and began to pick up speed. Lluava wished she knew where they were going.

"Are you okay?" Apex muttered. Lluava could hear him moving. She lay on her stomach and found it hard to position herself in any comfortable way while the sleigh bounced over snowdrifts.

"I'll live," she retorted. "Do you think we are going to their camp?"

"We'll find out."

"Could you try to be comforting?" she griped.

"I said, we'll see."

She was left to ponder the possibilities in silence.

***

Lluava discovered it was easy to lose track of time while blindfolded. Every time she tried to move around, someone pushed her back down. She was careful not to aggravate her old shoulder injury. If she had to make a break for it at some point, she preferred to have two functioning forelimbs.

When the party made camp, they refused to remove her blindfold or bindings despite her pleading. On the first day, she was tied to the sleigh. On the second day, she was given some lukewarm gruel; on the third, frozen jerky; goat, of course.

Unable to see, Lluava lost track of the turns they had made. Yet without her sight, she could focus on her other senses. During their fourth day, she picked up an earthy scent that began to penetrate the crisp smell of snow. Shortly thereafter, the meager light that filtered through the blindfold disappeared, and she was suddenly thrust into total darkness.

Lluava was pulled quickly off the sleigh. An extended commotion ensued, during which she was forced to stand still. No word was spoken; the threat from the spear points made it unnecessary. Finally, she was shoved onto another sleigh. At least this one had a thick layer of straw to cushion the bumps. No, wait. Could this be a wagon? Once jolted into motion, the creaks and groans sounded just like the wagon her mother used in Rivendale.

Inching her way to the wagon's side, she bumped into Apex. She was relieved, and having him with her was comforting. However, she wished more than anything else that Varren were here instead.

Gradually the light returned, along with the sound of crashing water. Something else had changed: the temperature. The frigid air had dissipated almost immediately. Not only was it not cold, it was actually hot, she realized, and the air was thick with an abundance of moisture. Although Lluava had grown up in southern Elysia, she had never felt humidity like this.

Sweat beaded on her chest and back; her clothes clung tightly and added to her discomfort. More sounds were heard. A large insect buzzed past her ear. Were birds singing? She was completely confused.

Through her blindfold, the light began to flicker. Lluava slowly realized they were traveling through some sort of forest, the only clue the sound of a breeze ruffling leaves. But how could this be? They had been traveling through arctic tundra. What had happened to all the ice and snow? And what was the source of this abysmal heat?

The wagon stopped.

"Take those off," a voice ahead of them commanded.

Clumsy hands pulled away her blindfold, catching a few strands of hair.

"Ow!" she yelped. Ignoring her, the man removed Apex's blindfold.

Looking around, Lluava saw thick, tall trees covered in ferns and vines. She did not recognize any of the vegetation.

"Where are we?" she asked, not expecting an answer.

Apex was wide-eyed. "Lluava, turn around."

Rolling onto her other side, she saw what had captivated Apex, and her own eyes widened, too.

Ahead of them, in the middle of the jungle, was what could only be a city—but a city unlike any she had ever seen. The buildings towered over them, the architecture appearing strangely fluid, lacking the rigidity of uniform vertical and horizontal lines and right angles. Stone buildings with roofs shaped like teardrops reminded Lluava of conical towers. Other structures were intricately carved layers of stone stacked into step pyramids. Door and window openings were arched rather than rectangular. Somehow, the city seemed to rise organically from the jungle. Here and there stood giant statues of the Theriomorph goddess Crocotta, Queen of the Gods; the carved images seemed to watch over the city like caring mothers. Amid the dense tree canopy, the city glittered—exotic, foreign, different from anything constructed in Elysia. The pair gazed in wonderment. What was this place?

Abruptly, Lluava and Apex were pulled to their feet. She recognized the small, white-haired man and his now familiar heavy accent.

"Welcome to Leucrocotta," he told them, smiling. "The greatest Theriomorph stronghold left on this continent."

Chapter 4

Ruire's Ruling

Lluava couldn't speak. What she saw and heard was unbelievable. How could this be? A Theriomorph city existing outside Elysia? And what about this jungle? Where did it come from? Had she died? Was she dreaming? None of this could exist. Could it?

Apex slowly turned to face her. "A god's city. I thought they had all been destroyed in the wars."

Lluava knew the tales of the Landon Wars, when Varren's ancestors had crossed the ocean, laid claim to the Theriomorph land, and instigated centuries of bloody conflict. The ancient Theriomorph cities were destroyed, abandoned or replaced by human ones. A few monuments and temples remained—but nothing like this. This seemed like an intact civilization.

Lluava noticed a thin, spidery individual glaring at them. "For a Theriomorph," said Spider, "you know very little."

"They are from the Banished Lands," countered the small man. His large, ever-watchful eyes continued to observe the girl like a housecat observing a lizard. "What did you expect?"

He turned to his captives and gave them a long, searching look. "We will take them to the ruire. He will sort out what is to be done."

Hands on Lluava's shoulder pushed her forward. "Move!" one of the men barked out. "Get going!"

The party of ice bearers split up. The wagons filled with their frigid cargo groaned as the larger group hauled them away, along with the now empty wagon that had borne Apex and Lluava. The few remaining men slung packs on their backs and prepared to leave. From this point on, they would need to travel on foot.

As they approached the city, Lluava was overwhelmed not only by what she was seeing but also by what it meant. If this place existed in the Outlands, could others exist as well?

As they moved off through the jungle, the city seemed to rise effortlessly out of the vegetation and vanish back into it. There were apparently no walls for protection, no guards watching with wary eyes. Did these people really feel so safe, so secure, that they had no reason to defend themselves?

While it was hard for Lluava to turn her gaze away from what lay ahead, she tried to take in her immediate surroundings as well. The thick jungle canopy encircled them and obstructed her view. Only the opening above Leucrocotta permitted glimpses of the brilliant blue sky. The sun had slipped past its peak and could not be seen from the gap in the foliage.

"Watch your step," the small man warned.

The trail suddenly turned into a stone avenue. Unlike the few rough, cobblestoned roads scattered throughout Elysia, this was made from flat rocks that interlocked perfectly.

"Is this the border of the city?" Apex asked. There was no reply.

Buildings loomed before them. Entire structures were covered with bas-reliefs depicting stories from the *Karmasana* and *Virisinu*, the Theriomorph holy books. Other scenes depicted events unknown to Lluava. Could these represent tales she had not yet studied? Or were they of people who had built this city long ago? Was the history of Leucrocotta scattered across the walls of the city? Lluava's curiosity grew, yet she did not voice her questions. Their escorts did not appear willing to respond to strangers.

Curious faces appeared at open windows and doorways—faces similar to those of Elysia yet far different. Many displayed piercings or strange tattoos and brandings on their exposed skin. Others had intricately inked designs covering their facial features.

The markings reminded Lluava of her friend Yamir and the rogue clans that refused to conform within Elysia's borders. Was their custom a long-lost practice from the time before? Were those bands of thieves remaining true to an ancient past, continuing a tradition whose meaning had been forgotten?

"This way," Spider hissed as he led them to a road that veered left. Lluava could sense his dislike. His steely gaze cut into her like a butcher planning how to slice a slab of meat.

Lluava asked the small, catlike man, "Are they afraid of us?"

"Afraid?" he reiterated as he looked over the city dwellers. "No. We just don't have many outsiders here."

They had arrived at a domed building built on a tall, raised platform and encircled by a row of columns.

"Wait here." After climbing giant steps, each twice as high as a normal one, he passed through an open door.

The remaining men watched Lluava and Apex closely as if expecting them to run. Even Spider seemed on high alert. With hands bound and weapons confiscated, Lluava would hardly be so foolish. Nor would Apex, she hoped.

The small man eventually appeared at the top of the stairs and waved them up. Spider followed behind the two captives while his other comrades turned and then dispersed.

At the top of the stairs, Lluava could see into the building. Rows of tiered seating descended to a flat stage. About forty men, each wearing a cloth wrapped about his waist, were seated around the chamber. Apex stared at several females also in attendance; their garb was too sheer to be considered modest. One male had a Tyrian purple sash draped over his right shoulder and a matching ribbon knotted like a fabric crown around his blood-red hair.

Everyone stared as Lluava and Apex followed their small leader down the aisle to the center of the arena. This place and its occupants reminded her of the High Council and how they manipulated the Elysian government. This parallel could not be a coincidence. She and Apex were going to be put on trial and judged.

"Ruire Thoth," the catlike man began with a bow. "Two Theriomorphs from the Banished Lands were discovered following our sleighs. Uncertain of their intent, we captured them. I respectfully present them to you for judgment regarding their disposition."

The man with the purple sash looked down at them, his face devoid of expression. But there was not a lot of time to wonder what he was thinking.

"Why have you come here? What made you leave the comfort and familiarity of your home in the Banished Lands?"

"You mean Elysia?" Lluava couldn't help but ask for clarification.

"That is the name *you* know it by," responded Thoth. Lluava struggled to understand what he was saying. It seemed that everyone spoke with the same thick accent.

Glancing at Apex, she began, "We left Elysia to search for other Theriomorphs so we—"

Apex cut in. "We were tired of being forced to cast away our beliefs and live under human rule. It's been very hard to pretend to believe their foolish ways in the hope that one day we will be accepted."

Apex spoke so sincerely that Lluava almost believed his lie.

"We were not sure," Lluava played along, "that we would find any others outside the kingdom, but we had to try. We stumbled upon those men," she nodded at her two captors. "Having no food, water, or means of shelter, we followed them, hoping they would lead us to safety."

"Why did you hide?" questioned Thoth, who clearly knew more than he let on. What had he been told?

"For fear that they might harm us."

"What are your names?" Thoth looked down his long, rather sharp nose. His eyes were lined with thick dark powder like the kohl used by the aristocrats in the capital, which made them extremely prominent. He scrutinized the pair.

"I am—" Lluava was cut off again as Spider hissed, "That is the ruire you are conversing with! Call him by his title or be punished."

"Ruire Thoth," Lluava began again. "My name is Lluava Kargen, daughter of Haliden Kargen, and this is my travel partner, Apex."

Thoth merely continued to study them.

"Ruire Thoth, they were traveling with these." Spider dumped out the contents of a sack. With loud clangs, Issaura's Claws and Ullr's Fangs skidded over the stone floor.

Lluava was horrified at the handling of their weapons. "Be careful! Those belong to us!"

Thoth's eyes widened at the unexpected sight. He stood abruptly and strode down the aisle to look at the artifacts more closely.

"Where did you get these? Why were you traveling with them?" he asked as he carefully picked up one of the Fangs and inspected its flawless craftsmanship. Spider seemed curious at the ruire's strange reaction, yet he did not interfere.

"We purchased them from traders before we left the Outlands," lied Apex. "We needed to defend ourselves against the unknown."

Thoth whistled, and several men descended from the seating area. "Take these to the temple for safekeeping."

"But those are ours," Lluava objected, once more wishing her hands were free of their bindings. Spider slapped the back of her head, but the teen was not concerned with shows of respect.

"These holy relics have been lost to us for centuries. They will be returned to their rightful place," stated Thoth coolly.

"You have no right!" Lluava snapped back as the Claws disappeared from her sight. Swiveling, she quickly dodged another slap aimed at her head.

Thoth raised a hand and Spider stepped away. "You have come here claiming you seek refuge. I do not believe you, not for a moment."

Had her quick action alerted Thoth to their lie? Lluava forced herself not to give Apex a worried glance.

Thoth continued, "Yet as the current ruire, I will not jump to any initial conclusions. You will remain here, in Leucrocotta, until we judge you trustworthy. I am sorry for this inconvenience, but you must understand that I do this for the protection of *my* people."

Several heavily built Theriomorphs descended the stairs and grabbed hold of Lluava and Apex. As they left, Thoth exchanged words with the small, catlike man.

***

"This way," Apex's guard barked as he escorted the huntsman into one of two identical buildings. Both had double-peaked roofs in that magnificent teardrop shape. Lluava was ushered to the second building, where waited two expressionless women with gauges in their ears and tattoos of birds on their cheeks. As she stepped through the doorway with hands still bound, Lluava realized that this was a bathhouse.

The clearest water she had ever seen lapped at the edge of the mosaic pool. More mosaic images of the Mother Goddess surrounded the base. At one end, water trickled from a trough in the floor to fill the gigantic bath, while at the far end another dip in the ground allowed the excess to flow away. Lluava had not had a proper bath in a long while. The closest she had come was that terrorizing swim through the icy river. She did not realize how ready she was to be clean.

"In there," one of the women instructed, inclining her head toward the pool. Neither she nor her counterpart appeared to be in any mood for conversation. Yet as Lluava took a step toward the pool, the terse attendant snapped, "Take your clothes off! You are no beast."

Not meaning to be rude, Lluava raised her hands to display the rope bindings. This simple action caused the woman to sneer. "Take those off of her," she ordered her partner, who complied, giving Lluava's wrists a temporary reprieve. After a hurried and rather embarrassing bath, Lluava quickly dressed as instructed in a sand-colored shirt and pants. Her hands were tethered once more.

As they left the bathhouse, Lluava implored the women who were taking away her Endun clothing, "Please don't throw it away."

The woman holding the rank items sighed reluctantly. "They will be washed and returned. Though I don't see the need."

Outside, Lluava rejoined a somewhat cleaner-looking Apex. Accompanied by their guards, they continued on their way without speaking. Their destination was one of the smaller common buildings, its structure almost identical to those nearby. Lluava wondered if it was a tiny household. Square and with a peaked roof, this building's windows were of an unusual design, comprising a series of small, diamond-shaped cutouts the size of Lluava's fist and grouped in patterned sections along the stone walls.

Prison bars, Lluava thought sourly. A different shape but the same result. Once again, she would be locked up. Caged like an animal.

Their escorts stopped at the front door and untied their hands.

"Inside!" one ordered.

As soon as they entered, the wooden door shut behind them. Lluava and Apex found themselves in a sparsely furnished room illuminated by the three perforated windows, one on each of two side walls and a third near the door. A table with three chairs was positioned in the center of the space. Probably once beautiful, these pieces had been used and worn down over time. Decorative paint had chipped away, scratches marred the surfaces, and one of the animal-like beasts that formed the chairs' legs had had its head knocked off. The rest of the space was barren. There was an alcove in the back with three rows of stone ledges on either side, each positioned high enough so the lowest could be sat upon without one's head scraping the ledge above. Lluava wondered if those were to be used as their beds. However, there were no blankets or pillows. Perhaps, as the climate was warm and humid, there was no need. Were these actually their living quarters? Were all households in this vast city as basic, spare, and plain?

"Well, they are a talkative bunch," Lluava said, attempting to lighten the mood as she rubbed her chafed wrists.

Apex was not amused. He moved purposefully to one of the slotted windows and peered out. "Of course, they are standing guard," he sneered.

"Maybe if we wait until night," Lluava offered. Without weapons, knowledge of the city, or any profitable plan, she hoped that having a few extra hours to strategize might prove fruitful. Apex continued to stare out at the city. After a while, he moved to the second window and then to the third.

"What are you doing?" Lluava asked as she sat down on one of the chairs. She was glad to rest. The stress of the journey had been more tiring than the lack of sleep.

"Observing," Apex responded. As he stared out of the window, Lluava knew the huntsman was working something out. Like any predator observing its prey, he would wait patiently to find the point of weakness and then strike.

"Anything in particular?" she asked as she moved to stand beside him at the window. The city outside was thriving, to judge from the number of Theriomorphs moving about in the afternoon heat. How many were there?

"How are we supposed to find the other Incarn in a place like this? We can't just ask them, can we?"

There was a quick rap at the door before it opened to reveal another small man, younger than the one who had led them here although similar in build and facial features. Could they be brothers? As the guard motioned him to enter, the man almost tripped over the slight step up into the house. He swerved clumsily to prevent the scrolls he carried from falling out of his arms.

Looking around, he crinkled his nose in distaste. "And all they could provide was a vacant storage space." He tsked before returning his attention to the other two in the room.

"Hello," he said perkily. "Welcome to Leucrocotta. My name is Leo Pardus. I have been assigned to be your pedagogue during your stay here."

"Our what?" Lluava asked curiously as she watched the man dump the scrolls onto the table.

"Pedagogue… ah, your *teacher* in all things Theriomorph," explained Leo. "As you were raised in the Banished Lands, I was asked to assess you both and decide where to begin your education. Little is expected, to be sure." He shuffled through the parchments. "No offense."

"Why do we need to be educated?" demanded Apex brusquely. He walked over and stood next to Leo in a most intimidating manner. "I don't remember saying I wanted any schooling."

"Well…this…" stuttered the frightened teacher, "is in case you receive permission to enter Leucrocotta as a welcomed visitor and potential citizen. Please forgive my manners. I was told that you, Apex, and your companion, Lluava, both wanted to become Free People."

Apex leaned into Leo, who seemed to shrink. "What if we don't pass your tests? What if your *leader* thinks us frauds? Or *dangerous?*"

"I am only a pedagogue." Leo looked from Apex to Lluava with worried eyes, his pupils narrowing to slits. "A teacher."

Lluava felt sorry for the man. "Give him room," she said, pulling Apex back. Leo looked at her gratefully, but she had already turned her attention to the pile of scrolls. "What do you want us to do?"

With that, Leo straightened up and unrolled the scroll in his hands.

"Well, all right," he began, "what do you know about this event?"

Lluava looked over his shoulder. The entire parchment was covered in the ancient runes. Though she recognized some, it would take her a while to decipher their meaning. Apex had no knowledge of this part of their heritage.

"We don't read the ancient language," she acknowledged.

"Oh." Leo let go of the page, and it rolled up on its own. "Right. You use the barbaric lettering. We should start at the beginning, then. Basic reading and writing can be studied alongside oral recitations of politics, religion, and social etiquette."

Etiquette. Lluava hated that word. It was as if she were back at the capital again, learning social graces but without the swordplay. At least this time, Apex would be learning alongside her. She glanced over. His expression was dubious; this clearly was not in his plans.

Leo said, "Tonight I want you both to tell me everything you know about our religion. That's as good a start as any. Tomorrow we will commence early and explore other subjects."

Knowing that the huntsman was not in an agreeable mood, Lluava took the lead. She recited the creation stories, just as her grandfather had taught her. When she had finished, Leo shuffled the tall stack of notes he had written with a charcoal stick.

"Very good," said the pedagogue. "That was very good. You seem to know the *Karmasana* very well, though little can be said about the *Virisinu*. We will get there in time."

"I also have been told," Lluava added, "that the gods would return to Earth using Theriomorph vessels."

"In what sacred text did you read that?" questioned Leo, bemused.

"Nothing written. Just tales passed down to us." She nodded at Apex, who thankfully kept his face serious.

"Both the *Karmasana* and the *Virisinu* refer to Issaura's promise to one day return on the brink of the Theriomorph race's destruction."

"Just her? No other gods?"

"No others were written about in our holy texts." Leo looked over at the window and sighed. "The sun set some time ago. I shall take my leave and return in the morn. Goodnight to you both."

"Goodnight, Pedagogue Pardus," intoned Lluava. Leo seemed pleased with her response as he slipped past the guards and into the night.

He had barely gone when Apex huffed out, "Rubbish!"

"What?"

"If he thinks he can lecture me about his life here, he's clearly delusional." Apex moved to one of the windows.

"Don't you want to learn about this place?" questioned Lluava.

"No."

Although Apex was still calculating his escape, Lluava had a new perspective on their mission.

"We should play along," she told him. "This Leo fellow might actually end up telling us what we want to hear. He might know about the other Incarn. We could use this to our advantage."

"It didn't sound like he knew much when you questioned him about the prophecy."

"No," she admitted. "But he might know others who have a god's dual form. We can learn a lot from him if we only open our ears."

"Schooling and I have always been at odds," grumbled Apex. "And it's a waste of time. You have been the one saying how valuable our time is. Now you want to cozy up and settle down in hope of getting some sort of useful information. No. Not me. I will get out of here. The only way we will find what we are searching for is by searching the city."

"And how do you expect to do that? Break out? In a city like this, how long do you think you could avoid being found?"

Apex glared at her. "If anyone in the city knows about the Incarn, it will be their leader."

"That might be true," acknowledged Lluava. "But if you want to talk to him, you need him to trust you. What better way to earn his trust than by willingly taking advantage of the opportunity he has presented? If Leo vouches for us, we could be released. We could meet with Thoth."

"There are other ways to get someone to talk."

"Really?" scolded Lluava. "In a city filled with his followers?"

Apex stared out the apertures that formed the window. At last he sighed and turned to her. "I will play this game of yours for now. There are Incarn here, I can feel it. Once released, I will find them."

In the silence after their conversation, Lluava realized for the first time that the city was filled with the sounds of beasts, the voices of a people—a race, hidden all these centuries. They would find the other Incarn. They had to.

Chapter 5

Voice of the Goddess

At a respectable time in the morning, there was a knock at the door. Lluava and Apex had long since finished the breakfast the guard provided and had begun to strategize ways to convince their teacher to trust them. The sound of the door opening stopped their talk.

Dressed in a tawny cloak smudged with splotches of ink, Leo entered, carrying another bundle of scrolls. "I think we should start today's lesson," he began excitedly as he lowered his treasures onto the table, "with a discussion about this city itself."

"Fascinating," griped Apex. Lluava sent him a warning glance: *Be nice!* What was his problem?

Leo seemed unperturbed as he sifted through his papers. The daylight caught in his short golden hair as he unrolled a map and declared, "This is Leucrocotta, our ancestors' magnificent architectural feat."

Lluava sat down next to him and peered at the city's plan. Apex stood a slight distance away. Why was this so hard for him? The information could only benefit them.

"Leucrocotta," explained Leo, "like all of the first eleven Theriomorph cities, was designed to worship a specific patron god or goddess."

"Crocotta, of course," Lluava said.

Their pedagogue smiled, exposing a set of very small, sharp teeth. "Exactly. Of course, we worship the entire pantheon, but we claim the Temple of Crocotta." There was a hint of pride in his voice.

"This building?" Lluava pointed to a large structure with several inner courtyards and smaller rooms.

"Yes. The *pronaos* is the large outer vestibule for public worship, the *cella*

30

is a smaller structure for private devotions and ceremonies with the priestesses, and the *adyton* is the inner sanctum restricted to the priestesses."

"Is Thoth allowed in the inner sanctum?" Lluava asked. She had always enjoyed school, and this intrigued her. Was this where the Claws were kept?

"Unless invited into the inner sanctum, even Ruire Thoth cannot enter."

"Not much of a supreme ruler, is he?" scoffed Apex as he moved to the front window and stared outside.

"Would you join us, Apex?" asked their teacher. "You will learn quicker if you study the diagram."

Lluava gave the huntsman another warning look. Apex grudgingly took a seat across from Leo. The pedagogue shifted uncomfortably under Apex's grim gaze. "Um…ah…where was I?"

"Explaining why Thoth is not able to enter the inner sanctum," Lluava reminded him.

"Please refer to him as Ruire Thoth. He is deserving of that title."

"Is a ruire a king?"

Leo emitted a small, rumbling laugh. "No. No. No. A ruire is a title that designates our city's ruler."

"What's the difference?"

"Please hold your questions until I finish this short lesson," he said pleasantly. Leo clearly enjoyed having a student as interested in his lecture material as he was. His surprisingly long black eyelashes perfectly framed his eyes, which widened even more in delight. "From what I know, a king inherits his authority. Ruire Thoth earned his and can even lose it. The ruire oversees our governmental rulings and proceedings. He is not in charge of religion; that is the responsibility of the priestesses. The high priestess has supreme authority over everything in both our religious and our secular lives."

"Everything? Even the ruire?" Lluava wondered if Leo would be angry at her questions, but this was important. Leo grinned and shook his head.

"High Priestess Yena has authority to overrule anything the ruire says, as she alone communicates with the goddess Crocotta herself."

"She talks to the gods?" Now it was Lluava's turn to be skeptical.

Leo put on the pair of black spectacles that hung from a chain around his neck. Somehow, wearing them made him look far older than he was. "She is Crocotta's high priestess. Crocotta speaks only with her."

Leo rerolled the map, then selected another scroll. "We have veered away from the point of this morning's lesson. I will get to our hierarchy in due time. Right now, let's learn more about the city."

For the remainder of the day, while Lluava listened to Leo lecture on the history, city plan, and architecture of Leucrocotta, her thoughts kept wandering back to the high priestess. Maybe she and Apex should focus on gaining more than just Thoth's attention. The high priestess could have valuable information, too. Perhaps their best bet was to speak with both the high priestess and the ruire. Could Yena know anything about the Incarn? Maybe she was a Guardian—that is, if they existed outside of Elysia.

When Lluava voiced her thoughts that evening, Apex countered, "How long will all this take? I'm not sure how much of this drivel I can stand. Who cares which architect designed the temple?"

"Even I don't care about that," agreed Lluava, in a partial lie. "But we need to appease Leo so we get a chance to visit the city."

Apex emitted a low growl.

"At least it isn't warfare."

"I think I prefer the latter," huffed the huntsman.

Rolling her eyes, Lluava said, "Our best chance to find the other Incarn is to talk candidly with the city's two authority figures. You must realize this."

"Thoth didn't seem too excited about having us in his city. Even if he could point out the Incarn, why would he want to help us?"

Lluava felt strangely compelled to stand up for the man who had confined them to this house. "Thoth may not want strangers running around his city, but he is confining us to protect his people. Think of it this way, Apex," Lluava argued, seeing that her companion obviously wished to disregard her words, "just because someone doubts your character doesn't mean you can't prove him wrong. Things change, people change, and the views we have of people change. Mine have on many occasions."

Lluava retired to her sleeping alcove and left Apex to watch Leucrocotta slowly settle down through his window.

***

Morning arrived with one big change: Apex's demeanor. He seemed almost content to be trapped in this household.

"What's going on?" Lluava inquired as she spooned down the nutty porridge that had been delivered. She added a few pieces of fruit from the neighboring platter to sweeten the concoction.

"Nothing. Just taking your advice," he said, as he swallowed his portion in three bites.

Wrinkling her nose, Lluava declared, "You're disgusting."

"You're stuck with me, sweetheart."

"Hopefully not for long," Lluava half teased under her breath. She wondered what his real motive was.

Almost on cue, the pedagogue arrived.

"Good morning," Leo chirped perkily. "Ready to begin?"

"Of course," replied Apex, earning a skeptical look from Leo.

Judging him to be in earnest, Leo rhetorically asked, "What topics shall we discuss today?"

"How does one meet the high priestess?"

Lluava was worried about Apex's blunt question. Would Leo think they were up to some foul plot?

Thankfully, Leo laughed. "One does not just *meet* the high priestess. She spends the majority of her time in holy prayer behind the walls of the temple. She makes her presence known when she speaks for the goddess, but that rarely occurs. However, she does appear at public ceremonies."

Now Lluava was intrigued. "So when is the next ceremony?"

"Well, there are no major celebrations scheduled for several moons," acknowledged Leo, as he absentmindedly adjusted his ink-stained cloak. "However, there is a minor ceremony at the next new moon, an initiation into adulthood. This formal rite occurs each season, although the Spring Initiation Ceremony is much larger, as it includes the annual citywide Matching Ceremony. High Priestess Yena is not required to attend this minor rite, but she typically makes an appearance to congratulate the new initiates."

"He clearly doesn't care about his appearance," sneered Apex in a whisper. "Or maybe he doesn't notice."

Lluava forcibly stepped on the huntsman's foot, causing him to grunt. She was afraid to draw attention to Apex's insult, or she would have snapped back, "Look who's talking." Instead she focused on the disheveled teacher.

"Thoth said—," Lluava began, but Leo interrupted.

"Ruire. His status is ruire."

"Ruire Thoth mentioned something about becoming members of society. Would we be participating in that?"

"That ceremony is only two weeks away," Leo pointed out. "There is no time for you to learn everything. There is simply no time."

"But what if we could?" Lluava pressed.

"There is a series of examinations that are both physically and mentally challenging. I really do not believe that—"

"Leo," Apex interrupted. "Are we not even able to try?"

"Undertaking these examinations would be extremely difficult. Passing them would be a tremendous feat."

Leo paused for a moment, and a grin cracked his face, exposing the tips of his tiny canines. "Okay." He nodded. "All right. We will do this, but you will have to work nonstop until the examinations."

"That's not a problem for me," said Lluava. She looked at Apex. He might not have been thrilled, but he was willing. This would be the perfect way to prove to Thoth that they were truly interested in becoming citizens of his city. They might even have a chance to speak with Leucrocotta's high priestess or find an escape route. At the very least, they would leave their quarters for the first time since their confinement.

"Let us begin," said Leo, and he unfurled his first scroll of the day.

***

When the pedagogue said he would push them, he was not kidding. The amount of material produced by their enthusiastic teacher was massive. Past rulers, codes of ethics, reviews in religion, to name only a few subjects. There was no way to cover everything in depth, but Leo did his very best. Each day was the same. The pedagogue arrived early in the morning, seeming to race the rising sun. He lectured them on various topics, drilled them on the ancient runes, and had them recite from memory the material he had assigned the day before. At night, they studied the scrolls Leo entrusted to them and quizzed each other until they fell asleep.

Apex struggled to retain the wealth of information, but he remained undeterred. An unspoken urgency drove both him and Lluava forward.

As the two weeks came to an end, Apex grew more restless. Lluava felt the same way. They had not been outside these four walls since they entered Leucrocotta. Worse, they had not discovered any beneficial information about the Incarn, the Guardians, or how to help save Elysia.

This morning, however, Leo seemed to fly through the door without pausing for a warning knock.

"Come here, come here, both of you." He waved them forward. "After spending many hours convincing Ruire Thoth, I am pleased to report that he has agreed to let you take the exams with the other students. He said if you pass and all has gone well, you will receive the same privileges as those born in Leucrocotta. You may not, however, go traipsing off into the surrounding jungle unless you receive permission. Very few are allowed that freedom, so do not be offended by this restriction."

"That's great news," Lluava said with a grin.

"And there's more!" said their tiny teacher, beaming. "Word is that High Priestess Yena will make an appearance for the Initiation Ceremony. How marvelous would it be for you not only to be initiated but also to meet our high priestess so soon!"

Even Apex looked pleased at this.

Leo acknowledged, "Since fortunately this is the case, we must hurry to complete your studies in time. Today, we will talk about gender roles and how they shape our society."

This topic was one that had always disturbed Lluava in Elysia. The patriarchal kingdom cared little for women who were powerful, physically or mentally. The few who did exist learned to play by rules made by men. Lluava held her tongue and waited to hear what Leo had to say. His declaration caused her to gasp.

"We are matriarchal," he told them.

"Matriarchal?" Lluava had to make sure she had heard correctly.

"Yes," affirmed Leo. "Let me start with our family units and work up. The ceremony you hopefully will partake in welcomes new members into our adult community. In addition to the academic examinations, we include a test of physical prowess. The assessment of your knowledge indicates whether you are ready to be treated as an adult. Your physical skill and abilities help determine your ranking."

"What do you mean, ranking?" questioned Lluava.

"If you would hold your questions like your partner does, I can provide the answers more rapidly."

Lluava eyed Apex. Always a man of few words, he rarely asked questions. And he was no partner of hers. That title was reserved for Varren.

Leo continued, "Every man and every woman is ranked at graduation. One keeps this ranking until the Spring Match, at which time it can change. In addition, it is possible to receive an outside challenge, but I will explain that another time.

"You see, our society views breeding pairs as greatly important. The ranking one receives helps with the selection of a mate."

"Marriage," clarified Lluava in terms she understood.

Leo shook his head, bemused. "I am unfamiliar with that term; it sounds human. Now may I continue?"

Lluava nodded.

"I have said that we are matriarchal because the females choose their mates. The top-ranking females have the right to select any partner they desire. The top-ranking males are typically their best matches. Males perform feats of strength to impress females, hoping to be chosen. Lluava?" Leo acknowledged the young woman's desire to speak up.

"Do you not mate for life?"

"Sometimes, yes," acknowledged Leo, "but not always. Each year during the Spring Match, the female has the right to select a new partner if she finds the current one no longer desirable."

"What if—" Lluava cut herself off.

"Go on," urged Leo, who clearly was not angry at his interested pupil.

"What if several females desire the same male?"

"That is when female rankings come into play. The female with the highest rank has first choice. If a male refuses a match, he is no longer eligible for that season's breeding and must wait until next year's Spring Match."

"Now, the top-ranked male becomes that year's ruire, and he maintains that title as long as he continues to be the top-ranked male in subsequent Spring Matches. The ruire is always paired with the high priestess."

Lluava jumped in. "And the high priestess has power over everything?"

"In a way, yes, she does," agreed Leo. "In Leucrocotta, High Priestess Yena chooses to govern only the religious aspects of our society. The ruire oversees the rest."

"How does one become the high priestess?"

"Well, all priestesses are selected at infancy. Crocotta reveals her choices to the current high priestess, and the infants are brought to live in the temple. When the high priestess dies, a successor is selected by rites unknown to those outside the fold."

"She cannot be challenged?"

"No. As the physical voice of the goddess, the high priestess can never be challenged."

There were so many questions to ask about this strange culture, but Lluava knew time was precious. "So why do females have the power to select mates and the males do not?"

"It is the female who brings life into existence. For this, your gender is revered. Throughout our history, the female has had the right to select her mate. The male provides for the female and protects her and her children, as he had the honor of fathering offspring. This, in a sense, is a symbiotic relationship between mates."

"Do you view females as weak because they do not fend for themselves?"

"No. But they are worth dying for."

Lluava smiled. "I think I am beginning to really like this place."

"So, if we pass these tests, what happens once we are ranked?" Apex's question came as a surprise, as he had been silent during the entire exchange.

"As you are male, and this is not the citywide match, you might be selected by one of the female initiates. I would advise you, as a new member of our society, to accept an offer. All pairs will more than likely change during the citywide Spring Match."

Lluava's stomach turned somersaults. This would only feed Apex's sexual appetite. He was a grown man and one Lluava cared little for, yet this proposal was far from appealing. Seeing Apex's smile made Lluava unhappy. What a vile creature.

"That brings me to my next point," said Leo almost sadly. "I feel dreadful for not allowing you to work on your physical skills. Please do not be discouraged if you receive an initial low ranking. Once you are accepted into our society, you can improve that component before the Spring Match."

Apex gave a rumbling laugh. "I'm not worried about anything physical."

He couldn't end up with another woman, Lluava thought sourly; they had a mission to complete. No distractions. *None.* Another female would only cause problems. Maybe this initiation was the wrong thing to do. But they couldn't very well back down now. They had already lost two weeks and were still no closer to finding any of the Incarn, not to mention escaping.

Lluava had to make sure Apex was undesirable. But how?

Chapter 6

The Ranking

The morning of the exam arrived in a mix of sunshine and clouds. The house arrest was lifted, and Leo Pardus led the pair through the winding streets to the Temple of Crocotta. Along the way, the pedagogue pointed out the various buildings and monuments they had covered in their whirlwind studies.

"Is it just me, or does the air smell sweeter?" Lluava asked exuberantly. "It's like blooming flowers and ripening fruit all at once."

Leo gave her a pleasant smile, although Apex remained impassive. Lluava slipped in front of the huntsman. Walking backwards, she teased, "What's wrong? Nervous?"

His only response was a quick glare.

Lluava began to laugh but then wondered if maybe the mighty Apex really *was* nervous. All they had to do was recite a few lines of script and answer some questions on politics, history, and culture. This wasn't even the hard part. The physical exam would take place the following day.

On the other hand, how much schooling had he had? This might be Apex's first major exam. Was he truly worried about it? A new thought crossed Lluava's mind. If he did not pass, there would be no matching for him, no mate selection, and he could focus on their mission. On the other hand, he might be imprisoned in the house once again. Lluava could look for the other Incarn on her own. This might be the perfect solution—unless his failure meant hers as well. Could Thoth condemn her if Apex flunked? Maybe it was better if he did pass.

Moving to the huntsman's side, she leaned over and whispered, "It'll be fine. It's only a few exams. You don't need a perfect score to pass."

Apex walked stiffly forward. Lluava could see her words were not helping and might be making things worse.

"We could meet High Priestess Yena today," Lluava said with a smile. Apex's response was the same blank gaze.

Before she could think of anything else to say, Leo announced, "The Temple of Crocotta."

Even though Lluava had studied the map of the city, observing the temple in person was impressive, to say the least. Although nowhere near as large as the royal castle in Cronus or Elysia's northern palaces, this structure was enormous. The beautifully carved white marble columns were the same hue as the rows of oaks that led to the main stairs.

Lluava recognized the bone-colored trees. She knew from legends that these oaks, once found at all Theriomorph holy sites, had been all but obliterated in Elysia during the Landon Wars. The last one had been destroyed after the Raiders attacked her kingdom.

Although the full-bodied trees were beautiful with their ivory leaves flickering in the slight breeze, Lluava shivered in disgust. The association with these wondrous trees and the massive oak that had held the hanging corpses of the entire city of Therial was too strong. Lluava hurried inside and away from the sight of these oaks.

Crossing a small porch, they entered the largest chamber of the temple. Only a few spaces remained at the tables and long benches where students were seated. Since they all seemed about Lluava's age of eighteen, she felt comfortable around them. However at twenty-five, Apex looked out of place, and she wondered if the age gap would make him even more nervous.

Lluava seated herself next to Apex, who was muttering under his breath. *"Pronaos, cella, ad—, ady—"*

"Adyton," whispered Lluava. Knowing the architectural components of the temple was of little importance, but she was quite impressed that Apex was studying everything.

"Good luck," Leo said, as he and the other adults left the room.

After the temple doors closed, a dozen women in pristine white linen tunics entered from the inner sanctum. Their hair was covered by a white cloth so sheer Lluava could tell that the one about to speak was a blond.

"Welcome to your initiation examination. We are about to begin." The priestess spoke in a voice like a musical whisper, while the other priestesses handed out ink, quills, and parchment.

"May the Great Mother, Crocotta, be with you all…"

There were a series of tests throughout the day. First history, followed by government; then current culture, including literature and artistic achievements, and finally science and anatomy. After each session, several priestesses offered ladles of chilled water to sip, collected the parchments, and refreshed materials.

During a minor section on the local ecosystem, one boy was pulled out of his seat so quickly by a dark-skinned priestess that he spilled his vial of ink, splattering the nearby students. Although the priestess spoke in a reserved manner, everyone heard her.

"You will remove yourself from this exam. Cheating will not be tolerated. Pray hard tonight for forgiveness."

The wide-eyed boy pulled down his sleeve to cover the runes scribbled on his arm and left the temple in shame. The priestess turned to the rest of the class. "You may continue."

During the afternoon session, Lluava's stomach began to rumble. Ritual fasting during these examinations was mandatory. Forgoing breakfast and lunch was bothersome, but she had been through far worse. Could the other students say as much? Several of them looked weary and frustrated.

Ignoring her hunger, Lluava mentally prepared for the oral exam on religion. Each student was paired with a priestess in a different area of the temple, where the student was asked multiple questions. Lluava knew she was next. Apex had been called some time ago.

"Lluava Kargen," called the dark-skinned priestess. Lluava followed her to the back corner of the chamber.

"I want you to tell me about three major relationships between Crocotta and the other members of the pantheon," said the priestess.

Aware that this was a warm-up question, Lluava began, "Crocotta is the queen of the gods; her mate is Giahem, the supreme ruler. She is independent and fierce, and it took several attempts for Giahem to woo her successfully. Together they reign over the entire pantheon as well as all living things."

Not knowing how much detail to provide, Lluava moved on to the next two parts. "Crocotta and Giahem's child was Ullr, the warrior and sun god. As told in the *Karmasana*, because the boy brightened their lives he was permitted to control the sun to brighten the earth and warm its people. Crocotta loved her son and wanted him to be paired only with the best mate. However, Ullr desired the one goddess Crocotta despised: Issaura, the moon goddess."

"Issaura, as the illegitimate daughter of Giahem, had been in disfavor with Crocotta since birth. Yet Crocotta could not harm the child-goddess, who was under the protection of Giahem. Worse, Giahem raised the two children together as playmates in his home. When the sun god and moon goddess matured, another bond formed, one that only strengthened their relationship: they were both gods of war. When word reached Crocotta that her son was courting Issaura, she placed a curse on the pair that prevented them from consummating their affection. To this day, the pair have never mated."

Lluava paused, hoping to receive some sign that all was well, but her questioner merely requested, "Now tell me what you know about *The Twins*."

***

Late that evening, the doors of the temple were finally opened to crowds of cheering citizens. A row of torches was lit, and the exhausted test-takers were escorted through the city to a large square, where tables and long benches had been set up. Mounds of food awaited, a feast for the weary students.

Leo managed to find Apex and Lluava among the bustling crowds. "How do you feel?" he asked, clearly curious about his two pupils. His large hazel eyes were full of excitement.

"Hungry," Apex and Lluava said in unison as they reached for the food.

As he was not allowed to sit with the students, Leo congratulated them on their efforts and then moved to a nearby table. Lluava sensed he had something else to tell them. Maybe about tomorrow? Her stomach soon regained her full attention and held it for the better part of the next hour.

After their dinner, a strange thing occurred. All the test takers were escorted back to the temple. Candles had been lit to illuminate the alcoves that contained figurines of the goddess Crocotta. Rows of unlit candles were aligned along one side for those who wished to pray for help during this process. The entire central area had been cleared of furniture, leaving bare the polished marble floor. Only the students were summoned to spend the night in the house of the goddess. Leo and the other adults were not permitted entry.

Apex sat down apart from the others and scrutinized each person carefully. Lluava walked over to him. He was the only one she knew. Though the other students were friendly, tomorrow they would all be competing for their initial ranking. Was Apex sizing up his competitors? There were a few well-built young men in the group, but Lluava knew none would be able to contend with Apex. Physically, at least, he would be superior. The thought of a dozen of these women vying for his attention was somehow unsettling. Lluava had noticed more than one young woman looking over at them, looking at him.

Sleeping on the cold stone floor was less than ideal; she got very little rest. When she did doze, dreams of clanging metal and ear-shattering screams woke her. Somewhere else, far away from the calm of this place, the war raged on. Her friends were fighting. Varren would be doing his best to protect the kingdom.

The slight rumbling snores coming from the huntsman did not ease her sense of loneliness. Together, she and Apex had to prove their worth tomorrow, meet High Priestess Yena, and find a way to talk candidly with both her and Ruire Thoth about the other Incarn. Time was slipping away, and so was Lluava's patience.

Morning's light brought with it a new day of trials. Required to fast one last time, the group of hopeful initiates lined up before a dozen priestesses of varying age. About a third of the students' names were called out. Lluava's wasn't, nor was Apex's. What did this mean?

The blond priestess from the day before spoke out, "Those of you whose names I have called, please leave the temple. The scores on your exams fell short. I will see you again next season."

The disheartened group left the temple with heads hanging. Beside her, Lluava heard Apex's sigh of relief.

"Didn't I tell you you'd be fine," kidded Lluava as she poked the huntsman in the side.

His eyes flashed with excitement. He must already be thinking about what was going to happen today.

"The rest of you," the priestess continued, "will follow Etha to your final examination."

Etha was the dark-skinned priestess. Smiling pleasantly, she ushered the students out of the temple and through the streets of Leucrocotta. Lluava had already figured out which building they were heading for.

The coliseum was larger than either of those in Durog, where she had trained as a recruit. The entrance was similar, through an arched underpass into a central arena. However, instead of weapons racks, a pyramid of identical stone orbs was stacked at the far end. There were also two wooden stakes with colored ribbons wrapped down their shafts positioned at opposite sides of the vast space.

"What do you think we are supposed to do?" Lluava whispered to Apex.

"Win," grunted her gruff companion. With his unshaven beard, Apex was starting to look quite wild. He had asked her once, "What? You don't like it?"

Lluava had replied, "If that's what you like…"

Apex had laughed. That was one of the last times Lluava had heard him laugh. How many weeks had it been? Everything felt so long ago.

Etha gave instructions as observers filled the multitude of seats. "All males to the stone pile. All females to this marker." She pointed to the stake nearest her.

"Good luck," Lluava said as she moved to join the women.

Apex's lip curled. "I don't need it."

"Such a confident—" Lluava shook her head to expunge the foul words she had been about to say. She hoped one of the stone balls would roll down and crush his foot.

"Each male," the priestess continued, "will take one of the orbs. All weigh the same. Once you line up, I will give the command. Starting with the male farthest to my left, each of you will throw the orb as far as you can."

Lluava was not surprised that Apex's throw was neck and neck with the best. He was strong, even under that smug persona. Couldn't one of those boys knock him down a peg? Was that too much to hope for?

While the men retrieved their projectiles, Etha announced to the women, "You are to line up beside this marker. On my command, sprint to the far marker and back."

Lluava had been a fast runner once, but she was certainly out of practice. For the first time, she noticed how fit the teens were. Actually, all the Theriomorphs she had seen since arriving in Leucrocotta were fit. What if she wasn't good enough? What would happen then?

"Go!"

Lluava sprang off half a second late. The girls *were* fast. Pushing herself forward, she began to elbow her way through the cluster of flashing legs and swinging arms. Right before she reached the marker, she began to slow down to prevent skidding too far past it, as some of the girls had just done. Spinning on her heels, Lluava took off after the three runners in front of her.

Come on, she willed herself. Faster!

Bounding forward, Lluava slipped into second place as the four flew past the final marker. This was no good. She had to do better. Lluava bent over and gasped for breath. She had not run that hard in a long while.

The dark-skinned priestess was speaking again, "The males and females will switch positions, and the males will line up for their sprint."

Lluava looked up in time to see Apex charging into the lead, yet when he reached the far marker, he struggled to turn quickly. Unlike some of the others, his build was not that of a runner. Apex came in fifth. Lluava breathed a sigh of relief.

When it was the women's turn to toss the stone balls, Lluava's confidence grew. She could do this. She knew it, and she was right. Her orb landed a cat's length ahead of all the others. This would certainly improve her score.

"Thank you," Etha said as she moved to the center of the arena. "Now let the test of strength begin!"

"What?" Lluava gasped, but her question was drowned out by the applause of their onlookers. The entire coliseum was filled with excited faces. It seemed that tossing stones and running sprints had only been a warm-up. Now their true test was about to occur.

The priestess shouted above the din, "All females will remove themselves from the arena floor!" Etha gestured to a pair of double doors that were slid open by several men. As Lluava followed the girls, she looked over her shoulder at Apex. He was stretching his arms out before him. She suddenly knew that no contender would be able to defeat him.

Lluava missed some of the priestess's speech as the group scrambled up an inner staircase to some vacant seats. However, she caught the very end: "May Crocotta bless you all." As Etha stepped through the double doors, she shouted, "You may begin!"

Chaos erupted from below.

The stone orbs and the two stakes from the arena had been removed. The entire space was bare except for the multitude of young men wrestling among themselves. There seemed to be no rules, no semblance of order. Soon, animals began to appear as the Theriomorphs shifted into their dual forms. In seconds, one young man had transformed into a lynx, another into a water buffalo, and a third into a crocodile. Flecks of red streaked into the sky.

Were they going to kill each other? A whistle was heard; two adult men dressed in red ran onto the field, lifted an unconscious victim, and carried him out. Spectators throughout the coliseum cheered, shouted, and applauded the pandemonium. Another young man tried to crawl away from the melee, but a second figure grabbed his legs and pulled him back.

"Crocotta!" he screamed and was released. The double doors slid open, and he stumbled through them.

A safety word, Lluava realized. Competitors were given a way out when they could no longer continue. At least there was some mercy in this horrid display. All around her, the young women seemed enthralled by the brutal show. At first, Lluava was disgusted. Was the sight of all this pain entertaining? Then she remembered Leo's words. This was all part of a matchmaking ceremony. These females were watching to see which males would prove the most powerful, the most elite, the most desirable.

More and more shouts of "Crocotta!" were heard as the fighters were whittled down. One scruffy fellow shifted into a maned wolf. His ruddy fur flashed around unprepared victims. A water buffalo charged at a limping puma. A coyote bit into a boar.

Apex had not shifted. Lluava thought she might know why. His dual form was unlike any she—and probably the others—had ever seen. Then again, it could be because—

Suddenly, as the large water buffalo turned its eyes toward the huntsman, Apex shifted. The bull skidded to a halt and then tentatively backed away, the whites of its eyes flashing. No wonder. Who could blame the buffalo from backing away from a wolverine that size? Apex's bronze fur glistened, and a low growl slipped past his bared fangs.

Lurching forward, the wolverine grappled with the horned beast. In only a few movements, Apex had flung the buffalo onto its side. Just as the animal bellowed out "Crocotta!" the maned wolf leaped onto Apex's back and bit into the wolverine's neck. Blood spurted from the wound.

Then Apex faltered.

Chapter 7

Growing Darkness

The wolverine crumpled to the ground.

Had the maned wolf won? Was Apex all right?

In a burst of movement, the enraged wolverine leapt to his feet and spun furiously in a circle.

Poor little dog, Lluava thought as Apex tossed the animal off. Closing her eyes, Lluava waited until she heard a drumbeat. The fight was over. She already knew who the victor was.

As the male champion, Apex would be the most desirable match. Several dozen young women would all want him to be their initial mate. The idea was revolting. If these girls only knew how vile he actually was. Then again, would they care? Maybe they would *want* a male with all that…experience.

Lluava had to prevent this from happening. She could not let him be chosen. That was not acceptable. No distractions. No outsiders. No other women. Their mission was too important; success required their full concentration. Moreover, her best chance to meet the high priestess would occur if she herself was the winning female. Just a chance to converse with the priestess could change everything. She had to win, regardless of Apex's ranking or her shoulder acting up. She could not afford to let that old injury hinder her.

Following the other contenders back to the arena floor, Lluava could hear the low moans of some of the less fortunate young men echoing through the underbelly of the coliseum. Where was Apex? Was he taking a seat to watch her? Maybe the plan to impress the high priestess was a mistake. Maybe they should have lain low and not pushed for notoriety.

As she approached the over bright doorway, Lluava heard Etha's voice announcing the next round. Why were these lithe women so unusually fit?

Did they train for this day? The need to earn a high rank in their social pecking order might drive them to do so.

Lluava stepped into the arena. The sun shone brightly, and the heat was tremendous. Combined with the dense humidity, her skin was already coated in a film of sweat. This was going to be anything but pleasant.

Etha continued, "Each participant will stay in the arena as long as she can and will only leave if wounded or incapable of defending herself. Whoever wishes to voluntarily step away will call the Great Mother by her name, Crocotta. May the winner be worthy, honored, and blessed."

The priestess moved to the doorway. Lluava glanced around. All the other young women seemed to be watching her. Raised together from childhood, these women knew each other's weaknesses and dual forms. Lluava was an unknown. Maybe she could use this to her advantage.

"Begin!" Etha cried out as she exited the arena. The girls were left to fight. And so they did.

Several women rushed Lluava. Had they chosen to target her? Whether prearranged or just circumstantial, Lluava would have to defend herself against poor odds. One thing she had on her side was her training as a soldier.

Using the oncoming force of the first girl, Lluava grabbed hold of her dark shirt and flipped her onto the ground. Dropping low, she tripped a second attacker. The third collided into her crouched form, forcing her to the ground.

The impact caused Lluava to gasp as the female on top of her began beating her fists against Lluava's chest and face. Moving an arm to protect her eyes, she tried to grab hold of the flailing hands. She needed to get this woman off of her, and quickly.

Grounding her feet, the teen bucked her hips upward. As her assailant jerked up, Lluava collapsed her own right leg, grabbed the woman's left arm, and pulled her around to the ground on Lluava's right side. This basic wrestling move worked. Before her opponent could react, Lluava swung her left leg around, kicked the stunned girl, then jumped to her feet.

She had only a moment to enjoy her upright position. Another adversary, dressed in gray, charged forward as the last one grabbed at her legs. Springing away from her prostrate foe, she lurched at the new one, whose hair was as platinum-blond as her own. Such a tiny thing! Lluava almost felt sorry for her, since she knew her own strength was clearly far greater. But just as Lluava grabbed the slender torso, her rival shifted. The girl's minuscule form took to the air. A mockingbird.

Of course these young women would be shifting, Lluava thought sourly as she ducked a swinging fist. A girl with a mane of orange hair jumped onto Lluava's back and in an instant had wrapped her legs around Lluava's waist. Struggling to keep the redhead's hands away from her throat, Lluava was now defenseless from aerial attack by the enraged bird.

All about them, crowds of people cheered and screamed out names of their favorite contenders, encouraging their family and friends. Nobody called Lluava's name.

Twisting, Lluava flung off the redheaded parasite just before the other shifted into a red panda to escape another angry participant's attack. The dratted bird, on the other hand, would not leave Lluava alone and continued to dive at her eyes and tug her long hair.

If Lluava shifted, the mockingbird would be severely injured or possibly killed. If only…but she would not. There was too much risk; the danger was too great. A few more women began to shift into their dual forms. Lluava wondered if their hesitation was due to the fact that most female dual forms are weak compared to those of males. Though there were exceptions, like Lluava's white tigress, their meeker forms provided a less impressive show than the men's battle. Many girls attempted to complete this ceremonial brawl without using their dual form at all. At least Lluava was not alone, though her rationale was far different.

As Lluava batted away the vile avian, she took note of the dwindling number of women left on the field. This battle would end far sooner than the men's at the rate the girls called out "Crocotta!" and ran to the available doors. However, those who were left would definitely stay the course.

"Ahh!" Lluava huffed as the small bird pulled a clump of her hair out with its beak. That girl was becoming a nuisance. She had to go.

Calculating the exact moment, Lluava swung at the mockingbird and knocked it out of the air in mid dive. The small beak hit the palm of her hand, piercing the flesh. As the bird fluttered to the ground, Lluava shook off the droplets of blood that ran down her arm.

Suddenly, a beautiful golden dog pounced upon the bird. There was a crunch, then a scream, as the mockingbird's wing snapped in the canine's mouth.

The sound of the girl's screams continued, yet she did not cry out the goddess's name. Was she in too much pain to think straight? The dog shook its head wildly, flinging the poor, feathered creature about.

Lluava couldn't watch any longer. Gripping the dog's tail, she pulled it toward her. As the canine looked around, Lluava grabbed its jaws and pried them open. The bird flopped to the ground, and as it shifted, the young woman cried out "Crocotta!" She cradled her mangled arm to her chest and stumbled to the exit.

There was no time to feel sorry for the girl or disgusted with the competition as the dog wrestled itself free. At that moment, Lluava felt a strong hand grip her right shoulder and jerk her backward. Maybe it was the quick, forceful movement or the angle at which she fell, but her shoulder, her weak link, dislocated. Although this had happened before, the pain was always horrendous.

The teenager standing over her looked like a giant. She was very tall, six feet or more. Grabbing Lluava's injured arm, she yanked her to her feet.

Lluava muffled a cry. Behind her, two more competitors shouted

Crocotta's name. Very few girls were left in the arena. She was so close to winning! She had to persevere, despite the throbbing pain.

The dog returned, its face now splattered with blood. Lluava couldn't tell if the blood was the animal's or that of one of the poor teens who was being assisted out of the arena. The canine snarled, guard hairs raised. It was about to attack, and Lluava was helpless, pinioned by her captor.

The giantess twisted Lluava's arm at the worst possible angle, positioning the injured teen in front of her like a living shield. The pain from Lluava's arm was searing, and she felt her pupils narrow like a housecat's. Her inner heat rose, and a rumble slipped past her lips.

No! She mustn't shift; she mustn't succumb to the darkness that manifested inside her. These young Theriomorphs only wanted rights to a good rank. She could not let loose her inner demons. She must not destroy them!

In the stands, people were on their feet, shouting and urging the fight to a finish. Apex was there, but he remained seated, his face like stone. What was he thinking? Did he want her to continue, or give in? Did he even care?

The dog lunged.

Contorting herself, Lluava screamed in agony but managed to avoid the snapping teeth that instead sank into the chest of her tall adversary. Tears ran down her face as she stumbled away from the wrestling pair.

She tasted blood. In that moment of excruciating pain, she had bitten her tongue. Something inside her stirred. Her inner heat continued to rise. Lluava forced herself to breathe slowly as she concentrated on controlling herself.

"Lluava! Watch out!"

She didn't know how she'd heard those words over the roar of the crowd. Apex's warning came none too soon. Lluava had only a moment to turn, react, and shift. There was no thought involved. Swinging its spiraled horns, an eland charged her. There was no time to defend herself in human form, especially with an injured shoulder.

Allowing her body to shift, Lluava yielded to her inner heat as it scorched through the very fibers of her being. Fur sprang out, fingernails became claws, bones realigned, a tail emerged. Despite her injured limb, the tigress met the eland head on. Lluava sank her fangs into the back of the animal's head as she dug her claws into the thick shoulder hide. She had to hold on, for though the animal stumbled, it continued to charge. If Lluava slipped just a little, she would fall beneath those sharp hooves.

The large antelope was not deterred. Lluava felt the animal's strong neck muscles try to shake her off. She instinctively allowed her grip to slacken. She knew what pain would come of this but hoped the end result would be worth it.

Lluava's injured foreleg could no longer hold on. She let her body slide down to the underbelly of the eland as her rear paws struggled to cling to the beast's side. Suddenly she felt small daggers slicing at her ribs. The eland's hooves were kicking at her larger form.

In another moment, she would fall to the ground. She sank her teeth into the eland's throat, not to tear but to clamp down and slowly suffocate the beast. The seconds dragged on. Was it working? Would this antelope give in? Not willingly, apparently.

The animal bucked and kicked as it struggled for air. The eland's haphazard movements forced Lluava to clamp down harder. Come on, she willed the animal. Give up.

The eland slowed and stumbled. One foreleg sank to the ground, followed by the other as if it were kneeling. Unfortunately, that meant Lluava was now pinned beneath the heavy beast.

Concentrating on the animal's weakening heartbeat, Lluava counted down the moments until she could release the giant eland, hoping that the Theriomorph would call out the goddess's name. All this young woman needed to do was admit defeat, and it would be over. Lluava would ensure that no female would mate with Apex during their stay. They could continue their search in peace. This Theriomorph had to give up.

A thrusting jerk enabled the eland to spring to its feet. Lluava felt her body tear away and fly off sideways. Emitting a high-pitched cry, she landed on her right shoulder. Immediately she shifted and curled into a ball. That was it. There was nothing more she could do. The pain was too great.

All around the stadium, onlookers cheered, shouted, and screamed. Their individual features were blurred behind her veil of tears. The throbbing pain running up and down her arm was so intense that she could hear each thump of her heartbeat; its rapid rhythm drowned out all other sounds. She rolled over to face the wall and did not see the command given to quiet the overexcited crowd.

Etha's voice broke through the sudden silence. "We have a champion."

Lluava didn't care how smug was the tall young teen who had defeated her. She only wanted to cradle her arm until she could realign her shoulder. She wanted to hide away and mourn in private. She could sense the stares of all the eyes upon her. It was too much. She had failed.

"Someone, help our winner to her feet," said Etha emotionlessly.

Footfalls. Two figures in red approached Lluava and carefully assisted her so as not to aggravate her injuries. Wiping her eyes, she turned around to see that the eland had shifted back to human form. The tall young woman sprawled on the ground. Several more people in red were positioned around her. One held a drenched cloth to the young woman's neck. The other closed the teen's vacant eyes.

"No," Lluava murmured as she almost sank to her feet. The attendants held her erect as they moved her around the corpse.

"I didn't mean…" Lluava murmured as she passed the rigid Etha. "It was an accident."

Etha ignored her. As the dazed teen was ushered to the doors and led into the darkness, she heard the priestess announce, "Our winner, Lluava Kargen."

Chapter 8

A Warrior Now Known

urderer.

Lluava could have sworn that was the word shouted by many of the onlookers as the doors were shut behind her. The sudden darkness terrified her to her core. She knew her enhanced night vision would help, yet that did not eliminate the almost physical pressure of the oppressive blackness.

The attendants led her through the underbelly of the coliseum to a series of subterranean compartments. Arranged like stalls, the small rooms were filled with injured competitors and adults who appeared to be local healers. The moans and cries of the afflicted echoed throughout the catacombs. Those who were uninjured or not badly hurt seemed to have been moved elsewhere. Lluava was taken to one of the rooms, and a pair of healers entered to inspect her shoulder.

A gangly male departed and quickly returned, rolling a device very similar to one Lluava had seen—and used—before. This wooden contraption was going to reset her arm. She shuddered.

"Bite on this," said a female healer as she handed Lluava a wooden bit.

With no energy left to argue, Lluava placed the rod in her mouth as the healers carefully manipulated her arm and shoulder into the slots and strapped them down. Sweat peppered her forehead. She blamed it on the heat.

A lever was turned, followed by a muffled pop. Lluava tried desperately not to scream out in agony. Fortunately, it was soon over. Once unstrapped, Lluava spat the bit out.

"Where is Apex?" she gasped.

The healers did not bother to look at her face but studied the ribbons of red running down the side of her clothes. The lanky man said, "Take off your shirt."

"I'm fine," Lluava hissed.

"No time for modesty. Take off your shirt," the man ordered testily.

"It's okay," the woman added. "We need to inspect your wounds."

Lluava reluctantly peeled off her tattered shirt, the only one she had that was made from Endun. As the man balled up the ruined item, the woman said, "Go get her a new one."

Of course, Lluava suddenly realized. These Theriomorphs would all wear clothes made from that same material. How had she not understood this earlier? Apex and Lluava had been using some of the clothing provided to them during their house arrest, but both had chosen to wear their personal outfits during the Matching. The other competitors had been shifting back and forth during the whole appalling ceremony. Then again, she had not been focused on clothing.

Once the man left, the woman said, "Lift your arms, please."

Lluava did as she was asked, and the woman took note of all the lacerations the girl had received during her fight with the eland.

"Where did this one come from?" the woman asked, pointing to the long pink scar that stretched down the side of Lluava's torso.

"Hunting a deer, actually," replied Lluava honestly. There was no point in delving into the severe infection that had resulted from that wound. The scar was the physical reminder of how close to death she had come, as well as how Apex had risked his own life to save hers.

As the woman cleaned the cuts with some liquid that burned, Lluava asked again, "When can I see Apex? He fought earlier today."

"You can see your friend tomorrow at the graduation ceremony. Tonight you will rest here until you are better."

Lluava balked. "I'm fine."

"Until tomorrow," affirmed the woman gently.

The gangly man returned with a white top to replace the one Lluava had destroyed. This one's design was more form fitting, and the texture was softer to the touch. "Is this Endun?" Lluava inquired.

"One variety," said the man as if expecting her disapproval.

Though the material clung to her body, it absorbed much of the sweat that still covered her. "I like it," she admitted.

The healers left her lying on the low stone bed. Though far from comfortable, Lluava calmed her mind. A short while later, the man returned with warm broth.

"Drink up," he said as he handed her the bowl.

Lluava took a sip and instantly spat it out. Splashed with her spittle, the man was not amused. "Drink!" he ordered more harshly.

Forcing herself to swallow the vile liquid, Lluava paused to make sure it did not come back up.

The man shook his head. "All of it."

Unable to keep from glaring at him, Lluava finished off the bowl. Why couldn't it have been smaller?

Apparently satisfied, the man left her to go and force more of the cursed broth on other victims. Lluava took several moments to calm her now volatile stomach. As she was drifting off to sleep, a cry from the adjacent cubicle woke her.

What was that? Lluava rose to her feet. The hallway was empty, so she slipped around to the neighboring room. A small girl with platinum-blond hair and wearing a clean gray uniform was tossing on a stone slab. The mockingbird. Her mangled arm was tightly bound in some sort of large leaf. The tropical plant had dried out to form a hardened case.

Lluava wondered what Rosalyn would think of this. Her friend had been trained as a healer in Elysia. This would interest her greatly.

Stepping closer to the small teen, Lluava could see she was in a great deal of pain.

"Hey," Lluava whispered. "How're you doing?" She felt a bit stupid for asking the question when the answer was so obvious, but what else was she to say?

The young woman's eyes fluttered open. "You," she gasped.

Lluava felt she had to explain why she was there. "I heard you, since I'm next door, and—"

The young woman interrupted. "You saved me."

"I mean, you were in far too much pain."

"You saved me," she said again.

Lluava eyed the cast. "How bad is it?"

"Because of you, I will be able to attend the ceremony tomorrow," chirped the young woman as her face contorted in pain again. "Thank you."

"Uh, you're welcome." What else could she say? Lluava flashed a quick smile and started to return to her own cubicle. "I'm Lluava."

The teen in gray replied, "I'm Maruny."

"Maruny," reiterated Lluava. "That's a nice name. My sister has that name." Lluava returned to her cubicle and forced herself to sleep.

***

"Yep. That's her."

The voices rang in Lluava's ears as the touch of fingers awakened her. Startled, she instinctively jumped up, grabbed the intruder, and slammed him into the stone wall. Behind her, another voice broke the silence.

"Take it easy. You have been summoned to the Council of the Ruire. Your presence is requested immediately."

Blinking, Lluava saw that four men, including the one she still gripped, had entered her cubicle. Releasing the unfortunate man, Lluava quietly followed her escorts back through the underground corridors and out of the coliseum. But she remained alert. She had been tricked on more than one occasion and was not about to let it happen again.

Her escorts led her through the city to the public amphitheater to which

51

Lluava and Apex had been taken that first day. Thoth was waiting. He did not look pleased. Scattered around the large space were other unhappy faces. Several appeared to have been crying.

Lluava already knew what this meeting was about. But she had no idea what to tell them. She had not meant for the young woman to die. It was an accident. A horrible, tragic accident.

"Lluava Kargen," Thoth motioned her to approach the center of the floor. "You are here to discuss your actions in the arena today. Our law states that the candidates at matching ceremonies should never risk the lives of the other participants. We are not bloodthirsty savages that kill our own kind. A Theriomorph *never* kills another Theriomorph. That is the law passed down from the gods. The question stands: Did you kill Okran Corna to better your standing in the Match?"

There was a sob from the stands. In the torchlight, many faces cast dark looks or were veiled in shadow. Lluava couldn't tell who was crying. Was it Okran's parents? Was her family there to pass judgment? Her mouth felt dry.

"I didn't mean to kill Okran," stated Lluava earnestly. Her voice sounded shaky; her stomach was still on fire from her vile supper. "I did clamp down on her throat in order to slow her down. She was running so fast. She wouldn't stop, and I was slipping." Lluava took a breath. Her nausea was increasing. "I just wanted her to stop, to give in. I was about to let her go, hoping she would call the goddess's name."

"You tore her throat out!" a woman screamed from behind her.

The teen turned to face her accuser. There were several people standing in the dark. By their unusual height, she knew they must be Okran's family.

"I didn't mean..." Lluava tasted bile in the back of her mouth. "It all happened so fast. Okran jumped up. I wasn't expecting that. I remember being flung into the air and landing on my injured shoulder. I thought I had lost. I thought she had won. I had no idea until..." Turning back to Thoth, Lluava insisted, "It was an accident. I didn't mean it to happen. I... I..."

She could not hold it in any longer. Suddenly Lluava began to vomit.

Thoth spoke out, "If there is anything you think I should know about you or why you and your friend are here, tell me now."

Acid tainted Lluava's mouth as she stepped back from the chunky puddle before her.

Another voice asked harshly, "How is it you fight so well? Who are you, really?"

Lluava's heart was racing. She tried desperately to think.

Thoth stood up. "This is your last chance."

She finally got out, "I was an Elysian soldier."

"And your companion? Is he a soldier as well?"

"No. But once we decided to leave Elysia, I began training him. We didn't know what we would find outside our kingdom, but we needed to be prepared."

"Why are *you* here?" Thoth scrutinized Lluava.

"We came in search of other Theriomorphs," she said simply. Everything she had said was true. She had been a soldier, she had trained Apex, and they were looking for Theriomorphs. She chose to be honest, even though only halfway. Should she ask him about the Incarn? Given the current situation, this was not that time. Not yet. If she knew things Thoth thought she shouldn't, she might be in even more trouble.

"Take her back to the coliseum," ordered Ruire Thoth.

Her escorts returned and began to lead her away. Lluava would have to wait for another chance to talk to the ruire.

"But what of her punishment?" a voice called out in the amphitheater.

"This is not the first time someone has been killed in these ceremonies," Thoth acknowledged. "Tragic accidents do occur. Lluava Kargen, rest up tonight. Tomorrow is meant to be a joyous occasion."

Somehow those words were anything but encouraging. Lluava couldn't help but feel as if someone else was going to wake her in the night—perhaps to abduct her, or worse. From his responses to her actions thus far, Thoth did not like her. Was he planning something sinister? Or did he believe what she had said? If the latter, maybe he was beginning to trust her. She needed his trust. Somehow, she would have to broach the subject of the Incarn soon.

Not long afterward, the healers arrived to awaken all their patients. Lluava stretched. Though a bit worn out, she felt surprisingly well. Not a muscle ached; her wounds were not sore. Actually, there were no wounds. Lifting her shirt, Lluava saw that her cuts had entirely healed. The only mark that remained was the long, fleshy scar from the stag, and even it looked less prominent.

From what she could see of the other young people leaving their cubicles, the majority of injuries seemed to have vanished. Even the severest wounds had begun to heal, the pain now bearable.

"How?" Lluava muttered to herself just as Maruny bumped into her. The young woman's arm was now wrapped in a sort of gauze, but it was clearly usable again.

"You okay, Lluava?" asked Maruny, seeming to read the shock in Lluava's features.

"I don't understand any of this."

Maruny laughed. "You drank Idun last night. It makes you better."

"That disgusting broth?"

Maruny nodded. "You didn't think that half the attendees in the Matching would be unable to attend their own ceremony, did you?"

"I had no clue," acknowledged Lluava.

"Wherever you are from, it must be a strange place. Welcome to our enlightened world."

How strange to think that her own kingdom was not as advanced in medicine as this ancient society. Were there other things that Elysia did not know? Had this knowledge existed before Varren's ancestors crossed the ocean? What would he think of all this? Lluava felt pride in the knowledge of her own people.

Once again, Lluava was led to the square, where several large tents had been erected. Beneath them, tables were laden with food, and extra seating had been provided. A semicircle of flags, each displaying a rune, flapped around the main tent, where several priestesses held court.

Lluava searched for Apex in the crowd. Although the candidates were kept in a specially designated area separate from the general public, Lluava could not see her companion. At last she caught a glimpse of him. Surrounded by a group of young women, Apex was happily entertaining his entourage. Seeing Lluava, Apex squeezed past the women and approached.

"There you are. How was your sleep? Was the stone bed comfortable?" he asked, looking bemused. He had trimmed his beard to a low bristle.

"Where were you?" she returned the question briskly.

"Crankiness doesn't suit you," noted Apex as one young woman caught his eye. She smiled at him coyly. He winked back.

Lluava gagged.

"Don't tell me you have something against a little fun?"

"Apex—" she began.

"The Matching hasn't happened yet. Technically, I'm still a free man."

"Be serious."

"*Sweetheart*, of all people, you should know the value of a little fun." Another young woman moved past and purposely brushed up against Apex's arm.

Lluava had had enough. "I was summoned to appear before Thoth last night. It was some sort of hearing."

This got his attention. "What happened?"

"I was on trial for killing that girl yesterday. They asked if I did it on purpose."

Apex was quiet.

"It was an accident." Somehow, she still felt defensive.

"What did the ruire say?"

"I think he believes me." Lluava looked around and spotted Thoth's purple turban. He had arrived and was taking a seat under a tent. "But I told him I had been an Elysian soldier. He wanted to know how we could fight the way we did. I said I'd trained you and that was it."

Taking a breath, Apex scanned the crowds. "So, what now?"

"I think," began Lluava, "we have to be extra careful. Focus on fitting in and blending with the people. I don't want to cause alarm and raise suspicions. I have a bad feeling that Thoth will not like the fact that we want to bring *certain Theriomorphs* back to our 'Banished Lands'."

"I don't think he will ever trust us," said Apex as he glared over at Thoth.

"Well, we have to get him to talk with us somehow," said Lluava, her frustration showing. "Until then, we need to try to not cause trouble."

"I know what you mean," said Apex. "Our purpose should remain secret. But Thoth is not our answer."

"What do you mean?"

"Thoth is only the ruire," explained Apex. "The ruire can change during the Spring Matching Ceremony. His authority is never guaranteed."

Lluava had not thought of that. "What, then?"

"We know that knowledge of the Incarn is not openly taught. If it were, we would have been informed over the past two weeks. Right?"

Nodding, she agreed.

"If the Incarn truly were created by the gods," continued Apex as Lluava tried not to scoff, "and the knowledge is meant to be kept secret, there is only one person who might have the answers we seek: the high priestess."

"Fine," said Lluava. She needed time to think about this. If talking with the high priestess was now their single goal, they had to gain *her* trust. The problem was that she rarely interacted with the public. Worse, she had not attended the ceremony.

"Do you think Yena will show up?" Lluava asked him. Since the high priestess had not met them yet, maybe she would take more of a liking to them than Thoth obviously had.

"I don't know."

Almost all the seats were taken, so Lluava and Apex were unable to sit together. When Thoth began to speak, Lluava barely paid attention to his words about the ancient ceremony, the right of the female to select her mate, and more insignificant rubbish. There had to be a way to meet the high priestess. Waiting until the large Matching Ceremony in the spring was not an option, even though Yena would assuredly observe all challengers to her current mate's title as ruire. There was no time for them to waste.

The young man sitting next to Lluava nudged her side. She looked up and discovered that people were staring at her. "That's you," the young man said. "Stand up and approach the ruire."

Thoth looked directly at her. "As the alpha female in your class in both knowledge and skill, you may select your mate first."

The eyes of the entire city were upon her. Several young men looked up hopefully from their tables. Lluava did not hesitate. Rolling her eyes, she walked over to Apex and pulled him up off his bench. The irony of this selection might have made others laugh, but not her. Nor Apex either, though he did venture a smirk.

"Well matched," acknowledged Thoth. "Now stand to the side."

As the Matching continued, Apex whispered into Lluava's ear, "Now, how rigorously are you going to follow the local practices? We *are* trying to blend in."

"We are not consummating anything," hissed Lluava, though she knew Apex was just teasing. At least, she hoped that was the case.

"You drain the fun out of life," sighed the huntsman. He smiled at some young women who were looking longingly at him.

After the new candidates were matched, Thoth announced, "Leucrocotta's new mating pairs!" Cheers erupted from the onlookers. After the ruire quieted his citizens, he spoke once again. "Now it is time for the second part of our ceremony: the matching of our castes."

Lluava and Apex exchanged looks. Neither one knew about this part of the ceremony. What else did they not know?

"Each of the candidates will receive a scroll from the priestesses of Crocotta. The scroll contains a rune identifying the caste that is judged to be your best match."

Once everyone had received a scroll, they were commanded to break the wax seals. Lluava unrolled hers and stared at the rune. Fortunately, this was one she recognized. Looking at Apex's scroll, she realized it was identical.

"That's—" Apex began, and Lluava confirmed, "Yeah. Warrior."

Chapter 9

Casting Doubts

"I t might be a little harder to hide who we are now," noted Apex as he rolled up his scroll.

"We have to blend in," restated Lluava, looking not at him but at the ruire.

Thoth was speaking again. "Behind me, the flags of all the major castes are displayed. Now that you have seen which caste you best match based on your rankings in the exams and the competitions, you must make a decision. Accept the caste matched to you, or choose a different caste, one that you prefer. The masters of each caste are stationed at their respective flagpoles. They await your commitments. You have until the end of our celebration to decide. Once you have declared your choice, you will be accepted as adults in our society. Congratulations."

The ruire regarded his people. "As High Priestess Yena could not attend the ceremony today, I am acting on her behalf. May Crocotta's blessing fall on each of you. Now, let the festivities commence!"

Drums erupted in a wild and frantic rhythm. Dancers cavorted about the tents in scantily clad costumes that revealed intricate designs painted on their bodies. Leaping, vaulting, and spinning in the air, the performers captured the wild frenzy of the animal kingdom. As Lluava watched in awe, she began to see a story emerge from the bestial movements. Some aspects reminded her of animals on the hunt, and others their fleeing prey. Several dances mimicked the fanciful courting displays of exotic birds or the encounters of males competing for a place in a pecking order.

Lluava soon realized that not everyone was captivated by these performances. Some of the initiates made their way toward the flagpoles to affirm their chosen caste. Others found seats with their new mates. Platters of food were brought to the tables. The attendants wore brightly colored feathered and furred outfits. Jingling bells were strapped around their ankles.

Lluava was served a dish of boiled goose eggs on a bed of steamed greens alongside a sickeningly sweet fruit. As she ate, she continued to watch the intriguing entertainment.

"What do you want to do about our choice of caste?" asked Apex.

"Ah, well," Lluava tore her eyes from the acrobats to look at the huntsman. She had never known him to ask for advice. "That is up to you."

"I think we should accept the Warrior Caste," said Apex. "Since we need to blend in, it would be unseemly to reject their recommendations."

Pausing to think about this, Lluava was hesitant. What if they were viewed with suspicion because of their prior knowledge and skill? She had told Thoth the truth—at least partly. Did he have anything to do with their placement in the Warrior Caste? And what about Apex's dual form, as well as her own? Though she could not speak for her companion, she still struggled with her inner darkness. Whatever it was, it might destroy much more than she wanted to consider.

"Plus," Apex added, "wouldn't it be fun? I thought you liked a challenge."

"I don't know, Apex—" Lluava began, then stopped. A new thought came to mind. "Okay," she said.

"Okay? Just like that?" Now Apex was skeptical.

"If the…um…*you know*," began Lluava as one of the attendants refilled her glass with a honeyed liquid, "are here, they would be strong, right? They would have to be. We are. Maybe they have also been placed in the Warrior Caste."

"One would hope," noted Apex as he turned to watch a new set of dancers.

As time passed, more platters of food were brought out to replace the now empty ones. It seemed this event was an all-day holiday. Children ran about the open green spaces, and the laughter of old friends mixed with the talk of new pairings. Torches were lit, and fire dancers thrilled onlookers.

Lluava and Apex headed to the warriors' flagpole, where a well-built man stood near a podium with quill in hand. The scruffy-looking youth whose dual form was the maned wolf had just signed his pledge to the Warrior Caste. He passed Apex with a wary look.

"The alpha couple," acknowledged the man at the podium, appraising them with hooded eyes. His overly muscular build reminded Lluava of the grand master chief who had trained her in the southern camps. That seemed so long ago, yet it had been only half a year. So much had happened in so little time.

The man asked expectantly, "Here to register?"

"Yes," said Apex assertively.

Lluava was less enthused. One day, she hoped she would be done with this sort of training. She was weary of fighting. "Yeah. Sure."

The man wrote their names on his parchment. "You will begin at sunrise. We meet at the coliseum gates."

Nodding, Lluava turned back to the festivities. Part of her wished she had chosen differently. This was a new place, one where she could have started off afresh. Surely they needed people to grow crops. That's what Lluava would have done before the draft. She would have completed her studies and helped her mother work the family farm.

After her father died, she and her mother were left to take care of things. But she had school to attend, and Gramps was too old to be much help, so her mother had trouble keeping everything in working order. Who could blame her? With infant Tomius and little Maruny, there was always too much to do. Now that Gramps had passed away and she was far from home, Lluava wondered if having two fewer mouths to feed made it any easier.

Lluava sighed.

"What are you sulking about?" asked Apex.

"Do you really care?" she hissed as she found a seat close to the dancers.

"For some unknown reason, I do," snarled Apex; he moved away from her.

Lluava shouted at him, "That's nonsense!"

As she watched the dancers whirl around a small fire pit, Lluava wondered why she was so angry at Apex. He was helping both her and Elysia. She was certain he wanted to return as much as she did. She longed to see Varren again. Apex would see…who? Was anybody waiting for him? Did he have anyone to go home to? Did he even have a home?

Realizing that she had never asked about his past, Lluava suddenly felt guilty. She had never delved into Apex's former life nor asked about his interests and passions. He was just a traveling companion, one she begrudgingly put up with. Yet they had been traveling together for weeks. What did she really know of him? He was still very much a stranger to her.

All right, Lluava decided. I'll try to be nicer to him.

Standing up, she attempted to move through the growing crowd. The onlookers appeared to be more and more enthralled. Lluava paused for a moment to watch the Theriomorphs dance. The performers were quite flexible, their movements frequently erotic. Leaping and jumping over the flames, they effortlessly shifted into their dual forms and back again. The dance was breathtaking.

"Isn't it amazing?" asked a small voice to Lluava's left. Maruny had spotted her in the crowd.

"Yes," acknowledged Lluava.

"Do you like to dance?"

"Yeah. But I've never done anything like that."

"Nor have I," laughed Maruny in a shrill, high-pitched way. "The non-ceremonial dances are about to begin. Care to join me and my mate?"

"Sure," smiled Lluava, "but I didn't see who you selected."

"Zeek," said Maruny with a grin. "He is a good match."

"I'm glad. Let me find Apex, and we'll find you and Zeek."

Moving through the crowd, Lluava heard the music change. Now, the sounds of string and wind instruments mingled with the beating drums. She recognized the melodies of some of the dances she had learned over the summer at Durog.

Where was Apex? She looked but didn't see him anywhere. Then, in the flickering firelight, Lluava spotted him conversing with a woman about his own age. Lluava approached, but when Apex looked up at her he shook his head ever so slightly. He obviously didn't want her interfering. But he was *her* match, wasn't he? She had chosen him.

Moving closer, the woman, who had dark, thick locks, glanced over at Lluava. She whispered something into Apex's ear, turned on her heel, and left. Before Lluava could speak, Apex reached over and ruffled her hair like a small child or his mutt and said, "Go enjoy yourself."

Apex didn't want her around! Suddenly Lluava was embarrassed. She, the female with the highest ranking and the honor of selecting a mate, had been turned down by her chosen partner. Had anyone seen this? She could almost hear the gossip begin. Turning quickly, her face reddened. She needed to get away.

Tears welled up. What was that about? Wiping her brimming eyes, Lluava took off at a trot toward their quarters. Once inside, she began to sob. Alone, she wept in the quiet darkness until she fell asleep in exhaustion.

***

When morning came, Apex was snoring in his stone niche. The sun was just beginning to rise, barely illuminating the small room.

"Up!" Lluava shouted as she jumped to her feet. "We can't be late!"

Apex's bloodshot eyes sprang open. Who knew how long he had stayed at the celebration? Seeing him so groggy made Lluava grin.

"Let's go! Let's go! Let's go!" she shouted, and clapped in his ears as he stumbled to his feet in a tangle of sheets. "Training starts today!"

Lluava was out the door and halfway down the street by the time Apex jogged up behind her.

"Wait until the day *you* sleep in," he huffed as he slipped on a new shirt. Lluava had to admit, he was very well built in a barrel-chested sort of way.

A decent-sized group of people already waited outside the coliseum doors. The man who had signed them up last night was calling out names. They arrived just in time to hear him shout out, "Apex!"

"Here!" responded the huntsman.

"Lluava!"

"Here!"

Lluava and Apex exchanged looks. "Well, that was close," she whispered as they shared a smile.

The coliseum gates opened, and everyone filed inside. In all the movement, Lluava spotted Maruny walking beside the scruffy young man.

"That must be Zeek," noted Lluava as she nodded to the pair.

"The maned wolf?" questioned Apex. "Do you know them?"

"I know her," said Lluava as she waved to the young woman. Maruny waved back as the command to line up was given. Due to her prior military training, lining up was nothing new to Lluava.

Once everyone was in order, the master of the Warrior Caste shouted out, "I am Master Hon, and I will oversee your progress as you train. We will begin each morning with a stretching routine. Everyone will follow accordingly."

For a man as muscular as he, Hon was able to maneuver his body into some impressive positions. The morning routine was reminiscent of one she had learned from Colonel Ojewa, an instructor in the training camps. Beginning from a standing position, the group learned how and when to breathe as they shifted their weight fluidly into each pose. Although not extremely flexible, Lluava was better than many of those around her. One man even stumbled, causing a ripple effect as trainees toppled onto one another.

Balanced on one leg, Apex snickered. When she jabbed him lightly in the ribs, Lluava didn't mean to make him lose his balance. Unfortunately, he pulled her down with him in a heap on the hard-packed earth. Master Hon passed by them, shaking his head.

"What was that about?" Lluava whispered testily as she unwound herself from him and stood up.

Apex replied, "If I go down, I'm taking you with me."

He was playing with her. Lluava was not amused. "We need to be serious about this."

"Loosen up, for once."

"Look who's talking!"

"Are our young lovers having a spat?" Master Hon asked with mock incredulity. "No? Good, since we are about to begin our dual-form training."

As Hon walked away from them, Lluava cast Apex a worried look. He alternated his gaze between his partner and the master.

Hon shouted, "I want everyone to shift so we may begin combat training!"

At once, the coliseum filled with wild and fierce beasts. The few females among them were as impressive as their male counterparts. Lluava spotted Maruny. Her form did not appear threatening, but her spunk and drive compensated.

"You can do this," encouraged Apex as he shifted. The massive bronze Yorrick wolverine drew the eyes of everyone. His form was quite rare. Lluava wished she felt as confident as a tigress. What if the darkness took control again?

"Is there a problem, Lluava?" questioned Master Hon.

"In Elysia, we rarely trained in our dual forms," she lied. "How are we supposed to use weapons?"

"We are not in the Banished Lands," explained Hon. "Here, we train as we have for centuries. Theriomorphs do not need the assistance of weapons.

They themselves *are* weapons. You must learn to battle in your dual form."

Lluava tried to argue, and pointed out that even the gods had their mythic weapons. However, the look on Master Hon's faced confirmed that a refusal on her part would prove meaningless. She would have to shift. She would have to learn to control herself, and fast.

Apex watched her warily. He knew what was worrying her. Wasn't he afraid, too? He had said he faced the same problem. Had he figured out a way to master himself? He would tell her if he had, wouldn't he?

Taking a breath, Lluava shifted. Immediately the tigress felt the change in her senses. Sounds she would not normally hear were as clear as Apex's steady breathing beside her. Her tail swished agitatedly as she made sure her sight had not altered. She could not lose control and black out again. How could Apex be so calm? She wished she shared this trait.

Hon, still in human form, said, "The first thing I want you to do is to fully submerge yourself in your dual form. Notice the differences your animal form offers, differences that you would not have otherwise. Take note of all your physical senses. How have they changed? Feel the sensations and signals you receive through your feathers or fur. Notice how your scales or claws feel on the ground."

As the master spoke, Lluava began to tense up. If she acceded to Hon's request, let herself become the tiger completely, what would happen to her? She knew what the tigress was capable of. She did not dare explore its potential further.

"Now, move around," ordered Hon as he shifted into a large white rhino. He continued to instruct the new initiates. "Pay attention. How do these movements vary from your other form? Do your muscles react differently? If so, how? Are they more fluid, or unusually restricted?"

There was one thing Lluava did find quite different: her breathing. It had become extremely rapid. While everyone else seemed to be in a relaxed, almost meditative state, Lluava felt her agitation grow.

"Relax, Lluava," observed Hon. "You must relax. There is nothing to worry about. Trust me."

"None of this is helping," she argued. If she had spoken in this manner to a commanding officer in the Elysian training camps, she would have paid a heavy price for insubordination. Fortunately, that was not the case here. Instead, Hon looked directly at her. "You must become one with the animal within. Trust your instincts."

Did he know what he was asking of her? Of course not! Lluava's claws dug into the hardened earth. "A Theriomorph must be careful not to lose herself in her animal form, lest she never return."

Hon laughed. "Who told you that rubbish? What will tear you apart is ignoring this vital aspect of who you are." The master became serious. "Now, concentrate, Lluava. Let your inner tiger out."

"No!" screamed Lluava. Suddenly, the colors around her seemed to warp. As if someone had splashed water onto a new painting, color bled out, leaving a blue-green-tinted world. Flashes of red could be seen in bits of fur or feather patterns, but all other warm hues had vanished.

"No!" Lluava screamed again. "No!"

"Lluava!" A voice rang in her ears. Apex must have realized what was happening. The giant wolverine raced across the coliseum toward her. But he would not reach her in time.

"Stay away from me!" Lluava screamed, but the more she thrashed and warned, the more the other trainees pressed toward their panicking comrade. She felt her control wavering. She was losing her inner battle. Whatever evil was locked inside her was going to make itself known.

Lluava let loose a roar.

Chapter 10

Night Summons

The sound echoed off the stone stadium's high seating. Before the air had stopped reverberating, Lluava roared again. She could feel that thing—that presence, that darkness inside of her—stir. Why didn't the others near her understand her warning? They had to get out, run, escape.

"Lluava!" Apex shouted once more. He was almost there, but she was already slipping into the darkness.

Suddenly, Lluava was tossed into the air. She had not realized the rhino was upon her until it was too late. It didn't matter that Hon chose not to gore her with his horns; the desire to fight her opponent was too strong. As soon as she landed on her feet, Lluava sprang at the pale-gray mountain.

Screams erupted all around her. Theriomorphs in both forms were racing for the doors. The reality of this fight sank in. As Lluava's sharp claws grazed Hon's thick hide, her eyesight began to cloud. In only moments, she knew she would be lost.

Sharp nails dug into her shoulders. In a single, jerking motion, Lluava was torn from her position and pulled toward another large body. Turning with a snarl, she faced the enormous wolverine.

The creature bared its teeth and snapped at her. Its guard hairs rose up in a mat of bronze spikes, making it appear to double in size. A normal animal would be terrified, not to mention intimidated. But Lluava was not a normal animal and certainly not afraid.

As she readied herself to spring, the wolverine opened its mouth again. Was it preparing to bite? The tigress was more than ready. Her claws would give its muzzle a nasty scar.

Instead, the beast spoke. "You don't want to do this."

Lluava's mind reeled as the wolverine continued. "You can stop this. Remember who you are. Remember why you are here. Think, Lluava. Think of…Varren."

Varren. A name that represented a face, the face of a man. Varren was the reason she was here, in this place. She was trying to get back to him. He was waiting for her. As Lluava visualized her partner's dark wavy locks, his kind cool eyes, and the smile that could brighten any dark soul, color bled back into her vision. The world normalized. She shifted.

A large body shoved her against the stone wall, and Lluava let out a gasp as the wind was knocked out of her.

"Don't hurt her!" Apex's voice urged

In his human form, Master Hon shouted, "What was that about?"

"She has a problem," Apex explained. "She has trouble controlling herself in her dual form. She forgets who she is."

Hon continued to pin Lluava against the wall. She did not resist. Instead, she let her body grow limp. What could she say? Once again, she had almost killed innocent people. Was she any better than the enemy army threatening Elysia?

Releasing her, Hon said, "You are excused for the rest of the day and until further notice. I must decide how to proceed. Volatile behavior such as this will not be tolerated."

Nodding her head in understanding, Lluava slunk off. As she walked through the city, she could feel the hidden looks as well as the obvious stares of the people. Word spread fast, it seemed. Or was this all in her head?

A small man in a long, ink-stained robe crossed the street in front of her. Lluava instantly recognized him. "Pedagogue Pardus!" she called.

The teacher turned and smiled as she jogged to his side. "How are you, Lluava?" he asked. "You do not know how proud I am of you both! Who knew I could take two strangers and teach them enough, in such a short time, to become the winter class's alpha couple?"

Leo was beaming.

"I think I made a mistake," confessed Lluava.

"How so?"

"I chose the wrong caste. Is there a way for me to switch? I should be working in agriculture, not warfare."

"Well," began Leo, "there is a way, but you would have to discuss the issue with higher authorities. Switching one's caste is not typically encouraged."

"Yeah, I would expect as much. What do I need to do?"

"You will need both your current caste's master and the master of the caste you wish to join to agree to the transfer. Ruire Thoth must also assent to this modification."

"That's a lot of effort," sighed Lluava, although she was almost certain that after today Master Hon would agree.

"Yes. They don't make it easy," said Leo kindly. "They want you to be certain of your decision. You can only change once."

"I'm pretty certain."

"Let me make some inquiries."

"Thank you."

"Anything for a good student and a friend," said Leo with a smile. "Now, what are you up to for the rest of the day?"

He had to have known something had happened. How could he not? She was clearly not where she should be.

"I have no plans."

"Would you like to join me in the library? You have always seemed interested in your studies."

With nothing else to do besides to sulk, Lluava said, "That sounds just fine."

***

By the time Lluava left the library, she had discovered the Theriomorph legends that had arisen during the Landon Wars. Fierce fighters had protected family and clan. Magnificent warriors had laid down their lives in futile attempts to protect their cities. Great sacrifices had been made. Theriomorphs living in territories conquered by humans accepted voluntary banishment so as not to lead their enemies to the remaining Theriomorph cities and strongholds, of which Leucrocotta was one.

Leo was not only a pedagogue but also the city's finest cultural anthropologist, and he was thrilled by the extent of her interest in their culture. With his consent, she was able to take as many scrolls as she liked with her for further study.

The sun had set, and Lluava fumbled with the door to their quarters in the darkness. Several scrolls slipped from her grip, and she realized she might have gotten a bit carried away. Luckily, the door opened without her help. Apex stood there looking disgruntled.

As Lluava entered, she began excitedly, "You won't believe it. I bumped into Leo Pardus. He invited me to the library with him. I found out that he is probably going to be the next Master of Studies. He said he would put in a good word for me and that I might be able to— What's wrong?"

Apex was staring at her strangely. He gave a small nod and focused on something behind her. Turning, Lluava realized they were not alone. Etha and the blond priestess stood silently by the back wall.

Lluava gave Apex one last, questioning look.

He just shrugged.

"Lluava Kargen," began the blond priestess. "You have been summoned by High Priestess Yena."

Was this because of the incident earlier? wondered Lluava. Her mouth dropped open, but she didn't care. This day was taking yet another strange and possibly problematic turn.

"It is advisable," Etha stated sternly, "to attend the high priestess immediately." She locked eyes with the teen.

The touch of Apex's hand on Lluava's back reassured her.

"Okay," she agreed, and followed the priestesses out the door. Behind her, Apex watched her go, his eyes aglow in the dark.

***

Once inside the temple, Lluava was led through the grand public pronaos, where several devotees reverently knelt before individual shrines, and into the smaller cella used for private council. The light from flaming sconces clearly showed that no one else was there. Lluava studied the tall, throne-like chair that sat atop a high dais. Carved from a silver-hued marble, the empty seat conveyed a hard, cold presence.

"Wait here," commanded the blond priestess. The pair disappeared behind the dais leaving Lluava alone in the sanctuary.

As time passed, the teen became more anxious. Where had the priestesses gone? What were they doing? Where was High Priestess Yena? Why had they summoned her like this? Had she done something wrong? Lluava knew the training had gotten out of hand that morning, but no one was hurt; she would apologize if that's what they wanted.

Unable to stand still any longer, she paced around the room. The walls of the inner sanctuary were covered in bas-reliefs of the goddess Crocotta. Lluava ran her fingers over the carved form of the figure nearest her. The goddess was depicted as about her mother's age, but her timeless features made it impossible to tell. In this relief, the smiling goddess held out a piece of fruit, an item of food, a source of life. Crocotta was the eternal mother, offering life to all.

As she neared the throne, Lluava noticed a small passageway opening directly behind the stone dais. Peering in, she saw at the other end a golden light radiating from an open doorway.

So that is the inner sanctum, she thought, where all the priestesses reside. Where Yena was now. The light seemed to beckon, and she moved closer. Were they testing her? Were there other plans afoot?

Slipping quietly down the hall, Lluava approached the doorway. She would take just a small peek. What did they keep hidden away from the world that was so special? An esteemed statue of the goddess? Some ancient relic?

Suddenly, Lluava remembered the weapons that had been taken from her. Issaura's Claws were here! She wanted them back.

As she reached the doorway, a sultry voice called out behind her.

"Who gave you permission to step on hallowed ground?"

Lluava whirled to face a figure draped entirely in a silver garment that revealed only the white irises of the woman's eyes.

The teen tried to speak, but no words came out. They stuck in her throat.

"You will return to the outer chamber," commanded the woman.

Lluava quickly hurried down the passageway and around the dais to her

67

original position. Although she knew the high priestess was walking behind her, she could hear no footfalls. Turning to look at the dais, Lluava saw that the high priestess was already seated on her marble throne.

Yena's voice resonated through the sanctuary. "Do you know why I asked you here tonight?"

"No," admitted Lluava.

"How do you feel you are acclimating to our way of life?"

Lluava recognized the topic had been changed, yet she did not know why. "As well as can be expected, High Priestess."

"You chose the Warrior Caste. Why?"

"It is what I know, High Priestess." Lluava wondered if she should bring up her desire to switch castes. Yet overstepping Ruire Thoth's authority might end poorly for her.

"You are a great warrior."

"I fought for my kingdom."

"Do you like war?"

"No, High Priestess," Lluava quickly countered. "War is a terrible thing. Every life touched by war changes; many are damaged irrevocably."

"Then why do you continue to fight?"

"I took the recommendation given to me. The scroll indicated I should join the Warrior Caste."

"I am not referring to your choice of occupation."

Lluava wished she could see Yena's expression behind the folds of cloth.

The high priestess continued, "Your spirit is strong, Lluava, yet you are at war with yourself."

Had Master Hon told her? Some gossip must have come Yena's way. How else could she know about what had happened earlier? Of course, as one of the city's rulers, she must have informants everywhere, since she rarely ventured beyond these hallowed walls.

"Your struggle is great but unnecessary."

Lluava did not know what to say. "I try to control it."

"You sound as if you regard your dual form as a separate entity. But it is part of who you are."

Shaking her head, Lluava said, "You couldn't understand what's going on with me. It isn't my dual form I am fighting. It is something else. Something evil."

"Child," Yena began, making Lluava feel far younger than she was, "you must first realize that your inner struggle is something *you* have instigated to separate you from one aspect of yourself. You are fighting yourself rather than embracing who you are. You are building walls where walls need not be. Tear them down, Lluava. Allow yourself to be whole again and not divided."

"If that is who I am, what I am," objected Lluava, "I don't want to be that anymore."

"In the end, the choice is not fully yours. To continue on this path means certain destruction for you. The only way to master the darkness is to let it in. You *must* let it in, Lluava."

"I don't want that," hissed Lluava.

"What *do* you want, then?"

Lluava answered without any hesitation, "I want the weapons I possessed when I arrived in Leucrocotta."

"Issaura's Claws," mused the high priestess. "They can only be bestowed upon one who is worthy. To wield a weapon as powerful as these requires more than skill. Do you deem yourself worthy, Lluava?"

"Yes." There was no doubt in Lluava's mind that the Claws should be returned to her.

"I do not," countered the high priestess. "Not yet."

Balling her hands into fists, Lluava bit her tongue so not to say the vile things that came to her mind. Regaining her composure, she asked, "What can I do to prove I am worthy?"

"There is a test," said Yena. Excitement emanated from the priestess's form. "To pass it, you must be one with yourself. You must face your demons."

Lluava wanted to scream. This woman clearly had no idea what she was asking. How could she? She was nothing more than a relic of a long gone mythology. She had no comprehension of reality. And especially no clue about what was going on inside Lluava's being.

"How do you expect me to do this?"

"Come each evening to the temple. Helena and Etha will guide you in meditation techniques."

"Meditation?" Lluava was skeptical.

Yena was undeterred. "Meditation will allow you to have full control of your mental, physical, and emotional states. Your mind is capable of much. Wait and see. It will be the sledgehammer you need to break down those walls."

"Or the sword to combat the darkness," offered Lluava.

Suddenly laughter erupted through the chamber. The sound climbed higher and higher into the lofty ceiling. Yena's pale eyes flashed at Lluava in the gloom. "I like you, Lluava Kargen. Soon you will understand what you are meant to be."

Lluava fervently hoped so.

"What of Apex?" she asked, suddenly thinking of her companion. "What of *his* weapons?"

"He will face the same test to earn the right to Ullr's Fangs."

"He will. We will," said Lluava.

As Lluava left the temple grounds, thoughts of Issaura's Claws filled her mind. She would wear them again; that was certain. And what better way to earn the high priestess's regard than by taking and passing this test? She finally felt they were close to discovering where the other Incarn were. But first she must face the darkness inside. Lluava hoped it would not consume her.

Chapter 11

Claimed

Apex was not at their quarters when she returned.

Strange, thought Lluava. It was quite late, but then, like her, he had always been one to act on his own. Lluava hoped he had wandered off by choice and not been dragged away at someone else's command.

The next morning, Apex was fast asleep on one of the stone ledges. Lluava woke him up and, without much talk, followed the huntsman to the coliseum. Along the way, she wondered if she had missed a great opportunity. She had been alone with the high priestess; Yena had even asked her what she wanted. But instead of inquiring about the Incarn, Lluava had asked about her own weapons. Would she have another chance? Should she have asked then? Would Yena have trusted her enough to share information? Had she made a poor choice? Then again, she now knew there was a way to regain Issaura's Claws.

Anyhow, it was a new day for new beginnings. Lluava wasn't sure if Master Hon would see her, but she needed to talk with him. When they arrived, Hon acted as if nothing unusual had happened the day before. Maybe he wanted to give her a second chance. Or had someone ordered him to?

Not everyone was as welcoming. Lluava felt the wary looks of the other trainees like claws running down her back. Should she leave? Although training would be beneficial, the Warrior Caste conducted regular drills in dual form, and she was afraid of what might happen. She could still switch castes. In fact, she liked the thought of Leo taking her under his wing.

Lluava eyed Apex as they began the morning stretching routine. She had not told him about the opportunity to earn back their weapons. She wanted Issaura's Claws in her hands and knew Apex felt the same about Ullr's Fangs.

If she wished to earn back her weapons, she would have to learn to control her actions, especially in dual form.

When everyone was told to transform, Master Hon approached Lluava. "I want you to shift with the others, but if you begin to… panic, change back. Challenge yourself to stay in your dual form as long as you can, but don't overdo it. We will gradually increase the length of time you are able to stay in your dual form." Although Lluava was a bit embarrassed, she gratefully followed his advice.

In dual form, trainees worked on building up their physical strength. They had to become comfortable in animal form. Each needed to know the capabilities and limitations of that other body. Though skeptical, Lluava began to notice some benefits. For better or for worse, she began to relax a bit in her tigress form once again.

That first evening after training, Lluava headed toward the temple.

"Where do you think you're going?" Apex's gruff voice inquired. She still had not told him about the night before, partly because she did not want to admit she had lost an opportunity to inquire about the Incarn.

"That meeting last night," Lluava began, knowing that the huntsman must have been at least a little curious, "was about my loss of control yesterday. I was told that I need to learn to meditate and see if that can help me control…myself."

Pausing, she waited for Apex to laugh. Yet he did not. He did not even look like he wanted to poke fun at her expense. Instead he was serious. "Meditate? For how long?"

"Every evening, until—*if*—I can get myself under control."

Apex clearly was thinking about something.

Lluava quickly added, "I don't think they understand what actually happens when I black out. I wasn't about to try to explain it."

"Yeah. Okay," said Apex as he ran his calloused fingers through his hair. "You do that. Let me know if anything helps."

"So, you're still struggling with it too?" said Lluava, now quite relieved. "I thought—"

"You'll be late, and so will I," said the huntsman as he turned his back toward the temple.

As Lluava headed off, she glanced over her shoulder. "Late for what?"

But Apex had disappeared.

Should she have told him about the possibility of earning their weapons back? No. There really wasn't any reason to do so unless she was certain that they could overcome the darkness inside them, whatever it was.

***

"Meditation," began the blond priestess Helena, once Lluava was situated on a pillow on the ground, "is meant to help one to gain full control of one's mind and thus full access to one's emotional and even physical aspects."

Even though the priestess's garment was not as sheer as the material worn by city folk, Helena's silhouette revealed a lithe form. She sat down cross-legged before Lluava.

"We are going to start an exercise today," explained the priestess. "To begin, I will give you a word…well, more of a sound actually, and I want you to memorize it."

After a moment, Helena said, "Shring."

"Shring?" Lluava repeated the sound to make sure that was what she had heard. She did not recognize it as a word.

"Yes. Shring," replied Helena. "*Shring* will be your mantra, your repeated word to focus on during your initial meditation practice. Close your eyes."

Lluava did so.

"Now," Helena said softly, "I want you to mentally repeat your mantra over and over again at whatever pace you see fit. Don't vocalize it. There you go. Just think it."

Shring, Lluava thought. Shring.

Helena broke in once more. "Your goal is to continue to focus on repeating that word and nothing else. Your mind will wander often in the beginning, but once you recognize that it is wandering, refocus on your mantra. I want you to do this today until I tell you to stop."

Lluava was left in the silence of her thoughts. Shring. Shring, shring, she repeated mentally. Shring. How was this supposed to help her? Shring. What could repeated words really do? Shring. Were they making fun of her? Shring. Why did they want her to focus on one nonsensical word? Focus. Oh, crud. Shring. Shring. Shring.

By the time Helena told her to stop and open her eyes, Lluava was appalled at how easily her mind had wandered. The task was such a simple one, yet she struggled more than she had on the coming-of-age exams. How could that be?

Helena inquired, "What do you think? How do you feel you did?"

"Horribly," muttered Lluava.

The priestess nodded. "It will take practice. You need to strengthen your mind just like any other part of your body. We will resume tomorrow."

***

Next morning, Lluava woke up groggily. This time, Apex was out of bed before her. He looked vibrant and seemed actually to be enjoying the warriors' physical training. Lluava remembered a time when she, too, was excited about learning the art of war. Not anymore. Even though this style was different, essentially it was all the same. Learn to master a weapon, be it oneself or an actual item; work first as an individual, then as a unit; learn to strategize, et cetera, et cetera.

Anyway, why did the city need a Warrior Caste if no one except the ice bearers set foot beyond the valley's protecting mountains? What was the purpose? Defense? Since their existence had been kept secret for so long, did they actually fear invasion? By whom? They were invisible to the rest of the world. Or was this just a means to keep the citizens' minds at ease?

That day, the trainees were led to a part of the forest beyond Leucrocotta. There they found several natural-looking formations, including a deep ravine cut into the earth, mounds of boulders, and thick-stemmed vines hanging down from large, exotic trees.

"Today you will learn to manipulate your dual form in and around these formations. You must become comfortable maneuvering as animals."

For Lluava, these tasks were fairly simple. The hardest part was overcoming the fear that she could suddenly lose control. However, nothing unpleasant happened that day. In the evening, Lluava resumed her meditation training. Again, she was asked to silently repeat her mantra. Her mind wandered every half-dozen repetitions or so. Was she ever going to improve?

Over the next few days, the dual-form drills became increasingly harder. Trainees had to focus on how to use their physical attributes as military weapons. Occasionally, Maruny would talk to Lluava. Zeek, Maruny's ruddy-haired mate, would accompany her, though he was clearly intimidated by Apex. Yet, as the days ebbed away, even Zeek and Apex grew comfortable with each other. Lluava had never known the huntsman to have friends, but the four of them worked well as a unit during their training sessions.

In the evenings, Lluava continued to struggle with her mantra. The assignment hadn't changed, yet her thoughts seemed to wander more often. Her concentration was not helped when she returned to find Apex out and about. What was he up to?

One evening, frustrated with the lack of progress of her meditation, Lluava decided to skip the session. Something else was on her mind, and saying *shring* would not prevent her from thinking about it: just where did Apex go at night?

Lluava knew that he would not tell her even if she asked. He rarely told her anything personal. But why would he? Although they were partnered for this mission, that was their only tie. Well, that and supposedly that both were Incarn.

After their warrior training, Lluava pretended to head to the temple. Once out of sight, she doubled back. Apex headed away from their quarters and began to wander through a heavily populated area. He stopped at one of the street vendors and purchased several skewers of hot meat. Where had he gotten the money?

Lluava knew they were both on a stipend that would provide food during training and at their quarters until they had become fully working citizens. But neither of them had received any coin, or so she had thought.

Next, Apex made his way to a shop that sold various meads. He's drinking again, Lluava thought sourly. No wonder he did not want her to know. Stupid idiot! She was angry and disappointed. Sighing, Lluava decided to leave him to his old habits; she almost turned back, but someone else caught her eye.

A woman about Apex's age approached him—the woman from their graduation ceremony. In the light of day, her hair shone vibrant red, not dark as Lluava had originally perceived. The woman strode up to Apex and kissed him full on the lips.

Lluava gasped. In a foolish fear of being heard in the crowded streets, she ducked behind a moving cart full of produce. When the cart had passed, she saw the pair walking down the road arm in arm. The woman pulled Apex closer, and he laughingly leaned in and kissed her again.

Apex is mine! thought Lluava angrily. She had claimed him. She had earned that right. The teen followed the couple. This insult was too great to ignore. Without understanding exactly why, she had to see where they were headed.

Lluava stealthily tracked the pair. Despite the bustling cityscape, several times she dove around a corner of a building or ducked behind a group of people to prevent being seen. Yet none of this really mattered; Apex and the woman were enthralled with one another. Yet Lluava stayed vigilant.

Though the woman was clearly leading the way, Apex also seemed to know where to turn. Had he done this before? How long had this been going on? Since the ceremony? Lluava felt nauseous.

Eventually the woman opened a door to one of the houses. The building looked identical to those beside it, so Lluava made sure to note its location. Once the pair was inside, the door was shut.

Looking around, Lluava realized there were very few people in this neighborhood; yet no one seemed to notice the girl's presence. Taking a big breath, Lluava strode up to the door. She would confront Apex. This might be a misunderstanding. This might be—

The sounds that emanated from behind the door were all too clear. Lluava stumbled backward. Her heart beat so rapidly that her breath came in short, sharp inhalations. All of a sudden, she wanted to be as far from this house as she could. She took off running toward her own quarters.

As she passed the library, she heard Leo's voice call out from the library steps. "Lluava! Over here. I have a wonderful scroll for you!"

She ignored him and continued on her way. Instead of crying, she entered her lodging, slammed the door behind her and screamed. What was Apex thinking? He was ruining everything! He was...this could....

Taking several breaths to calm herself, Lluava knew she had to find the Incarn and leave this place. If the Incarn existed here, there had to be a clue somewhere. She had not seen High Priestess Yena again, so talking to her was out of the question for now. However, Leo had access to all the ancient scrolls and documents. Maybe somewhere in the dusty archives was a scroll on the Incarn and the prophecy involving them. Someone had to know. She would confide in Leo. He was her only true friend here.

That night, Lluava plotted how to get out of the city. With Leo by her side, she was sure to find some scrap of information that could benefit her mission. Yet, instead of being consoled by that notion, she grew more agitated. Apex had still not returned. She decided to wait up for him.

Hours passed before Lluava heard the door open. She sat up and growled, "I told you we had to focus on finding the other Incarn!" She jumped out of bed and walked straight over to the surprised huntsman. "I said we had to stay focused! I said no distractions!" She jabbed her finger at Apex's chest. "And then you go and bed any woman you see fit! While I am doing everything I can to help us, you are off philandering! Do you even care about why we are here?"

Lluava was seething. She shoved Apex against the door. "Do you even care that I'm stuck out here with the likes of you when I could be in Elysia with my friends, my family? No! You don't! I said—"

"You said to blend in with the society." Apex's face darkened. "You made me promise to do everything I could to avoid drawing attention. That's what I have been doing. Keeping the promise that I made to *you*."

"What promise was that? To sleep with anyone you liked, just for amusement?" snapped Lluava.

"I am following the local protocol for mate selection," growled Apex. "Just like you asked me to."

"But you're *my* mate!" shouted Lluava. Her anger was overwhelming.

"No. Not anymore," said Apex sullenly.

"What?" Lluava did not understand what he meant. She had beaten all the other contenders. She had won. He was hers by Theriomorph law.

"I am technically Vissa's now," Apex explained gently. "The law states—or don't you remember—that all initiates are ranked lower than all other adults until the Spring Match, when the entire adult population is re-ranked. As Vissa has competed in the Spring Match several times over, she is ranked higher than you. Her claim overrides yours. She saw how I fought in the coliseum and claimed me shortly after the ceremony."

Lluava was dumbfounded.

"You told me to do everything I could to seem to be one of them," he reiterated. "This is their law. I am keeping the promise I made to you. In order to fit in, there is nothing else I could have done. I could not denounce her claim. You know this. I have yet to move in with her, because I'm hoping you and I will find what we need before then."

Lluava turned away. Her face felt hot. She was grateful for the darkness. Climbing onto her stony bed, she turned to face the wall. As she forced her eyes to stay shut, she heard Apex say, "I was just doing what you asked."

The next morning, nothing went right. Everything about her training was off. At the temple, Lluava felt drained, but she endured Etha's lecture on responsibility and commitment.

"If you cannot appreciate and respect the aid High Priestess Yena has offered you, then do not waste our time," finished Etha.

Fair enough, thought Lluava. She had made the wrong choice. Oh, how she wished she hadn't! To be blissfully ignorant would be better than this. No wonder this meditation practice was one of her worst yet. Her mind remained on Apex. What were he and the red-headed woman doing right now? Lluava knew she had to clear her mind of distractions if there was any hope of winning back the Claws. Yet Apex filled all her thoughts.

After leaving the temple, Lluava went to the library and found Leo working in the archives.

"I'm so sorry about yesterday." She apologized for her blatant slight when she had refused to acknowledge him and his friendly chatter. "My mind was on other things."

"Is everything all right?" the small man kindly purred.

"Yes," Lluava lied, then began to cry. She hated doing so.

"What's wrong?" Leo asked consolingly. He left his mound of scrolls to drape an arm around Lluava's shoulders, and they took seats on a bench.

"It's Apex." Lluava's voice quavered. "He has been claimed by an older woman, and I can't do anything about it."

"That is not uncommon for the alpha male in minor matches. They are highly sought after. Are you actually attached to the man?" asked Leo earnestly.

Wiping her eyes, Lluava answered, "Of course I am." Her lie sounded convincing even to her. "But he is gone now."

"Hush, hush," comforted Leo as he patted her on the shoulder. "You can win him back."

Lluava blinked.

"There is a way."

Chapter 12

Course of Action

The weekly holy day fell two days after Lluava's conversation with Leo. All regular work was banned, as was all training. The priestesses read excerpts from the holy books to devotees in the temple. There were three sessions that people could attend, but the morning session was clearly the most popular.

Lluava made herself scarce, which enabled Apex to position himself next to Vissa. As Helena recited the well-known verses, Lluava's attention was drawn to the new couple. This was the day to reclaim her mate. This was the day she would strip the redhead of her smug expression.

As everyone began to file out through the grand temple doors, Lluava made sure to be one of the first to leave. She stood on the bottom step and waited. Amid the crowd of people, she spotted her rival. It was time for her to act.

"Vissa!" Lluava shouted, loudly enough to draw the attention of more than a few. Walking straight up to her opponent, she announced, "I make a Challenge to your Claim."

"You can't do that," barked the redhead.

"Oh, yes, I can," countered Lluava. "And you know it."

"How dare you!" snapped Vissa, as if she had been publicly insulted.

Apex stared at Lluava. "What are you doing?"

Ignoring the huntsman, Lluava shouted louder than before. "I said, I am making a Challenge to a Claim!"

Several curious city folk began to gather around the trio. Vissa did not appear amused.

"Quit being petty," she said. "It shows off your immaturity."

"No," said Lluava. "I think I'm about to show off my strength."

77

Realizing that Lluava was not going to back down, Vissa's eyes darted about. They flashed angrily, causing several onlookers to step back. "I'm not going to play your little game."

Looking up at the temple doorway, Lluava realized that several priestesses were observing them. She smiled at the angry woman. "I think you must accept."

When Vissa saw the priestesses, she seemed to understand the seriousness of the situation. Glaring at Lluava, she asked, "You want to fight for him? Then have it your way."

Ignoring the growing crowd pushing in around them, Lluava's full concentration was on the redhead. Apex seemed to have been swallowed up by the crowd. Oh, well, he didn't *really* need to see this.

Vissa balled one hand into a fist while Lluava rolled her shoulders back. The redhead swung first. Her fist missed its mark, while the other hand clawed the air in front of Lluava's eyes. She quickly noted the length of Vissa's sharp nails.

Crouching to lower her center of gravity, Lluava swung a left hook, followed by an uppercut. Vissa jumped back to escape those blows yet was unprepared for the multiple jabs that quickly followed and collided with her jaw.

"A real fighter, are you?" spat Vissa as she sprayed blood into the air. "A real animal? Let's see how animalistic you can be!"

Vissa shifted into a red fox. The vixen sprang at Lluava's leg and bit her lower thigh.

"Get off me!" yelled Lluava. She felt her skin tearing as she tried to shake loose the scarlet parasite.

Releasing her foe, the canine barked, "Shift, why don't you? Are you scared?"

What had Apex told her? thought Lluava. How could he!

Since the incident with Master Hon on her first day of training, Lluava had not attempted combat practice in her alternate form. If she shifted, would she lose control again? She would have to stay focused and be ready to shift back at any moment, even if she lost this duel.

The vixen bared her teeth and snapped. The fox prepared to spring again.

"So, you want to see a beast?" snarled Lluava. "Be careful what you wish for."

Lluava shifted, and the white tigress roared.

The fox's eyes were suddenly filled with fear. Vissa must have thought that Lluava would not fight in her dual form. She was wrong.

The vixen raised her hackles to inflate the appearance of her size. The attempt was useless. Lluava's dual form so obviously overpowered the small canine that everyone knew this fight was now one-sided. A single slap from the large pad of Lluava's paw sent the fox sprawling. The tigress pounced on the poor animal and grabbed the furry scruff in her jaws.

"Enough! Stop!" squealed the writhing vixen. "I renounce my claim!"

The tigress released the red fox, who began to slink away as the cool voice of High Priestess Yena was heard. "Be it here known that, since this woman has renounced her claim, she no longer has mating rights until the Spring Match."

Any smile that Lluava might have displayed was dispelled. Seeing the pitiful look of the fox, she realized this ordeal would affect Vissa for several more months. But this was fair, right? Vissa had overstepped Lluava's rights. Lluava followed protocol. Yes, challenging a claim was rarely done, but it was allowed.

Standing at the top of the stairs, the high priestess's gaze fixed on the white tigress. Yena's eyes—the only thing not covered by her silver garments—flashed with power. Lluava shivered. The city folk began to disperse and return to their homes. Vissa had disappeared, probably to mourn her wounded pride. Only Apex remained. He stared at the silhouette of the high priestess as she turned back to the sanctuary of the temple.

"I'm glad that's over," sighed Lluava as she returned to human form. "Now things can get back to normal."

Her words seemed to have broken Apex's spell. He spun on her, "What have you done! You idiot!"

"What?" Lluava replied quite defensively. "I brought you back to reality, so we can finish what we started. No distractions."

"You fool!" snarled Apex. "Vissa was feeding me information about everyone's dual forms. She was looking into anyone who might have a god's form. That knowledge would have helped us identify any Incarn, and you ruined it. You selfish little brat!

Lluava felt her jaw drop.

"We could have been heading home soon. You just trapped us here even longer!" Apex stormed off, leaving her to contemplate the repercussions of her actions.

Was he right? Had she waylaid them? Suddenly, guilt engulfed her. There had to be something she could do, and she knew the perfect person to help her.

***

In the archives of the city's library, Leo was wiping down his spectacles, which were coated in a film of dust. Upon seeing him, Lluava said jokingly, "I thought this was a city holiday. You know—a day of rest and worship?"

"I think you have me all wrong," Leo responded with a purr. "This is what I do for pleasure."

Lluava laughed. He was such a bookish fellow. Of all the people in Leucrocotta, Leo might actually be the one with the answer.

"There's something I have been wondering about for a while. How many other Theriomorphs have a god's form?" Lluava watched Leo intently. She couldn't tell him the whole truth behind her questioning, but she needed him to trust her with the answers. "I mean, Apex and I both have one; since it was so easy to find him, I'm assuming there are others."

Why, wondered Lluava, hadn't she done this earlier? She had been so focused on talking to the high priestess that she had not thought about questioning others. At least not until Apex told her he had been making inquiries.

"Well," began Leo as he replaced his spectacles. "You two are the first I have seen with forms such as those."

"So, there are no others in the entire city who have a god's form?"

"None in Leucrocotta that I know of."

"But you can't possibly know everyone here," argued Lluava disappointedly.

"True," countered the small man. "The city is vast, and I know only a few citizens. But word would have gotten around of a person with a god's form. Some note would have been made in our city's birth registry. Occasionally, there are rumors, yet all are eventually disproven. Your forms are quite rare. It is very lucky that your paths crossed. The probability of that happening is extremely slim. The gods must smile on you."

Ignoring the last remark, Lluava asked, "Can I look through the old birth records?"

Leo laughed. "If that's what you wish." He led her into a large annex and gestured about him. "All these scrolls document births. Newest to oldest."

"This could take years to sort through," sighed Lluava in exasperation.

"I do not know about years," noted Leo, "but it will take a good bit of time."

Eyeing the scrolls, Lluava asked one last time in the hope of hearing a different answer, "So there are no known Theriomorphs with gods' forms?"

"None that walk the streets of Leucrocotta."

Had she and Apex wasted weeks in this city searching for other Incarn when none existed? The thought was depressing. Worse, they had surrendered their weapons to the priestess. Lluava knew one thing for certain: she was going to get Issaura's Claws back.

That evening, Apex was waiting for her return to their quarters. Once again, Lluava's guilt knotted up in her chest. But wasn't it partially his fault? If he had trusted her and explained what he had been doing, then maybe—

"I'm sorry," Lluava spoke first. "If I had known…I do bring news as partial compensation."

"Good or bad?" questioned Apex gruffly.

"Both," Lluava sighed as she rubbed her weary eyes. "No Incarn have been documented here in the past thirty years. I went through all records that noted the dual form of each Theriomorph who entered or was born in this city during that time span. This means we can leave Leucrocotta. Maybe go home…"

"Elysia was never my home," Apex corrected her.

Why was he saying such things? Did he want to hurt her? He was clearly still angry at Lluava's morning escapade. "We can leave here."

"Not without Ullr's Fangs."

At least they both felt the same way about their weapons.

"We can get them back. The high priestess will grant us the rights to our weapons if we pass her test."

"And what test would this be?" questioned Apex. His look of utter loathing directed toward Lluava momentarily vanished.

"I am not sure of the details, but I do know we have to prove we can fully control ourselves and not fall victim to our inner darkness. Yena said she wants us to prove we are one with all aspects of ourselves. I just have to maintain control—"

"—of the gods who use us?" questioned Apex dubiously.

Lluava quickly replied, "You don't believe that."

Apex remained silent for a time before asking, "So what does the priestess know about our little issue?"

"She knows that we, or at least I, fight some aspect of ourselves, and she wants that to stop."

"And how are we supposed to do that?"

"This is why I have been practicing meditation. Yena believes it will help."

Apex looked skeptical. Was he angry that she had lied to him? After all, he had kept secrets from her. "And has it?"

"Well," hesitated Lluava. "Not exactly. I had other things on my mind that were greater distractions."

"Do you think it could work? The meditation, I mean."

"I don't know," said Lluava. "I hope so. I'll give it a few more days."

"Tell me what you have been doing, so I can try it," said Apex as he sat down on his ledge.

Lluava studied him a moment to make sure he wasn't teasing. He seemed sincere. "Okay, then."

She walked Apex through her meditation routine, and for the rest of the evening they practiced together.

The following day, dual-form training in the coliseum went well. The other trainees were starting to accept Apex as one of them, though they were not so welcoming to Lluava. This didn't bother her as much as it might have because Maruny continued to be friendly with her.

At meditation practice that evening, Lluava worked hard to clear her mind of extraneous thoughts. She could return to them soon enough. Right now, she needed to focus on one thing: her mantra.

Shring, she began. Shring. Shring—

The voice of Helena broke her focus. "That is enough for the day."

"But we have barely begun," noted Lluava sourly.

"The timing has not been altered," replied Helena as she escorted Lluava to the grand doors.

Lluava thought for a moment. Her mind had drifted a bit, but her mantra had been the primary focus. Was she actually improving? Did alleviating her primary worries allow her a greater level of concentration? This was exciting to think about!

She half ran to their quarters to tell Apex the good news. When she reached the lodging, Lluava realized the huntsman was not alone, for he was talking to someone inside.

"Not again!" snarled Lluava as she threw open the door, only to discover Apex conversing with Maruny and Zeek.

"What's the matter with you?" questioned Apex. "Stung by a bee?"

Lluava realized she must have had an angry expression on her face as she stood in the doorway. "Nothing. Why the visit?"

"I've been told that's what friends do," said Zeek with a wry smile. "Spend time together."

Friends. Lluava had never associated that word with Apex before, but seeing him with Zeek and Maruny might change her mind on the matter. Was Apex her friend now? Or did Zeek merely assume this since she and Apex were supposedly mates?

Smiling, Lluava moved beside Maruny while Apex and Zeek continued their previous conversation. Lluava observed the way Maruny looked at Zeek. "You like him, then."

"I didn't think I would, at first," admitted Maruny in a whisper. The girls moved to the back part of the room. "He is cynical and so rigid in his beliefs. But since we were the most logical match as mates, there is something between us." Dropping her voice even more, she admitted, "I'm beginning to worry, come spring, whether I will be able to keep him."

"Can't you both choose to stay mates?" questioned Lluava.

"Yes, but someone with a higher rank than mine could take him away."

Lluava thought of the vixen she had fought a few days ago. Maruny took one of Lluava's hands in her own and said, "I wish I was as strong as you."

"Hey, Maruny," Zeek called out. "We should go. Our first challenge in training is tomorrow."

"Yes," added Apex. "We should all get some sleep."

Once they left, Lluava turned to the huntsman. "It worked. The meditation is working. I'm finally making improvements."

Apex looked relieved. "That's great, but we both need our rest for tomorrow. You go ahead. I'm going to meditate for a bit."

As Lluava lay down, she watched Apex for a long while as he silently meditated. He looked so calm and reserved. All his muscles relaxed. Lluava had never seen him look more serene.

Tomorrow was just another minor challenge. In the whole scheme of things, it was not worth stressing over. Beyond this valley, over tundra and mountains, a kingdom was being ransacked by war. Her kingdom. Elysia. Even thinking about the war, her friends, and Varren made her heart race. Lluava recognized that the time to return home was drawing near.

Chapter 13

Fighting for Life

The entire group of warrior caste trainees was led into the jungle that bordered the city nearest the coliseum. The trek was short, allowing little time for talk. Moreover, Master Hon required silence; it seemed they were not to theorize about what the challenge might entail. All Lluava knew was that this task would push the Theriomorphs to the limits of their individual dual forms.

Lluava's best guess was some sort of obstacle course, since their only training in the forest so far had involved practice in navigating around natural formations in their dual forms. If that were the case, this shouldn't be a problem for her.

However, her fellow trainees all seemed worried. Were they aware of something she was not? Or were they just nervous about their first trial? Regardless, Lluava felt fairly confident of her own skills.

She wished she had had more time to practice meditation, but she had awakened early and worked on her mental concentration. This exam could not be that hard. It was early in training, and all they had worked on was becoming comfortable in their dual forms.

Hon raised an arm, signaling everyone to halt. Before him was a three-forked path, each fork leading in a different direction.

"Everyone shift."

Lluava followed this command a little less tentatively this time.

Hon was still speaking. "I will send three of you at a time, each down a different path. Your mission is to follow the entire path in your dual form and come out safely at its end. Each path has its own set of tests and trials that must be overcome.

83

"I want to see how you think, how you react, and whether you can remain calm in your dual form. Depending on that form, some may want to flee, others to fight. I will have eyes watching your progress and will be informed of your reactions. This is not a graded exercise, but it will help me assess your strengths and weaknesses in order to make you better warriors. However, you will be judged on how quickly you move through the course. Let us begin."

Hon called three names, including Apex's. The three lined up at their respective entrances, and the master barked out, "Go!"

Each trainee took off down the narrow footpath through the vine-clogged jungle. Lluava watched the Yorrick wolverine disappear from sight behind the trees. After several minutes, Hon lined up the next group, then gave the command to begin. As wave after wave set off, Lluava could almost tell how deep into the jungle the front runners were by the sounds of disturbed birds and other fauna in the distance. Other than that, there was no clue what lay in the murky depths of the woods.

"Lluava," Hon's voice called out, "you take the rightmost route."

Standing at the edge of the path down which Zeek had disappeared a few moments earlier, Lluava awaited the signal to begin. There was no real reason to show her full range of ability, at least not yet. She knew her own skills and did not feel the desire to plow headlong into whatever trap or test lay in wait. Instead, she took off at a steady gait.

The jungle humidity was extremely uncomfortable. The entire group had been in a full sweat before arriving at the jungle's edge. Now, at this faster pace, she felt as if she were forcing her way through sticky syrup rather than air. The trainees had been permitted little water prior to the run, and now Lluava's body craved liquid. Was this part of the test, or just an added challenge? She would have to be careful not to push herself too much in her dehydrating state.

Lluava felt the oppressive air change a moment before she heard the sound. Lurching to the ground, she ducked under a tree trunk that swung down from the canopy. That impact would have caused a bit of damage. How had she missed the tripwire?

Taking a moment to collect herself, Lluava could not help but grin. Though her heart was pounding rapidly, there was a thrill in an obstacle course challenge. More important, she had guessed correctly. Knowing a little more about what to expect, she moved ahead.

Keeping a wary eye about her, the tigress was still calm. She knew her large form could make her an easy target, but if all the devices were sensor triggered, she had a good chance of evading them—that is, as long as she stayed alert. If she had to deal with Theriomorph-controlled contraptions or engage in combat, this might be more difficult. But what was the likelihood of that happening?

Before her, the path ended at a deep ravine, one too wide to jump. A series of vines dangled over the gap. If she had been in human form, Lluava could have swung across the pit; but she was not.

Should she shift? It would make this easier. Looking around, Lluava could tell that this was the only access to the path on the other side. Did Master Hon expect her to jump over? Climb down the steep side of the ravine, cross at the bottom, and ascend the other side? He had said he wanted them tested in their dual forms, but did he actually mean they were to stay that way for the entire course? This obstacle was better suited to one of the monkey or avian trainees.

Still, Master Hon had seemed adamant. Well, since both he and Lluava wanted to see how she could handle herself as a tigress, a tigress she would remain. She would have to find another route to the opposite side of the ravine.

Leaving the path, Lluava trekked to the right. She soon picked up the scent of a fellow competitor. Zeek had also gone this way. As a maned wolf, he surely had the same difficulties as she in crossing the chasm. Had he found another path?

Lluava followed the canine's hearty musk through the underbelly of the jungle. Eventually she came to the end of the ravine and crossed to the far side. Yet Zeek's scent continued to veer off farther to the right. What had he found? What did he know that she did not? Lluava decided to follow him.

She finally spotted the ruddy-colored wolf skulking ahead. "Zeek! Wait up!"

The wolf turned to look back, then sat down on his haunches. "Lluava! I could have guessed that you would be thinking along the same lines."

"I'm not sure", Lluava admitted. "I figured you were looking for a way across the ravine. But having done that, you are continuing to head in the wrong direction. Actually," Lluava admitted, "I have no clue why you are this far off the path."

Zeek barked out a laugh. "And I thought you were—oh, never mind. Actually, I *am* trying to find the path."

"But it's back there." Lluava nodded behind her.

Zeek shook his mane. "Think about this. The three paths can't cross, or the competitors would get confused. Since ours was on the right, more than likely it will eventually veer farther to the right until it loops back to the city's edge. Nobody's allowed to breach the valley's walls, so all three paths would have to reconnect with Leucrocotta at their end."

"Um," Lluava said, thinking "I guess. But that means you are trying to cut ahead of the group."

"So?"

"But that's cheating!"

"No. It's acting *very* smart."

"I'm disappointed in you," asserted Lluava rather sullenly.

Zeek blinked. "Master Hon is testing our cunning. Don't you see? What I am doing is brilliant. He will appreciate that."

"I'm heading back," said Lluava. Too much time had been wasted.

"So be it," said Zeek as he padded off. "But you will see. Master Hon will like my strategy."

Grumpily, Lluava left him to pursue his own path, all the while muttering to herself. How much time had she lost? Had Master Hon's "eyes" seen her take the obviously wrong direction? What would he think? And what about Apex? The word would get out. Instances like this always had a way of surfacing.

There was a yipping bark behind her. Lluava halted. Was that Zeek? She thought back on her training in the Southern camps. The entire forest was rigged with booby traps. Was that true here? If so, had Zeek been hurt by one? Lluava turned around and went in search of her red-furred friend.

Up ahead, Zeek yipped again. Where was he? Bounding forward, Lluava heard a trap trigger behind her and a series of darts whistle past. One dart pierced her rear haunch, and she let out a yowl.

Lluava slowed down. She knew she needed to be cautious. If that trap had been any worse, she would be in big trouble. Grabbing the feather-trimmed dart with her mouth, Lluava pulled the irritant from her hide before continuing, this time more warily.

There was another muffled shout.

"Zeek!" Lluava called out. "Zeek, where are you?"

"Lluava? Lluava!" Zeek definitely sounded distressed. "Be careful…"

Lluava could not distinguish the last few words, for a sudden slope caught her by surprise, and the tigress's heavy body slid quickly to its base. Nearby was Zeek—or half of him. This didn't make sense.

"Zeek!" Lluava called, but as she tried to move toward her friend's torso, she realized she was sinking. This was very bad.

The maned wolf faced away from her. His half-buried body flailed about for a moment as he tried to twist around to see her. Lluava struggled to reach any sort of solid ground, but every movement sucked her down farther.

"Stop that!" Zeek snarled. "You are making things worse for us."

"What's happening?" Lluava asked. As she did, her voice cracked. Was she really that scared?

"Quicksand of some sort. Well, more like a bog," explained Zeek. "I should have seen it, but that slope caught me off guard, and when I tried to leap over, I landed, well, in the middle."

A third of Lluava's body had already disappeared under the surface. "Let's call for help."

The pair shouted as loud as they could, but to no avail. Zeek had slipped in up to his shoulder blades; Lluava was halfway submerged.

"Okay. Okay. Let me think," said Lluava. She looked around for any possible natural aid. Suddenly, she felt hardened earth. "I'm standing on the bottom!" she exclaimed excitedly.

"At least one of us is," complained Zeek. "Are you able to move?"

Trying to shift her weight, she felt as if she were packed in solid stone. "Ugh. It's going to be difficult."

"You okay?" asked her scruffy friend. "You sound different."

"I'm fine," she countered. "I just need to…"

Using her strong forepaws, the tigress clawed for the bank. Though only a whisker's length from the edge, she felt so far away. With all the strength she could muster, Lluava pushed herself forward. She felt momentarily dizzy; then her head cleared as color shifted around her. Everything looked more green and blue.

Her paw touched the damp underbrush. "There!"

She forced herself forward, and her other paw landed firmly on the bank. For a few moments, her claws scrabbled with the loose topsoil and finally caught hold. Heaving herself up had never been such a struggle before. It felt as if three other people were trying to drag her back down.

Once on the bank, she looked back at Zeek while she caught her breath. As her vision regained its normal hues, she saw that his head and shoulders were loosely bobbing on top of the mucky surface.

"There are vines nearby. I'm going to get one and be right back."

"Lluava, you're not making any sense," said Zeek. His eyes had widened in fear. "What's wrong with you?"

"Vines," reiterated Lluava. "I'm going for vines." Yet that wasn't what she'd said at all. Instead of words, her voice came out in slurred rumbles. What was happening? She did not try to speak again. Turning to climb up the slope, Lluava's paws felt like they had lead weights attached. She stumbled upward; then, at the peak, she collapsed.

The ground seemed to undulate like waves on the ocean. She crawled ahead, digging her claws into the earth, clinging for dear life lest she be flung off. Hanging vines dangled from trees and swung wildly as though before a storm. Lluava clawed at one of the vines, but it continued to whip around her, and she could not grab hold.

Feeling herself sliding, Lluava pressed her body closer to the shifting ground. Was this an earthquake? The rapid motion nauseated her. Flipping onto her back, she watched the canopy swirl faster and faster above her. She closed her eyes and wished this would all be over.

When she felt hands on her fur, Lluava's eyes shot open. Men encircled her. She did not recognize any of them. Lurching to her feet, Lluava snarled until she heard Hon's voice order, "Back up! Leave her to me."

"Master Hon!" Lluava exclaimed as she shifted back into human form. Still on hands and knees, Lluava crawled over to the familiar figure, still wary of any possible movement of the ground. Thankfully that seemed to be over.

"What are you doing out here? Why did you stray from the path?" questioned the master harshly.

"Zeek!" gasped Lluava as she stumbled over to the edge of the slope. Hon's large hands grabbed her shoulders.

"Watch it."

"Zeek's down—" Peering below, all she saw was the illusion of solid ground. "You found him. You got him out."

Hon turned her toward him. "Where's Zeek, Lluava?"

"Down there!" Lluava pointed a shaky finger. She held a slight hope that he had somehow found a way out of the death trap.

One of the men carefully made his way down the slope. "It's some sort of quicksand," he reported after testing the ground.

Hon's expression was bleak. "Escort Lluava to her quarters and return here with grappling hooks."

"But Zeek…" murmured Lluava as she was forced away from the scene.

***

It seemed that "her quarters" actually referred not to her own room but to one of the cubicles located under the coliseum. The two red-clad healers met her on arrival. She had to strip down so they could examine her for injuries. Lluava was mortified as the gangly man stood watching. The plain-looking woman lifted the teen's arms and inspected her ears.

"Where did this come from?" asked the woman as she pointed to a splotchy pink mark the size of Lluava's fist on her right thigh.

"I was hit by a dart."

The man whispered into the woman's ear and left while his partner finished her inspection. "Stay here," she said as she handed Lluava a blanket. Lluava's uniform was taken away, and the humiliated teenager was left to wrap herself in the cloth.

Eventually, Lluava heard noises down the hall. Peering out of her cubby, she saw a draped form being carried in on a stretcher. The sheer cloth that covered him could not disguise the distinguishing details. Zeek was dead. A pale arm, crusted in mud, hung over one side of the stretcher until an attendant noticed and gently repositioned it.

A man stepped up, blocking her line of sight. He was very tall, leather-skinned, middle-aged, and entirely bald. When he spoke, Lluava noticed his unusually large mouth. "Get dressed quickly and follow me," he intoned. "You have been summoned."

Lluava had a feeling that she knew where she was headed. She quickly donned the black outfit handed to her by the strange man, then followed him to the amphitheater. There, standing once more in front of the stoic ruire, Lluava waited.

Ruire Thoth nodded to Lluava's tall escort, who moved to the lip of the stairs. The city's leader turned his sharp nose to the teen. "Lluava Kargen, daughter of the Banished Lands, you are once more brought before me under an accusation of murder."

Lluava's stomach dropped.

"Ammit, present the case against her."

The tall man with the wide mouth spoke. "Lluava Kargen and Zeek Jund, a fellow trainee, were assigned a test during Warrior Caste training. Although both were specifically told to stay on the selected path, they were found far off the trail. Zeek died by suffocation in a quicksand pit; Lluava was found conscious nearby. It is claimed she could have gone for help, yet she stayed near the scene."

Ruire Thoth turned to Lluava. "What say you to this?"

"Zeek wandered off the path and fell into quicksand. I tried to help him, but I fell in as well. I was able to escape the pit, but something happened to me. I—I think it was the dart that hit my leg, but the world began to move, to spin, and I couldn't save him."

"If he wandered off, why did you follow him when you had been told to stay on the path?"

"At first, I wasn't sure what he was doing. When he told me that he was trying to find a shortcut, I argued with him and then headed back. Moments later, I heard him cry out for help."

"What of her physical examination?" Thoth asked someone behind Lluava.

The wiry healer stepped around her. When had he arrived?

"She was hit by one of the tainted darts."

"So, she was incapable of saving Zeek?" questioned Thoth.

"There is that possibility," the healer affirmed. "The hallucinogenic properties of the substance found on these darts has been known to cause violent behavior and even homicide."

"What are you implying? Be specific."

"There is a possibility that Lluava Kargen, under the influence of the poison, killed Zeek Jund by pushing him into the quicksand and waiting for him to die."

"But—" Lluava interrupted. Ammit began to reprimand her for insubordination, but Thoth raised his hand, silencing him. Lluava continued, "Did you not see the bank? There had to have been claw marks where I climbed out."

"If that was the case, why did you not save your comrade?" asked the ruire, his face impassive.

"I was trying to get some vines to pull him onto solid ground when that drug took effect."

Thoth sat back in his chair for a while and considered the given facts. Then, looking about, he stood to give his decision.

"Lluava Kargen, if this had been your only case of suspected murder, I would discard it as an accident. However, since your arrival from the

Banished Lands, you have been associated with two deaths. I hereby sentence you to judgment by the Tucala."

The name of the harsh punishment rang in Lluava's ears. She had barely survived this severe combat trial when training in Durog.

"Do you know what the Tucala entails?" questioned Thoth sympathetically. Something in his eyes seemed to make Lluava question her certainty. Perhaps this challenge was different in Leucrocotta.

"You might want to refresh my memory."

"Since I am unable to make a clear judgment, and this accusation is quite severe, I am turning your fate over to higher powers. I am allowing the gods to pass their judgment upon you. During the Tucala, you will defend your honor and your life in battle against an opponent who challenges your claim. The pair of you will meet in the coliseum and fight to the death, without weapons, in either form you choose."

"I'll be fighting for my life?"

"Do not look so frightened. This is out of our hands now," noted Thoth. "The gods will protect you if you are honorable. If not, you will die."

Chapter 14

Tucala Revisited

We fight to the death?" Lluava was aghast.

"Do not look so upset," said Thoth. "If you are innocent, you will live. The gods will protect you. Now, who will speak for the gods?"

Ammit stepped forward.

"Very well," said Thoth easily. "We will hold the Tucala at dawn. I suggest you both rest."

How can I even consider sleeping? thought Lluava angrily. She had been falsely accused. There had to be proof of her innocence, if only they would make the effort to look for it. What of Master Hon's "eyes"? Had they seen nothing? What good were they, then? A friend was dead, and everyone seemed too eager to blame her. This was not fair. This was not just.

Lluava felt their reasoning was biased because she was still an outsider and therefore not to be trusted. What did she have to do to prove them wrong? Hadn't she passed their inspections? Hadn't she passed their tests with flying colors? What did they think she was keeping from them? Some big secret?

But she was.

She had been lying to them since her arrival, and so had Apex. They were not here seeking sanctuary. They were looking for other Incarn, hoping these Theriomorphs and their exceptional strength could somehow save Elysia. Should she have confided in Thoth? Would brutal honesty have prevented all of this?

Suddenly, Lluava confronted the nagging fear she had pushed aside for so long. This mission that Councilman Hyrax, their supposed Guardian, had given them was ludicrous; it wasn't holding up. Even if they found another

Incarn, how would that help? What could another Theriomorph, who was probably struggling with his or her own inner darkness, actually be able to offer? Incarn were not magical beings. They did not have supernatural powers or miraculous strengths. They might have dual forms of the gods, but they were not gods themselves.

As Ammit led Lluava back to her cubicle underneath the coliseum, she wholeheartedly regretted her decision to leave Elysia. She should have stayed at her military partner's side. Varren loved her, and she loved him. She had left to help save him and Elysia. But that choice was wrong. It had been eight weeks, maybe more, since she had departed. What might have happened to the kingdom, to him, in that time?

Sobbing echoed through the underground catacombs. As Lluava approached her cell, she glimpsed figures in the cubicle where Zeek's body had been placed. Once inside her tiny room, Ammit nodded in farewell and left. There were no doors to hold her in, no gates, and no key. It seemed Lluava was to remain there based on some sort of honor system. She could make a run for it. Unless this was yet another test.

A figure approached. It was Maruny.

"Lluava," Maruny's voice was raw. "Did you see him?"

"I saw him trapped in the quicksand. We both were. I couldn't save him."

Lluava saw that Maruny, through her tear-blinded veil, wanted to ask a different question. Lluava added, "Tomorrow, I face the Tucala."

Maruny's lower lip trembled; she took another ragged breath. After a moment, she said, "The gods are never wrong." She turned away, leaving Lluava alone in the oppressive darkness.

That was that. Her new friend had turned against her. Her mission had been a failure from the start and probably one of the biggest mistakes she would ever make. She had lost the Claws, and now she might lose her life.

Vowing to leave Leucrocotta if she survived, Lluava tried to prepare for the task set before her: to kill an innocent man. Could she do it? She had killed before, men with families and friends in their homeland across the ocean. Yet these men were enemies who had come to Elysia to pillage, destroy, and conquer. She had been forced to kill them. Their lives had *had* to be lost.

But what of Ammit? He was only fulfilling a duty of ceremonial law. He was innocent. Could she kill him?

What did she know about him? Not much more than she'd known about any other man she had slain. And Ammit, like the Raiders, would not hesitate to take her life. If she reacted instinctively and defended herself, she could justify a fatal injury based on pure self-preservation.

What of the Tucala? This ceremony clearly had originated in ancient times. How could this "only one survivor" regulation be considered fair? She was innocent, so the gods must make sure she wins. But then, what of her opponent? He was innocent, too. He was only respecting the rules of this bloodthirsty event. Wouldn't the gods, if they did exist, take pity on him as well? If there could be only one winner, how would either her death or Ammit's prove anything?

Lluava's head began to spin. None of this seemed ethical. None of this made sense. Was she truly to die in a barbaric battle of strength? She was overwhelmed by different emotions: anger, frustration, confusion, fear, regret. Why had she come to this place? Why had she left the kingdom's boundaries? The old tales warned that none returned once they voyaged beyond Elysia; Lluava was beginning to understand why.

Torchlight came and went as people sporadically visited Zeek's body. His friends and family continued to trickle in through the night.

Early in the morning, one of the visitors walked down the hall toward Lluava's cell. She prepared herself for an explosive encounter with a grieving family member. Instead, Apex's bristly face appeared in her open doorway.

"I figured they were keeping you here," he said ruefully.

"I didn't do it, you know," Lluava defended herself.

"I know."

"They are going to make me fight for my life today."

The flickering flame from the torch in his hand cast eerie shadows on the huntsman's face.

"We need to leave this place," Lluava said in a whisper. "No good has come since our arrival. There is nothing here for us."

Motioning Apex to step into her cubicle, Lluava cautiously stated, "We should make a run for it. Tonight."

"And what, exactly, is your plan?"

Lluava stared almost horrified at the man before her. "We make a break for the jungle, in the dark. Nobody would see us. Then we… then…"

"Then what?" questioned Apex. His voice was methodical. "We have no weapons. No way of knowing where the opening to this valley lies. The jungle is filled with booby traps, or have you forgotten? They would capture us before we even had a chance."

"I might die tomorrow. I can't do that. Not here." Lluava realized she was trembling. At least in the dark, maybe he wouldn't notice.

Apex reached out and stroked Lluava's pale hair. "You won't."

Lluava wanted to ask why he seemed so sure, but she didn't want his reassurance to end, charade though it might be. Afraid to speak, she kept silent, and Apex left her cubicle. As the light of his torch dimmed, so, too, did her hope.

***

No sirens called the citizens of Leucrocotta to the stadium in the morning; no city-wide announcement proclaimed this archaic judgment ceremony. There was no notification at all. Two men arrived at Lluava's quarters and ordered her to follow them, then led her to the coliseum's grounds. Everything seemed unusually calm, reserved, quiet.

This stadium was not filled with people as had been the case when Lluava faced the much milder version of the Tucala in Elysia's training camps. In addition to Ruire Thoth, a few seats were filled by councilmen and advisors. Only one priestess was present; Helena, draped in sheer white cloth, stood behind Thoth's seat. Neither family nor friends gathered on behalf of Zeek. No wayward bystanders had shown up to observe a bloodthirsty spectator sport. This was not a punishment meant for public ridicule. No, this was different. This was treated with the utmost seriousness.

The sun was barely creeping over the mountaintops, but the heat of the day was undeniable. Along with it came the hellish humidity. Lluava was in a full sweat by the time she stood in the center of the arena. Although her parched mouth was due in part to her fear of what was about to occur, she quickly recognized that she was also dehydrated. She had not been given food or water for a day and suspected the oversight was intentional. Combined with the merciless humidity and yesterday's exertion, she felt lightheaded.

Thoth stood up and announced, "Lluava Kargen, you have been sentenced to the Tucala based on your suspected involvement in two deaths since your arrival in this city. You will defend your innocence and affirm your worthiness as a new citizen of Leucrocotta, or you will die."

The last part of that statement made Lluava fidget. She hadn't been honorable. She had lied. Would this affect her outcome? Ridiculous! Lluava scolded herself. If she believed that, she might just as well believe that the gods actually had a hand in her life and that she was nothing but a pawn in the deities' game.

The ruire continued, "Ammit Pra'un will serve as the gods' speaker."

Lluava heard footsteps behind her. Ammit was in the arena. Everything was all too real now. Why hadn't she tried to run last night? She should have tried.

"The pair," Thoth decreed, "will fight to the death in either form they desire. No outside weapons are allowed. In this most ancient of ceremonies, the gods will determine the virtue of the accused."

Thoth looked from one to the other, then lifted his hand. Lluava turned to look at her opponent just as Thoth's hand gesture set Ammit in motion. She vaulted backwards. The upturned corners of Ammit's large mouth no longer revealed a wry smile. Instead, they exposed sharp, pointed teeth. Lluava looked at his well-muscled body and knew he would not be as agile as she. She would use this to her advantage.

Ammit lunged again, and Lluava leaped away. His strong, leathery hands were ready to squeeze the life out of her. In a hand-to-hand fight such as this, he clearly had more physical strength. Maybe she could wear him out? Maybe she should shift?

Just as that thought crossed her mind, Ammit transformed into a large crocodile. The giant reptile ran at her with snapping jaws. In this form, he now gained needed speed.

As Lluava turned tail, she also shifted. It was her only chance to evade the sharp teeth. What did she know about crocodiles? Lluava tried to remember her schooling. They were quite fast, but only in short spurts. There was a chance to escape his charges. Even now, Ammit was slowing.

There was no water in the arena, so she would not lose sight of him. Yet if he did bite her, his barrel roll would certainly do damage, as would a slap from his meaty tail. Evasion was the key until she could wear him down. Then she would strike.

There was a fur-raising snap as unruly teeth closed on the air beside her. Lluava sprang away from the reptile. One bite would be enough to severely maim her. If that occurred, it would be only a matter of time until it was all over.

The heartless sun beat down upon them. The humidity seemed to wrap her in a moist, heavy blanket, yet her throat felt parched. Had she been able to sweat in her dual form, she would have been drenched.

The crocodile seemed quite comfortable in the unearthly heat. If Ammit had been just an animal, wouldn't he seek a water source to escape the sun? Too bad his full attention was on the teen and her struggles.

Why did she have to have so much fur? Despite beginning to shed her thicker winter coat as a result of dual-form training in the jungle climate, her fur seemed to soak up the heavy air. She began to pant.

Ammit stopped his attack.

What was going on in his scale-bound skull? Well, crocodiles didn't have true scales, but his rough flesh looked as unappealing as his intent. Ammit's dark, shiny eyes followed her as she paced the perimeter of the arena. Her own thirst for water was growing. Was his?

Lluava knew that she had to make a move or continue her struggle to stay ahead of those strong jaws. What advantage did a tiger have? Her claws were sharp enough to hook into his hide—at least she hoped so. Her limbs were capable of grappling with an animal, while the croc's short legs limited that tactic. She had a strong bite and decent ability to jump. She had to attack.

What better time than now?

Lluava leaped.

Landing on the reptile's large, spiny back, the tigress tried to dig her claws into his flesh. His hide was tough, yet she was able to maintain a grip.

Ammit did not like this. He thrashed and snapped at the air. His powerful tail whipped around behind him. Each time he jerked, Lluava could feel her body slip. If her position shifted much more, the crocodile's jaws would find an unwilling target.

There was only one option left. She had to prevent the crocodile from using his mouth.

Two more loud snaps were heard as the animal underneath her

desperately tried to bite off the tiger's muzzle. After Ammit's third snap, Lluava retracted her foreclaws from the crocodile's hide and simultaneously stretched forward to grapple with the beast's head. Shifting to human form, she dug her heels into Ammit's ribs and clung there. Lluava clamped the animal's mouth shut and hoped she had not made a mistake.

The sensation of the giant croc's muscles straining under her arms felt strange, yet the brute was unable to open its mouth. Lluava sighed in relief. Ammit could not harm her like this. Once his jaw was forced shut, he had no strength to open it. The only remaining weapon was his tail, and it was a formidable one.

Ducking her head low, Lluava listened to the thick appendage slap the ground. She did not risk losing her grip to take a peek. She had the croc held down, but for how long?

The muggy heat was unbearable. The air was supersaturated, making breathing difficult. Compounded by the physical exertion, she was tiring.

Lluava realized she had to make some sort of move. She could not hold down this beast forever. Besides, the longer she waited, the more rested Ammit likely was. What could she do?

She was growing dizzy. Was it the constant movement of the crocodile's body under her as he tried to break free? Or perhaps a side effect of her growing dehydration?

The reptile lurched again. The teen slid sideways. The thick film of sweat now coating her body caused her grip to falter. She had to do something. The next logical move would be to kill the croc, but this vicious animal was a Theriomorph. Could she—

Crack!

The muscular tail of the reptile finally hit its mark and sent Lluava sprawling. Her vision momentarily spun as her head slammed against the hard-packed earth. As she struggled to focus, the blurred shape of an oncoming creature began to register.

Lluava shifted. Pain seared up her left rear leg, and she yowled. The beast had her limb secured in his jaws. There was no way to force the croc's mouth open unless the creature was willing. As bones crunched and muscles tore, Lluava felt the ground sliding out from under her. She was being pulled backward. Her claws dug into the earth, leaving deep gouges.

Fighting the pain, Lluava twisted her body around in hope of clawing the reptile's dark, shiny eyes. He seemed to expect as much and made his cruel counteroffer. There, in the center of the arena, the crocodile began to corkscrew his body. Twisting around and around, Lluava's only choice was to roll with him, at his remarkable speed, to prevent her leg being torn off.

As the animal bit down harder, Lluava's vision wavered again. This time, cooler hues glazed everything except the atypically brilliant reds that spattered the ground around her.

A sudden confidence flooded her system. She *would* kill this creature. "Halt the trial!"

At first, Ammit continued to roll, jaws still clamped on the tiger's leg.

Thoth's angered voice replied, "How dare you interrupt this holiest of rituals! Someone escort—"

Lluava could not make sense of all the shouting. The pain was searing. Her leg could not handle much more. She only caught snippets of words: "dealt with later," "superior to current ruire," "challenge to rank."

Ammit stopped. Lluava's mangled leg was suddenly released. Despite the fiery pain, she readied herself to lunge at the crocodile. He would die for this.

Shifting, Ammit stood there, mouth dripping with blood, staring at Ruire Thoth.

Left on her back, Lluava rolled over onto her three good limbs. Ammit was vulnerable now. She could dispatch him. Everything would be over.

At that moment, Lluava finally realized that Apex was standing right below the ruire.

Apex shouted again, "You heard me! I challenge your status as ruire. I believe that I am far superior to you in *every* way."

Thoth laughed. "You think this would save your mate? Is that what you are doing? The gods have already decided her fate. She is to die."

"No," asserted Apex. "She is not dead yet. Your trial is not over. And as the next ruire, I will revisit this matter with fresh eyes. There might be a different sentence."

"You are not ruire yet," stated Thoth.

Apex did not back down.

Thoth inquired, "Are you fully aware what you are asking? Do you understand all the risks? The punishment for challenging the ruire out of season and losing is quite severe."

The fire in Apex's eyes was astonishing.

"I. Never. Lose."

Chapter 15

Means to an End

Out of the corner of her eye, Lluava saw the gates to the arena opening. Figures were moving toward her and Ammit. She shifted back.

Thoth ceremoniously stripped off his tunic, turban, and purple sash. His blood-red hair flamed in the sun as he said, "Very well. Let this be a lesson to you and all others to come."

Hands reached for her. Lluava screamed as she was lifted and placed on a stretcher. Among the faces were the pair of coliseum attendants with whom she was all too well acquainted.

"Hold still!" the woman ordered as the team hoisted Lluava into the air.

Lluava's gaze had not moved from Apex. The huntsman was following Thoth to the stairway. They were heading to the arena. What had Apex done? Had he thought she was about to die? If he had only given her a little more time, she would have killed Ammit. That darker part of her would have gained full control. Apex had never been patient.

Lluava realized she was being taken to the underground cells. She would not be able to watch the fight unfold.

"No!" yelled Lluava as she rolled off the stretcher. Her brutalized leg hit the hard ground; she screamed again.

"What are you doing?" snapped the thin man as he reached for Lluava's arms.

"No," Lluava choked out. "I will see the fight."

"Nonsense," huffed the man. "You can barely walk. You'll losing blood."

"I will see the fight," snarled Lluava as she slashed at the attendants. Though partial shifting rarely occurs, her claws emerged. She still had some fight in her. When those around her stepped back, the injured girl began to crawl to the stairs.

"She's absolutely out of her mind," the man exclaimed, while the woman proffered, "She probably can't think clearly. Look at the state she is in."

No one came near the injured girl as she began to pull herself up the steps. Careful not to put pressure on her leg, Lluava hobbled to her feet. There was neither railing nor banister for her to hold. She leaned against the wall as she hopped up the narrow stairs on her good leg.

"Come back!" called the woman. "You will trip and fall to your death."

Lluava ignored her.

She struggled with each step. How many were there? Would she ever reach the top? Tears brimmed in her eyes.

Strong hands grabbed her shoulders. Lluava wanted to shake them off, but the fear of slipping and falling on her leg was too severe. The grip held her in place.

At the base of the stairwell, the thin man asked, "What are you doing?"

"Helping her to her seat," replied Ammit. The man who moments before had been trying to kill her was now assisting Lluava in her time of need. "If you wish to treat her, you can do so in the stands."

"But our supplies, the protocol!" blubbered the man below.

Ammit ignored them and lifted Lluava up each step. Finally, they reached the top of the lower level of seats. It was not the best vantage point, but she could go no farther. Ammit helped her to one of the seats lining the top of the arena's inner wall.

Easing onto the stone bench, Lluava found herself saying, "Thank you."

"We may not yet be done with our fight," cautioned Ammit as he sat next to her, "but mortals cannot predict the will of the gods."

Lluava stared at the leathery-skinned man. She didn't want to hate him, but he had destroyed her leg and was the cause of all her current pain. He would take her life in an instant if given the right orders. Such a heartless fellow.

Below, two figures emerged through the dark entry just as the gates slid closed behind them. Thoth and Apex took positions opposite one another in the arena. Seeing them from this angle, Lluava could not understand how a man as wiry as Thoth had been able to wrest control and maintain his standing for so long. Compared to Apex's muscled body, he seemed quite slight. Apex would crush him. Ammit could have destroyed Thoth, too, yet he had not. Why?

Now that Thoth was shirtless, the intricate designs tattooed on his chest could be seen. Swirling lines, ancient runes, unknown symbols, flowed from his right shoulder down to his left hip and possibly continued under the clothing. Was this a cultural ritual, a clan identification, or a supernatural protection? Lluava thought she recognized the runes for truth and honor interlinked on his torso. Yet none of this seemed intimidating.

Helena took the seat in the ruire's stead and announced, "There has been a challenge made for the title of ruire. Both men will combat each other until one submits, is unable to continue, or is killed. The victor will claim the title as ruire and will serve as fair overseer to this great city. Let the gods pass judgment on the one who is deserving."

There was a pregnant pause before Helena lifted her hand to the heavens. The fight began. Apex charged. Lluava's eyes flashed to Thoth, who stood waiting. In a spinning aerial kick, Thoth sent Apex stumbling to the side. Thoth was fast, almost lightning quick.

Apex approached more cautiously. He used his raw strength to punch at his opponent, but Thoth easily ducked the incoming hands. In return, the ruire sent a series of quick jabs at the huntsman's face. One broke Apex's nose, and blood ran over his facial hair.

"Come on, Apex," urged Lluava under her breath. "You can do this."

Focusing on the swiftly moving bodies was hard. Lluava tried to follow every maneuver, but her attention kept drifting. Thoth clearly had the upper hand. If only Apex would shift!

"Your leg is bleeding too much," Ammit warned.

Lluava turned to look at her limb. The sight was revolting. Peeled flesh, exposed muscle, everything coated in coagulating red. It was amazing that her leg was still under there somewhere. She quickly turned away. Staring at her wounds made the pain worse and her stomach queasy. Lluava gritted her teeth to stave off any vocalization of her own agony.

"I'll be fine," she lied.

Disregarding Ammit's concern, Lluava looked back upon the men in combat below. Except one was no longer a man. Apex had shifted into the Yorrick wolverine. His massive bronze form shone metallic in the sunlight. She had to squint to make sense of all the moving fur.

The wolverine lunged at the lithe man. Thoth somersaulted away. Then, leaping to his feet, the ruire turned to face the snarling beast. In the middle of a spiraling jump into the air, Thoth shifted into a magnificent sarus crane almost six feet tall. The bird's red mask and white cap shone brightly against the dark soil on which he landed.

"It will be over soon," said Ammit matter-of-factly.

"What do you mean?" questioned Lluava as she eyed the bird.

"This is where Thoth always wins," replied Ammit. He must have seen Lluava's look of confusion, for he added, "Thoth will attack his opponent's eyes. First, he will pluck them from their sockets; then, if the challenger does not submit, he will begin piercing vital arteries while his opponent cannot defend himself. Your mate has made a life-altering mistake. I sincerely hope he concedes early."

Lluava wanted to scream out a warning, but Ammit snapped, "Do *not* do it. There can be no outside aid in this battle, or your mate will be charged with cheating and severely punished."

"Apex…" moaned Lluava as she felt herself growing dizzy. Between dehydration and loss of blood, how much longer would she be able to hold on? Had Apex done this all for nothing?

The attendants approached her. Carrying bindings, vials, and tinctures of all sorts, they hastily tended to Lluava's gruesome wounds. She paid them scant attention, as all her energy was focused on the fight in the arena.

Thoth soared over Apex's head just high enough to stay out of range. Apex kept a wary eye on the gliding bird. Although the crane circled the wolverine almost indifferently, Lluava knew he had a darker plan.

"Coward!" snarled Apex. "Come down and fight me!"

The bird landed directly in front of Apex. This seemed to surprise the large wolverine. For a moment, neither the bird nor his opponent moved.

Lluava realized Thoth was about to strike. He would take Apex's eyes. It would all be over. She could not shout a warning. All she could do was watch.

Jerking up from the stinging pain in her leg, Lluava glared at the attendants who were cleaning her wounds.

"This will hurt," warned the woman as she poured the entire contents of a small vial onto Lluava's leg. Lluava screamed.

There was a roar from the arena.

Turning her tear-blurred eyes back to the contenders, Lluava observed blood flowing down Apex's face. At first, she could not see where it was coming from.

The wolverine slashed at the jabbing crane.

Had Apex lost an eye? Had Thoth hit his mark?

Lluava wiped her eyes with her arm to clear her vision.

Thoth took wing.

Apex turned and followed the bird's trajectory. He could see! The blood was coming from a long scratch down the side of his face. Thoth had missed.

Thank the gods, thought Lluava before realizing what she had done. No. Curse them! This was all because of them. They were the real villains.

Thoth dove at his foe but pulled up just in time to escape the claws of the enraged animal. Apex was furious. The wolverine leapt and swatted at the bird. Neither animal was getting anywhere. Something had to change to alter the course of the battle.

The world started to sway.

"Lluava?" the female attendant said worriedly. "Lluava, can you hear me?"

Lluava realized she was the one moving. She tried to hold still, but she suddenly felt faint. The large, rough hands of Ammit grabbed her once again.

"She has lost too much blood," the woman cautioned.

The wiry man stepped into Lluava's view. "Drink this." He poured the vile-tasting liquid down her throat.

Lluava coughed and gagged.

"We have to take her inside."

"No," she argued. "I can stay—"

"Hurry, or she will go into severe shock."

Suddenly, Ammit grabbed her and tossed her over his shoulder. Lluava hung there like a rag doll. All her strength seemed to wane.

"Hurry. Inside," implored the woman. Lluava saw the ground move as she was carried away.

"No," Lluava cried out though her voice seemed to be leaving her. "Apex!"

As they descended the stairs, she heard an echoing snarl from the wolverine, and then Lluava's world went black.

***

"Let me inside."

"She's not ready."

"I need to see her."

"I said—"

"That's an order!"

Lluava heard familiar voices. She wanted to open her eyes and look, but her lids felt so heavy.

"I'm not sure she will hear you." Lluava recognized the female attendant's voice. "She is still heavily sedated."

Someone approached her.

"She will be fine," the woman added. "Her recovery will be complete. We are monitoring her. Do not worry. Besides, you have wounds of your own that need to heal. Go and rest. Your induction is tomorrow."

Hands touched Lluava's forehead and brushed back hair that had fallen over her brow.

"Lluava." The second voice was Apex's. He had survived. He was alive, at least. "Can you hear me?"

Lluava tried to open her eyes. They fluttered but remained shut.

"It's done," he said wearily. "Everything will be okay. I promise."

The woman spoke up. "She really should not have visitors. She's too weak. I insist that you leave."

"And I *order* you," growled Apex, "to back off."

Someone left.

"Apex?" Lluava croaked.

"Yes. I'm here."

"Do you still have your eyes?"

There was a gruff laugh. "Yes. Yes, I do."

Lluava found the strength to open hers. The room was dimly lit by a torch in a nearby sconce. She was back in her cubicle beneath the coliseum. The huntsman was looking down at her. A bandage covered the long cut down the side of his face. There were bandages on his arms, visible bruises, and a now-crooked nose.

Apex acknowledged, "If you hadn't yelled out, I would not have looked away, and I would have lost at least half my sight."

"You turned to look at me?" asked Lluava still partly in a daze. Her thoughts were foggy. Her injured leg felt numb. What drug had they given her?

"Thoth renounced his rank as ruire."

"Why did you challenge him?" inquired Lluava.

Apex ignored her question. "My initiation ceremony is in the morning."

Lluava stated sullenly, "I know why. You didn't think I would survive."

"I think," he replied gruffly, "I know a way to get our weapons back."

This caused Lluava to drop her accusations. "How?"

The huntsman explained, "The ruire has access to every place in the city, including the vaults where they keep their so-called relics. Our pedagogue shared some information. As ruire, I will be able to retrieve our weapons."

"Oh, that's perfect!" Lluava exclaimed excitedly, although her voice still sounded rough and faint. "We can get them and leave this cursed placed and never look back. Elysia, here we come!"

"I need to talk to you about this," said Apex. "I'm not going to abandon what I have just accomplished."

"Wait, you want to stay?"

"I have real power now. I have vast sway over these people."

"What are you talking about?"

"Think about this," said the huntsman as they heard footsteps approaching. "I can ready an army to march on the Raiders. I have made some initial inquiries and found out that the number of trained citizens is far greater than either of us might have expected. We might not have found other Incarn, but we now have the opportunity to change the balance of the war for the better. I'm not leaving here with nothing."

The male attendant poked his head inside the room.

"I'm going," grunted Apex as he gave Lluava's hand a quick squeeze.

The wiry man stepped in once the huntsman was gone. "You're awake. Unusual. Now, let's have a look at your leg."

As the man unwrapped the bandage encasing her calf, he asked, "Did you say your goodbyes? Perfect time as any, I guess."

"Goodbyes? What are you talking about?"

"Your mate," replied the man, clearly not interested in the topic. "After his initiation tomorrow, he will be the new ruire. His mate will be High Priestess Yena."

"He can't! He won't!" blustered Lluava.

"He has to, and he will," countered the attendant tonelessly. "He must consummate his position as ruire, or he will be charged with public humiliation of authorities, insubordination, and disrespecting our most ancient law. He will be executed."

The angry scream that followed reverberated through the entire catacomb of underground cells.

Chapter 16

Crocotta's Hackles

After her outburst, Lluava kept quiet and brooded. The mission had been straightforward: find the Incarn, return home. That was it. Quick and clear-cut. How had it gone so wrong, become so complicated? As they'd found no Incarn in Leucrocotta, she and Apex should have been on their way back to Elysia by now. But without their weapons, they had been compelled to stay. And the longer they stayed, the more problems arose. People died. Fingers pointed at her. She could have proved her innocence if Apex hadn't underestimated her. On the other hand, he had defeated Thoth. That should have been the end of it. As ruire, Apex could retrieve their weapons, so now they could leave.

Lluava snarled under her breath as she thought of her cocky companion. Apex was greedy. He wanted more than easy access to their weapons; he wanted to command an army. Did he think this new plan would compensate for the time wasted? For their obvious lack of success? Did he know what he was obligated to do to gain the power he thirsted for? Should she just sit around while he fulfilled his duty? No. If that's what he wanted, fine. She would not be waiting.

The last torch was finally doused. Lluava slid off her stone bed. With hands outstretched, she carefully felt her way out of her room and down the corridor. She couldn't risk getting lost; if she did, more time would be wasted. Her extraordinary night vision required a light source, however slight. In the catacombs, it was pitch black. As she shuffled along, she was thankful that her injured limb was almost numb. Perhaps this was due to the salves the healers had used. They had told her to stay off the leg until fully healed, but there was no time. Morning was fast approaching.

Thump.

Lluava bit her tongue to keep from crying out. She had rammed her bad leg into the base of the stairs. Half crawling, half stumbling, she eventually reached the top. She breathed an audible sigh of relief. Starlight illuminated the doorway, and she hurriedly left the coliseum.

Observing the empty streets, Lluava thought, Now what? Should she try to talk with Apex? He wouldn't listen, and he might even order her back to her cell. There had to be a loophole. What was she missing? What had Leo taught her?

The ruire was the strongest, most powerful individual in the city, with one exception: the high priestess herself. Yena was the only one who could overrule the ruire. Yena could stop the ceremony. Lluava had to talk to the high priestess.

***

Arriving at the temple, Lluava regarded the steps. She had never paid attention to how many there were. She took a big breath, gritted her teeth, and half climbed, half hauled herself up. The doors were open, and she carefully made her way into the second room.

Etha was there with another priestess Lluava did not recognize.

"Lluava," inquired Etha, "what are you doing here at this hour, and with your injury? You should be resting."

Ignoring the question, Lluava walked as quickly as her leg would allow toward the obscure doorway behind the throne-like seating.

"You can't go back there."

Hearing the priestesses' approach, Lluava turned and growled, "Are you going to stop me?"

Etha held her companion back. "Crocotta does not look fondly upon those who enter her sanctuary uninvited."

"Who said I wasn't?" sneered Lluava as she turned toward the doorway. Light poured through, a light so bright that Lluava was as blind as in the coliseum's catacombs. She stretched out one arm to feel her way down the corridor, shielding her eyes with the other.

"Lluava Kargen." A throaty voice reverberated around her. "Why have you intruded into my sanctuary?"

Lluava squinted as she tried to spot the speaker. Brilliant light flooded the space. There was no single source; the light seemed to emanate from the walls, the ceiling, the floor. At first glance, these appeared to be made of translucent crystal, but a second look showed they were made from the purest white stone.

Carved from this same stone, a larger-than-life statue of the goddess Crocotta stood watch. Her bared breasts hung full with milk. One hand rested over her swollen womb; the other, outstretched, beckoned observers. Her dual form, the hyena, matriarch of the animal world, lay curled asleep at her feet. Lluava stood there, in awe of the mother goddess.

"Why are you here?"

She still couldn't tell where the voice was coming from, but the question stirred Lluava to respond.

"I must have a word with you, High Priestess." Lluava looked behind her. A few of the minor priestesses had appeared, including Etha, who looked quite displeased behind her sheer veil. But no Yena.

"It pertains to the ceremony tomorrow and Apex."

"What are your concerns?"

Turning toward the statue, Lluava now saw that the gray-robed high priestess stood in front of the goddess.

"Tomorrow, Apex is to become ruire. But I have come here to ask that you stop this."

"Why do you ask this of me?" Yena inquired, not unkindly.

"He is my…mate," Lluava asserted. "I earned that right. I fought for him again when he was stolen from me." She hated talking about the huntsman as if he were property, but she had to explain in terms these Theriomorphs understood. "Please, do not take him away from me again."

"Apex is strong, courageous, fearless. There is no doubt why you favor him." The high priestess approached Lluava. "A fine specimen. A prime example of his gender. I can easily see why you love him."

"I —" On the verge of contradicting the priestess, Lluava realized that to explain that she loved another would only complicate things and cause her request to be denied.

"I do," she affirmed.

Yena stood so close that Lluava could see her white irises sparkle. "As high priestess of this temple and this city, I have many undisputed rights," she said, "including the right to mate with the strongest male. I have been waiting for a worthy mate for a very long while. Apex will be my mate."

"No!" Lluava objected. "You can't."

"I can."

With that, Yena turned away in silence and moved back to the base of the statue. From some obscure doors, other priestesses entered. Helena had entered the room and now stood near Etha.

Under the gaze of all these eyes and the stone goddess herself, Lluava called out, "Yena! I make a challenge for your rank. I challenge you to fight for the title of high priestess."

"That cannot happen," warned Helena quickly as she moved toward Lluava. "You do not know what you are saying."

Several priestesses crowded around Lluava, grasping her arms and shoulders to force her out of the inner sanctum. Struggling against all those hands, Lluava roared, "I challenge you, High Priestess Yena! Prove your worth! I challenge *you*!"

"Release her!" rapped out the high priestess. The order was promptly obeyed. "Is this man worth dying for?"

"Yes," responded Lluava without pausing to think.

"You will have your fight," said Yena. She nodded to Helena. "Bring the weapons."

Facing Lluava, she continued, "We will conduct this duel here, before Crocotta herself. We shall each choose a weapon. We shall fight in dual form. There can be only one winner. There can be only one survivor. This is your wish, is it not?"

Another challenge, another battle to the death, thought Lluava sourly. She should be used to being thrust into these archaic situations. This time, however, she was not physically ready. Her leg was not healed, and her old shoulder injury put her at risk.

Lluava nodded, hoping this would be the last time she would be required to participate in such ceremonial barbarism.

"Very well," said Yena. Several priestesses encircled her and began to disrobe the high priestess. Although her view was partially blocked, Lluava saw the silky garment drop to the ground. When they stepped back, the woman now revealed was striking.

Yena appeared youthful, although she was probably much older. Like Lluava's, her form was athletic. Her skin was smooth and polished, so black it resembled obsidian. Her hair was cut short, close to the scalp; its gray color matched not only the discarded garment now being folded by the priestesses but also the opaque, short-sleeved bodysuit she now wore.

The high priestess saw Lluava's expression and laughed. The loud, high-pitched, staccato sound built upon itself and rose into the rafters.

Helena and Etha quickly left the chamber and returned with the weapons. Etha handed Lluava something she had feared never to see again: Issaura's Claws. The golden weapons shone in the brightly illuminated room. Lluava slipped the Claws gently over her hands and fitted them to her knuckles. She inspected each one's three curved blades. Issaura's Claws were back in her possession. She promised herself they would never be separated again.

Turning her attention to Yena, she observed the high priestess's chosen weapon: a whip. The handle's sturdy silver pommel was shaped like a snarling creature, but she couldn't determine which one.

Yena flicked the weapon in her hands. The whip made a loud crack that reverberated throughout the sanctuary. The second time, she flicked it at a rotating angle. The ends unwound in the air. Nine barbed tips reached out for their waiting victim.

Lluava's heart sank. She knew this weapon and now recognized the animal on its pommel. Yena possessed Crocotta's Hackles—one of the gods' weapons. Lluava suddenly regretted her choice for this fight.

Did Yena know how to use the whip? With each crack, it became more obvious that she did. Lluava gripped Issaura's Claws tightly, feeling the cool metal in her hands. At least her weapons were familiar to her. This was of some comfort.

Yena smiled at Lluava. "A word of advice: fight in your dual form. You are stronger that way. Perhaps the goddess Theri will protect you."

"I don't need your advice," retorted Lluava.

The high priestess's expression was reminiscent of a mother observing her unruly offspring. Yet Lluava was no child in need of education. One thing she knew she was naturally good at in this world was bloodshed.

Helena, along with the other priestesses, gave the pair a wide berth. The blond priestess hesitantly said, "You may begin."

With three flicks of her whip, Yena approached. Her weapon crackled in the air. Lluava focused her attention on the barbed tips. If one hooked into her skin, it would rip out a chunk of flesh.

The girl ducked as the whip slashed the air above her. She felt like an animal in a traveling circus, being forced to perform tricks. Another *snap* by the side of her head as a clump of hair was yanked from her scalp.

As much as she hated to admit it, her best option was to transform. In human form, she could not get near the priestess as long as those whirling barbs bit the air. Lluava shifted. As she did, she heard Yena say, "Good."

Lluava hoped the priestess would be caught off guard. Issaura's Claws shifted along with her, gilding her foreclaws in metallic sheaths. This time, when Yena slashed out, the tigress batted the barbs away and closed the gap between them.

"Very good, Lluava," encouraged Yena. She swung her arm down. The whip wrapped itself over the high priestess's back, down her chest, and up her back again. Lluava winced as the barbs bit into flesh. Yena did not seem to mind, not even when small halos of red oozed from her wounds.

Then she shifted. Yena's mass shrank to reveal a spotted hyena with a silver coat. However, her whip had also shifted; the beast boasted a metal-tipped mane and hackles.

"You're—" Lluava was almost too dumbfounded to voice the word, "—an Incarn."

"A what?"

"You're an Incarn, like me." Lluava suddenly realized she could not fight Yena, for the high priestess was one of the very Theriomorphs for whom she had been searching. She had to explain. She had to stop this battle.

"You were born with a dual form resembling a god's. You're Crocotta's Incarn, just as I am Issaura's—Theri's—and Apex is Ullr's."

"What did you say you were?"

"I'm the Incarn of Issaura."

"And you believe that?"

"Yes, I do."

Yena laughed in the animal-like way of her species.

Lluava was completely nonplussed.

Abruptly, the high priestess shifted back to human form. In a simple move, all the barbed tips of her whip detached. Handing her weapon to Helena, Yena announced, "She is ready." Turning to the confused teen, she said, "Come with me."

"You know what we are, then?" Lluava asked, still confused. "Do you know why Apex and I are here?"

Yena turned to her and smiled sweetly. "Child, *I* am the one who brought you here."

Chapter 17

Words of the Prophetess

W e came here of our own accord."

"Did you, now?" Yena motioned Lluava to follow her. "Explain to me how you found this place."

Lluava followed the high priestess through a concealed doorway unnoticeable from the front of the room. In truth, there were many such doors, cunningly designed to create the illusion of a solid wall. The door Yena chose led down a curving stair.

"We, Apex and I, came upon a group of men harvesting ice. They were the first people we had seen in weeks. We followed them, but we were overheard, captured, and brought here."

Yena and Lluava walked down a brightly illuminated corridor constructed from the glowing white stone. Arched doorways opened off the passageway. Glancing into several of the rooms, Lluava wondered if they were bedrooms. Each had a small table and a stool, a simple dresser, an oil lamp, and a rug. However, instead of beds, some rooms had pillows of varying sizes, while others contained what looked like perches.

"What happened before that?"

"The ice…" replied Lluava as she recalled the horror of the river for the first time. "We were stranded on a large block of ice as it floated down the river. We had been hunting when we were caught by a sudden blizzard. Our provisions were lost, and we were desperately tracking a stray caribou. We began to suspect it was a Theriomorph, so we continued to follow it, and then the ice we were standing on broke."

Yena stepped into one of the rooms. It contained the same items as the others, but no bed. Lluava entered behind her.

The high priestess studied the teen. "It was the caribou that broke the ice, was it not?"

"How do you know that?"

"Kani was following my orders to send you this way. He is a Guardian, one of—"

"I know what Guardians are," snapped Lluava. "They are supposed to find and watch over the Incarn."

"And," added Yena, "not to intervene unless deemed necessary. You were heading the wrong way, so Kani corrected your course. I needed you to come to Leucrocotta."

"If you knew about us, if you actually steered us here, why didn't you tell us when we arrived? We have been here for weeks."

"You weren't ready, Lluava." Yena pulled out a drawer and changed into a clean set of silver-colored robes.

"Weren't ready for what? And how did you know where to find us? Or who we were?"

"Theri is said to be among the most inquisitive of the gods. You certainly are her mortal instrument. Would you help me with this?" Yena gave Lluava one end of a cloth.

"Wrap it around my back and over my other arm. Just like that. Yes. Thank you." To secure the cloth, the high priestess pinned a silver brooch, the silhouette of a hyena, to her shoulder, then said, "I can answer only one question at a time.

"I have been bestowed with the gifts of my goddess. Crocotta is the goddess of many things: motherhood, childbirth, mating vows, prophecy, and foresight. At her will, I have visions of what is happening in this land, as well as revelations of what is to come."

"So, you could see us? You have been watching us all along?" Suddenly Lluava felt as if her privacy had been violated. What had the priestess seen? How much did she know about them? How long had she been watching?

"I have seen only what Crocotta wanted me to see. It was time for you to be brought here so that the prophecy could come to pass."

"Are the others here?" demanded Lluava angrily. She was infuriated that she had not been told the truth.

"Others?" asked Yena innocently. "What others?"

"The *others*," repeated Lluava. "Where are all the other Incarn? We need them to save Elysia."

"That is not why you are here, Lluava."

"Apex and I came to save Elysia, to bring back help." From the look on Yena's face, however, Lluava guessed that finding the priestess may have brought an end to her quest. Would Crocotta's Incarn, alone, be enough to help? Or, through her, would Leucrocotta's Theriomorphs come to their aid?

"High Priestess, you are able to lead all of Leucrocotta under your command," continued Lluava as Yena adjusted her garment. "Will you help Apex and me, your fellow Incarn, and lead an army of Theriomorphs into Elysia to defeat our enemy, the Raiders?"

"Elysia was relinquished for good reason. Humans leave nothing but destruction in their wake. They drove many ancestors from our lands and slaughtered countless others. I will not lead my people into bondage."

"You are wrong," countered Lluava. "Not all humans are evil. I know the king, and he is working to undo the wrongs that have been done in the past. He wants equality for both races."

Yena looked doubtful.

Lluava persisted, "If King Varren loses this war, then your claims will be true. The Raiders will kill or enslave all Theriomorphs living in Elysia. You believe that Theriomorphs do not wish each other ill; why, then, do you wish your brethren ill by leaving them to die when their only fault was to be born in the Banished Lands?"

"You are correct that I want what is best for our people. As high priestess for the Blessed Mother, I am here only to do her will." Yena rested a hand gently upon Lluava's shoulder for a brief moment. "But I cannot lead an army into a kingdom that is ruled by the very men from whom we have hidden all these years. Friend or not, your king is no friend of mine. How do I know that there will not be a trap waiting for my people once we arrive? How will I know that the Elysians will protect *us* if we need it?"

"I promise you, no harm will come from the Elysians. King Varren will place all of you under his protection."

"You are not in a position to speak for your leader. You have not spoken to him about this matter."

Elysia desperately needed help, and Lluava was not about to lose this opportunity. "Please, High Priestess, let me talk with him. I will send you a message that everything is well."

"A message," mused Yena. "Hmm. If what you say is true, and the human leader is willing to accept our aid as well as provide protection if we need it, that would do. It would be a blessing to once again return to our homeland." The priestess paced, obviously thinking hard. Lluava waited, desperately hoping to hear the answer she sought.

At last, the priestess stopped her pacing and turned to face Lluava. "All right," she said. "I will gather my army at the border of the Banished Lands and wait for your messenger. But if I do not receive word after one month, we will return to Leucrocotta."

"Thank you!" Lluava cried. She wanted to hug the priestess, but she dared not insult the one person who could provide an army. She did not want Yena to change her mind after so quickly agreeing to Lluava's terms. But was this all too easy?

The high priestess reached out and stroked Lluava's cheek. "I will require something in return." She looked into Lluava's eyes and held them. "I need you to fulfill your destiny."

She held up a hand to forestall Lluava's question. "You are part of the prophecy," she explained. "Wait here."

The teen was left in the strange room until her hostess returned carrying a simple scroll. Unrolling it on the top of the bare dresser, Yena placed her finger on the scroll and said, "Read this aloud. Start here."

Lluava looked at the excerpt from the *Virisinu*, the religious book concerning future revelations, for a moment and then began. Although she stumbled over some of the less familiar runes, she read aloud, "The magnanimous goddess, Theri, known also by her false name, Issaura, will return to the mortal world to…"

"Fulfill," prompted Yena without looking at the scroll.

Lluava went on, "…fulfill what was prophesied before the beginning of the mortals' time. Through her, the Theriomorph race will be saved from destruction."

As Yena explained the context of the scripture, Lluava turned to watch the high priestess.

"Crocotta had birthed the most perfect of children, the one child she loved most, Ullr. Soon afterward, her life-mate, Giahem, King of Gods, strayed from her bed and fathered an infant daughter, Theri.

"Fearing his mate's wrath, Giahem passed Theri off as another's child and gave her the false name Issaura to prevent her from being found. Yet Crocotta discovered his deceit. To placate her in her rage, Giahem decreed that females had the right to select and to leave their mates. Crocotta was henceforth deemed protector of mating rights."

Unsure where this was going, Lluava waited patiently.

"In a prophecy, it was revealed to Crocotta that if Ullr, her child, ever bred with Theri, their child would become the most powerful creature in existence. Crocotta's hatred of the illegitimate goddess grew, yet she could not harm her mate's offspring. Instead, Crocotta found ways to keep the siblings apart. She sent Ullr to oversee the sun, and Theri, the moon. Unfortunately for the Mother Goddess, the young pair reunited during an eclipse and became enamored of each other.

"Yet Ullr, like his sire, had a wandering eye and could not remain faithful. Theri, heartbroken, vowed to remain a virginal goddess for all eternity, never again to be deceived by the false promises of the male sex. Crocotta's wish came true: no child would be born of her son and Theri."

"I know that story," Lluava interrupted. "That is from the *Karmasana*. I know those scriptures backward and forward."

"Do you know the second part? The one from the *Virisinu*?"

"No," admitted Lluava.

"The *Virisinu* is extremely complex and multilayered. As a result, only the most popular passages are taught in school. The complete text is studied only by the priestesses or members of the Scholar Caste.

"Listen to me, Lluava. This is important. Crocotta eventually realized the misery that engulfed her only child after Theri made her vow. Ullr renounced all other mates. The Mother Goddess felt her son's pain and regretted her earlier hatred of Theri. Although an immortal's vow could not be broken, she sought a remedy.

"Crocotta approached her mate and implored Giahem to give Ullr and Theri a second chance. The all-powerful King of the Gods promised her that the entire pantheon would be given mortal instruments, through which any wrongdoing could be undone. They would have a chance to begin again.

"This is what we are, Lluava: vessels used by the gods to redeem their wrongdoings." Yena pointed to the scroll. "Read the next line."

"Through her life's blood, Theri will conceive the savior of the Theriomorph race." Lluava paused. "Does that mean what I think it does?"

Yena smiled. "You and Apex are to mate. The child you bring forth will be the prophesied savior."

Yena wanted Lluava to have a child by the huntsman! Lluava's head began to ache. "Then why do you want Apex as your own mate?"

"Apex is not meant to be my mate."

"Then why wouldn't you grant my wish earlier?"

"You needed to prove to me that you were ready." Yena rolled up the scroll. "When you first arrived in Leucrocotta, you were not. You had to accept that you were the Incarn of Theri, or else you would continue to struggle against your fate. In the sanctuary, you said that you were that Incarn. I know you do not wholly believe that, yet you are now open to the possibility.

"You must consummate your choice of mate. You chose Apex. You fought for him. Now mate with him. Bring forth our savior. That is what I ask in return."

The idea of bedding the huntsman caused the hairs on the back of Lluava's neck to stand erect.

Yena continued, "Kingdoms rise and fall, but the future of our race is much greater than that. The Guardians will say and do what they must to keep you on your preordained path. You and Apex were sent here to fulfill this, our greatest prophecy. You were designed for this purpose: to bring forth a new life and a new era for the Theriomorph species. This is your true destiny."

Lluava wondered whether she could lie and say she had already slept with Apex. But what if the priestess had watched them in their quarters? She would know that Lluava and Apex had no romantic interest in each other. Would any of this matter to Yena? She was clearly adamant about her beliefs.

"You still doubt," observed the high priestess. "Every Theriomorph in existence knows this prophecy in some form or another, even though they may not have heard it in its entirety. At the very least, it is taught that Theri promised to return and save the Theriomorph race in their hour of greatest need. This child, which you will bear for her, will secure our salvation."

Lluava refused to think about that course of action. Instead, she asked, "What of you, then? What is your purpose as an Incarn if you are not part of this prophecy?"

"Each god has an Incarn. I believe they use us, their mortal instruments, to provide them a second chance to undo all the wrongs they have engendered—perhaps even to relive their greatest triumphs. Crocotta mistakenly wished Theri ill and prevented Theri from becoming her son's mate. My purpose is to right that wrong."

"So, there *are* other Incarn?"

"Yes."

"One for each of the gods: Slypher, Valcum, Shennue, and even Giahem?"

Yena stood as still as the statue of Crocotta herself upon hearing Lluava speak the last name. Lluava pressed on. "Is that who you referred to when you said that you had been waiting for a worthy mate? Have you been waiting for Giahem's Incarn?"

The high priestess's gaze lost focus momentarily.

Lluava baited the hook. "That is why I am here, Yena—to find the other Incarn, including Giahem's. Help me find them. You said you have gifts. Use them to help us unite all the Incarn."

Yena's distant gaze suddenly turned dark. "That is not the goddess's plan."

"How do you know?" protested Lluava. She was losing Yena. "Can't you ask Crocotta? You said you speak with her. If she would allow you to find the others, you could find Giahem's Incarn."

Abruptly, the high priestess silently left the room. Lluava took a seat on a large circular cushion lying on the ground. When Yena returned, Lluava felt she needed to alleviate some of the tension.

"What is this?" she asked as she patted the comfortable cushion. Although soft, it seemed to be coated in a fine layer of dog hair.

"That is my bed. We all," Yena gestured toward the rest of the temple, "sleep in our dual forms."

"Always? Why?" Now Lluava wondered if she should stop asking questions.

But the high priestess did not seem to be annoyed. "In public, we must be seen only in our human forms, yet we know the importance of being in tune with our animal natures. In order to keep a balance within ourselves, we sleep in our dual forms. In truth, I prefer my dual form. When I am not making public appearances or performing a ritual, I stay in mine." Yena's voice deepened. "Fulfill your destiny, Lluava. I cannot force you to do this, but I will provide the army you seek once it is done."

At first, Lluava wanted to shout, *Absolutely not!* Yet as she stood there, she began to realize the true power she held in her hands. If she said yes,

Yena would send an army to help Elysia. An army to eradicate the enemy and save her kingdom, her family, and her friends. In return, she must sleep with Apex. The huntsman was not unattractive. He had bedded many others. What was one more woman to him? Yet, could *she* do such a thing?

No. If she did, how could she ever look Varren in the eye? How could she look at herself in the mirror? An army for her honor? Didn't love mean anything?

Her thoughts turned to her little sister and her baby brother. If the war continued, would they live long enough to find love? What about her friends? Talos and Rosalyn had just married. Didn't they deserve to live out their days together and to raise a family of their own?

But what about her and Varren? How could they ever hope to marry if she bore this offspring, the blood price for the army? How would Varren feel about her? Yet if Elysia lost the war, would she ever see Varren again?

On the other hand, how would Yena know that she and Apex had mated? Conceiving a child could take time.

"I'll do it," said Lluava. She would lie to the end of her days, as long as the army was sent to Elysia. Surely, when she explained everything to Apex, he would go along with her scheme and pretend to be her mate. This was the answer to all their struggles. "I will mate with Apex."

Nodding toward a small table, Yena said, "See the knife? Prick your thumb, then stamp it on the scroll. This signifies your agreement."

What did Lluava care? She would have an army. Wincing at the sharp pain, she smeared the bloody thumbprint onto the blank parchment.

Yena looked pleased. "Follow me."

"Where are we going?" asked Lluava as she walked out of the room behind the high priestess.

"I want to show you something," was her reply.

They came to a dead end. Yena reached out and touched the stone, at the same time whispering inaudible words. The wall began to move.

Wide-eyed, Lluava quickly stepped back.

A heavy section of the wall seemed to break away, then swing back like a door on a hinge, yet there was no sound of stone grating upon stone. In awestruck silence, Lluava followed the high priestess into blackness as the wall closed behind them.

Chapter 18

The Dark One's Return

The black curtain that seemed to cover Lluava's eyes began to lift. Her hypersensitive vision was enabled by a single source of illumination that entered from a minute hole in the ceiling.

The small, domed room of black polished stone might have been a natural cavern before deft hands had found ways to improve upon it. In its center was a pedestal that flared out at the top to form a shallow basin. Lluava could not tell what the basin held.

She wanted to ask what they were doing in this room, yet the heavy silence swallowed her voice. She stood next to the high priestess and waited.

For a time, neither spoke nor moved. Then a thin beam of moonlight lit the floor and slowly moved toward the pedestal. For some reason this simple, incremental movement captivated Lluava.

When the stream of light touched the base of the pedestal, Yena began to hum, a strange vocalization that arose from deep within the priestess's throat. The heavy sound began to rise and fall in an unearthly melody.

When the moonlight encroached upon the lip of the basin, High Priestess Yena moved toward the pedestal. Some inner sense told Lluava to follow. The priestess began to speak in a strange language. Lluava realized what it was: the ancient tongue. Though she could read the written words, understanding the spoken language was entirely another matter. She had heard the words uttered only in ancient ceremonies.

Suddenly, Lluava realized that a ceremony of some kind was taking place. Shouldn't she have been asked first if she wanted to participate? Shouldn't she have been told what this was for? Shouldn't she...

Yena dipped her finger into the liquid in the basin, a shimmering, unforgiving black fluid. The high priestess lifted her finger, and dark droplets slid down her arm before falling back into the basin.

"Crocotta, O magnanimous Queen of the Gods and all that lives, Prophetess, Matriarch of the Blessed. I have come to learn your will."

A chill ran down Lluava's spine as she observed the moonlight strike the dark liquid.

Yena continued the ritual. "Bestow upon me, your servant, keeper of your word, the knowledge you wish to instill."

The ripples created by the fallen droplets subsided as the moonlight pierced the center of the basin. Lluava gasped. At least she thought she did, but no sound was heard. She was mute, held in the absolute silence that demanded her respect.

The fluid's murky blackness faded like curtains being parted to reveal a window. A figure appeared, one that had haunted Lluava's dreams. However, Varren's face was not as she remembered. This man looked thinner, paler in complexion. Yet it was the prince. The girl reached out to touch the lips she knew so well. Yena quickly grabbed her hand and held it in her strong grip.

Lluava blinked away tears. All she wanted was to be at Varren's side. His kind blue eyes were tinged with sadness. What had happened?

The image changed. There was a jungle. Lurking in the shadows and hiding among the vines was a dark creature. Yena's grip tightened, causing Lluava to winced.

The image vanished. The beam of moonlight had moved beyond the basin, leaving only the liquid blackness.

Lluava regained her voice.

"Varren," she called out. "Varren. Varren!"

The high priestess pulled Lluava away from the basin and quieted her with a withering glare.

"Your human is alive. Take solace in that," commanded Yena as she watched the moonbeam approach the opposite side of the chamber.

"What was that?" Lluava asked, once her emotions were under control.

"It's called scrying. One of several ways the goddess communicates with me."

Hoping for another glimpse of her military partner, Lluava asked, "Can I do that?"

"No."

"What if you taught me?"

"That is not your gift," Yena said seriously. Then she smiled gently. "All Incarn have one."

"I don't have any gift." Lluava was confused. With the exception of her dual form, there was nothing special about her.

"Your gift will manifest when the time is right. Have faith in that."

The priestess turned to the seemingly solid wall and traced an image on the stone with her finger. Lluava leaned over and glimpsed the profile of a bird hacked into the rocky surface.

"These birds protect the darkness," explained Yena. "Even the All Mother, Crocotta, acknowledges that."

Looking closer at the crude carving, Lluava wondered about Onyx. What had happened to her dratted bird? Was the doughty thing still alive? Did she actually miss that creature? Lluava hoped not. Anyway, the raven was doubtless long gone.

As before, the wall opened. Stepping into the corridor, Lluava shielded her eyes from the glowing light until they adjusted to the brightness. As her sight began to return, she heard Yena speak to someone.

"The Dark One has returned. Find him."

Although the girl wondered what Yena meant, she was too concerned about Varren to ask questions about the new visitor.

"Lluava." Only the high priestess's ivory eyes were visible through her silver garb, but they looked kindly at her. "Go back and rest." Yena eyed Lluava's still-bandaged leg. "There is much to be done. Do not worry. I will ensure that the ceremony does not take place in the morning. Ullr is your mate, not mine."

Before Lluava could protest, several priestesses joined them. How had Yena summoned them?

"Please escort Lluava to the coliseum, where she can rest and heal."

Outside the temple, the sky was beginning to brighten. The pale moon still clung to its position high above, but the sun would make its appearance soon. Somehow, the sight of the moon was comforting. Returning to the coliseum cell, Lluava quickly fell asleep on the slab that was her bed.

***

For Lluava, waking up in the dark was always unnerving because there was no sense of time. When she finally arose, she could not be sure how long she had slept. Had she missed the ceremony? Had Yena kept her word, or was Apex the new ruire? Chastising herself for not staying awake, Lluava quickly left her cubicle. Her leg had improved remarkably; she hoped to one day share this knowledge with Rosalyn.

Footsteps approached. She heard the chittering attendants before a third voice growled, "Leave me be! It's only a scratch. I'm not going to die. You should see the other guy."

Apex!

"Umph." Turning a corner quickly, Lluava ran into the huntsman himself. In the flickering torchlight, she saw that he held a reddening cloth to his neck. The two attendants and four other, apparently injured people trailed behind him.

"Lluava?"

She responded with a question of her own. "What happened to you?"

"Long story," grumbled Apex before snapping at the female attendant who was reaching up to his neck. "Stop that!"

"Take a seat in here," the woman ordered, gesturing to an open cubicle. The huntsman reluctantly acquiesced.

"Apex, what happened?" Lluava asked again as she followed him and one of the attendants into the room.

"The entire Warrior Caste was sent to find an intruder," he explained as the woman pulled a vial from the pocket of her red apron. "A former ruire, who had been banished, returned uninvited."

Apex snarled at the woman as she pulled off the bloody cloth, exposing several nasty claw marks that cut deep into the bruised flesh around the huntsman's collarbone.

Apex looked darkly at the attendant. "He was quick and cunning; we chased him all over the jungle. When we finally captured him, he certainly put up a fight. Of course, this had to happen the day I was to become ruire."

So Apex hadn't been able to complete the ceremony. Lluava breathed a sigh of relief. She could see that he was trying not to wince as the woman dripped medicine into his wounds. She felt sorry for him.

"Apex, I have something to—" Lluava began, but her thoughts turned to the intruder and the image she had seen in the basin. "What was his form?"

"A black panther. Kept disappearing in the understory, but we got him." He gave Lluava a shrewd look and added, "*Not* one of us."

Lluava was unnerved. "What did he look like?"

"Large, black, furry," replied the huntsman sarcastically.

"No, I mean, did you see his human form? What did he look like?"

Apex gave her a serious look. "Tall. Very tall, like six-six. Maybe more. Angular features. Very black skin."

"Did he have an accent?"

"I'd call it that. But it matched those from here, so nothing special."

"Did he say why he had come?"

"No," admitted the huntsman as the woman began to wrap his wound with clean cloths.

"Where is he, Apex?" questioned Lluava hurriedly. "Where'd they take him? I need to see him."

"The temple."

She spun on her heel and made for the stairwell. Behind her, Apex called out, "Leave this alone, Lluava!"

There was a shattering of glass on stone, and the woman attendant snapped, "Sit back down!"

Leaving Apex's argumentative voice behind her, Lluava took the stairs three at a time. If the man awaiting punishment in the temple was who she thought he was, she had to do something.

She was dripping with sweat by the time she left the coliseum. The sun hovered over the treetops, and a glorious pattern of orange and red hues haloed it as it sank. Forcing her legs to move faster, she wove through the city's narrow streets and past the intricately carved stone architecture. Finally, the temple was just ahead. Unable to slow down, Lluava ran into a man pushing a cart full of jewelry as he left the market area. Bangles and nose rings flew into the air.

The man cursed her clumsiness, but Lluava was already on her feet, dodging rolling anklets and beads. There might not be time to risk helping collect the merchant's goods. She left him to complete the job himself.

Bounding up the stairs of the temple, Lluava hurried past several worshippers in the pronaos and darted into the cella, which was crowded with many familiar faces from her caste. Maruny was there, and the look she gave Lluava made her stomach churn. Would Maruny ever forgive her? It hadn't been her fault.

Pushing through the crowd, Lluava saw Master Hon holding one end of a thick iron chain that encircled the neck of a handcuffed man who knelt before him. She didn't have to see the face. She recognized him instantly.

"Ojewa!" she cried out. Hon stopped conversing with the high priestess, who was reclining in her throne-like chair. Faces turned toward Lluava.

"I know this man!" Lluava protested as a pair of seasoned warriors started to pull her away.

The high priestess raised her hand, the only part of her body that was not shrouded, with the exception of her eyes. The men released Lluava.

"Do you know this traitor?" Yena asked.

"I don't know that he is a traitor, High Priestess," stated Lluava as Ojewa looked over his shoulder at her. A slight smile cracked his bleeding lips. "But he is an old friend, one who helped train me in the art of war during my time in Elysia."

"This man is raising an army against us," snarled Hon as he jerked the chain and almost caused Ojewa to fall backward.

"No. No. It's nothing like that," stammered Lluava, although now she wasn't sure. These people knew Ojewa. He had come from Leucrocotta. Did she really know this man at all?

"The way I see it, he switched loyalties after his banishment. Maybe he is planning to bring those cursed invaders here," bellowed the master of the Warrior Caste.

"True!" A voice arose from in front of Hon.

Lluava moved to a different angle and spotted Thoth standing at the base of the dais. This somehow made sense to her. Until Apex fulfilled the ceremony, Thoth still served as ruire.

Thoth continued. "Yet, knowing that death would meet him if he ever returned, why would he have come alone? Where is his army?"

"A spy!" someone proffered.

"I wish I could say I had more respect for you than that—but, Ojewa, I do not know you anymore," Thoth acknowledged.

"He will not stand up for himself," stated Hon. "He has not said one word since he was captured."

Above them, the high priestess's voice rang out. "What say you about this, Ojewa? Why have you returned?"

"I left Leucrocotta..." Ojewa began. His thick accent perfectly matched Yena's. Why hadn't Lluava made this connection earlier? Yet, she had not seen the colonel since she followed a band of Raiders away from the battles at the Southern Camps. Half a year had passed since she had last seen his all-knowing face.

Ojewa was still speaking. "I left Leucrocotta with full knowledge that, if I returned, it would cost me my life. I have not forgotten the terms of banishment, nor will I deny your rights."

He paused. No one spoke while they waited for his explanation.

"I have not come to bring war or to spy on old friends. I have simply come in search of the one who might be able to save the Banished Lands, of which I have grown fond."

Speaking directly to High Priestess Yena, Ojewa admitted, "I have come for Lluava Kargen."

Hon looked in Lluava's direction, while Thoth kept his eyes on their prisoner. Lluava felt questioning stares on the back of her neck. Ojewa was here for *her*, risking his life. What was happening in Elysia?

"Did you really expect us to let you go?" questioned Thoth.

"As I said," answered Ojewa, "I am willing to give you my life as long as I am permitted to deliver a message to the one called Lluava Kargen."

"Leave us," ordered the high priestess.

The room began to empty. Soon only Master Hon, Ruire Thoth, Colonel Ojewa, Lluava, and the priestesses remained. With a hand gesture, Yena granted permission for someone to enter. Lluava, focused only on the high priestess, did not turn toward the door.

"Tell me, Ojewa," Yena asked, "what message is important enough to sacrifice your life for?"

Ojewa stood up. Hon was clearly disgruntled as the man towered above him, yet he allowed it. Turning to Lluava, the prisoner explained, "I have come in search of you, to implore you to return. Elysia is in peril. The enemy is marching toward the capital's gates. King Varren refuses to act. He is not only your king, but also your military partner. You must make him understand that war is at hand. He needs to rally the people and lead the troops. It is imperative that you return and bring him to his senses, or the kingdom will fall."

"You have sacrificed yourself for that message?" huffed Master Hon.

Ojewa turned to Hon. "I will sacrifice one life to save many."

"What's happened? What's wrong with Varren?" Lluava hastily asked. She didn't care if those around her realized that she had not abandoned the Banished Lands. Elysia was her home. Varren was her king, her partner, the man she loved.

Ojewa's eyes darkened like the bruises on his obsidian skin. "The king seems to have disregarded the need for defense against our enemy. His mind is obsessed with his upcoming nuptials."

Lluava felt as if someone had punched her in the stomach. She took a step back as Ojewa continued.

"All his attention and all the capital's resources are being directed toward his wedding, which will take place on his twenty-first birthday. By then, I fear, it will be too late."

All thoughts of her mission, the Incarn, war, and those around her instantly disappeared as Lluava screamed out, *"To whom?"*

Chapter 19

The Amulet Revealed

O nly one name came to mind. Only one person could have manipulated Varren into marriage with another: Head Councilman Themis. Lluava thought little about him lately, assuming that the power-hungry man and his evil plans had been curtailed.

As head councilman, Themis held more power than anyone in the kingdom except the king. Certainly, he had pulled strings to make King Thor dance like a marionette. Yet Thor was dead, and Varren now wore the crown. Themis must have found a way to force Varren to bend to his will. What was it? Some forgotten rule that worked in his favor? But the king could amend rules. Blackmail, perhaps? Blackmail was just up Themis's alley.

Lluava's outburst still reverberated through the room. Ignoring the sharp looks of those around her, she strode up to Ojewa and stood before him. "Who is he to marry?"

Ojewa's clear disappointment in her could not be misread. Lluava knew she should be concerned about the war, about Elysia, about her mission; yet she had to know.

"The Lady Selene Fárbauti."

Suddenly Lluava couldn't breathe. She opened her mouth, but no air entered. Dizzy, she doubled over, lungs burning. Someone approached and held her shoulders. Hot anger seared through her, rising from her core. Fiery tears stung her eyes. Rage bubbled up like bile. Lluava let loose an enormous roar.

The intense release of emotion drained her strength, and Lluava sank to her knees. She would have hit the floor if those strong hands at her shoulders hadn't grabbed her tightly and eased her down.

"It can't…" Lluava's voice sounded weak, pathetic. "She wouldn't…"

Her thoughts spun out of control. Selene was her friend; she would not do that. Didn't she know how Lluava felt about Varren, how he felt about her? Yet, Lluava had never told her friend about those feelings, out of the need to keep them secret until Varren amended the law so he could break his betrothal to Illia and marry Lluava. Varren was going to do this for her, for them, not for anyone else. How ironic. The law no longer needed to be changed because Illia had been killed during the battle for the North.

Varren would never condone this marriage. He would refuse. He would never consider this match. He loved *her*, not Selene, not Illia. He would not. He would *not*! Varren would fight Themis. Themis…

Why would Themis advocate this match? Selene was a Theriomorph, and Themis hated Theriomorphs. It was true that Selene and her brother had been adopted and raised by a human family of noble blood, but Selene's blood was pure. Theriomorphs would defile the royal bloodline. Theriomorphs were the scum of the earth. Themis would never agree to this union. What was really going on?

"I have to go home," rasped Lluava, finally looking up through tear-blurred eyes. "I have to return to Elysia."

The figure behind her bent low and snarled in her ear, "Stop that."

It was Apex. Had her companion turned against her? Couldn't he understand that she had to return to stop this horrid wedding? She needed to be by Varren's side. Varren! It was Apex's fault that she was so far away from her rightful partner. Apex believed in this foolish endeavor; she didn't. It was Apex, not Lluava, who wanted to find the other Incarn. He—not Lluava—was perfectly content to stay with these people. *He* was the real problem.

Apex studied Thoth's grim face.

"Clearly you can see that Lluava is not well," said Apex.

Thoth glowered at the pair. "What I *see* is two people who knew more than they admitted, who came here for reasons I neither knew nor ever believed. What I *see* is a threat to my people and our way of life."

Yena spoke. There was danger in her voice, sharp as a blade's edge. "Have you come to do us harm, Apex, huntsmen of the wood and wilderness?"

Apex stepped around Lluava. The bandages about his neck, which had been hastily wrapped, had fallen low about his collar, exposing the fleshy wound. Blood still oozed and slowly congealed.

"No." His response was quick and assertive.

"And you, Lluava, daughter of the Banished Lands, do you wish to save your people, your race? Will you fulfill the promises you have made?"

For a moment, Lluava considered the implications of the high priestess's words. Yena's question was less a request than a demand—a demand Lluava could not bear to fulfill. She knew what Yena wanted of her but could not oblige.

"I will when the time is right. This is not the time."

"Are you rejecting your duties?"

Lluava warily eyed the angered ruire, then glanced at the confused expression on Apex's face. "No. But I can't fulfill them yet."

"There you have it," sighed the high priestess. "Apex, tomorrow you will fulfill your rights and become the ruire." A look of longing briefly flared in Thoth's eyes as he heard the priestess's decree.

Lluava understood that this was just a bluff. The high priestess didn't mean what she said; she was trying to manipulate Lluava into doing her bidding, just as Themis had Varren. But the teen would not give in. Yena would never allow the ceremony to be consummated.

Lluava needed time to tell Apex everything. Away from all these eyes, they could lie about their mating. The army would be sent, and Elysia might be saved. "I cannot fulfill that promise now. Soon, yes. But not now."

Yena's eyes looked at the teen sadly. "Lluava has publicly rejected the wish of the goddess. Take her and the Dark One to the holding cells, where they will await their punishment."

"What?" gasped Lluava as Ruire Thoth motioned and members of the Warrior Caste gripped Lluava's arms. "No! You can't do this!" As she kicked and struggled, she shouted, "I've done nothing wrong! Yena! Apex! *Apex!*"

The huntsman didn't even turn around to watch her leave. As Lluava stared at his strong back, her hatred blossomed.

***

The cells were nothing more than barred cubicles in another sector beneath the coliseum. Once they may have held beasts for ancient rituals, but now they served as a dungeon of sorts. The ancient claw marks of imprisoned animals still scarred the walls. Though warm and dry, the place offered little comfort. It was the birthplace of loneliness and despair.

In silence, Lluava sat for a time and remembered the recent past. Apex had been locked up in the dungeon in Alcazar Castle and sentenced to the executioner's blade. Nonetheless, Lluava had found a way to save his life. He owed her as much, didn't he? Yet he had stood there and let them drag her away like an animal. When that had happened to Apex, she had fought for him, argued for his release. Did he do the same for her? No. He had not moved a muscle.

Lluava had gotten in his way more times than she could count, but did that entitle Apex to wish her ill? Everything she had done was to make sure they stayed on track, to make sure Apex did not lose focus. Was that wrong? Did he judge her for that? Was he angry for what she had done to Vissa? Lluava didn't believe the man could feel real emotions. Apex was motivated by lust and power. She never gave into him. He was just desirous. Why had she been forced to work beside him?

"Lluava?"

Ojewa's voice drifted down the hall. His cell must be nearby.

"Yes?" she replied, realizing she wasn't alone.

"You need to return to Elysia." Ojewa was still focused on his own mission. "You must talk to the king."

Varren. The thought of him made her heartsick. What had happened?

"Lluava, listen to me." Colonel Ojewa's voice was cool yet stern. "The enemy has won the North. They are moving toward the capital. King Varren needs to focus on the dire issue at hand. He is not well."

Remembering the sight of Varren's wan face in Yena's scrying basin, Lluava's worries were confirmed. "Have the healers seen to him?"

"This is not a physical disease," Ojewa replied. "His mind is clouded. He rarely eats or sleeps. His thoughts are only on his marriage."

"That does not sound like Varren."

"True. The High Council has discussed the Wasting Disease his grandfather had. They wonder if it has been passed onto him."

"Do you think that is the case?" Lluava was worried.

"There are darker things in the world than the Wasting Disease."

"What do you think it is?"

"I know not."

What could be wrong with Varren? When they parted, he had wanted to travel with her. Yet they both knew that if he did so, Themis would seize control of the government. Knowing Themis, nothing good would come of it, at least not for the Theriomorphs. Varren had returned to the capital to assume his proper place on the throne, to save Elysia, to help her. What had happened? What?

"Can't they provide more torches in this place? It's abysmal down here," stated the mild voice of Leo Pardus.

"No point in that," noted a second voice with a distinctly nasal twang. "Those who come never stay long. You know how it goes."

"Could you be any more cheerful?" questioned Leo sarcastically as he and his companion approached the area where Lluava was imprisoned. "You're becoming like these walls—cold, hard, and dark."

"If only it *were* cold down here," sighed the second man. "She's over there. Down to your right."

"Thank you," said Leo, moments before his tiny form appeared in front of Lluava's cell. "Aren't you a sight!" he exclaimed.

"Leo!" Lluava greeted him excitedly. "What are you doing here? You have to get me out!"

"Shush, shush," soothed the man as he motioned her to be quiet. "We can have none of that right now. I am not even supposed to see you." His eyes darted about the place.

"Then why are you here?"

"To help." He leaned in close and dropped his voice. "If I can."

The other man, probably a guard, could be heard moving in the corridor. Leo pulled out a handkerchief and wiped the sweat from his brow.

"I have only a moment. In order for you to be released, Thoth needs to know he can trust you, and I fear that will be a difficult hurdle to overcome in itself. The Warrior Caste fears you will try to escape, which is the last thing you must do. I will try to have you moved to the Scholar Caste and have you placed under my supervision. At least you will be out of this dreary place."

Lluava wanted to interject but allowed Leo to finish. "Follow your mate's lead. You must make a vow in Crocotta's temple that you will never leave the city. You can still have a good life."

"Apex won't be my mate much longer," noted Lluava dryly. "He is to be ruire, remember?"

"He is not the only male who walks these streets. You will find others," Leo pointed out. "You are strong and young and beautiful. Most important, you are smart. Choose to work with me, and I can teach you many things. You can be happy. You can stay with me and my mate until you have a roof of your own. You do not want to spend the rest of your days locked in this godforsaken place."

Even though Leo was in earnest, Lluava declined. "I can't, Leo. I belong in Elysia, not here."

"But this is where you are meant to be," argued Leo, as he would any other fact he had taught.

"You don't know what I'm meant to do."

"But I do," Leo said as his hands brushed a point on his chest.

"Really?" said Lluava, her voice dripping with skepticism. "How is that?"

"Trust me."

"I'm losing trust in people rapidly."

"Lluava, you must remember that I serve as your advisor."

"I thought you were my friend."

"I am, but my purpose is to guide you."

"To what end?" inquired Lluava darkly. Something about their conversation had aroused her sixth sense. *Advisor, guide*—these words seemed to be freighted with some implicit burden.

"To help you."

She sighed. "What aren't you telling me?"

Leo tapped his chest again. Was there a slight bulge under his shirt?

"What is that?" Lluava demanded. "Show me."

The torchlight that glimmered off Leo's spectacles prevented Lluava from seeing into his eyes. Slowly Leo tugged at a ribbon around his neck. Soon she saw a familiar amulet, a radiating eye surrounded with ancient runes. Just like Hyrax's.

"You're a Guardian!" hissed Lluava. "You knew we were Incarn all along!"

"Lluava, your voice," he motioned for her to quiet as he rapidly tucked the amulet back under his shirt. "Please."

"Was it an accident that you were assigned to transition us to

Leucrocotta, or did you make the decision yourself?" Lluava felt her anger flaring, igniting the inner heat at her very core.

"High Priestess Yena asked me to work with you, to get both you and Apex ready for your task."

"To breed with one another," snarled Lluava. She was exasperated that this issue had come up yet again. The feeling of betrayal had never been so strong.

"If you agree to stay, to work under my supervision, everything can return to the way it should be," assured Leo hastily.

"Apex will be ruire."

"No. Not if you agree to fulfill your destiny—your birthright, as it were."

"You lied to me," growled Lluava. Her hands grabbed the bars framing the top of the door so hard that her knuckles turned white. "You tried to manipulate me. You tried to use me."

"No. No. No!" countered Leo, clearly worried by Lluava's growing anger.

"You work for Yena!" shouted Lluava. "Leave now! Never see me again!"

Leo backed away from Lluava's cell. "As you wish," he said and hastened off down the dim hall.

Lluava sank to the ground in despair. She half expected to hear Ojewa ask about her conversation. Despite the knowledge that he would be executed, he had come to Leucrocotta to find her, to send her home to save Elysia. Now he would die in the morning, and his life would be forfeited for nothing. Elysia was falling to the Raiders without any opposition, Varren was suffering from illness or madness, and he was going to exchange vows with Selene. Imprisoned in the dark cell, Lluava felt helpless. She had lost both Varren and her homeland.

What else had she lost? Everything. Her life here was ruined. The people with whom she had formed relationships in the Warrior Caste, including Master Hon and sweet Maruny, now hated her. Pedagogue Leo and High Priestess Yena had proved to be manipulators for their own arcane purposes. Thoth distrusted her more than ever. Even Apex would rather become ruire than stand up for her. That power-hungry savage!

As hopelessness shrouded her, Lluava sank into a fitful sleep, nightmares through which laughing hyenas and fork-tongued creatures slithered and crawled. There, in the jungle of her mind, Lluava ran wild. Leaves and vines slapped at her face, causing her cheeks to smart. Her feet were bare and picked up splinters and thorns.

Yet she ran on.

She had to keep going. She couldn't stop. Was it because something was behind her, following her? Or was she heading somewhere? But where? The jungle seemed endless. Every tree and fern looked just like the last. How long had she been out here?

She could hear Yena's high-pitched laugh. Was she being watched? No matter where Lluava ran, she could not escape the high priestess's voice.

Maybe Yena was watching her in that black liquid. Lluava wanted to hide from the invisible gaze.

The forest came alive with movement. Creatures lurked in the shadows—enormous snakes, hungry black dogs. Where was she to turn? How could she get away? Where should she go? Not back to Leucrocotta. Anywhere but there.

The forest began to break apart. The shapes of stacked, domed roofs loomed before her.

No! thought Lluava. I don't want to go back!

Turning, she took off into the depths of the jungle. Yet the city reappeared. No. No. No!

Everywhere she turned, the city rose in front of her, calling to her, demanding that she stay.

Her piercing roar of despair shook the trees around her.

"Here! Here! This way." The voice startled Lluava. "Follow me. Quickly."

Comforted by the familiar deep purr, Lluava followed the sound through a narrow gap in the forest. She would escape the city and all the troubles that lay within it.

"Hurry. Quickly, quickly."

Lluava would escape this place as long as she could keep up with the voice of the dark form leading her through the shadows.

"Someone's approaching."

Lluava froze. Which way to go? Where was the guiding voice? Lluava's eyes darted about her. The voice returned and screamed, "Awaken!"

Her eyes shot open, and Lluava sprang to her feet. A figure stood just outside her door. She pressed herself into the back corner of her cell and hoped the darkness would shield her. Ojewa's order still rang in her ear. Had he actually spoken those words, or had she dreamed that, too?

Someone was fumbling with keys. She was foggy-headed from exhaustion, yet she could not have been asleep for more than a few hours. Morning had yet to arrive, so who was paying her a midnight visit?

Lluava looked around to see what she could use in her defense. The straw-stuffed mattress would be of no help. She could see nothing else. Since Issaura's Claws had been taken from her, she was left with only one choice: hand-to-hand combat. Fortunately, she had claws of her own.

An irritated rumble in her throat was hard to stifle as the key finally turned in the lock. With a click and a rasp, the heavy door was flung open.

Chapter 20

A Life Saved

We have to go," the hushed voice demanded. "Now."

Lluava let loose a breath of relief. Looking at the huntsman, she could not be happier to escape her imprisonment. As she stepped out of her cell, Lluava hoped this would be the last time she was thrown behind bars.

"We're leaving," Apex said again.

Lluava still hesitated a moment in disbelief at this unplanned release. "I thought you wanted to stay, to be ruire."

Ignoring her, Apex adjusted a large duffel over one shoulder and moved down the corridor. How was it that even when he attempted to do something nice, he found a way to be insulting? As Lluava started to follow him, she halted.

"Wait," she hissed as quietly as possible. "We have to release Colonel Ojewa."

"The panther?" Apex repeated in disbelief. "No."

"Yes," countered Lluava. "He's a friend."

"And the one who tried to take my head off," snarled the huntsman. Lluava had forgotten about the oozing wound at the base of Apex's neck.

"I'm sure you gave him some of those bruises that I noticed."

"He attacked me."

"You went after him."

"He's an outlaw."

"So are we—now."

Apex turned to glare at her. In the dim light, his eyes flashed yellow-red. "Do you want to remain here until they decide on your fate—a traitor's fate?"

"Of course not."

"That man betrayed his people. He was banished for life because of the

131

crimes he committed. How can you trust someone like that?"

Lluava chewed her lip. Ojewa had been banished for something he did. He was never to return. What could he have done to deserve such punishment? Could he be trusted? Recently, Lluava had found it difficult to trust anyone. No one was who they seemed to be. Even worse, some of her closest confidants had turned out to be actual traitors and had sought her life. Was Ojewa one, too? He'd been the first person to believe in her abilities. Yet for years he had worked alongside General Kentril, the traitor who had attempted to kill both her and Varren.

From Apex's rigid posture, Lluava knew he would not easily change his mind. How could *he* be so judgmental? He was Apex, the wild huntsman of the wood; Apex the rogue.

Lluava spat out, "I trusted *you.*"

They glared at each other. Lluava continued, "Remember, you were—are—an Outlander. Elysians never looked kindly on them. And you were also sentenced to die for murder. How quickly you forget!"

"And the panther is innocent?" snapped Apex.

"At least he never killed a child." Lluava realized she had said too much. Apex turned to leave.

Suddenly Lluava felt sick. "Apex, they'll kill him. Because of me, he'll die."

"Leave me, Lluava." The thickly accented voice of Ojewa trailed down the corridor. "While you still can. I completed my mission. I did my duty."

"There," Apex said. "He agrees. Let's go."

As he turned the corner, Lluava demanded, "Give me the keys."

"You can't be serious," sighed Apex, clearly exasperated. He lowered his arms, and the duffel over his shoulder nearly slipped off before he righted it once again.

Lluava remained undeterred. "You have them. Give them to me."

"We're running out of time."

"Just hand them over."

"We have to leave. Now."

"And go where?" snapped Lluava. "Into the jungle? There are booby traps all around. The Warrior Caste will be tracking us. We are surrounded by impenetrable mountains. Do you know the hidden path out of this valley? Because I certainly don't."

There was a long pause as Apex considered Lluava's words. She spoke once more. "But Colonel Ojewa does."

Another pause.

"Ojewa came back on his own. He knows how to get in and out of this place. Without him, we are lost."

The keys jingled as they were tossed through the air. Lluava's quick reflexes helped her catch them before running to Ojewa's cell. There were a few tense moments as she struggled to find the right key. Then, with a click she released the captive.

With a quick nod of thanks, Ojewa followed the other two down the labyrinth of passageways underneath the coliseum. Suddenly he stopped short.

"Wait," he said. "This way."

He began to double back. Lluava looked at Apex's perplexed expression.

"He's going the wrong way," said the huntsman.

Was Ojewa leading them into a trap? Had Apex been right all along?

Lluava made a snap decision. She followed Ojewa into the coliseum's depths. Apex followed grudgingly.

Sometime later, they emerged through a hatch in the ground. Ojewa had led them through several long tunnels that opened into the jungle. The thickly tangled canopy blocked the view above. Lluava could not tell how soon morning's light would appear, but she knew they were running out of time.

Ojewa shifted. The lithe black panther seemed to disappear into the shadows. There was no more fitting camouflage in the animal kingdom.

"We should do the same," noted Lluava.

A hand touched her shoulders. "Take these first," Apex said as he lowered the duffel to sort through its hidden contents. He pulled out two objects Lluava had given up hope of seeing again—Issaura's Claws. Before she could gasp out her thanks, he shoved them into her open hands and said, "No time for that. Shift. Let's go."

Lluava slid the Claws over her knuckles. She felt whole for the first time in a long while. Then, allowing the heat from her core to take over, she shifted into her dual form. Fangs and paws emerged as her body reformed. Her foreclaws took on a gilded hue as Issaura's Claws shifted with her, encasing her own razor-sharp instruments.

Beside her, the massive form of the Yorrick wolverine appeared as if out of thin air. The beast used his bronze-encased muzzle to pick up the now much lighter duffel. So, he also had Ullr's Fangs. She wondered how that thievery had been conducted, as she hurriedly followed Ojewa through the darkness.

Her eyesight was much keener now, and she easily pursued the feline through the jungle. She was careful to place her paws exactly where the panther's had been, lest she trip a wire or fall into a trap.

There were several tense moments when Ojewa seemed unsure of what path to take next. Their movements were surprisingly slow and calculated. Lluava kept peering back, half expecting to see an approaching party of angered warriors. Yet, if anyone in Leucrocotta realized they had escaped, Lluava and her companions were too far away to hear the sound of an alert.

Ojewa led them up the base of one of the mountains whose craggy top loomed over them. Digging her claws into the stony ground, Lluava climbed as rapidly as the panther would allow.

Large, jagged shards of the mountainside stuck up like broken teeth where they had fallen ages ago. Ojewa led them on a winding path around one rock fall, then back around another. Lluava could not tell whether this was the only way to approach the hidden entry, or just a tactic to keep them hidden as much as possible from searching eyes.

The sound of crashing water was picked up by her hypersensitive ears. Far ahead, Lluava spotted a waterfall that plunged from a high crevice to smash onto the stony ground in a torrent of noise and spray. The cloud of steam hovering at the top of the rocky ledge meant that this was one of several hot springs that vented from the mountain depths. A swollen river formed at the base of the falls, where the churning water cooled in a basin larger than any of the pools she had seen at the capital, before winding downstream to be lost under the canopy of the jungle. Ojewa steered them toward this waterfall.

By the time they had followed the most obscure path to the base of the falls, the sun was rising over the jagged crown of the mountain range. The cascading water sparkled in the early light.

Ojewa looked back at them, flicked his long tail twice, and then disappeared. Apex followed with duffel still in his strong jaws. Approaching the spot where Ojewa had stood, he, too, seemed to evaporate into the misty spray that rose from the waterfall.

Lluava took a final look at the strange beauty of the valley. From stony wall to stony wall, vibrant jungle flourished. Several thin streams of glimmering silver poured down the mountains. The waterfalls gave this valley its life. Without these mountaintop hot springs, the humid bubble of air would never have existed, and this valley would be a frozen desert.

Maybe the gods did protect this place after all. Or maybe her ancestors, who had stumbled onto this hidden salvation, were just lucky. As she cast her gaze over the stone domes that appeared to pop up in the jungle's heart, she understood why they had stayed. Lluava had never seen the likes of this valley's beauty before, yet she hoped she would never have to see it again. A moment later, she followed her companions into the mist.

At first, Lluava could not see anything and carefully inched forward. The roaring wall of heated water fell to her right as she pressed her body to the stony wall on her left. Soon she emerged into a tunnel behind the falls. In the gloomy light, the glowing reflection of two pairs of eyes shone back at her. Then they turned away, disappearing into the darkness. Lluava followed the sound of their breathing and the scent of their hides. The temperature plummeted. Soon after, a thin crack of light appeared before them.

As she stepped out from behind a boulder that served to shield the cave, Lluava instantly resumed her hatred of cold and ice. They were back where they had started, back in the nothingness of white. Suddenly, Lluava longed for home. She wished to be tucked in bed next to her little sister in their broken-down farmhouse. She wanted to walk through the year-round green gardens with Varren at Cronus, the capital, and delight in all that was beautiful and pure. But she was here in the horrid, frozen white.

"The underwater bridge has yet to resurface at this time of year," explained Ojewa as he uncovered a hidden parcel buried under a layer of freshly fallen snow. "We will have to cross the river by other means."

As the sun continued to rise, it illuminated more and more shapes, and Lluava realized they were still in the mountain range—at least in the beginning of it, for she could see glimpses of tundra far to the northeast. Her haphazard trip down the river in the dark had been disorienting; the water flowed far more rapidly than she had ever wanted to experience. Though it had taken several days to travel from riverbank to mountain, Lluava wondered where exactly *here* was.

After shifting into human form, Ojewa unwrapped his own parcel. He shook out a fur coat, snow-gray in color. Suddenly, Lluava missed her own pristine white coat, which had been claimed by the river. Apex had spent days sewing it for her from furs he had trapped and tanned. The huntsman had already resumed his human form. He wasn't all that bad, thought Lluava. After all, Apex had set her free.

After she shifted, the trio shared scraps of blankets that Ojewa had hidden, then made their way over the snowy expanse to the river's edge. As they followed it downstream, they trekked in silence, and Lluava's nagging thoughts took hold once more. Apex had saved her—but how?

"Where did you get those keys?" she asked quietly when Ojewa was a good pace or two in front of them.

"You make strong friends," he replied gruffly as he ran a hand over the hilt of one of Ullr's Fangs.

Lluava shivered. What did he mean? What friend did she have back there? Or was he making a jest? Had he killed the guard and taken the keys from the cooling corpse?

Apex studied her face. "Leo Pardus. He filched the keys from the guard."

"Leo?" Lluava exclaimed in surprise. "Why would he—?"

"I didn't hurt anyone to get them," mumbled Apex at the same time.

"I didn't say you did."

"But the thought crossed your mind."

"Then how did you get the weapons back? Yena?" asked Lluava dubiously.

"Leo had them when he gave me the keys."

The realization that Leo actually was her friend upset her. She had been so mean to him. If he really was her friend, all that she had said….

"Why would he want me to escape? What purpose was there? He wanted me to stay in the city." She did not mention that Leo was a Guardian.

Lluava's foot slipped, and Apex grabbed her before responding. "He said he needed the guard to think you and he were at odds so that nobody would suspect him. I owe Leo more credit then I gave him. It seems he has more than just book smarts." The huntsman made a hand motion as if pickpocketing.

Lluava did not like any of this. Yet what was she to do?

"What were you and Yena talking about in the temple?" questioned Apex as he continued to help her down a slippery slope.

Lluava gently touched the tip of the thumb she had pierced with the dagger. Surprisingly, it was still very tender. She glanced back at the mountain with its hidden entrance and admitted, "It does not matter anymore. That's behind us now."

***

Over the next few days, Ojewa guided them to the river's edge while always keeping watch for potential pursuers. Fortunately, there did not seem to be any. The only possible threat came from within their little group. Apex's dislike of Ojewa could not be concealed, no matter how much Lluava asked him to.

When the river was in sight, Ojewa started digging into the snowbank. "Help me," he ordered, and Lluava drove her hands into the frozen powder. Just when she felt that her fingers could not get any number, she touched something solid.

"Here," she said, still unsure what they were uncovering. It took all three of them to pull out a crystal canoe from its snowy prison. Except the canoe was not crystal but ice—a very substantial canoe chiseled from a solid block of ice.

"This is how we get across," explained Ojewa as he began to drag the heavy object toward the raging river. Apex picked up one end; Lluava reluctantly gripped the middle. She loathed the idea of resuming her venture downriver. The occasional shard of ice floated past, although not nearly as many as before. Even so, she glared at the sparkling surface.

"Will this thing hold us? Won't it melt?" Apex's questions indicated that he, too, resented the idea of water travel.

"It will serve our purpose," answered Ojewa as he placed Apex's duffel in the center of the boat. Lluava stepped cautiously into the bow. As Apex placed a foot inside, Ojewa asked, "Can I trust you?"

Apex blinked.

"Can I trust you not to leave me as I shove off?"

Apex did not trust Ojewa, but he still gave his word. "I won't leave you."

"Then hold on." Ojewa pushed the canoe farther into the water. With a jerk, it pulled away from the bank just as Ojewa leaped inside.

At their feet were four wooden paddles; each picked one up. These won't help you steer much," acknowledged Ojewa, "but they might prevent us from crashing into other debris."

"How comforting," grumbled Apex as he batted away a floating branch.

The current suddenly grabbed them, and they hurtled downstream away from the jewel-like place hidden in the mountains. Lluava wondered if the tension in their little boat might be too much for the cramped space.

"Colonel Ojewa," she asked, "why were you banished? I think we deserve to know, if only to establish some sort of real trust."

Lluava could not see Ojewa, as she was in the front of the canoe and had to concentrate on anything bobbing in the water that might hit its bow.

"I was ruire once."

Apex squirmed behind her as Ojewa continued. "According to our doctrine, each year at the Spring Match, all males compete, with the exception of the ruire. The male with the best combination of intelligence and physical power must challenge the current ruire. My scores far exceeded not only the males in my class but also the rest of the males in Leucrocotta. As a result, I had to challenge the existing ruire, a kind man who wanted only the best for his people. I won the match and the title."

The canoe listed sideways for a moment, then corrected itself.

"I never wanted to be ruire. My heart was not in it. My dream was to be the next master of the Warrior Caste. I wanted to teach, to instruct others, to make them better. I had no desire to deal with politics and the issues of the city.

"My predecessor was far better than I in that respect. Although I soon realized I could not continue as ruire, I was never successfully challenged, and as ruire I remained.

"I approached High Priestess Yena and asked her to find another. This angered her. The law states that only the strongest male should be ruire, and I was undefeated. She said I was to remain ruire or die. I chose death. I would not live a half-life. I would not attempt to rule knowing well my decisions would not be the best for the people.

"I was ready to sacrifice my life. Yet on the morning of my execution, the high priestess's public decree changed. She said that the goddess Crocotta had ordered my banishment from the city because my work for her was not yet complete. I was never to return, or I would forfeit my life. I left."

"What purpose did Crocotta have for you?" questioned Apex.

"I know not. Yet because of the banishment, I was able to find my true calling as a military instructor in the Southern training camps for Elysia. That is where I met Lluava. I always knew she was special and would do great things."

A new chill overwhelmed Lluava, caused by something other than the cold air around her. Ojewa had been banished because Crocotta had a plan for him. Had the goddess saved him so that he could later train Lluava? Had the Theriomorph goddess known that without Ojewa's help to get the young female recruit transferred to the men's camp, General Kentril would have killed her in Thowcelemine? How long had the gods been playing them like pawns? And if the gods were able to control so much, why had they allowed them to escape?

Was this part of a bigger plan?

CROCOTTA'S HACKLES

PART II

Chapter 21

Verta

On your right!" barked out Apex.

Lluava had to maneuver quickly to push the bow away from an oncoming block of ice. The boat was approaching too fast. As Lluava wedged her oar between the icy boulder and the canoe, there was a loud crack. Her blade splintered in her grip. The chunk of ice veered away, and Lluava threw the broken remains of her paddle overboard.

The crisis averted, Lluava's thoughts returned to what Ojewa had told her. Could she believe all the implications? If so, she would have to accept that the gods were real. Even more unsettling, could she acknowledge that the Incarn existed and that she was one? Yet she had proved to be different.

A solemn loneliness swept over her. She wanted to be back in Cronus; she needed to talk with Varren. He was always ready to listen, always there for her. The day wore on with no source of solace—as did the next day and the next. Though the water in the river was drinkable, they had no food. The pangs of hunger soon became her first concern. A relentless ache in her thumb, the second.

That first night, they made it to shore to rest before resuming their journey. But on the second evening, the current was too strong, and they were forced to bounce between the floating ice blocks all night.

Lluava did not complain about her empty stomach or her limbs that were numb from the cold. She did not even grumble about her pathetic bouts of sleep. What made her finally speak up was the sight of icy water rushing directly under their canoe.

"How much longer do we have to ride this thing?" she asked, more worriedly than she intended.

"Another day, at least," responded Colonel Ojewa from behind her. "We are traveling much faster than I had hoped. This is all well and good."

"Does this look right to you?" Lluava turned and pointed to the bottom of the canoe, which was so crystal clear she could see a school of fish swimming below them.

"It must be melting faster than I anticipated," Ojewa acknowledged calmly.

Apex examined the hull. "The seven hells with that! We could break through at any minute. We should head for shore."

"Much time will be wasted if we do that," countered Ojewa.

"I'd rather waste time than myself," growled Apex. He tried to shove the boat sideways by pushing his oar against an ice floe, but the current pulled it back to its original course.

"There is not much we can do," said the colonel. "The river has us. Even if we reached the bank, we would be stuck on foot in the middle of the Verta Mountains."

"The Verta Mountains?" Lluava echoed. "So, we really have been heading south? I wasn't sure."

"Yes. This river is the quickest route home. Its headwaters lie in the area where the Borren and Verta mountain ranges meet. Its course flows south and parallels the Verta Mountains. In a few hours, we will branch off toward Elysia."

"I doubt we have a few hours," snarled Apex as he bent down to inspect their icy floor.

"We do. We must," insisted Lluava, despite her lack of knowledge about their fragile watercraft. The ice-capped mountains loomed over them and cast shadows over much of the river. Apex's silence was agreement enough, and they continued their hazardous journey down the rushing river.

All went well until evening, when a loud cracking sounded, accompanied by the canoe careening sideways.

Her balance lost on the slippery floor, Lluava tumbled into the water. She was forced to shift into her tiger form as she paddled to the churning surface. Water blurred her vision. As she gasped for air, she desperately sought her companions. But all she could see was water, snow, and ice.

One of the frozen islands, too small to serve as refuge, slammed into her. Lluava dug her claws into its frigid surface, carving divots that splintered off rather than held. The ice was not strong enough; she would have to try to swim to land.

But paddling her way to shore was just short of impossible. The current kept pulling her back and under. Nonetheless, she fought on. Finally, having used her last stores of energy, she reached shallow water and heaved herself onto the bank.

Too exhausted to stand, Lluava lay limp and weak as a newborn kitten and wondered what had happened to Apex and Ojewa. Stars appeared in the growing darkness. Somehow, shivering on the bank, she fell asleep.

A feeling of warmth first alarmed her. Had she been dragged back to Leucrocotta? The fragrant smell of flowers added to her sudden terror, yet the tiered earth around her could only be the capital's royal gardens. She had made it back!

She heard a familiar flutter of wings in the treetops and spotted the stone footpath that led to the bench by her favorite tree, where she and Varren had often met. Maybe he was there, around the bend, waiting for her....

Lluava approached the bench. She was in her human form. A figure was seated there, dressed in pure white linen and silk. Loose, dark locks seemed to caress the breeze rather than the other way around. Though the young man was looking away from her, she instantly recognized him.

Varren! she wanted to shout, but instead she hurried toward him on leaden legs. She knew she was exhausted from her own journey, but she did not care. The man she loved was so close! As she drew closer, Varren—without so much as a glance at Lluava—raised his arm and pointed ahead of him.

What was he trying to show her?

Suddenly, something stirred in a nearby tall azalea bush, which had long since finished blooming.

Lluava froze in mid step.

A long, green tentacle emerged from the bush and descended slowly toward the spot where Varren sat. Its vivid color was striking, making all the other greens in this lush environment appear dull and lifeless. The tentacle was thicker than Lluava's forearm, yet it continued to broaden. Suddenly, she realized what it was. This was no tentacle—it was a tail. So where was its head?

Slowly putting her other foot down on the path, Lluava inched toward her military partner. He was so calm, so unnaturally calm. As she kept her eyes on the encroaching tail, Lluava heard leaves rustle above. In a flash, the enormous body of an anaconda dropped from the canopy and wrapped itself around Varren. His struggles resulted in the snapping of bones.

No! Lluava wanted to scream, as she realized that Issaura's Claws were not on her hands. Then all her breath left her as the tail end of the serpent enveloped her, and she, too, was being suffocated. The pressure on her chest was incredible. She gasped and gagged for air. The teen watched in horror as the light left Varren's eyes, and he disappeared behind a wall of coils.

Lluava heard a yelp as she struggled to escape the coils. No—not coils, but fur. The wolf-mutt loped away from her flailing limbs as she blinked and shivered. She was in her human form. She had been dreaming again.

"Sköll! To me!" barked Apex. The mongrel trotted to the huntsman, who continued to talk to his dog as he looked at Lluava's perplexed expression. "She doesn't like help."

"How did—"

Apex stopped her before she could even ask. "It seems he was led here by that." He pointed.

Lluava heard the flapping of wings as a ratty-looking raven plopped down in front of her. Its ugly head tilted so it could peer at Lluava with its good eye. The other eye was blind, marked by a long scar.

"Onyx!"

The raven pecked at a dark spot in the snow. Lluava knew she could not inquire further about this inexplicable ability of their pets to find them. The result would be only mutterings from the half-blind bird.

"Where's Ojewa?"

"Around," answered Apex. "If you want to look presentable, get to it. We are not alone."

"Wha—?" began Lluava as she looked about and tried to understand what she was seeing. Silhouettes of a number of men were scattered among the evergreens at the base of the mountain.

Jumping to her feet, Lluava quickly brushed off the wolf-dog's fur that still clung to her clothes. Pulling a loose thread from her shirt, she tied her long, matted hair back to keep it out of her eyes. The rising sun glinted dangerously off Issaura's Claws. Shielding her eyes from the snow's reflection, Lluava saw that tattoos and piercings adorned the bodies of the men around her.

Despite all their efforts, they had been discovered. Lluava began to growl as someone approached.

"Have you gone rabid, or is this a new way to greet an old friend?"

"Yamir?" Now Lluava was truly in shock. The spiky-haired youth smiled widely. She noticed he had added a gauge to his left ear to accompany his collection of facial piercings. His coppery skin seemed far darker against the background of snowy white landscape.

"In the flesh," Yamir responded. Ojewa appeared behind him as some of the silhouetted figures began to disperse. "We were worried for a moment that you would not be returning this way." Anticipating Lluava's next question, Yamir explained, "Though my clan avoids leaving Elysia's borders, they were more than agreeable when they heard it was you they were looking for."

As the strange figures returned with fresh mounts, Lluava began to grin. The Cloven-Hoofed Clan, one of a score of traveling bands of thieves and sideshow entertainers, had aided Lluava and her friends over the summer during the seaside battles. Although openly rebellious against the kingdom's monarchy, they did understand the greater issue at hand when it came to the Raiders and the war. As a result, Yamir, who had enlisted before the war, was still accepted as one of the clansmen rather than identified as a deserter of his people. Actually, he seemed to be rather well liked by his clan's leader.

"I thought the clansmen, of all people, would be too superstitious to leave Elysia," Lluava said as she nodded toward several men who were peering warily about. "I mean, if even the army would not venture into the Outlands, why would they?"

"That is why Father let me take charge of some of his men. He and the rest of the clan are waiting in Elysia." Yamir leaned closer. "But we both know this rescue mission was only possible because of Grandmother."

"She's still alive?" Lluava questioned in awe. She remembered the withered, ancient, blind woman who somehow could "see" everything that was going on and knew far more than she should have known.

"That old crone will outlive us all," Yamir responded with a laugh.

Suddenly, the striking similarity between the clan's infrastructure and that of the citizenry of Leucrocotta was undeniably apparent. Father was their ruire, while Grandmother took the place of the high priestess. Grandmother always had the last say. Were the clansmen descendants of Theriomorphs from Leucrocotta who had been forced to remain in Elysia after the Landon Wars? Did the clans retain vestiges of their people's forgotten past?

Yamir nodded and said, "From the look of things, you might want to visit her as well."

Lluava suddenly realized how she must appear. Her clothes were smeared with blood and dirt. The knife cut on her aching thumb had reopened. Lifting her hand, she said in mock seriousness, "I don't know if I will survive this wound."

Her coppery-skinned friend laughed. "It looks fatal to me."

As Lluava was handed the reins of a shaggy horse, she shook her head. "I'm still confused. How is it that you knew to be here?"

"That was Colonel Ojewa's doing," admitted Yamir as he swung up on his horse. "When he said he knew how to find you, we offered assistance." Lluava assumed he must be referring to Talos, Byron, and maybe even Rosalyn, but not the clansmen. "Yet, as it happened, I was the only one who could break away. The colonel had need of extra mounts and supplies, and I knew how to get them." Yamir grinned.

"The clans helping the kingdom yet again," said Lluava as Onyx fluttered down to perch on her shoulder. "Who would have thought?"

Apex rode by on his new horse and gave Yamir a quick nod as he followed others; the caravan had started back toward Elysia. Yamir's grin slipped away. "I still don't like him."

"Nor do most people, I think," retorted Lluava with a slight chuckle. Then she became serious. "What's happened to Varren?"

Yamir's expression darkened. "Something occurred shortly after we arrived at Cronus. Varren was working with the High Council on plans that included a more offensive strategy. Then he just stopped. He announced not only that traditional betrothals were to be renounced, but also that he was going to marry some Theriomorph lady."

"Selene," Lluava proffered.

"Yeah, that one," concurred Yamir. "Ever since the announcement, Varren has been *off*. He rarely eats or sleeps, as far as I can tell. He talks only about his love for his wife-to-be. The High Council could not persuade him to refocus on the war effort, so Talos and Cronus's commanding general took it upon themselves to fight in the name of the king."

"If Talos is fighting, then Byron must be with him as his military partner. But where is Rosalyn?"

Yamir spurred his horse over a fallen pine tree. "At the capital. In the beginning, we thought Varren was sick, so Rosalyn stayed behind, hoping to somehow help cure him of his ailment. But he is not sick. I know that just by talking to him."

"Then what do you think is wrong?"

"I think it's mind control."

Lluava would have laughed had it not been Varren to whom he was referring. Yamir had always been the one in their group to entertain conspiracy theories. This one, along with many of his others, was too impossible to believe. "Who would—or even could—control Varren's mind?"

"One of the Berserkers or their leader, Alcove something or other. Think about it. If the king loses interest in the war, our enemies could stroll right up to the capital's gates and conquer the kingdom easily. These people get superhuman abilities from something they smoke. Who knows what else they can do?"

Though Yamir seemed convinced of his fabricated explanation, Lluava was more than doubtful. "Couldn't the High Council blackmail Varren somehow? After all, the head councilman is power hungry." Themis's smirking face appeared in her mind. She wanted to claw that smirk right off.

"As far as I can tell, they are all furious at Varren's recent decisions. Mind control by the enemy. That's what's happening, Lluava. Mind control."

***

Even after setting up camp that evening, Onyx continued to cling to Lluava's shoulder. The bird seemed almost afraid to lose sight of her. She wondered if perhaps the raven actually had some feelings toward her. As if in response to her thought, Onyx began to pick at loose strands of Lluava's silvery hair.

"So why a bird?" Apex's question referring to her choice of pet cut through the cold. He had ignored her the entire day and was only now attempting to exchange pleasantries after sharing one of the clansmen's bottles.

"Why a mongrel?" snapped Lluava. The only logical reason for her snide remark must be her growing exhaustion. She didn't really mind the wolf-dog, just his owner.

Apex didn't take offense. "He hunts with me." Sköll thumped his rear foot reflexively as Apex scratched behind an ear. "I saved him when he was a pup. I killed the bitch when she attacked me. I discovered her den afterward, with several pups in it. I left them for the woods to claim, but this one followed me. He has followed me ever since."

Lluava did not know what to make of the huntsman's story. Should she be appalled that Apex left the pups to die, or relieved that he had taken pity on his soon-to-be pet?

"The bird was not mine." She felt Onyx shift his weight. "Not at first. Chat, a boy of eleven years, was drafted with me. His innocence and compassion may explain why he took in the injured raven. This bird was his until he died. I let the thing go, yet it somehow found me at the capital. My chambermaid named him Onyx."

"I'm sorry for your friend," Apex said earnestly. The huntsman left to check on the roasting mountain goat he had helped catch earlier. Lluava headed over to several people huddled under travel blankets.

"There are a few things I'm still trying to understand," said Lluava. She took a seat next to Ojewa. "I thought you were in charge of Thowcelemine. Why were you at the capital instead of training the new recruits?"

"I received a letter from Grand Master Chief Domar alerting me that they had need of all capable soldiers in the North and instructing me to have them congregate at Cronus to receive orders."

Lluava remembered the capital's grand master chief. Domar was one of a handful of generals who had earned that elitist ranking. Based on what Yamir had said earlier, she realized that Domar was working with Talos to combat the encroaching Raiders' army.

"Okay. Then how did you know I was in Leucrocotta. Are you a Guardian?" Lluava had to ask, since it seemed that everyone around her was turning out to be a member of the secret society.

"I know not what a Guardian is," Ojewa purred. "But I do know Yena, and I know she would desire someone like you on her side."

"Did you ever love her?" Lluava was uncertain why she asked him such a personal question.

"Once. But no more."

"What if she took you back?"

"There is no going back," said Ojewa. "Only forward."

Ahead of them lay the last line of mountains before they reached Elysia's western border. Then, after a longer ride than Lluava wanted to make, they would arrive in Cronos. She would finally see Varren. Too anxious to sleep, she was thankful that by morning's light they had already begun their journey.

Shouts were heard ahead of them. Well, more like the whooping of strange beasts. The rest of the Cloven-Hoofed Clan awaited them with their caravan of covered wagons. Even though they were still in the Verta mountain range, they must have crossed into Elysia.

"Son, over here!" From a distance, a massive man bellowed at Yamir. Lluava recognized the purple cloth tied like a turban and was again reminded of Ruire Thoth. Father, though not actually related to Yamir, referred to the swarthy youth by paternal terminology. As he looked over Lluava's party,

Father's wattles seemed to vibrate on their own.

"Father," Yamir nodded curtly to the chief of the clan. "The mission was a success, thanks to you."

"I see that," he said, grinning at Lluava. "We meet again."

"Hello, Father," said Lluava. She remembered that the last time she had dealt with the clan leader, his real son had been slain. If the clan leader still held a grudge toward her, he did not show it.

Father turned to Yamir once more. "Ya will return our horses to us."

"Of course."

"Good."

"Father, are you leaving us so soon?" Lluava put in.

"Sweet girl," he began. "Ya are headin' directly to the one place my people try to avoid. We're headin' south."

"I didn't think that was your territory."

"No, but since all lands above Lake Palal are overridden by those sea brutes, our fellow clans must share with us."

"So all the North is actually gone?" Lluava gasped out. She had heard this but had not realized how much land must have been conquered.

"Aye," acknowledged Father.

Yamir added, "The brutes would have continued south if the Middle Camps had not sailed upriver and set up a blockade that prevented longboats from heading toward Pern and the capital."

"They could be at Cronus's doorstep in weeks!" exclaimed Lluava, aghast.

"Or sooner," said Father. "So south we go."

"Apex!" Lluava waved the huntsman over. "Elysia has lost far more territory than I had realized."

Apex steadied his horse, for the gelding kept shying away from Sköll. "How much?"

"A third of the kingdom."

Apex looked disbelieving. Lluava could barely believe it herself.

Chapter 22

Waiting Without

Apex?" questioned Lluava when the huntsman failed to respond.

As Apex led his horse off to be picketed, he muttered, "The king has some explaining to do."

The thought of Apex and Varren going at it head-to-head was one nagging worry Lluava had hoped to put to rest. If Apex chose to aggravate the situation, he might be thrown into a dungeon far worse than the one at Castle Alcazar.

"You don't think he will cause trouble, do you?" she asked the spiky-haired youth.

Yamir scoffed, "That's one thing I do not doubt."

"Come, my friend," Father chimed in cheerily, attempting to divert the conversation to less serious topics. "We have much to catch up on since we were last together."

As Lluava followed her host into the midst of the circled wagons, she noticed that many of the wagons with bars for animals were empty. Had they released the poor creatures after the incident with the dancing bear? The likelihood of that was slim.

Around the cook fires, musicians played strange and captivating songs, almost all of which were foreign to Lluava's ears. Her mouth salivated from the aroma of roasting pig. Father motioned Lluava to sit down on one of the wooden benches that had been placed about the area.

The whale-sized man looked her over again as he absentmindedly twisted one of the two long strands of facial hair that sprouted over each corner of his lips. "You must be famished."

He waved over a small boy who carried a platter of dried fruit and hard cheese and placed it in front of them.

"Eat," he commanded.

She did not need to be told twice. Lluava picked up a wedge of cheese and began gnawing at its tough center.

"I am glad that my son chose to come to me for help," admitted her host. "It is what a father always wants. Yet the circumstances, you must understand, are strange."

Lluava swallowed slowly.

"What were you searching for? What did you find?"

So, Father had not been informed. Lluava glanced over at Ojewa, who was conversing nearby with Yamir. Did the teen know? What had the colonel told them? It now made sense that the clansmen had waited so far away: Ojewa had not wanted them to discover Leucrocotta. The city remained hidden. He had protected his home.

"We went in search of a fantasy. A difficult and dangerous wild goose chase that caused us to lose valuable time. We were ill advised." The sourness in her tone was unmistakable.

"That man traveling with you—Yamir tells me he is a great hunter from the North." Father looked at her curiously.

"I needed someone who knew the Outlands, that's all."

"And he is accompanying you to the city?"

For the first time, Lluava realized, Apex did not have to go to Cronus. He was free to leave. But where could he go? If the North was lost to the Raiders, what home could he claim?

"He said he wanted to talk with the king."

"Is that wise?"

"I don't understand what you mean," Lluava answered as she slowly resumed chewing her cheese.

"A wild animal roaming the capital's streets never ends well."

"He isn't a wild animal."

"You know him better than I." Father clapped his hands. "Bring us some goat!" The waiting boy ran off to get the meat.

After dinner, Lluava realized she had not seen Apex all evening. She felt suddenly panicky. Had he left? He had no obligation to stay, but...

As she wandered away from the camp in search of the huntsman, Apex's gruff voice spoke up behind her.

"You should rest."

"I—uh—" Lluava turned, relieved at the sight of him. "Where did you go? I did not see you at dinner."

"I met the one they call Grandmother."

A shiver ran down her spine as she remembered the weathered old crone. "What did she say to you?"

"Nothing that made sense. Her age clouds her mind."

Lluava remembered the prophecy she had been given: That someone she loved would die within the fortnight, that she would send him to his death. Lluava had thought it was Varren of whom Grandmother had spoken, not poor Chat. The boy should have lived.

"What did she say, exactly?"

Apex shook his head. "Get some sleep. You don't need to worry yourself with crazed words from an old woman. You sleep poorly enough as it is."

"I'll see you tomorrow as we ride to the capital?"

"Of course."

***

Lluava smiled at the look on Apex's face when he caught his first glimpse of Cronus. The soaring walls could not contain the teeming metropolis, for once the burgeoning city had begun to press against those stony borders, many households had sprung up outside the walls. In the center of the city was the castle. Each spire and tower seemed to reach higher than the next as the land terraced upward. The tallest towers brushed against the heavens like the fingers of hands lifted in worship. Flying buttresses splayed out from the sides of the magnificent castle like lovers' entangled limbs. Its solid iron doorway could easily be secured, forming an impenetrable defense.

Their days on the road seemed to wash away now that their destination was at hand. The outer gates of the city were wide open to welcome trade. They would be shut at dark, but that was half a day away.

"Follow me," Lluava said as her horse began to trot down the road. Apex would certainly get lost in the labyrinth of streets. This design was intentional, for Cronus was, in truth, a maze. Its extremely narrow streets would force an attacking army into a bottleneck. With no direct path to the castle, enemies would easily become lost in the labyrinth. Lluava hoped she remembered the correct route to the castle's gates.

Ojewa and Yamir had chosen to accompany them to Cronus, as Lluava had hoped. They were all united by the same purpose: to end the war by whatever means necessary. For many, this meant dealing with a dysfunctional king. Varren was in the castle. She would make certain to see him at once.

Halting her horse, Lluava looked about the bustling streets. Cronians were everywhere, hawking their wares, weaving through the open food stalls, hurrying from one chore to the next. A few boys kicked an inflated pig's bladder down the cobblestoned lane.

Left or right? Furrowing her brow, Lluava tried to think back to the autumn, when she had last been here. Right or left?

Yamir seemed to understand her plight. He nodded to the right, and Lluava continued on at a dismally slow pace. She should have guessed Yamir would know the city's layout. The young clansman had been living here until he left to help Ojewa with his search.

With so many citizens crossing the road in front of them, they were moving at little more than a fast walk. Didn't these people know how urgent it was for her to reach the castle? Didn't they recognize the prince's—no, the king's—military partner? Of course they didn't, but Lluava's anxiety increased nonetheless.

Onyx cawed and flapped his wings, smacking her face with his feathers. Once the bird settled down on her shoulder, Lluava looked about, wondering what could have caused his disturbance.

Nearby, standing next to a vegetable merchant, Lluava spotted Hyrax, wearing the dark robes of the council. His cloak now displayed three brown stripes. His station in the council must have changed—better for him, worse for her. He was no friend, just another powerful opponent.

He nodded at her as she passed. The two white stripes running down his short beard shone extra bright in the sun. Lluava wondered if Hyrax remembered what she had told him the last time they met. She had undertaken this fruitless mission because of his false advice. Did he realize he was partially responsible for what was happening in Elysia? With the enemy? With Varren? As she cast her scowl away from Hyrax, the castle suddenly didn't look so inviting.

Onyx muttered in Lluava's ear.

"At least I still have you to help me keep watch for the enemy," she said as she reached around to stroke the raven. Maybe she did like having this animal around.

Unfortunately, Apex had not been as lucky. Once again, Sköll had refused to leave the forest at the edge of the Verta Mountains. He whined and paced but could not be coaxed to follow. Apex did not call him. For a man who seemed to love the animal, it was strange that he cared not whether the beast wandered off.

Ahead, the heavy gates of the curtain wall, which surrounded the castle as a protective defense, stood open. It was nice to know that the citizens could enter and leave as they wished. Still, was all this good faith misplaced? Shaking her head, Lluava chastised herself for such suspicious thoughts. She had been a happy person not that long ago. Had the war changed her so much?

Upon their arrival, stable boys, along with several stewards, ran up to the small caravan. The elder steward welcomed them. Clearly recognizing Lluava as well as Yamir, he directed the others to carry the travelers' belongings to appropriate quarters.

Apex seemed wary as he watched his few supplies disappear with strangers. He absentmindedly fingered the pommel of the Fang on his left side.

Lluava wore Issaura's Claws. The last time she had been at the castle, she thought someone had attempted to steal her weapons. Yet it had been only Hyrax, inspecting them to see if they were genuine.

"If you will follow me," stated the head steward as he led the weary travelers into the enormous foyer.

Apex craned his neck, his expression full of awe as he took in the spectacular sight. For Lluava, the vaulted ceilings, the numerous inner columns, and the polished black marble floor were the least of her concerns. As the sound of footfalls reverberated in the vast space, Lluava said, "I wish to speak with King Varren at once."

The steward slowed for a moment, then continued. "The king has been apprised of your presence. I will show you to your quarters, where you may await him at his convenience."

Lluava did not like the sound of that. "Is he in the Closed Council? I can see him there."

The steward shook his graying head. "His Majesty is preoccupied with other matters. He will see you when he is ready."

Before she could balk, Yamir's hand touched her shoulder. A silent warning, but one she understood. She remained silent. Apex was also surprisingly complacent when another steward led him off in a different direction. Yet the look in his eyes as he turned the corner warned Lluava how uncertain he was of this place. Of all people, he should be quite content to be alone, shouldn't he?

Yamir headed off to find Rosalyn. "She will want to see you," he told Lluava with a grin.

"And I, her," Lluava admitted, but her thoughts were still on Varren.

Lluava was led to the suite of rooms where she had stayed in the fall. She looked about the main chamber; everything seemed the same as when she had left, all those months ago. Velvet couches and cushioned chairs beckoned her travel-weary legs. The open archway to the right led to a pillow-laden four-poster bed, its emerald-green curtains tied back with black silk ribbons. Yet it was the balcony across from her that made Lluava smile. Stepping out through its double doors, Lluava relished the sight of the capital from her private perch. This was where Varren had kissed her the first time. He loved her then and still did. She knew it.

Someone approached behind her, and June's sweet girl's voice cooed, "Welcome back, Lady Lluava."

Lluava turned to look at her little chambermaid and saw that June had grown a bit in her absence. The seven-year-old smiled widely as tufts of thick auburn hair fell over her brow. "Can I get you anything? Food? Wine?"

The girl grinned even wider when she saw the raven she had named. "And what about you, Onyx?"

"A tall glass of water and something to snack on would be nice," Lluava admitted. "And some corn for the bird." June, excited to be of service, almost ran out of the room. Onyx fluttered to the tall falconer's perch the little girl had given him. He hopped sideways along its length and bobbed his head, seeming to nod in contentment.

"Glad you're happy," said Lluava, only somewhat sarcastic as she rubbed the sore tip of her purpling thumb.

"Oh. I *am* thrilled!"

Rosalyn ran into the room, skirts billowing behind her, and threw her arms around Lluava's neck. Raven-haired and porcelain-skinned, Rosalyn's doll-like physique matched her slight body weight. Lluava could have easily lifted her and spun her around. As beautiful as she was, Rosalyn always looked delicate, almost fragile. Yet stress lines had somehow had the impertinence to mar her perfectly polished features like cracks on a doll.

Once Rosalyn released her grip, she stepped back to inspect her old friend. "I cannot believe how dark you have become out in the snow."

Glancing down, Lluava realized that her naturally olive-hued skin had indeed tanned. "The sun is a strange thing," Lluava commented, wondering if she should confess what had actually occurred in the Outlands.

Yamir entered the room but did not interrupt the women.

"Oh, come here," Lluava said, waving him over, and the three friends hugged once more.

When everyone took a seat, Lluava realized that both Rosalyn and Yamir were waiting to hear about her travels. Neither asked outright, but she could see they hoped to be filled in.

"You want to hear the whole story?" Lluava asked. The other two nodded.

These were the people she trusted. They had been with her from the beginning and had seen it all. It was time for them to know.

"I will explain," she began, "as long as you *swear* never to repeat this. I'll start at the beginning…"

Lluava paused only when June entered the room carrying a tray with a pitcher of water and a platter of fruit. The girl even had a small pouch of corn tied to her wrist. While June served everyone in the room, Rosalyn explained how June had become a handmaiden to the little queen. Lluava had forgotten about Enya, the former king's widow. That little brat was still up to nothing worthwhile.

Once June had finished hand-feeding Onyx, she left for the evening. Lluava resumed her story, from her blindfolded march into the hidden valley. Her two friends were strangely quiet through all of it, especially Yamir. Did they think Lluava was lying? Hearing herself telling the tale aloud, she had to admit it sounded like fiction.

"That's it," she finished at last. "That's when you and the clansmen found us in the mountains."

"So," Yamir finally spoke up, "you and Apex are vessels for the gods; you are sent to the frozen Outlands; you find a hidden jungle in the middle of mountains where Theriomorphs have lived for centuries, if not longer, where the ruler—also a god's vessel—is a priestess who not only speaks to the gods but also sees the future. Then Ojewa rescues you—he, who was their leader, having left to teach Elysians how to fight under a command of another. Now, you're back to help fight this war."

"When you say it like that..." Lluava sighed.

Rosalyn inquired, "You said Councilman Hyrax sent you on this mission. What do you think he will say when he learns what you have found?"

"I don't want to deal with him again," scowled Lluava.

"Do you think that is possible? He is on the High Council, and you are the king's military partner. He will want to know about this Yena."

"I will try my hardest to avoid him."

"Maybe it is in your best interests to talk with him."

"I want nothing to do with Hyrax and the other Guardians or their maddened quest. Just saying it aloud reaffirms how stupid it really was."

Yamir questioned playfully, "Why? Because you're supposed to breed with Apex?" He began to snort until the water he was drinking shot out his nose. "Ow! That burns!"

"I hope it does," replied Lluava brusquely.

"You do not choose whom you love," noted Rosalyn in her soft-spoken manner. "Nor can anyone else decide for you."

Lluava had been waiting to question her friends until she had told them everything. She wondered how Talos was doing. What was the latest report from the war front? Was Byron okay?

Rosalyn seemed to understand. "Talos has led his men farther south. The Berserker Legion has returned in full force. The Middle and Southern Camps have been working hard to train more soldiers, but both time and our resources are running out."

"And the Northern Camps?" questioned Lluava.

"Obliterated," replied Yamir darkly.

As her two friends were leaving to allow Lluava to rest, she asked Rosalyn, "Do you regret marrying Talos so suddenly?"

Though her friend looked forlorn, she said again, "You do not choose whom you love."

***

Lluava made her way to the women's baths. The room was filled with various large pools, several emitting steam, several containing floating ice, and others of a neutral temperature. She submerged herself in one of the steaming basins and relished the heat. Though it was not as cold as the Outlands, winter had definitely reached the capital.

Yet even now, submerged in warmth, she could not relax.

Why was Varren making her wait? How much longer before she would be summoned? He should have hurried to see her right away. Was something or someone keeping him from her? Of course, Themis would hate the fact that she had returned. Was it him? And what of Selene? Her friend should be ashamed at what she had agreed to do.

Stepping out of the pool, Lluava quickly wrapped a towel around her dripping body. She decided that if Varren wouldn't come to see her, she would go to see him.

Changing into a more acceptable human dress, she hastily made her way down several winding halls before she abruptly stopped. She suddenly realized that Varren wouldn't be living in his old rooms. He was the king now, and his quarters would have changed. Altering her course, Lluava found her way to the royal chambers.

No guards presided without. This was good, yet odd. She entered. The antechamber, a long, private throne room, seemed as cold and indifferent as she remembered it. But this time, the decrepit old king was not slouched on the taller throne.

Due to the late afternoon hour, the Closed Council should have been dismissed for the day. Varren was almost certainly in one of the other rooms in this private wing. As soon as she placed her hand on the golden doorknob that led to the king's sitting room, it turned.

Then the door was flung open.

Chapter 23

The Puppet

Varren stood before her, his loose curls, though neatly groomed, falling over his forehead, framing a face that had grown gaunt. His eyes were mere sunken pits; yet deep within them the old blue sparkle still struggled to be seen.

"Varren!" Lluava gasped. Whatever anger she might have had toward him and his decision was replaced by a sudden worry. The way he had rolled up the sleeves of his shirt exposed his diminished muscles. His whole form looked thin. Too thin.

"Lluava," he replied as if in disbelief. Had he doubted her return? Did he think she had perished in the frozen wasteland? Varren stepped forward and embraced her. Lluava felt the warmth of his body, inhaled his scent—a mix of rosemary and fennel, a calming smell that reminded her of her mother's kitchen. She relished being back in his arms.

Eventually, she forced herself to step back from him.

"Have you been well?" she asked, wanting to know the cause of his deteriorating appearance.

"As well as any man who has worn a crown," replied Varren. His eyes looked lovingly at her. "You look well. Your age becomes you."

"My age?"

"Eighteen. A woman grown."

"I had forgotten about my birthday." While she had been wandering alone with Apex in the tundra, Lluava's birthday had come and gone unnoticed. Varren remembered.

"Maybe you should celebrate yours when mine comes around," said Varren with a smile. As always, his smile made Lluava's heart quicken. But that ceased when she remembered what Varren's twenty-first birthday would entail.

Looking into his eyes, Lluava saw no guilt, no sense of regret, not even a shred of embarrassment. Her inner heat began to manifest. How could he do this to her? How could he not have realized? What had happened to his feelings for her? They certainly were still there; she could tell by the way he looked at her, the way he held her.

"Is something the matter?" questioned Varren, completely oblivious to her growing anger.

Taking a breath, Lluava forced herself to broach the other issue at hand, supposedly the more important one. "What are you doing about the war? The Raiders are nearly upon Cronus."

Varren furrowed his brow. "No. No. That cannot be. You are wrong. The Raiders are stuck in the North. The Berserker Legion fled into the Yorrick Forest. Remember?"

"That happened before I left." Lluava gestured northward. "Talos and Byron have been there for weeks, a month maybe, trying to slow down the Raiders' march to the capital. Surely you have knowledge of this? Hasn't the High Council discussed this issue during their sessions, open or closed?"

"I—I—" Varren floundered. "I have rarely attended the Closed Council since I returned."

"That's been months!" exclaimed Lluava. "Spring is around the corner. What have you been doing all this time?"

Varren shook his head, sending his dark curls bouncing. "Talos was just here. Months? No. I've been working on the wedding." He rubbed his temples as if he suddenly had a splitting headache. "I need to take a seat."

The young king retreated into his private chamber, and Lluava followed. Many of the castle's wings of unused rooms were kept pristine just for show. This one, however, was actually homey. On the walls were portraits of Varren as a boy, of his grandfather in the prime of life, and many of the child queen, Enya. Lluava wondered whether, if one of the queen's portraits accidently fell into the blazing fire, it would be missed.

Lluava seated herself on the sofa next to her partner and began, "Varren, listen to me. You once asked if I would become your lead advisor when you ascended the throne. The head councilman, if you will. You trusted my judgment. If you still do, listen to me now. You must focus on defending the kingdom and defeating the Raiders."

Varren mused for a moment, then nodded. "The Raiders... yes. The Raiders must be defeated."

Lluava affirmed, "There is nothing more important than this."

Yet Varren shook his head. "There is. I am to marry the Lady Selene Fárbauti on the morning of my day of birth." His voice suddenly seemed flat, devoid of emotion. Was he upset about this? Was someone forcing his hand? Had he been threatened? He was king. He could command anyone.

"But the war! Elysia!" Lluava insisted. "Varren, this wedding, at this time, is ill advised. You are wasting money and energy that should go toward the war effort."

"I am to marry the Lady Selene Fárbauti."

"Do you love her?" Lluava demanded angrily. "Look at me! Do you?"

Varren lifted his head slightly, his eyes glazed. His words seemed practiced. "We are meant for each other."

This was too much; her words burst from her "You said you loved me!"

Lluava stood to keep from slapping the king. "What does she have that I do not? A pedigree? A title? Money? Beauty?" The last question hurt the most. She knew that she did not conform to the Elysian ideal of feminine beauty with her wide shoulders, her athletic body, her small breasts. But Varren had loved her despite all that.

Lluava's thumb throbbed violently.

Varren remained silent.

For a moment, she wanted to lunge at her partner. How dare he say such things? Didn't he love her anymore? Was this wedding really his idea? How could he be so obsessed with Selene? Was he being manipulated?

From the corner of her eye, Lluava could have sworn she saw movement among the shadows. Surely it was the fire, or ... the Obsidian Guard could be eavesdropping on their conversation. How could Lluava not have realized? Their only purpose was to protect the king. Now Varren was king and the last of his line. They would be watching him constantly.

Lluava backed away from him just as there came a knock at the door.

"Your Highness, dinner will be served shortly."

Lluava did not look in the direction of the voice. She concentrated on her angry breathing and stared at Varren, who slumped against the sofa as if suddenly drained of energy. At this moment, he resembled his grandfather, King Thor; he even had the same puppet-like look. But who was the puppeteer? Themis had controlled Thor. Did he have a hand in Varren's apparent inability to focus on anything other than his wedding? Lluava bristled at the thought as the steward escorted Varren from the room.

***

By the time she arrived at the private dining room, Lluava noticed that most of the people she despised would be breaking bread with her. Varren was seated at the head of the long table, while Enya anchored the other end. The young girl's thick, dark ringlets emphasized her pale skin and blushing cheeks. Her lavish lashes and chronic pout had always made Lluava think of her as a china doll whom it was forbidden to touch lest the pristine features be marred. Unfortunately, this china doll could speak. Thirteen and proud, she seemed to enjoy having the Lady Selene sit next to her, if only for her own amusement.

Selene, on the other hand, was the epitome of womanly beauty. Well-endowed where it mattered, her cinched waist, sumptuous curves, and unblemished, coppery skin were enhanced by the gold silk dress she wore. Her angular face perfectly suited her crimson-stained lips; black kohl lined her golden eyes, which observed Lluava curiously as she entered.

Lluava turned away from Selene to catch Finch Themis staring at her. The Head Councilman wore the dark, rainbow-striped robe that signified his title and authority. He was the oldest man at the table and, Lluava knew, one of the most cunning and dangerous. He sat at Varren's right, clearly not ready to give up his position to a young female Theriomorph.

Fortunately, the other two people at the table did not make her skin crawl, though she could have done without them both. Across from Selene was her twin, Luka. They were only siblings on paper, for both he and Selene had been adopted by a human lord during the time when it was fashionable to take in Theriomorph spawn after the merging of the races. Only a few months apart in age, the nineteen-year-olds were often referred to as twins, though their appearance was far from identical. Lanky and pale, Luka was average in every way compared to his stunning sister. Only his black hair with its white spots stood out. At least Luka's smile seemed genuine.

Seated at the center of the long table, like a small island alone in a large ocean, was Apex, looking terribly uncomfortable. His fashionable attire, so different from what he typically wore, added to his awkward demeanor. Lluava felt sorry for the huntsman as well as for herself, for she was seated to Varren's left, directly across from Themis. She hoped Apex would not leave the capital and abandon her among all these people. Father's words crossed her mind: "A wild animal roaming the capital's streets never ends well."

As Varren thanked his solitary god, dishes of the finest delicacies were brought to the table and presented to the king. Although Varren seemed excited at the stuffed peacock and heavily seasoned shark-fin soup, once they were laid before him he barely nibbled at the food.

"To celebrate your safe return," toasted Themis, his eyes carving into Lluava like a butcher's knife.

As much as her nose relished the wonderful aromas, Lluava was not very hungry. Apex glanced at her and seemed to sense her discomfort even as his own became increasingly evident.

"Is the saffron snake not to your taste?" Themis questioned Apex, hacking off the head of the serpent and placing it on his own plate.

"The journey was wearing," replied Apex cautiously. He fingered the top button of his collared shirt.

"Then you should seek nourishment," rejoined Themis as he dipped a forkful of snake into a thick red sauce. "We wouldn't want you to become *ill*."

"Thank you for your concern," replied Apex. "But mine is for those sea brutes, lest they attack this *fine* establishment."

"Is this appropriate talk for the dinner table?" questioned Selene. "Our new arrivals are surely weary from their travels. Although the war is important," she looked over at Lluava as if backing up an unstated sentiment, then turned to the king and continued, "there are many other wonderful things to discuss. Is that not right, my love?"

Varren's gaze seemed to fall deeply into Selene's. Seeing this, Lluava felt the fire in her core burn. Selene's stunning yet somehow ignorant gaze turned to Lluava, and the young lady happily added, "Have you heard the wonderful news? My sweet Varren has proposed to me."

Bile rushed up into Lluava's throat.

Then Varren said, "Our wedding is not far off. We still need to finalize the performers, both visual and musical."

Lluava found the topic unbearable. She interrupted, "But the war—"

Themis's glower shut Lluava up immediately.

Thenceforth the discussions at both ends of the table centered on the upcoming nuptials. Lluava could clearly see that Apex was more than ready to retire for the night. Nothing of the lighthearted chat was remotely of interest to the huntsman. Lluava looked forlornly at him when he caught her eye. This was one area in which they were both in agreement.

"You have a warrior's look about you, Apex." Luka seemed interested in the huntsman. "Say, old friend, tell us a story about yourself."

"I'm no friend of yours," grumbled Apex.

Lluava flashed him a warning look.

"I hunt and trap. I can skin an entire elk in an hour." He lifted his knife. "From throat to cock."

Luka shifted uncomfortably. "Well… that is a neat trick."

Selene's sensual voice rose over the others. "Clearly, brother, these two have had a long journey. They are tired. I think it best we end our meal early." She smiled sympathetically at Lluava, then announced, "No dessert tonight."

"But I want dessert," pouted Enya. "It's toffee cream on candied summer fruits."

"How about you and I have a bowl, just the two of us?"

The former queen smiled at Selene's proposal, if one could call the girl's tightly curled lips a smile.

Lluava did not care. She needed to talk with Varren. He looked miserable. With Themis nearby, he clearly was unable to discuss anything fully. This would not do. Themis might be the current head councilman and Varren's godfather, but Varren should not be swayed so easily. Varren held the power now.

As the dinner party was moving to depart, Lluava pulled Varren into a hug. Quickly she whispered, "Meet me in the garden. Our spot. In an hour."

Not wanting to draw attention to them, Lluava stepped away. If she held onto him any longer, it would seem improper in front of his fiancée. Lluava collected herself and kissed cheeks, not only the little queen's but also Selene's.

Selene spoke kindly. "I am so glad that you have returned. I feared there might be some animosity between us."

"And why would that be?" Lluava tried to veil her contempt.

"As you are Varren's military partner, I did not know if you would feel that I was pulling him away from his duties with you. Silly me. I get concerned over the smallest details regarding anything pertaining to the man I love."

Lluava wanted to scream, I do! I do hate you! You knew how I felt about Varren! You *had* to have known! But looking into Selene's lovely gaze, Lluava could not tell whether the woman lied. Did she know? She seemed genuinely oblivious.

Luka bowed and kissed Lluava's hand. "Oh, how I have missed you! It has been such a bore around here without your presence, especially since my dear sister's proposal. Thank the gods for sending you back to entertain me!" His eyes flickered mischievously.

A laugh actually escaped Lluava's lips. A brief hope flared that Luka might actually be a true friend to her. "We should plan to catch up soon."

Apex had already made his exit when Themis found Lluava by the door. "Allow me to escort you back to your quarters."

"If it pleases you." At least, Lluava had not forgotten all of the common courtesies that had been drilled into her during her stay in the fall. Of course, she did not dare let Themis see how much he revolted her.

He, in turn, did not even smile at her but wore a dreary look plastered on his face. At first, they walked in silence. Unfortunately, this did not last long.

"How was your little trip to the North?" he asked.

The falseness of his interest was plain. They both knew the councilman had found a way to legally summon Varren back to court and prevent him from fighting in the war—the war that Themis had intentionally covered up for all these months. Themis was the reason Varren had had to escape from the capital in order to personally lead a party to track the strange band of large Raiders, known as Berserkers, that had infiltrated the perimeter of the Outlands.

"Cold," she answered briskly.

"It is not much warmer here, as you can tell," noted Themis as they rounded a dark corner. "I am surprised that you are not defending this kingdom, which we both love, by continuing your fight on the front lines. I have heard you are much happier there."

"Varren is here. I go where he goes."

"Varren is king. It is his job to rule the kingdom, just as it is yours to fight its battles."

The light was dangerously dim in this area of the castle. Fortunately for Lluava, this was not a concern. Her heightened senses allowed her to see almost as clearly as in the daylight.

"We both know," Lluava asserted, "that Varren asked me to become his lead advisor. I will advise him here at the castle and on the council."

They were halfway down a winding staircase when Themis stepped in front of her, blocking her way.

"I have heard of this advice you give, your incessant whispers into His Majesty's ears about such things as ending the tradition of betrothals—the talk of mixing royal and Theriomorph blood."

In the gloom, Themis's eyes appeared dark and empty. "I looked into the cause of Illia's death. I know you had no fault in that." He pursed his lips in displeasure. "Varren's choice of Selene surprised me, I admit. I knew you were fond of each other, but it had not crossed my mind that *she* was the one. I am not usually mistaken."

Themis stepped aside, and he and Lluava resumed their walk down the stairs. Lluava's heart was thumping wildly. Was he saying what she thought he was saying?

The head councilman continued, "Many people who hold faithfully to the old ways are not happy with this match. People are strong-willed and hard to change. The idea of royalty, of the king, marrying a Theriomorph is considered blasphemous. During times like this, people often take it upon themselves to correct such a wrong."

Was he insinuating that he was planning a murder? It would not be the first time he had rid the kingdom of a perceived threat.

"The Lady Selene is wise, to her benefit. She has uncovered several of these plots before they could fully manifest."

They had turned down Lluava's hall, their soft footfalls reverberating. "I know many of your race believe humans have wronged them in the past. The fault does not lie with King Varren. Varren is not the enemy. It is the men from across the ocean, these Raiders. As a member of the High Council, it is my duty to do anything I possibly can to ensure Varren's and Elysia's well-being. *Anything.*" With that, Themis bade her goodnight and hastened off down the hall.

Lluava was alone in her rooms. This was the first time that Themis's threat had not been aimed at her. At least, not entirely. He wanted Selene out of the way. It seemed he had even tried several times. Themis knew the war was a serious concern and that this wedding was impairing Varren's judgment.

Yet, if it was not Themis who had arranged this match, then who was it? And why?

Chapter 24

Open and Closed Case

Lluava felt ill.

Something else was afoot, and the man she had thought responsible was as much in the dark as she was. Doubling back to the royal gardens, Lluava wondered if perhaps Themis honestly believed he was protecting Varren out of love for him. The councilman clearly thought that this wedding would tear the kingdom apart. He did not want Varren to wed a Theriomorph—Selene, Lluava, or any other. Although this line of thought could stem from the High Council's archaic conviction that the royal bloodline must be kept pure, Themis had to acknowledge that as this wedding approached, so did the Raiders.

A caring Themis. The thought made Lluava shiver as she stepped into the gardens. The lush foliage was different now though no less full. New flowers bloomed in the chill of midwinter where others had faded. Trees still held their leaves, though some were ribboned with the warm hues of fall.

Each level of the descending terraces revealed a new growth of beauty. The Mandrun castle was built on hot springs like those that gave Leucrocotta life, though on a significantly smaller scale. Here, even in the cold of winter, semitropical plants flourished. The almost magical nature of the gardens was one reason they were Lluava's favorite spot in the entire capital. Here she felt as if she were somewhere else, not in the midst of a bustling city on the brink of destruction. And there was another reason she thought of these gardens so affectionately: this was where Varren had always met with her.

Hurrying along the path as it wound downward through the tiers, Lluava saw Varren already seated on the bench under their tree. Irises still bloomed around its base. Varren was looking at her. In his hands, he held her favorite flower, the white-and-black striped Theri iris.

"For you," he said as he handed her the bloom.

Lluava breathed in its heavy, almost fruity perfume.

"I have missed you," was all Varren said. Yet his eyes spoke more. They told her that their love still existed. That this wedding was not his idea. That something else was happening.

"And I, you," replied Lluava.

Varren reached out and touched her hand. A tingling sensation coursed up and down her arm. As she looked deeply into his cool blue eyes, Lluava felt her mind grow fuzzy. She had come here to discuss something. What was it?

She rummaged for the thought, then grasped it.

"Call the wedding off," she implored. "Or marry me."

Women in Elysia never asked the man for marriage; that was the man's responsibility. For a woman to do so was, at the very least, highly insulting, and Lluava knew this well. Maybe some of Leucrocotta had rubbed off on her.

"I will marry Selene Fárbauti." His stern response demanded respect.

"Then tell me that you love her. Tell me that you don't love me!" Lluava felt herself begin to tremble with anger. Her thumb ached again.

"I am to marry Selene Fárbauti on the morning of my twenty-first birthday. We are meant to be together," he said doggedly.

"But why, Varren? Why?" Lluava was utterly lost. She held his hand tighter. "You don't love her!"

Extracting his hand, Varren put his head in his hands and tugged his hair. "We will be married. Anyone who wishes otherwise can leave Cronus."

"Even me?" Lluava asked weakly. Her fighting strength deserted her.

Varren's breath seemed labored, yet he puffed out, "Yes. Even you. Do not talk of this again."

Both numb, Lluava and Varren sat a long while trying to maintain calm. It took all her strength to neither cry nor run. There *were* other important topics to discuss.

"At dinner," Lluava finally began, "you ignored any talk of the war. Cronus will be attacked if nothing changes. You need to convene the High Council and confront this threat. Lives are at risk, Varren."

"The Raiders are nearing the capital," he said tonelessly, as if remembering something told to him in a dream. Had he not heard her the other night? Was his mind truly so preoccupied with Selene?

He continued. "Yes. Something must be done. Tomorrow, I will attend the Closed Council, where a possible solution can be discussed. Lluava, I want you there with me. Together, we can deal with these Raiders."

Lluava added, "We can overcome anything together."

When he looked at her, Varren's expression was sorrowful. Then, one corner of his mouth twitched, as if he had caught himself about to say something. What was he not telling her? They sat next to each other for a while longer, neither speaking. After a time, as was their custom, Varren left first so as not to draw attention to their meeting. Lluava would leave a few minutes later.

Alone in the garden again, Lluava observed a very large crow flutter down to a branch above her. Something wriggled in its beak. Lluava shivered.

A sharp cry came from higher up in the tree. A raven swooped in and chased away the crow. In its haste, the smaller bird dropped its meal. Onyx glowered at the retreating crow with his one good eye before claiming the prize.

Carrion eaters, Lluava thought sullenly. Some believed these birds were omens of death. Not exactly what she wanted to think about in light of the kingdom's current predicament. Yet ravens were also depicted on the royal emblem; maybe good fortune would come Elysia's way.

***

The next morning, Lluava awakened to find June already setting out the dress Lluava was to wear that day. The teen was thankful that her wardrobe had been kept intact even after she and Varren had departed for the North. She would never admit it, but there were a few dresses she was actually fond of.

The daily routine had not changed: sit and allow June to groom her— still such a strange experience—then off to the baths; then dress and eat. Afterward, hurry down to the Open Council, where commoners as well as aristocrats could ask the king for recompense for their grievances. Justice was what they sought, though to Lluava many of their complaints were simply that—complaints.

June was unusually quiet this morning. When she finished lacing up the corset, Lluava asked, "Are you all right, June?"

"Why would I not be? My Lady is back."

June excused herself as soon as possible, and Lluava headed to the Open Council alone. What was wrong with everyone? Varren was obstinately intending to enter into a loveless marriage. Themis was displaying deeply held emotions. June was acting completely out of character.

The trumpets sounded as the doors to the Great Hall opened. This room could easily seat several hundred people. Wonderful woven tapestries were hung between groups of three long, thin, arched windows. The councilmen in their striped robes sat on stiff, high-backed chairs on raised seating areas at either side of the room. The royal family was seated on a two-tiered dais at the very back of the Great Hall. From thrones higher than all other seats, they could look down on the courtiers milling about below them. Smaller thrones flanked the two grand thrones in which Varren and the widowed Enya sat. Themis, as head councilman, sat at the king's right hand. Lluava had to settle for sitting next to the little queen. Fortunately, this time her chair had a small cushion. Perhaps a few perks had come with the shift in power.

The heavy doors were closed and the council progressed in its usual, horrendously boring fashion. A trumpet sounded as the doors were opened. The head steward would escort some disgruntled person to the dais where

165

he or she would recount his or her woes and issues. Once Varren or Themis had announced a ruling, the steward escorted the individual from the room and the doors were closed. During the long intervals between petitioners, the rest of the court would gossip and banter lightheartedly until the trumpet sounded and the process would begin again.

Varren appeared fully lucid this morning. All his decrees were well founded. Though it was impossible to make everyone happy, he had a knack for rendering unbiased judgment. Somehow this only made Lluava's fears worse. Could he have the Wasting Disease like his grandfather? Since Varren's father had accidentally died when he was not much older than Varren was now, no one knew whether this illness had been passed down.

Those with the disease lost their awareness; memories would lapse, as would their sense of the present. Typically, mornings were the best time of day for someone with this affliction. Then, as the day progressed, the person's mental clarity diminished, only to be somewhat restored the next morning. Varren was clearly in his right mind now. Lluava feared he would begin to flounder as the day progressed.

Yet hadn't the healers agreed that whatever was happening to Varren was something else, possibly something new? Had he fallen ill on his journey home from the northern border? She would have to find the truth, and soon.

Lluava glimpsed Selene through a wall of male admirers. Regardless of the fact that the woman was engaged to the king, men continued to dote on her, and she reveled in their attention. Somehow, Selene must have sensed Lluava observing her, for she looked up and gave her a sweet smile.

Lluava tried to smile back, but it felt like a grimace. Turning away, she looked around the rest of the great room. Luka was there, talking jovially to Yamir. Did Yamir actually laugh? When was the last time Lluava had seen or heard him do that?

Rosalyn was clustered with some of the other ladies of the court. They chatted easily, and Lluava wondered if her friend had known them in the years before the war. Apex was nowhere to be seen. He must not have been forced to sit through this ridiculous ritual. Lluava was a bit jealous.

When the Open Council finally ended, the entire court made its way to the royal banquet hall. Slightly smaller than the Grand Hall, the room held numerous long tables placed perpendicularly to the royal banquet table, elevated on a dais at the back. Dark tablecloths complemented the silver tableware. Overflowing platters of amazing foods served as edible table runners. As before, Themis sat at Varren's right; yet Selene now sat at Varren's left, with Enya seated to Selene's left. Lluava had to settle for Themis's unfriendly presence on one side and Luka's on the other.

Roast turkey, glazed pork, and even stewed caribou shoulder were within reach, along with honeycombs, boards of olives, and a full, round wheel of a particularly pungent blue cheese. Bunches of grapes and a bowl of mixed fruits powdered with sugar gave the air a sweet odor. Now the question was, where to begin?

"Did you sleep well?" Luka asked as he peeled the meat off a turkey leg with his fork and knife. "You still look dreadfully tired."

Lluava gave him a sidelong glance. "I slept well." It was the truth; she had been so exhausted that she had slumbered without any of her horrid dreams.

"You must eat something. That stuff on your plate is edible, you know."

Her plate held her favorite food, tenderloin on the rare side. As Lluava was about to place a dripping forkful in her mouth, she heard a melodious peal of laughter. Selene quickly tried to regain her composure after whatever Varren had whispered to her.

Lluava's fork landed on the edge of the plate with a clatter before tumbling to the floor. Although a servant replaced the dropped utensil immediately, Lluava stood up and said, "Excuse me. I find I'm not terribly hungry."

Her eyes were brimming with tears by the time the double doors closed behind her. In the hall, she forced herself to take deep, slow breaths. She wanted to get to her room, lie down, and rest.

"He still loves you."

Lluava stopped walking when she heard Yamir's voice.

"Then what's happening to him?" she asked over her shoulder as Yamir caught up to her. At sixteen, he was her height, perfect for locking eyes with hers.

"Black magic." Yamir appeared to have moved onto a new conspiracy theory. Though many—like this one—were absurd, some of his notions were believable, and a few had even proved true.

"How? Who?" Lluava questioned skeptically. "Not Themis."

"That she-snake he is to marry." Yamir was always serious about his accusations, no matter how ludicrous they sounded.

"Selene?" Lluava wanted to laugh, then stopped. She asked again, more seriously, "Selene?"

Yamir placed his coppery hands on her shoulders. "Just watch the way they act around each other. Varren does whatever Selene wishes. Listen to their conversations. Look at their interactions. Something's wrong. She is controlling him."

"Through blackmail?" Lluava was aghast. She thought back to the forced tone of Varren's voice insisting that he would marry Selene.

"Magic," corrected Yamir.

"Magic doesn't exist."

"Then how do you explain Issaura's Claws or Ullr's Fangs? They shift when you do. That is not natural."

Lluava shook her head. "Those are just weapons forged using a forgotten technique with a forgotten material."

"Or," Yamir countered, "they are magic. Not everything in the world can be explained. You, above everyone else, should know that."

167

Yena's scrying bowl and Grandmother's prophecies came to mind. Could Selene really be manipulating Varren in some way? Lluava remembered how he had seemed to be sucked into his fiancée's gaze. If there was any chance that this could be true, Lluava would have to proceed very carefully.

"I might know where to find some material about—"

Luka's voice cut her off. "There you are, Lluava. I've been looking for you. You left so suddenly." Luka had turned the corner behind them. "Oh, hello, Yamir."

Lluava quickly reassured him. "I'm fine. Really. Readjusting is harder than it seems."

"Only to be expected," Luka replied, smiling. "Well, since you are in good hands, I will leave you and return to my turkey. It was crisped perfectly."

After Luka left, Yamir inquired, "Do you think he knows magic, too? If so, you might be in trouble."

"How?"

"He wants you."

"Be serious, Yamir."

"I am."

***

The Closed Council was held in a small meeting room where the entire council as well as the king could sit around a semicircular table. Guests were asked to take a seat on one of the benches along the walls. Lluava was used to all of this—that is, until Selene entered the room. The Closed Council was exclusively for governing officials and royalty: Selene was neither. Lluava was only permitted entry as military partner to the king.

Lluava tried not to gape as the ruler's fiancée entered the room, but she almost exclaimed when Selene took the single vacant chair at Varren's left. Lluava should have that position! None of this was right, and from the distasteful looks of other councilmen, she was not the only one who thought so. Yet nobody questioned Selene.

Perhaps Yamir was right. Maybe Selene *was* manipulating Varren somehow. Seemingly oblivious to the probing gazes, she smiled sweetly at everyone in the room as Themis smacked the gavel down, indicating that the Closed Council was to begin.

Varren repositioned his crown. He still wore Thor's old headpiece. The High Council would present the young king with a new crown, designed specifically for him, at a ceremony during his birthday celebration. "Head Councilman Themis, what matter will begin today's session?"

"The Council finds—" Themis started, just as Selene cleared her throat.

Varren looked over at his fiancée. "What is it, my love?"

A foul taste entered Lluava's mouth as she watched Varren, who clearly was hopelessly enamored by the woman beside him.

Selene said, "I know you will want to move onto more significant topics that I would find dull. I know little of politics and nothing of war, yet I have come to make a personal request of you, Head Councilman Themis. Would you stand up for me, since my father is not able to come to my wedding?"

Themis remained unnaturally composed as a general murmur spread around the table. This request was certainly of little importance when much more serious matters were in need of discussion. Moreover, it was better tendered in private quarters, not in a public arena.

One rail-thin man objected, "Your Majesty, a woman should not be at this table, clearly."

Another waspish figure added, "This council is meant to discuss the most crucial issues relating to the kingdom."

A third said, "Women should stay with their needlework and gossip. Keep the wedding out of this."

For the first time, Lluava thought she saw something flash in Selene's eyes, although the woman retained her light smile.

Varren continued to gaze at Selene. "She is to be my wife and should know what goes on inside this room. Themis will certainly stand up for her in the ceremony."

Now, even the head councilman looked ready to challenge the new king.

"Let us move onto our resource report," Varren began.

But Lluava had found enough of her voice to speak up.

"Excuse me, Your Majesty. May I be permitted to express my thoughts?"

Themis clearly wanted to quiet her, but Varren, finally tearing his eyes away from Selene, nodded.

"We should be most concerned about the war. May we discuss that now?"

"The Lady Lluava makes a valid point," spoke up Hyrax. He sat facing her, and Lluava could tell he was concerned. He had been at the battle of Castle Alcazar and had seen the devastation; yet this man had proved to have other interests. Was he backing Lluava's idea in order to befriend her once again? She loathed him and the rest of the so-called Guardians.

"Your Highness, our attention must be focused on the war." Themis, though he might not like Lluava, was agreeing with her in this matter.

"But on which enemy?" questioned Selene, not bothering with the appropriate protocol. "Any person who opposes the king and the throne should be viewed as an enemy of Elysia and thus an enemy of the kingdom. Do you not agree, Councilmen?"

"Any man who proves a threat to the king should be punished by death. This is our law," noted one of the few Theriomorph councilmen.

Others nodded in agreement.

"Then, before we can focus solely on one enemy, we must first deal with another." Selene was now receiving perplexed looks. She continued, undeterred, "We must force the clans to bend a knee once and for all, or we must wipe them off the face of Elysia."

Chapter 25

Tartarus's First Victim

Eradicate the clans? Now Selene had gone too far. Who was she to even propose such a measure? She did not know the clans. Although they refused to acknowledge the Mandrun family line as their rulers or to be bound by human laws, the clans were not the bloodthirsty savages that were laying waste to Elysia. It was true that they raided the trading wagons of the rich from time to time, but they tried not to harm anyone. Only a very few deaths had occurred. Fortunately, Lluava was not the only one in the room who opposed the proposal.

"They are only a minor grievance, My Lady," said the shortest man on the council. "We would do better to focus on the approaching army."

"If they do not fight for you," Selene told Varren, "they fight against you. How many enemies will you let roam your lands?"

The uproar that followed was thunderous. The entire council seemed to tear itself apart. Those whose hatred of the clans for personal reasons caused them to fervently back Selene's suggestion. Of course, none of those men had ever set foot on the front lines of war. In contrast, many Northern-born representatives insisted on focusing solely on defeating the Raiders. They had lost their homes and their lands, and they were furious, for good reason. Only a handful of members kept silent.

"Enough!" Themis bellowed as he banged the gavel down several times. "We are not animals! Compose yourselves."

The council quieted.

"We all know what a nuisance these thieving bands have been over the years," he acknowledged. Lluava knew Themis would welcome a chance to tear the clans apart. "In a more peaceful time, they might be of a greater concern. It is also important to point out that they have assisted the Elysian army periodically with our war effort. The clans must be dealt with, this is true; but as it stands, our greatest enemy is now marching on Cronus."

Varren glanced at the councilmen, considering all that had been said before turning back to Selene. "Yes. We must focus on the Raiders; but if any clansmen cross paths with the military, they must swear allegiance. If they refuse, they will be either thrown into Tartarus's depths or killed."

Lluava gasped. "You would condemn your friends to rot in the dungeons? After all they have done for us?"

The king seemed not to hear her. "This is my royal decree. Let it be known."

"Varren!" Lluava exclaimed. "What's gotten into you?"

Themis motioned to a steward. "Please escort Lady Lluava from the council," he stated gloomily. "She seems to have forgotten herself."

"Varren?" Lluava implored him once more as she was ushered out. As the doors closed, she observed Selene's sickeningly sweet smile as Varren bent to kiss her hand.

Lluava stormed to her quarters, where she immediately strode onto the balcony and let loose a roar. As the noise diminished, she heard Onyx cawing loudly in distaste.

"What's the matter?" she shouted at the ratty bird. "You don't like it? Then leave me alone!"

Onyx took wing and disappeared. The sun shone in the cloudless sky. A wisp of laughter floated up from the city below. "To the hells with all of you," muttered Lluava as she threw herself onto the bed.

That evening, June came to check on her. "Would My Lady like to dress for supper?" she asked timidly.

"No," grouched Lluava.

"Would she—"

"No. Just go." As Lluava rolled onto her side, she was ashamed of how she had just treated the little girl.

"June?" she called, but all she heard was the sound of the door shutting.

"Ah!" she cried out as she sat up and fumbled with the cords of her bodice. It seemed to take forever before she was able to pull the dress off. Throwing on her old training uniform—a white, short-sleeved shirt and black pants—she curled up on her bed, hot and angry.

Sometime later, there was a knock on the door.

"Lluava?" Luka's voice called from the sitting room. "Are you here?"

Groggy even though she had not slept at all, Lluava shuffled to the archway. "What do you want?"

Luka held a silver tray with a matching dome, goblet, and pitcher. That he had balanced the entire thing all the way to her chamber was remarkable.

"I brought you some dinner." He slid the tray onto her table and lifted the dome, revealing a plate of sliced pork in a raspberry sauce, a heaping mound of caramelized vegetables, and a heel of warm bread.

"I'm not hungry," Lluava lied, but her grumbling stomach announced her as a fraud.

"Come, now. Take a seat by me," Luka said, plopping down on the couch. "Unless you are in the midst of a religious fast, you really should enjoy some of this food."

Lluava had not eaten much of anything since she had arrived at the capital. The wonderful aromas enticed her. She sat down next to Luka. Forking some of the vegetables into her mouth, she realized she was ravenous. She ate rapidly, slowing only when she saw the young man watching her.

Swallowing, she said, "Thank you for dinner."

"Uh-huh," uttered Luka, completely amused. "Once you've finished licking your plate, will you tell me what is the matter?"

Lluava decided to eat more slowly. After a few bites, she admitted, "I think I hate your sister." She quickly blushed. "I mean, I—"

Luka laughed. "Selene has a knack of getting what she wants, even when it pisses others off."

"She wants to hurt my friends." Lluava pushed her plate away. "She wants to destroy the clans."

Picking up the pitcher, Luka poured a goblet of wine and handed it to her. "Well, that is unfortunate."

Eyeing the red liquid, Lluava said, "I'm not thirsty."

"Drink," ordered Luka. "You definitely need it."

Lluava swallowed a mouthful of the dry, heavy wine. She felt the fire run down her throat. "Selene is ruining everything."

"My sister will be much more relaxed after the wedding."

"I hate her."

"Oh, come on, now. Remember how much fun we used to have?"

"Can't you see what she is doing? She will destroy everything. How can you defend her?"

Luka, for once, looked serious. "She saved my life. I owe her my undying gratitude."

Lluava took another swallow of wine as Luka leaned comfortably back on the couch and explained.

"My sister and I were adopted around the same time. Lord Fárbauti and his wife wanted children and were strongly advised to adopt Theriomorphs, for political reasons."

This was not new to Lluava. Luka continued, "It seems the couple was undecided about a boy versus a girl, so they ended up adopting one of each. As infants, we were inseparable. We ate, slept, bathed, and played together. Selene was doted upon by Lady Fárbauti from the beginning. The gowns, the jewels, the best of the best. Unfortunately, this was not the case for me."

Luka grimaced for a moment as he silently remembered, then he sat up straight. "Lord Fárbauti hated that I was a Theriomorph. If he caught me shifting, he would thrash me. Later, he beat me for no reason at all. Once he beat me so badly that I was bedridden for several weeks."

Lluava was shocked.

"Selene realized that if this continued, I could die. This might have actually been the intent of our lord father, for he could not disown me outright. But if I died, he could name another heir. Selene convinced Lord Fárbauti to send us to live at court. Here, we are out of our lord father's sight, and I am safely out of his reach. We have been here for over three years.

"I cannot hate my sister. I owe her my life," admitted Luka. "But I can talk to her, if you like."

So, Luka could not help her oppose Selene. But he still needed to understand how dire the situation had actually become. Lluava ran her fingers through her hair until they were tangled in it. "The war is almost at our doorstep."

Luka reached out and tilted her chin up. "Then prepare for it."

***

Members of the court still dallied in the Great Hall when Themis said, "Send the first one in."

Swarthy and surly, Yamir strode to the dais so fast that the head steward, Howard, had trouble keeping up with him. Armed guards standing below quickly crossed their spears in warning.

Varren ritually began, "What is it that brings you here, my good—"

"You gave orders to throw my family into the dungeons?" Yamir asked, almost spitting with rage.

"If you are referring to the clans—"

"After all they have done for you! For your precious crown!"

Though the room was well lit, Lluava suddenly noticed that the few shadows in the room seemed to tremble. A new guard approached, whacked the back of Yamir's head, and sneered, "Such insolence!"

Yamir faltered from the blow, then straightened and stood tall. Lluava saw tears in his eyes. "If you ever valued me as a friend, you will retract your decree."

Themis spoke up. "Do you associate yourself with the clans?"

"They are my family. They will always be my family."

The head councilman seemed to expect that remark. "Then bend a knee and swear your allegiance to the one true king."

Yamir looked darkly at Varren. "I was born to the clans. No words can take that away."

"Don't do this." Lluava whispered her plea in the king's direction.

Varren's expression remained unreadable.

Themis announced, "Find this man suitable quarters in Tartarus. The same goes for all who oppose the Crown."

Lluava felt numb as she watched Yamir being physically removed from the hall. Should she follow her friend? What help could she offer if she did?

Lluava knew she could not provide much assistance if she, too, were tossed into the dungeons. But Varren wouldn't do that to her. On the other hand, he had just done it to one of their friends.

She felt empty, hollow. She could not focus on the rest of the proceedings, nor did she have any appetite for lunch. Rosalyn did not return to eat after she left the Open Council, and Lluava had a feeling she knew where her friend had gone.

Staring at her plate, Lluava wanted to remove herself from these men, these people, this hypocrisy, Varren. She excused herself as soon as possible.

Themis simply said, "If you do not like your designated seat, I can surely find you another position elsewhere in the room."

Lluava did not respond. Let Themis remove her from the royal dining table. He had imprisoned one of her closest friends in Tartarus, and Varren had done nothing. She returned to her room to think in silence.

Onyx had not returned since the previous evening. His perch remained bare, and the small bowl containing bits of corn and crackers was untouched.

"Is everyone abandoning me?" she cried. Tears bubbled up into her eyes.

As if on cue, June walked through the door carrying a vase. The vibrant bouquet was not as eye-catching as the single striped iris.

"Oh!" June exclaimed as she jumped in fright. Righting the flowers, she said, "I did not know you had returned."

"Take them away," ordered Lluava.

Perplexed, June began to explain, "They are a gift from—"

"I know who they are from. Take them away!"

June hurried from the room, sloshing water as she went.

How dare Varren? Lluava thought angrily. Curse him! Curse his family! Curse this whole place!

When it was time to return to the Closed Council, Lluava knew that she and Varren had to have a heart-to-heart talk. No excuses. No interruptions. No exceptions. But when she turned the corner, she noticed Selene entering the council chamber.

Again? This enraged her even more. A low rumble passed Lluava's lips. She envisioned herself tearing off that pretty smile with her teeth. It would not matter what form Lluava took, as long as Selene screamed.

Two guards were positioned outside. This time, the spears were crossed at her approach.

"Lady Lluava," the older one spoke coldly. "You are no longer invited to the Closed Council."

"I am the king's military partner," Lluava reminded him. "Let me pass."

"The king believes you are of better service training for the future battles."

"I will be allowed inside—"

"You are to report to the training yards at once."

Lluava eyed the spear tips. Against her dual form, neither guard would stand a chance. Her growl reverberated down the hall. Lluava could feel her pupils narrowing like a house cat's. Then she saw the younger guard finger the top of his hilt. She could kill them. She knew how. But slaughtering the castle guard? They weren't the enemy.

Lluava wheeled and nearly bowled into Themis. They both paused. Lluava could have sworn that the corners of the head councilman's mouth twitched.

"Enjoy your swordplay," he coolly remarked.

She could tear out his throat right here and now. With Themis gone, there would be one fewer threat to worry about.

Instead, Lluava went to her room to retrieve the Claws. Her sore thumb pounded with every beat of her heart. Why wouldn't the stupid thing just heal? Gripping the Claw in that hand was painful. But what did she care? She felt more whole with them on.

Out in the yards, the clangor of metal, the grunts of men, and the smell of sweat reminded Lluava of a far simpler time in Durog. Why had she complained so much about her life back then? Before everything became so convoluted, she had been happy. She had had some hope for the future.

The number of men training in the area, which now appeared small to her, was impressive. Lluava glimpsed Rosalyn off in a corner, parrying with another soldier.

"Come to honor us with your presence?"

Shirtless, Apex questioned her as he wiped the perspiration off his brow with one arm. Stepping over his fallen victim, the huntsman left the poor man to struggle to his feet. Giving her a closer look, Apex added, "I find that sparring often relieves stress. Come. I need a good challenge."

Putting up his blunted training sword, Apex picked up Ullr's Fangs from the ground where he had left them. As the Gladius swords were swung in the air, they seemed to sing in excitement.

Forcefully pushing all her worries from her mind, Lluava concentrated on the man before her.

"Let's," she said.

Chapter 26

Snada

Issaura's Claws glowed vibrant orange in the afternoon sun; Ullr's Fangs, red. Glinting like the flash of teeth before a bite, they hungered for their first swing. A flinching muscle, a sudden change in breath, and the two impressive figures charged one another.

Apex swung low, and Lluava vaulted into the air. The blade sliced under her soft Endun shoes. Lluava spun around to carve into Apex's back, but he lurched out of the way. They were both cautious, and rightly so. Each had seen friends and comrades die horribly in the war. Mistakes were lethal. Neither could afford one.

Controlling her rage and utilizing its fury, Lluava soon took the offense. Her strikes were strong, quick, powerful. Her focus was solely on the huntsman before her. Without fear of attack by a third party, she disregarded the fact that anger clouds the mind. That did not matter now. All she wanted to do was slash and tear anything her blades could touch.

The huntsman was forced back. He clearly did not like this. Apex shoved forward and thrust both swords in front of him. Lluava dropped to the ground and rolled out of the way.

Cocking his head, Apex inquired, "How is your shoulder?"

Lluava regained her footing. She attempted to strike, then moved away. "My arm hasn't hurt me since…" —she put her thoughts on hold as Apex swung his left blade at her; she dodged his attempt—"…since the ranking ceremony, I think."

Apex raised an eyebrow, or at least Lluava thought he did. They both were moving quickly.

Had it really been that long? Her arm felt fine even without the braces she had destroyed. When had the last incident occurred?

"Do you think," she began as she sidestepped another attack, "that that potion, the Idun, that we drank for our wounds back in Leucrocotta could have healed my shoulder?"

"I'm not sure," snorted Apex as he readjusted his right-hand grip, "but your scar seems to have diminished."

That was true. Once vibrant pink and raised, the scar running down her torso had faded to almost nothing. Her skin seemed smoother, too. Why had Apex noticed such a thing? It was a bit unnerving that he had been observing her so closely.

Lluava spotted an opening. She moved for the hit. Apex countered just in time. The scream of metal was ear splitting. Sparks flew off both weapons, and both combatants shouted out.

As soon as their weapons collided, strange engravings manifested up and down their blades. Ancient runes and archaic designs appeared miraculously. When the pair stepped away from each other, the weapons instantly regained their normal appearance.

"What was that? Did you see it?" Lluava gasped as she inspected the surface of Issaura's Claws where the phantom images had appeared.

Apex looked more ravenously than ever at Ullr's Fangs. "It seems there is still much we do not know."

"Let's get out of here." Lluava's whisper was almost swallowed up by the clangs and clashes of other weapons.

Flipping one Fang over, Apex ran his fingers down the blade. "Could it be their kiss?"

"What?" questioned Lluava. Had anyone else glimpsed the occurrence? She scanned the yard, but the other soldiers took no notice of them. "We should get inside."

Ignoring her, Apex said, "Let our weapons touch again." He moved forward with sword outstretched.

"No! Not here!" said Lluava as she stepped back. "Inside."

Lluava moved to the door. Apex followed, weaving around other sparring pairs. As they left the training yard, Lluava caught sight of Rosalyn once more. She was swinging at a straw dummy with Vjeran, a sword Lluava had lent her, one that belonged to General Domar. Lluava knew the general was serving on the frontlines with Talos and Byron, maybe even Lieutenant Vidrick Bern. She longed to be with them, but there was much to be done here first.

"Where are we going?" questioned Apex once they were inside.

"To one of the libraries. Our only hope is to discover more about this." Lluava paused to make sure she could not hear any footsteps. "It's quiet, seldom used, secluded. It also contains confiscated Theriomorph texts. It's perfect."

"And it has the documents we need?" Apex asked skeptically. Lluava could not blame him.

"There is only one way to be sure."

They quickly made their way through the castle's corridors. Lluava was pleased that she remembered so much of this massive structure.

"Where does that lead?" Apex's question caused Lluava to halt.

Glancing at the double doors, Lluava hastily replied, "That is the Burnt Wing, where Prince Damian and his wife died. It's off limits to everyone." The doors were ajar.

Apex looked curiously at the ornate wood. "I thought I saw something move in there."

"Don't think about it," warned Lluava, remembering when she had wandered in herself. She had taken a beating from an Obsidian Guard, the Shadow called Holly, who was often assigned to that area. "I've tried. You don't want to cross paths with one of the Shadows unless you have to."

"So, the rumors are true," noted Apex. His eyes glimmered excitedly even in the dull light, but he followed Lluava down the hall.

Once they arrived at their destination, she took hold of a rolling ladder and climbed up to inspect the circular shelves that bordered the inner walls of the tower. She selected various scrolls and handed them down one at a time to the huntsman, who placed them on one of the central tables.

"There," said Lluava after taking a seat in front of a mound of yellowed parchment. "That should be a start."

"What about the weapons?" Apex asked. "Can we see what happens when the blades touch?"

Making sure none of the dim areas in the room were occupied, Lluava nodded. Picking up the Claws, she laid them against Ullr's Fangs. Immediately the fluid designs and ancient runes appeared.

"What do they say?" asked Apex, who was still not adept at reading the archaic writing.

"I'm not sure," admitted Lluava. "I can only make out a few words. The names of the weapons are here and here." She pointed to the symbols. "The Fangs of Ullr. The Claws of Issaura."

Lluava gathered more scrolls. "Take these. Try to translate the runes with this guide; I'll try to find out anything that can help us understand...us."

As she unrolled her first scroll, Lluava hoped she might also stumble upon something to explain Varren's ailment.

As evening fell, candles were lit. Wax pooled around their bases. Unhelpful scrolls were put aside. Notes were taken with dripping ink and quills.

Suddenly, Apex pushed away the weapons, breaking their contact and almost causing one of the Claws to topple over the table's edge. "Someone's coming," he grunted.

The door behind them opened with a sigh. A single figure carrying a candlestick and a bundle of scrolls paused in the doorway.

"The gods are smiling. I was not expecting you both to be here."

A heavy perfume enabled Lluava to identify Hyrax before he spoke. The councilman entered the room and began to replace his scrolls and gather others. After a moment, he paused and looked back at Apex and Lluava, who were watching him.

"Are you looking for anything in particular? I might be of service."

"Maybe. Would you—"

"No!" Lluava cut Apex off before he said something they would both regret. Hyrax was a Guardian. She would not forgive him for lying to her or sending her on that ludicrous quest.

"Very well," said the councilman, his feelings apparently unhurt. He continued about his business. Before he left, he turned back to the pair. "Whatever answers you may seek, the gods already know. Pray to them for help."

"I don't believe in the gods," snarled Lluava.

"That does not mean they don't believe in you," he said.

After Hyrax shut the door, Apex chastised her. "You should have asked him. What are you waiting for? He is the only one here who knows anything about us. He might have answers."

"I don't care if he does. We can find answers on our own without Guardians or gods."

Apex went back to his work without arguing. Lluava knew he would have preferred to converse with Hyrax. That was just too bad. She had sworn never to associate herself with Hyrax again after he had practically forced her to abandon Varren and wander the wasteland. Had she stayed here, she might have been able to help her partner. Hyrax was no friend. He was just another manipulator.

Eventually, the huntsman rose to his feet and stretched. "It is time for us to turn in," he said, yawning, as he watched their last candle stub begin to sputter. "We can do more tomorrow."

"Yes. Yes," replied Lluava absentmindedly. "Go on. I'll follow shortly."

"Get sleep, Lluava," advised Apex before he disappeared down the hall.

Sometime later, the candle began to flicker so badly that it made Lluava's head ache. "Ah!" she roared, and knocked a bundle of scrolls to the floor, which scattered them into the shadows. Rubbing her sore eyes, she fumed as hot anger coursed through her.

"This is hopeless!" she cried out. None of the chosen documents held anything remotely useful. She was wasting time again. Could she bring herself to crawl to Hyrax for help? The thought of him caused her lip to curl.

No. Not him. Who else? The gods? Hyrax had advised her to pray, but to which one? Ullr? Issaura? If she and Apex were their Incarn, those two were no use. Crocotta was the same; her Incarn had not helped them. Which of the twelve would possibly assist Lluava in her time of need? The Twins? What good was Suada, goddess of seduction, or her brother...

Lluava almost overturned her chair as she jumped up. *The Twins.* Before she left on her stupid quest, Hyrax had mentioned that there were other Incarn in Elysia known to the Guardians. If that were true, then what were the chances that some might be in the capital now, unaware of what they truly were, shielded by the countless bodies that moved inside Cronus's walls?

The Twins. The two sibling gods were often known simply by that name, the Twins. Lluava knew of another pair of "twins," Luka and Selene, Theriomorphs both. They were the right age. Both were orphans. Luka had even said that Lord Fárbauti was influenced to adopt the pair even though he clearly despised the Theriomorph race. Could the Guardians have had anything to do with that? Hyrax was on the High Council. Did the fact that aristocrats were strongly encouraged to take in Theriomorph young have anything to do with him? With the Incarn?

Lluava had never talked with the twins about their dual forms. The subject was not important to them. Humans thought it strange that Theriomorphs typically cared little about what animal each of them became. Luka was clearly a mammal of sorts—maybe a dog, from his under-odor. Selene always wore perfume, which made it impossible to identify what form she took. Hyrax had used perfume to trick Lluava. Was Selene doing the same?

Quickly searching the library, Lluava found the thick tome of the *Karmasana* and lugged it to the table. Flipping through the pages, she stopped when she saw the elegant painting of the goddess Suada.

From the depiction, it was quite clear that this female was the goddess of seduction and lust. Full-figured and alluring in all regards, Suada's involvement in the mortal world was often the downfall of some young hero. She had even seduced the god Ullr, causing a dismayed Issaura to take vows of chastity. The goddess's animal form lay at her feet—the emerald anaconda.

Suada had the power to lure any man to do her bidding. Though not overtly evil, her interactions left destruction and waste in her shadow. Both she and her brother were children born from rape. The abilities of both gods, no matter how well-intended, only festered into vile and tragic outcomes.

Lluava shut the book.

She had found two more Incarn. They had been in the capital all along.

Chapter 27

The Jackal's Warning

The hour was late. Lluava could tell by the dying flames in the sconces in the halls. Several candles blew out as she hurried past, and the path behind her was swallowed by the dark. Let the shadows feed. Let them be disquieted, Lluava thought bitterly as she forced herself to recall the way.

"If you had only done your job," she hissed aloud to the earless walls. She was aggravated with herself.

Needing to know for certain if her theory was true, Lluava hurried through the castle to find the only one she trusted for the answer. If the twins were *the Twins*, Selene could be controlling Varren. Lluava was uncertain how, but it was as good an explanation as any. And if that were the case, Varren still loved her, not Selene. That was worth fighting for.

Lluava rapped on the door, thinking, Please let this be the right one.

Inside, footsteps stumbled to the door. It opened.

"Lluava?" questioned Luka as he blinked sleep away. "What in the gods' names are you doing here?"

"I need to talk with you. Privately. Now." She was still out of breath from her rapid walk from the library.

"Ah…yeah." He opened the door wider. "Come in."

Luka shuffled to the hearth and halfheartedly stirred up some of the coals using an iron poker with a canid-shaped handle. His chambers consisted of a single room large enough for a sleeping area against one wall and a sitting area near the other. Though the room had no balcony, large windows overlooked the dark silhouettes of Cronus below. A narrow spiral staircase made entirely of iron allowed one to climb to a small private library with a single cushioned chair.

Although the room offered comfort and relaxation, Lluava was certainly not relaxed. She sat down, but she was too restless and stood up as soon as Luka sank into a chair.

"What is so perplexing that it woke you up?" he asked in a drowsy tone.

"I haven't slept."

"Well, I was having this fabulous dream about—"

"Luka," Lluava did not want him to get started on one of his stories. "I need to know something. What is your dual form?"

The young man laughed. "What? This is the question that could not wait until morning?" Lluava looked dreadfully serious, and Luka quickly answered, "A jackal."

"Black?"

"But of course."

"And Selene? What is hers?"

"An emerald anaconda."

Lluava's heart skipped a beat.

"Luka, what I am about to tell you will sound crazy." She took a breath.

Luka just looked bemused. His sleep-tousled hair caused several of his white patches to stick out at odd angles. "You already sound crazy. But do go on." He smiled.

"There are special Theriomorphs that have gods' dual forms, like me. Like you. They, we, are known as Incarn. Incarn are—"

"Vessels of the gods," he said matter-of-factly.

"You know?" gasped Lluava. She sat down across from him. "How long?"

"Far longer than you, it seems. And yes, Selene is an Incarn, too. Don't look so surprised. You're smart. I have been rooting for you for a long time. Actually, you took longer to put two and two together, but—"

"You knew. Both of you. And you didn't tell me?"

"Whoa, whoa." Luka motioned for her to settle down. "We were not allowed to talk of this."

"By whose order?" She knew the answer before she asked the question.

"The Guardians."

"I should have been told!" She slammed a fist on the table.

"Come now, Lluava," he said calmly. "You weren't ready."

"What made *you* so ready?" she snarled.

"We matured faster than you."

"Matured faster?" Lluava's growl rumbled in her throat. "What do you mean, *matured faster*? We are practically the same age!"

"Can we talk like civilized adults?" Luka's eyes sparkled.

Trying to calm herself, which seemed to be harder and harder lately, Lluava confirmed, "So both you and Selene know what you are and have known for some time."

Luka nodded.

"Can't you see that your sister is up to something? She is forcing Varren, and thus Elysia, into a very dangerous situation."

"And how, pray tell, is my sweet sister doing such a thing? By marrying the king? By becoming the first Theriomorph with real power since the humans conquered our people? This is a benefit to us all."

Lluava tried to come up with a plausible answer. Selene had to be manipulating the situation. She had to be, but how?

"Varren does not love her. He loves—" Lluava cut herself off before she said it aloud.

"Who?" asked Luka as he steepled his fingers before him and leaned back.

Switching the subject, Lluava demanded, "You have to help me, Luka. You know your sister better than anyone. You know she is manipulating the king. Everyone can see that Varren has changed since he took an interest in Selene. You have to help me stop her. Whatever she is doing is not right."

"You want me to turn against my sister?" questioned Luka, raising an eyebrow. He looked intrigued.

"Yes," she whispered, knowing full well what she asked of him.

"For you, Lluava, I would do anything," replied Luka, "but that."

"But she—"

"I cannot do that. I am in her debt."

"I know this. You are my friend, Luka. But if Selene doesn't stop whatever she is up to, I will stop her myself."

"You can't, Lluava."

"Of course I can."

Luka restated more assertively, "No. You can't. You are not powerful enough. Believe me."

"Not powerful enough? Of course I am. I'm a soldier. I have engaged in active battles. I am supposed to be the Incarn of the goddess of war."

"You don't have the power."

As frustrated as she was, Lluava waited for him to explain.

"Remember the other day, when I told you how Selene saved me from our lord father? Well, there is more to it than that.

"Selene has always been beautiful. When she began to bloom, every male took notice of her. Well, almost every male; her charms never seemed to work on me. Anyway, we both had our talents. She always got her way. Men, young lordlings and stable boys alike, doted on her and gave her little presents. My only gift was to cause trouble. I like a good prank. What can I say?" Luka shrugged and laughed again. Lluava, still agitated, waited with difficulty for him to get to the point.

"Selene soon realized she had a gift to…let's call it 'influence'…men to do her bidding. She used that 'influence' on our lord father. Now, Lord Fárbauti might have been neutral toward Selene and loathed me, but he did love his wife. When the threat of what he had done with Selene was held over his head, he was more than happy to whisk us away to the capital so the truth would not come out.

"You see, Lluava, all Incarn have special abilities that separate us from others. These abilities make us, well, simply more powerful. Selene and I were first. When we reached the capital, the Guardians, realizing this, approached us and told us who and what we really were. We have known we were Incarn for years, because we were ready.

"I do not know why they informed you when they did. Your ability, whatever it is, clearly has not begun to manifest itself. This is why I am warning you, as your friend. You are not strong enough to take on my sister, and I will not help you with that endeavor. I owe Selene that much."

"Abilities..." Lluava repeated the word aloud to herself. Was Luka truly insinuating that all Incarn had some special magic? That was preposterous. Magic was not real. The gods were not real. It was just another lie.

"Take a moment," murmured Luka. He got up, stretched, and went over to his washstand and pitcher and poured a glass of water. He handed her the glass and paced about the room. Lluava watched as her friend attempted to shake off his sleepiness.

He did not seem out of the ordinary. Was causing trouble a power of sorts? Was being beautiful? What about Yena? She was able to scry in that black liquid. That was special. If they all had some sort of power, why didn't she herself? And why didn't Apex?

Placing her head in her hands, Lluava sighed, "I don't know."

"It is strange to think about. I know," admitted Luka. "I've been there. Acceptance comes with time."

"Do you know of any other Incarn?" questioned Lluava. She needed to be fully informed.

"We were told that there were four under the care of the Guardians. The three of us and that wild thing you brought back from the North. I don't think I quite like him."

"Few do," snorted Lluava. "So, no others?"

"We were told any others must be surviving in the Outlands somehow. How many did you find there?"

Luka's question made Lluava uneasy. She took too long to reply.

"My dear Lluava, you didn't think I was oblivious to your so-called mission? Why else would you and that wild man go off for so long, when you had seemed affixed to the king's side?"

"Luka, I—"

"Tsk, tsk, tsk. Secrets often fester with time."

Should she confide in him? He was a fellow Incarn. But not only had he kept secrets from her, he had also clearly sided with his sister. "Luka, is Selene using her abilities on Varren? Can you please tell me that?"

"She is."

Lluava stood up to leave. "I did find another out there. But she will be of no help to us."

Instead of questioning her further, Luka walked Lluava to the door and bade her goodnight.

***

The next morning, Lluava observed Selene's behavior, especially around Varren. Was it the way she looked at him that forced him to obey? If so, removing him from her proximity would solve the problem, right? Yet Varren had held true to the thought of Selene when Lluava met him in the garden after her return. Maybe Selene's power diminished the longer he was away from her. Could Lluava keep the pair apart long enough to break the bond? Then she and Varren could devise a plan to remove Selene from court.

Selene laughed at another jest the royal fool made in front of their table during the midday meal. The joker's hat jingled with little bells, adding their charming note to her laughter. The fool somersaulted into a handstand and began walking down the aisles. Absently touching the silver teardrop pendant on her favorite necklace, Selene was pleasantly amused.

"I would love a whole troupe of jesters at our wedding," she cooed.

Lluava contented herself by visualizing choking Selene with her own necklace. The thought caused her to chuff. Wait—was she turning into a monster? Despite Selene's manipulations, the woman surely didn't deserve that. Lluava just needed to find out how the Incarn's abilities worked. Well, Suada's at least.

Once the feast ended, Lluava and Apex returned to the library. After a short time, Apex grunted, "I now know for certain that I prefer shoving others around the yard with my Fangs in hand to this."

"Quit complaining."

"Do you really think the Guardians would leave scrolls pertaining to the Incarn lying about?"

"No, but this is the castle's private library, and it's rarely used. Anyway, they don't know that we can decipher the runes. If we can learn about the gods' weapons and their abilities, we might find information applicable to us."

"You're grasping at straws when you should be looking for a vine to pull you up."

"What was that? Some saying from your fellow huntsmen? What else would you have us do?"

"Fight the battle at hand."

Lluava grew rigid. Yes, there was a horrendous battle going on elsewhere in Elysia, but there were other battles here as well. They might not involve the use of blades and bows, but they were equally necessary for the preservation of the kingdom.

"What we are doing is important," hissed Lluava.

Apex let his scroll roll up and pushed it aside. "To whom? To Elysia?

To the king? Or to *you?*"

She was mortified. "How can you ask that?"

"We are built for war, you and I. What better place to be of service than on the battlefield? The king is safe here. Let him sit on his cushioned throne. Let him marry and be happy while he can."

Tears of fury boiled up from the searing heat inside her. As Lluava blinked them away, she snapped, "What I'm doing here will save Varren. If you can't realize that, then just go!"

The red flecks in Apex's eyes seemed to ignite. "I know that whatever connection you had with Varren was special once. But that is over now, and you can't have both."

"Both?"

"Lluava, don't you yet realize? You have feelings for me..."

Lluava wanted to laugh at the absurdity, though no sound slipped past her tongue.

"...as I have for you."

Chapter 28

Dealings in the Dark

D on't say that," hissed Lluava. "It's not true."

"Are you trying to control how I feel now?" rumbled Apex.

This was preposterous. Lluava did not like this situation at all. Didn't he understand that any affection between them would ruin whatever chances they had of being friends? She was not even certain she wanted to be friends with this man.

"You can't have feelings for me."

"Why not? Because I'm not the man of your dreams? Because I'm not the polished, romantic prince you originally desired?" A snide expression appeared upon Apex's face. "Other people have desired you, you know."

"Desire is not love."

"True, but I am not other people."

Lluava turned away and busied herself with returning scrolls to their places.

"Do not lie to yourself. You have feelings for me." Apex's voice floated up to her as she stood precariously on the top rung of the rolling stairs.

Trying not to lose her balance, Lluava pulled out a new tome. Climbing down, she said, "You are utterly mistaken."

"If you have no feelings for me," he countered, "then why does it infuriate you so to see me with another woman? Tell me that."

Glaring at the huntsman, she snapped, "We were on a mission. Your *women* would have distracted you."

"Would they?" Apex questioned. His dark hair seemed almost black in the dull light of the library. "Last I recall, it was you who slowed our progress when you refused to let me stay with Vissa. What you did disgraced her. Then there was the high priestess. You certainly didn't want me to mate with her.

187

And what about—"

"You're so narrow minded," griped Lluava as she intentionally dropped the book on the table. The resounding thump echoed off the tall walls.

"Me?" Apex laughed as he stood and gathered his things. "You are the one with all the obsessions, like focusing solely on following the Berserkers through the Yorrick Forrest. At least that benefited more than just yourself. But now that your entire world revolves around your human prince, you have lost sight of everything else around you. What about the war you claim to care about so much, or your kingdom? What about your friends? You have not even gone to see Yamir since he was thrown into the pits. I have."

At the sound of that name, Lluava was ashamed that she had forgotten so quickly about her friend. Yamir had been with her since the beginning. But was she there for him? Something loathsome gnawed in the pit of her stomach. Some of what Apex had said was true. What about the rest of it?

"I hope one day you will be ready to look beyond your narrow view and see the world in its entirety. When you're ready to move beyond your childish infatuations, come find me."

Apex left. Lluava felt as if she had been bludgeoned by one of the Berserkers. His bristly face haunted her even after he was gone. She shouted at the closed door, "I hate you! That's the truth of it!"

Leaving her books and notes on the table, Lluava went in search of the royal dungeons and her old friend. Chastising herself the entire way about having been so self-absorbed, she found the doors to Tartarus guarded by a respectable six men.

The dungeon was known for housing the vilest, most traitorous people in the kingdom. Those who entered rarely were permitted back into the sunlight. None ever escaped. As if in mockery of those imprisoned, Tartarus was located under the castle itself. Lluava wondered if knowing they were so close to the men who had condemned them had ever driven any of the prisoners mad.

"I am Lluava Kargen, daughter of Haliden Kargen, and I am military partner to the King," she said assertively to the guard. "I have come to visit a prisoner, the one called Yamir of the Cloven-Hoofed Clan."

For the first time in a long while, her connection with the king proved helpful. One of the guards, a young man with shoulder-length burgundy hair, led her into the depths of Tartarus.

The dungeon was designed like the inner workings of a beehive. Numerous corridors appeared at various levels surrounding a hollow central area. Each corridor was attached to some bridge or stair. Some corridors one had to walk down and across to reach; in others, one went down to go up. This chaotic structure was clearly intended to confuse any who escaped their cells. The complicated routes would double back numerous times, cutting through split tunnels and inner rooms before returning to the same corridors.

The air was moist and cool. There were signs of deterioration. Lluava wrinkled her nose. The atmosphere was disheartening, draining, and the gloom made her want to leave as soon as she could.

Yamir had been held here for almost two days. Why had she not tried to help him earlier? Was she so self-involved? What had happened to her compassion? What was she turning into? Would she wake up one day as some heartless thing? Or maybe one who could not see beyond her own desires? Apex's words stung her more sharply than a hornet. She must not waste more time on Selene; she needed to focus on her friends and the war. But could she let Varren go?

Somewhere in the bowels of this horrid monstrosity, Lluava heard voices drifting through the darkness. Holding up the torch she had been given, she and the burgundy-haired guard turned a final corner. Lluava saw Rosalyn standing in front of Yamir's cell. The light from Rosalyn's torch cast an eerie yellow hue on her pale skin. Another guard stood nearby.

The guard accompanying Lluava said, "We will return shortly to take you back up." Both guards left. They were not concerned that anyone might escape. It was rumored that one would starve to death wandering in the labyrinth of Tartarus before finding one's way out.

"Lluava," Yamir's parched voice croaked out. "I thought you had forgotten me."

Though he was teasing, Lluava cried, "I'm so sorry! I should have come to see you immediately."

She ran up to the bars and gripped them tightly. Yamir looked tired but not hurt, at least not physically.

"Well, you're here now. That's what matters."

His words may have been true, but her guilt remained.

"What's the word from above?"

"You won't believe what's been happening!" Lluava quickly told them about Selene's power to manipulate men, about Luka's refusal to stand against his sister, about her mistrust of Hyrax. She told them about her research with Apex and the strange symbols that appeared when the gods' weapons touched. She did leave out the huntsman's confession of love. Finally, she expressed her concern about Varren. "He is under Selene's influence. If I can find a way to break that, then he will certainly return to his senses and free you, Yamir."

"To the seven hells with him!" cursed Yamir. "He threw me in here to die. He has ordered the same treatment for my family, for the clans."

"But it wasn't him," argued Lluava. "This is Selene's doing; I'm certain of it. If I can remove Varren from her influence, her power over him will crumble." Turning to Rosalyn, Lluava implored, "You have to help me."

"What proof do you have that this hypothesis of yours will work?" questioned Rosalyn. "If Selene can control others, are you certain this power, as you call it, can be undone? Have you considered that Varren might be permanently under her control?"

Why were her friends so doubtful? If there was a chance to undo this, why weren't they willing to take it? Lluava scowled. Once again, she was focusing on the wrong end of the issue.

"If Varren stays under Selene's power, Cronus and all of Elysia are left vulnerable. Whether you like Varren or not, without him we have no leader to help us fight the enemy."

Rosalyn countered, "Selene never lets Varren out of her sight for long. How do you expect to get him away from her? If she is as strong as Luka says, then it might be dangerous to oppose her. At least, right now."

"Varren threw me in here. He does not deserve my help," snapped Yamir.

"It's not him," Lluava tried to explain. "Selene was behind your imprisonment." Turning to her other friend, Lluava implored, "Rosalyn, please. Talos is fighting the enemy, doing what Varren should be doing. If Varren—"

"I will not put Talos in harm's way. I want to see my husband again."

Lluava observed her friend's pale form and realized that she was frightened. Rosalyn feared for Talos's safety. Did she think that Selene or someone else might harm him? Was that out of the question? Yamir was no better. His rage at his current predicament was festering in the cell along with him. Until he was released, he would not agree to any plan to support the king. Yet the war was approaching. Something had to be done.

***

That evening, Lluava ventured into the Burnt Wing of the castle. Pushing open the unlocked door, she stepped into the large inner foyer.

"Hello?"

There was no reply. Was the place now abandoned?

Moving toward the inner room, Lluava passed the entrance to the spiral staircase. Scorch marks, untouched over the years, still adorned the archway. The furniture and paintings were covered in the same dusty drop cloths that Lluava remembered, although the painting she had once reviled was now shrouded.

"Hello?" she called out once more. "I know you're in here. The Obsidian Guard protects this place. Come out! Holly, are you here?"

Silence.

Had Varren terminated the guards' assignment once he was crowned? Where else could she find the Shadow called Holly, one of the elite and rarely seen Obsidian Guards?

"I need a word. This pertains to the well-being of the king."

Nothing moved in the gloom. This castle has too many dark areas, thought Lluava sullenly. Better for the Shadows to hide in, harder for her to find the one for whom she searched.

Moving to the archway, Lluava caught sight of the grooves in the stone left by the flying suns that had been aimed at her the last time she had entered this room. Was it possible that some of the Guard might not know who she was? What if he or she did not take kindly to her intrusion?

As she ran her fingers over the divots, a familiar voice echoed through the room. "Leave!"

"I need to talk with you!" Lluava said. "Varren's life might be in danger."

From the corner of her eye, a shadow emerged from the gloom. The figure was dressed entirely in tight black material that exposed only green eyes a shade darker than Lluava's. In the figure's hands were metallic, radiating blades. The fact that the Obsidian Guard could move so silently despite Lluava's hypersensitive hearing caused the hairs on the back of her neck to stand on end.

"Holly," Lluava acknowledged. Though shorter than Lluava, Holly was one of the most intimidating presences Lluava had ever met, including the Raiders.

"What is this threat?"

"It is his betrothed," explained Lluava. "Selene is manipulating the king. She is forcing him to do her will, by what means I know not," she lied. "She is using him like a puppet. With her around, Varren cannot be truly himself. You must know how he has been wasting away. He is not himself. Because the Obsidian Guard was formed to protect the king, I wanted you to know."

"Your source?" questioned Holly. There was neither skepticism nor belief in the tone of her voice.

"Selene's brother, Luka. But he will not betray his kin."

Holly's eyes seemed thoughtful above the black material masking her face. Lluava asked, "What will you do?"

"See what proof I can find."

Lluava knew that the members of the Obsidian Guard would not take lightly any possible threat to the king. Certainly, Holly and the others must have realized that something was wrong with Varren. Now that they were pointed in the right direction, some form of action might be taken. But was there enough time?

As Holly stepped back into the room's shadows, she asked, "The braces?"

"They helped me when I needed them. My shoulder is better now." Lluava left out the longer explanation. This was not the time, nor was Holly the person, to be detained by such a trivial matter.

"Good. Now leave." Before Lluava could thank her, Holly had vanished into the darkness.

Lluava returned to her room and pulled out her father's old copy of the *Karmasana* that Varren had brought with him from the North. She fumbled through page after page full of the creation myths of her people. These yellowed pages contained the tales of the gods she had heard while growing up, as well as many others. Yet she found nothing to help her. So much for turning to faith. Although the gods' weapons were mentioned a few times, there was nothing about vanishing symbols or controlling the gods' powers. Moreover, the *Karmasana* made no mention of the Incarn.

Lluava began to accept that nothing was to be gained by searching the scrolls and tomes in the rarely used library. She had to place her faith in Holly and the Obsidian Guard. Though Holly was only second-in-command, if she decided to investigate Selene, her commander, Regin, would most likely allow it. Holly believed in Lluava. Why else would she have vouched for Lluava to head north to battle, or given her the arm braces when she needed them?

But would that be enough? The Obsidian Guard was trained solely to protect the king. That was their only purpose. They were elite human warriors that few had ever seen; of those who had, many had not lived to tell of it. Since the Guard was founded, no attempt on any king's life had succeeded. But Selene wasn't attempting murder; she sought the power that came with the crown. Unfortunately, she had the means to force Varren to marry her.

Would the Guard believe Lluava's accusation? Would they deem it important enough to intervene? Was there sufficient time? Could Lluava wait patiently until the matter was settled?

She ran her fingers over the inner flap of the *Karmasana*, feeling a raised patch in its leather binding. Curious, she thought, as she bent down to inspect her heirloom more closely. She could not tell whether the raised patch was damage or had been caused by the engraving.

Lluava called for June and sent her to fetch parchment and coal. When the girl returned, Lluava made a rubbing of the mark. With June's little face peering over her shoulder, both of them watched as a symbol appeared.

"What is that thing?" June asked.

"That is an emblem."

"Of what?"

"Of the answer I have been seeking."

Chapter 29

An Unwelcome Welcoming

I'm surprised you came to me."

Lluava was more than a little surprised, herself. After all, she had refused to trust the Guardians because they had manipulated her life. However, until now she had not considered that she could do the same to them.

Hyrax reclined in a wing chair in an area he claimed was secure. "What made you change your mind?"

"My father, actually," replied Lluava. The best lies were told through half-truths. Hyrax raised an eyebrow. Pushing her father's copy of the *Karmasana* across the table to the councilman, she said, "Look at the inner flap. What do you see?"

Hyrax picked up the book and quietly inspected it. "The symbol of the Guardians is inlaid in its binding."

"My father was one of you," Lluava told him. "A Guardian sent to watch over me, to protect and guide me on my preordained path." Her words were tinged with sorrow. "I didn't want to believe it at first. I hated the idea that my own family was not truly mine. And I hated you for it as well. It was you who told me these things. You have been part of this scheme since the beginning.

"I want to trust you," Lluava said, staring at the ribbon that held the tucked-away talisman around Hyrax's neck. "But in order for me to do so, you must tell me everything you know about the Incarn—our purpose here, our abilities."

"Abilities?" Hyrax's eyes flickered.

Unwilling to reveal the extent of her knowledge about the Twins, she said, "Yes. I know that we all have, or will have, some sort of ability. I was informed of this and a few other things when I met another Incarn on my mission."

Now Hyrax was completely intrigued.

"I know that the gods' weapons have secret images that appear only when two of them touch. She even—"

"She?"

Apparently, Hyrax did not know about Yena. Now Lluava was the one with valuable information. "Yes. She even allowed me to glimpse her gift. She keeps the old ways. Her name is Yena."

"Which Incarn is she?"

"I said I *wanted* to trust you and the other Guardians, not that I *do*. I want to talk with your leader. Surely you have one."

Hyrax returned the book to Lluava. "Meet me here tomorrow night. When the moon reaches its peak. No later, no sooner."

This time, Lluava was the first to leave. For the moment, she had the upper hand. How long would that last?

When she returned to her quarters, she realized June must have tried to stay awake for her. The little girl was curled up in a nest of pillows on her chaise. Finding a blanket made of fox fur, Lluava tucked it around her. The girl breathed deeply, causing the entire blanket to rise and fall.

"Sleep well, little one," Lluava kissed her forehead. "I won't leave you again."

Taking a second wrap, this one a motley of rabbit fur, Lluava stepped out onto her balcony.

That's strange, she thought. The gates are opening.

She would never forget her first arrival at Cronus. The big gates were closed at night, no matter who approached, even the prince. A chill ran down her spine. By her side, a raven alighted on the railing. Onyx cawed once.

"Hush, you old bird," chastised Lluava. "You will wake June. Do you want that? She's the one that gives you corn."

Onyx cocked his head to the side, peered at the glowing lights on the road, cawed once more, and flew off.

"That little pest," she hissed, then stopped to note the sound of many footfalls on the cobblestones, of both men and horses. Watching warily, she realized they must be soldiers returning from war. Dashing to the door, she made sure to grab Issaura's Claws.

"Lluava, is that you?" June murmured, half asleep.

"Stay here!" Lluava ordered, and then departed.

She knew the soldiers would immediately seek audience with the king in his private meeting room. She waited outside the royal compartments.

Then she saw them. Grand Master Chief Domar, one of the highest-ranking generals remaining in the kingdom and her old swordsmanship instructor; Lieutenant Vidrick Bern, whose red hair was now splattered with darker hues; and her longtime companions, Talos and his partner, Byron. They were all exhausted, tattered, and bloodstained, yet none had sustained any severe wounds save for a nasty-looking gash above Domar's left eyebrow.

They said nothing when they saw Lluava. They didn't have to. The entire story was written on their faces. As they stood waiting for the steward to notify the king, Lluava stepped forward and hugged both Talos and Byron. Talos's dusty blond hair was almost long enough to shield his darkly circled eyes. Byron had shaved his own hair down to the scalp.

The door opened, and everyone filed inside. Varren remained seated on his throne as the others claimed chairs around the sides of the room.

"Your Majesty," began Domar, not even waiting for the hurriedly awakened High Council to assemble. "We have lost more territory. Our enemy has pushed us back to your gates. The war has come to Cronus."

After a moment of silence, Domar asked, "What is your command?"

"We defend our kingdom," stated Varren matter-of-factly.

Lluava was returning to war. Her fear of those brutish enemies resurfaced. Her apprehension only added to her other concern; even though she had opposed the royal nuptials for personal reasons, the point that she had made about the unpreparedness of the capital was true.

Lluava had never been a stickler for protocol. After hearing about the devastating loss of soldiers in the fight, she at once spoke out. "We need more men! We need to assemble all soldiers, everyone who is able to fight, here in the capital."

Varren agreed. "The struggle for Elysia will be determined by this battle at the capital. It is past time for the Elysian army to unite. This will be our last stand." Quickly, he began dictating a plan of action.

This was the Varren she knew. Whatever hold Selene had, the man Lluava loved still existed. She only hoped that Selene would accept the fact that her precious wedding would have to be postponed. Though the king might be under her control, the rest of the government, as well as the military, would focus on defending the capital.

"I am in full support of that plan," agreed Vidrick. "Yet, according to our best calculations, the Raiders, along with their Berserker Legion, will be upon us in days."

The last time she had seen the Berserker Legion, Lluava remembered sourly, they had been summoned back across the border into the Yorrick Forest. However, the Elysian forces were not responsible for their retreat. Had the enemy forces remained, Lluava and all her friends would have perished in the battle for Alcazar Castle. With the Berserkers' return, Lluava suddenly realized, once again they would be trapped by the enemy. This time, did they even have a chance?

"Get every Cronian inside the castle walls. Have a defensive line ready outside the gates." Varren spoke authoritatively. "They will be our preliminary defense, but when push comes to shove, we will call them back inside."

Lluava could see the strain on Vidrick's face. The red-headed lieutenant had lost the woman he loved in the Alcazar battle. All this was a horrid case of déjà vu. Varren also studied the young officer's expression. "Until our army is united, this is the best option. I will not lose more lives than necessary."

Byron shifted his bad leg to a more comfortable position. "Your Majesty," he said, "give me leave to oversee construction of catapults and defensive devices. Allow Talos, Yamir, and me to fortify our walls. You may remember that Yamir was in charge of this operation at Alcazar. We must expect the enemy to construct siege weapons once they arrive."

"Very well," agreed Varren. "You and Talos may begin as you wish. However, Yamir will not be assisting you."

Before the others could inquire further, Varren waved to a page who had been awakened for this meeting. The old man shuffled to the throne. Varren ordered, "Instruct Major Ojewa to return, and summon all our military strongholds in the South. Arrange for supplies to be gathered and stocked in the storerooms. I want an inventory of everything we have. I fear Cronus may be under siege for an extended time."

"Yes, Your Majesty," nodded the page before shuffling out of the room.

"Grand Master Chief Domar," Varren began, "I want you and your men to rest and recuperate. You have done our kingdom a great service."

The general nodded. "My son will continue to prepare those who have been training here." There was no further mention of Yamir. Everyone would be informed about the new policy soon enough.

As councilors and soldiers exited the room, Varren asked Lluava to stay. Even though she knew his request pertained to the war, her heart fluttered.

Moving to her side, Lluava's military partner said, "You are the one person I trust above all others. Knowing what we know and seeing what we have seen, tell me plainly: what do you think of our chances?"

After a moment, Lluava replied, "I am less concerned about the common Raiders. They are strong, but they are also slow and cumbersome. I do fear the Berserkers. Once drugged, they will be devastating. We will be cornered inside Cronus. They will surround us and attempt to break through the gates. If they breach the walls, our army, as it currently stands, will not be able to defeat them.

"The bitter truth is that while we await the rest of the army, Cronus can offer only limited resources, be it soldiers, supplies, or weapons. I do not think we have enough time to create substantial defensive devices, although by no means should we hold Byron back. If we had concentrated on reinforcing our defenses earlier—but we must now consider the present. You asked me how I thought we stood. I think both Cronus and the kingdom are at risk."

Lluava felt proud of herself for keeping her voice calm and steady. She wished she could scream in Varren's face about his stupidity; then again, he was not fully in control of himself. Although she also wanted to bring up Yamir's predicament, she knew it would be futile.

"Thank you for your council," Varren began. "You are a true...Lluava?"

"Yes?" For the first time, she could see that Varren was struggling with himself. He seemed deep in thought. His eyes glazed over. Although he was looking at Lluava, he did not appear to actually see her. His lower lip trembled slightly. Then, suddenly, everything cleared up.

"Just...thank you."

He was fighting a battle inside himself, fighting Selene's grasp. Lluava wished she could help, but this was one war in which she could not stand by his side. However, the war against the Raiders was something else entirely.

"Varren." Lluava reached out and took his hand. "Know that whatever I do, I do for you."

***

This was the right time—midnight—and this had to be the correct room, but no one was here. There were many similar areas in the castle; had she made a mistake? If so, she might have missed her chance.

Panicked, Lluava spun around to leave and collided with a man standing right behind her. In an instant, a handkerchief was shoved in her face. The odd odor reminded her of something, but what? Lluava tried to remember, but she was engulfed in blackness.

When her eyes fluttered open, Lluava jumped to her feet. Her first thought was of the Claws—where were they? She had brought them with her in case she needed them. Her second thought was, where was she? Both answers came quickly as she blinked away the last remnants of fog.

"See how quickly she moved?"

"Her reflexes are amazing."

"How did she wake so soon?"

Lluava was standing in the center of a doorless, circular room. There were no lights nor candles of any kind. The only illumination came from one tall slit of a window that allowed the moonlight to stream in like a pale dagger. Issaura's Claws were on her hands.

All around her, men in hooded robes peered at the young woman through obsidian masks. Each mask was different. Each portrayed a grimace of sorts. At first, Lluava thought the Obsidian Guard had abducted her, but then she began to think. The Shadows wore ceremonial suits of armor made from obsidian on formal occasions, but their heads and faces were covered by a helmet, not a mask. That meant these weren't Holly's men. They were the Guardians.

Lluava took note of the floor. Painted onto the stone was an enormous symbol of the Guardians, an eye with long beams emanating from it. Its immense size made it easy to count twelve such rays. At the tip of each was a rune representing one of the gods.

"Lluava," began a voice that sounded like crinkling parchment. "Incarn of Theri, we welcome you." After a wheezing breath, the voice continued, "You asked to converse. You must be ready to learn. What knowledge do you seek?"

Lluava managed to keep her voice from trembling. "I want to know more about the abilities of the Incarn."

The Guardians' speaker answered, "All will be explained to you—in time." Before Lluava could argue, the speaker continued. "Each Incarn manifests an ability that is a reflection of the god or goddess they serve. Each one is different but beneficial to the Incarn, both individually and as a unit."

Lluava had the feeling that she needed to be much more specific in her questioning. "What is my ability as Incarn of Theri?"

The old man's answer seemed to flutter around the cavernous ceiling. "You have the ability to be an extraordinary warrior."

"Is that my destiny? To do battle with the Raiders?"

"Not merely fight. Your destiny is to end the war, but that is only one part."

"What is the other?"

"To initiate the era of unending prosperity."

"And how do I do that?"

"Through the child you will bear."

So they knew about the prophecy. She had expected as much. "Is that the real reason you sent Apex and me to the Outlands? You wanted us to fulfill the prophecy. We were never meant to find other Incarn."

From behind her, a man spoke up. Lluava recognized Hyrax by his voice. "The timing of the prophecy is not up to us. You said you found a goddess's Incarn. Whose did you find?"

"Crocotta's." Observing the robed men, she pursued the topic that had brought her here. "I need to send her a message." Perhaps she could convince one of the Guardians to travel to Leucrocotta for her.

Whispers flitted like rustling leaves around the room. The rasping voice of the one who appeared to be their leader inquired, "Did she have her ability?"

"Yes."

"What is it that you wish to tell her?"

Lluava thought about her family and loved ones. There was so much at stake. It was past time for Lluava to stop focusing on herself. Elysia needed her. "That I will fulfill the promise I made to her if she fulfills her part. I will mate with Apex if she brings her army."

"This promise you made," said the elder. "Did you sign a contract?"

Rubbing her throbbing thumb, Lluava replied, "Yes."

"Then all is well."

A wizened, knobby hand emerged from the speaker's robes and motioned the others closer. One man carried a stone basin, another a pitcher. The first man set the basin on the floor, on top of Crocotta's rune. His partner poured in a thick, black liquid.

The speaker gestured to Lluava to approach. Peering into the basin, she half expected one of them to say that they could scry, yet the liquid remained totally black.

"Now what?"

"You must bleed," came the reply.

Chapter 30

The Jackal's Agreement

The hooded men backed away from her, their dark robes rustling.

"Lluava, Incarn of Theri, do not take offense. We require only several drops of blood."

Once the ancient speaker said this, Lluava became aware that her grip on Issaura's Claws had tightened and the Claws stood erect over her knuckles. Relaxing her hands, Lluava nodded to the watching Guardians. Her thumb throbbed violently.

One figure wearing a mask that portrayed droopy eyes approached and pulled out a short blade. He waited for Lluava to offer him her hand. A quick prick later, she watched as several unusually dark droplets at the tip of her purple thumb dripped into the basin. Somehow the sensation was coupled with a release of pressure. The pain was gone.

"Now what?" Lluava asked once they were finished.

"Your message has been sent. She will understand."

"Well, I don't," complained Lluava. She had expected that one of the Guardians would volunteer to deliver the message personally. How could this ceremony mean anything to anyone?

"You do not understand, but she will."

Would Yena actually know what this bloodletting meant? Would she bring the army she had promised? Their agreement had been made with a certain contingency. Would she understand that Lluava was ready? Or at least claimed that she was?

"So, what am I supposed to do? Wait for some sign? There is a war at hand. If I am to end it, how? And what about Apex?"

"Apex, as the Incarn of the God of War, would be most beneficial at your side. Since Ullr's specialty in warfare is to compel people to stand up and fight, he can help you build the army you seek. You will need every able citizen with you in this endeavor. You will need every Incarn by your side as well."

The Guardians had somehow helped her send a message to Crocotta's Incarn. But what did this mean? How long before help arrived? The length of time could vary dramatically if Yena's men were not already waiting at Elysia's border. That had been their original agreement before Lluava fled Leucrocotta.

"The time for questions is over." The speaker seemed to understand Lluava's convoluted thoughts.

"But I have so many more!" she argued.

"All will be answered in time," the old Guardian rasped out again.

Suddenly, Lluava felt dizzy. She had just enough time to throw her arms in front of her before she fell. When she tried to stand up, she noted a different floor. She was back in her room, with the morning sun peeping through the window.

She quickly dressed for the day, eager to have a word with Hyrax before the Open Council. She was more confused than ever.

Unfortunately, when June entered the room, the handmaid brought other news. "The Open Council has been canceled until the war is over." The little girl's voice was shaky. "People are talking about protecting the gates and wondering what to do if those fail. The Raiders can't enter Cronus, can they?"

Looking out the window, Lluava observed minuscule figures pacing on top of the parapets. She knelt in front of June and promised, "I will do everything in my power to keep them out."

There was a knock at the door. June opened it, allowing Talos and Byron to enter. Their expressions indicated that this gathering was for business, not pleasure.

Lluava said lightly, "I thought you were supposed to be resting."

Byron gave her a weary smile. "What could be more restful than indulging in your presence?"

"Always the flirt," laughed Lluava as she motioned for them to take a seat. June was just closing the door as Rosalyn appeared. "I did not expect a meeting this early," Lluava added.

While everyone was getting comfortable, June piped up, "Should I fetch more biscuits and jellies for everyone?"

Lluava knew her friends were not concerned with breaking their fast, but she needed privacy. "Please. That will be delightful."

When June left, Talos spoke in a voice on the brink of anger. "Varren has locked up Yamir, his priorities are not focused on the kingdom, and the war is turning dire." He looked at Lluava, hoping she had some inside knowledge about the situation. He added, "Rosalyn told me that you believe there is some magic afoot."

"Magic might not be the right word for it," admitted Lluava. "But there is something very odd happening to Varren. How much did you explain,

Rosalyn?" Before the woman could answer, Lluava continued, "Let me tell you what I know..."

Trying to be succinct, Lluava filled her friends in on the events of the previous night. Once she had finished, she waited for them to express their disbelief, but no one did. Instead, Talos asked, "What do you want us to do about Selene?"

"You believe me, then?"

"In our short time as friends, I have come to realize there is something special about you. And with this strange and sudden change in Varren, I have no other explanation for what is happening. If you say that Selene is controlling Varren's will, I believe you."

Byron and Rosalyn nodded in agreement.

"I am so glad you are my friends." Lluava bent in for a group hug. "There are several things that need to be done. First and foremost, we have to get Yamir out of Tartarus. No good will come if he stays down there."

"Nobody escapes from the dungeons," said Byron, for once quite serious.

"Nobody yet," admitted Lluava. "But there is always a first."

"What's your plan?" questioned Rosalyn, who seemed surprisingly willing to help.

Grinning wickedly, Lluava said, "I think I know someone who can assist us." Ignoring their puzzled looks, she continued, "Let me talk to him, and if all goes well, we can try to free our friend."

Moving to the next point, Lluava added, "*If all goes well*, we will have an army of Theriomorphs arriving in a few weeks. When this happens, the gates of Cronus must be opened for them. I need your help to ensure that."

Talos interjected, "The gates are shut and barred. I am not sure opening them will be so easy if Varren does not give the orders."

"They need to open, Talos."

Byron chuckled. "Miracles can happen, right? But first things first."

"Fine," sighed Lluava. They would all have to think about the problem of the doors. She moved on to her final point. "Now, while Varren is compromised, the military must work directly with the High Council regarding all things pertaining to the Raiders' attack." Lluava hated thinking that she and Themis would be forced to deal with one another, but their personal dislike was not the greatest concern. The safety of Cronus was.

"I can arrange for Grand Master Chief Domar to talk to the council," Talos suggested. "Varren has not been heard from since this morning. Do you think that has anything to do with his fiancée?"

Lluava did not like hearing this. "Let me deal with Selene."

"You're not going to try anything crazy," cautioned Talos.

"For once, no."

Talos stared at her doubtfully.

Lluava reminded him, "As you said before, you'll just have to trust me."

***

Knowing that she was expected in the training yards, Lluava needed to be extra quick. She rapped on the door three times. Clearly taking his time with his own meal, Luka opened the door in a leisurely manner.

After offering her some food, which she declined, Luka said, "As flattered as I am with all these unexpected visits, I do wonder if I am being used." His eyebrows flared upward.

"This time, you might be right," admitted Lluava honestly. "I do have several favors to ask of you."

Luka dipped the end of a piece of toast in a pot of honey and allowed the golden substance to be absorbed by the bread. "Always taking, never giving," he laughed. "What is it you want of me?"

"We both know you would never do anything to betray or hurt your sister. We also know your sister is controlling the king. The first thing I am asking of you is that you persuade Selene to loosen her hold on Varren just enough so that he can provide the best possible leadership during this time of war. If she does this, we have a better chance of surviving, which would certainly benefit her if she is that adamant about marrying a king."

"Selene doesn't care much for war," admitted Luka as he bit into his toast. He chewed the bread for a moment, swallowed, and wiped the corners of his mouth with a handkerchief. "Neither do I, but survival is one thing we both care about." He took a sip of hot tea. After blowing on the steaming surface, he said, "Very well. I will talk to my sweet sister."

Lluava was suddenly relieved. "There is one more request."

"Yes?"

"I need you to help me free a prisoner from Tartarus."

Luka's eyes flickered mischievously. "Now, that is one thing you didn't have to ask me to do." If wreaking havoc was Luka's special ability, then this would be the perfect mission for him.

Lluava asked, "What do we need to gather?"

"Let me be in charge of all that."

"When is the earliest we can set Yamir free?"

"Tonight, if you like," responded Luka confidently. He did not even seem surprised that the captive was Yamir, the person his sister's influence had sent to rot in the pits.

A mild groan made its way to Lluava's ears. Luka turned to stare out his window. "Did you hear that?" he asked as he stood for a better look. She followed him to the large glass panes. Another strange groan seemed to emanate from outside Cronus's walls. Puzzled, Luka asked, "What could that be?"

The hairs on Lluava's neck stood erect. "That is the sound of Cronus's gates under stress. We have visitors."

"Already?" questioned Luka. A tinge of fear resonated in his voice. "We do not seem prepared."

"We aren't," she agreed.

Hurrying out of the room, Luka said over his shoulder, "I will talk with Selene. Meet me outside my room tonight at dusk. Just us. We will rescue your spiky-haired friend. Now, go fight your war."

He was gone before Lluava had moved away from the window. The gates would hold for now. Yet a bad feeling was stirring deep inside of her, along with something else much darker. Seizing Issaura's Claws, she quickly ran down to the training yards.

Under the cloud-filled sky, men seemed to be moving with purpose. Most were still practicing their skills. She wondered if they knew how soon they would be tested.

"There you are, Lluava!" Talos waved her over to a small open door. "Quickly, now. We have to hurry."

"Do you know—?"

"The Raiders have arrived."

They both spoke at once.

Talos gave Lluava's arm a big squeeze before leading her to a tiny room in the back, where those of note were still gathering. Domar was there, along with his son, Daniel. Lluava had not seen the young mute since he had been her sparring partner in the fall. Ojewa, who must have returned during the night, stood crouched in the back corner, as the ceiling was too low for him. Vidrick was speaking to several other officers of varying ages and ranks.

Lluava stood next to Byron and Talos. Both blonds seemed completely in sync with each other when they moved, even when they breathed. Her military partner was nowhere to be found. By the grim looks Lluava received, others, too, were aware of their king's absence.

The door opened again, and another figure stepped through. To Lluava's great dismay, it was not Varren but Themis. All heads turned toward him.

The head councilman began, "His Majesty will not be attending this meeting. As representative of the High Council, I thank all of you for being present at this time. As many of you know, the Raiders have arrived at the capital's gates. I am not one to advise any of you how to deal with this opposition. I wanted you to know that we sent word to all other military assets before we had to seal the gates. I hope they come swiftly to give us aid. Until then, Elysia's future rests solely in your able hands."

Themis looked about the room. His graying features seemed to have aged since Lluava had last seen him. "The High Council wishes to assist you in whatever way we can; we will gladly support your decisions." Themis turned to look at Lluava, who suddenly felt her mouth go dry. The councilman went on. "In addition, we have addressed the issues regarding certain privates who have taken command without having the authority to do so."

Byron shifted his bad leg while Talos lifted his head high. Lluava knew, based on their past, that all three of them should have been punished harshly for various choices they had made while serving in the military. Was this why they had been called here? For their inescapable punishment? Yet hadn't those choices been made to save others?

Domar gave Themis a solemn nod in agreement. The head councilman said, "Step forward when I call your name. Byron Larson. Talos Cremwell. Lluava Kargen."

Now it was the general's turn to speak. Domar began while Vidrick moved to each of the three accordingly. "From this day henceforth, Byron Larson, Talos Cremwell, and Lluava Kargen will all be recognized as corporals in the Elysian army."

When Vidrick paused in front of Lluava, he pinned a ribbon on her left shoulder. Domar finished by saying, "Due to the current situation, we are unable to present you with the appropriate uniform for your rank. Instead, we are bestowing upon you these pins to indicate your new status."

Lluava looked down at the bronze pin bearing the royal emblem with the gold and moss-green striped ribbon hanging below. An officer's medal.

Themis spoke up once more. "The High Council has decided that with your personal knowledge and unusual experience in combating our enemy, you would serve us far better by taking up true commands. You are each deserving of your new rank."

Damn, thought Lluava as she looked at the head councilman and grinned. How could she wholeheartedly hate Themis now?

The rest of the meeting was turned over to Grand Master Chief Domar so that he could lay out his strategy. Once they had been dismissed, Byron followed Lluava out the door. Talos was ahead of them, engaged in a congratulatory talk with Vidrick.

Byron, limping to Lluava's side, inquired, "You said this morning that your shoulder injury had healed. How?"

"I think it was the nasty liquid the healers of Leucrocotta gave me," speculated Lluava.

"Got any more?"

"Oh, Byron," Lluava said, looking in sympathy at her friend. "If I had even a drop of it with me, I would give it to you." She meant every word.

Byron feigned a smile, then looked down at his bad leg. "Ah, well, people tell me women like a battle scar."

Before she could try to console the young man, Domar called to her. "Corporal Kargen, I need you to come with me, please."

"I think it will take me a while to remember my own rank," said Lluava with a mild laugh.

Byron waved her off. "Catch you later."

Domar was waiting for her in the entry to the training yard.

"What do you need of me, Grand Master Chief?"

He gave her a sidelong glance. "Have you forgotten that I told you just to call me Domar?"

"No, sir."

"Follow me then, Corporal. There is an emissary awaiting outside the walls. I suspect you might know him. I want you present when we converse."

As they were handed horses for their ride through the city, Lluava could not hide her distaste. She knew whom he meant: Ambassador Hadrian Alcove, the man she once thought led the Raiders' army. Now, she knew otherwise.

They dismounted at the city's main gate and climbed an inner staircase leading to the parapets. Lluava positioned herself next to the general. Beyond the city walls, she could see buildings and homes burning. In the distance, silhouettes of strange forms seemed to infiltrate the trees and clearings. More and more figures approached down the cobblestone road. She did not need her keen eyesight to recognize the burly men wrapped in layers of furs. Many wore their horned helmets. The Raiders were getting into position and preparing to attack, while staying well out of range of the archers on the walls.

Below them, several lizard-headed battering rams had been cast aside. Dead Raiders lay where they had fallen. So many arrows had found their targets that the bodies appeared to be covered in feathers from the fletching. One unfortunate victim had been rolled over by those enormous logs. A solitary man stood at the base of the gates.

This figure, though of average height and build, donned a wolf-skin cloak with a snarling canid head on each shoulder. He was not wearing the helmet that Lluava remembered, nor was his falcon in sight. The two patches of white hair over his ears glinted in the sunlight. The rest of his hair and beard, once well groomed, looked surprisingly disheveled.

As Lluava looked at Ambassador Alcove, she wondered if he were ill. Good, she thought. If he became too sick, he could no longer give orders to his men. Regardless, Alcove stood erect and began to speak. His voice sounded far stronger than he looked.

"I am Hadrian Alcove, Ambassador of Einherjar, true Emperor of Niflhel, Nemorosus, Mictla, Aaru, and the territory Elysia. I have come to treat with the one you call your king." Alcove looked at each of those staring down at him. Though thick of accent, he spoke clearly enough. "Where I am from, it is customary to invite one inside the premises to discuss matters of such importance."

"I am Grand Master Chief General Domar, current commander of the Elysian army stationed here at Cronus. When we have dealt with you in the past, your courtesies have been lacking. If you wish to discuss something, you may speak here, as we are now."

Alcove was clearly unmoved. "I wish to talk with your self-proclaimed king."

Not waiting to be invited into the conversation, Lluava shouted down, "Ambassador Alcove, you and I have had the pleasure of meeting on several occasions. Allow me to vouch for General Domar. He will listen to what you have to say with an impartial ear."

Alcove seemed to smile at her without actually doing so. "Ah. The shape-changer known as Theri. It pleases me that you are doing so well. I knew we would meet again. But I must insist on parleying with the ruler of this land. I will converse only with him."

Domar spoke up again. "King Varren cannot—"

"—apologize enough for making you wait." Striding along the parapet, Varren approached the others wearing his royal garb, his crown glinting in the sun. Luka had kept his word. For that, Lluava was extremely grateful. Her military partner continued, "Looking presentable was no reason to postpone our meeting. What have you come to say to me?"

For the first time that Lluava could remember, Alcove appeared surprised. Clearly, he had assumed he would be speaking with a frail old man, not the young one who had slipped through his fingers on several occasions.

"So, the prince has become the king," mused the ambassador. "May you be wiser than your predecessor." Brushing off some soot from his doublet, Alcove finally made his point. "As you know, we have taken the North, slain countless Elysians, and beaten back your forces again and again. We are now setting up camp outside the very walls of your capital. I have come to let you know that if you forswear your rule, son of Mandrun the Betrayer, and open these gates, we will permit those persons who bend a knee to keep their lives."

"I would be forfeiting my life, then?"

"You would be saving your people."

The greater good. The phrase was one that Varren had always embraced, but would he consider this? For a moment, his features appeared carved out of granite. Then he asked, "And whom do you recognize as people? Elysians? Or just humans?"

"Do not underestimate this charitable offer," stated Alcove.

"I will not condemn half my people to slaughter."

"I do not think you understand your current predicament. We have rations enough to wait without for as long as we need. We have the ability to pillage for more as well. You can be slowly starved out of these walls. Yet not everyone is as patient as I am."

What a load of horseshit, Lluava thought sourly, knowing the death and devastation Alcove left in his shadow.

The ambassador continued after a moment of self-reflection. "If you do not accede to this agreement, the Berserker Legion will tear down every stone from your walls and desecrate everything you hold dear."

"They do not scare us," Lluava bluffed.

"Then you are as foolish as you are brave," noted Alcove. "For with their commander now present, they scare *me*. He is the figure who haunts dreams."

Chapter 31

The City Below

H e haunts mine, too," said Lluava.

"If this person is so terrifying, why doesn't he come and talk to us himself?" questioned Varren.

"Trust me. That is the last thing you would wish." Alcove's words chilled Lluava's bones like ice in the wind.

"Your edict might say that we must make our contracts with you, Ambassador," Varren began assertively, "but I do not have to agree to your terms. I will not sacrifice the lives of my people, human or Theriomorph."

"Know this, Son of Mandrun the Betrayer: you have a fortnight to open your doors before the Berserkers destroy your city."

"Let them try." Varren's jaw tensed with the severity of his own words as well as their implications.

Ignoring the king's last remark, Alcove lifted his arm. Several of the Elysian archers raised their bows, but General Domar waved them off.

"To make sure you understand that time is precious, as well as to demonstrate how compassionate *you* really are," said Alcove looking directly at Varren, "I will have one wolf slain every day until you change your mind or time runs out."

What did he mean by wolves? Lluava warily scanned the panorama. There were three figures just beyond a human's normal range of sight, though Lluava could make them out clearly enough. Two Raiders held a tied and gagged prisoner, whom they forced to his knees.

"Someone hand me a spyglass," ordered Varren.

Not needing one herself, Lluava described what was happening. "The Raiders—they have someone. He looks like...like...one of Derrick's men!"

Lluava thought Derrick and his troop of wolf Theriomorphs had perished in the battle for Castle Alcazar. She was wrong.

Alcove swung his arm down. In that moment, one Raider took off the prisoner's head with a war axe. Lluava cried out, as did several people around her. Varren remained solemn.

"One wolf each day," Alcove reiterated. "A day is a precious thing." The ambassador departed for his camp down the road.

"Will you let him survive?" Lluava questioned harshly.

Varren turned to her, his features revealing his inner torment. "I must. If I had him killed now, who knows what would happen to the rest of his prisoners?"

"How do we know he has more?" asked General Domar earnestly. "To your best knowledge, do they keep many prisoners?"

"They have sometimes done so in the past," admitted Lluava. "But, Varren, he is the *Leader*."

"If we believe what he says, he never truly was," countered her partner.

Suddenly afraid, Lluava asked, "Do you think Derrick's alive?" She remembered her dark-skinned companion. Although she had not always agreed with his decisions, she knew that he truly believed in the man Varren would become and wanted the best for Elysia.

"If he is alive," commented General Domar sullenly, "he is as good as dead. We cannot risk the lives of the Cronians for a handful of soldiers. These are the harsh realities of rule, Your Majesty."

"I need time to think about all of this," admitted Varren. "Lluava, will you come with me?"

"Of course," she said. She would always follow him, no matter what.

They mounted their horses and rode through the labyrinth of the city.

After a time, Varren said, "For the first time in a long while, I feel as if I am thinking with a sort of clarity, yet everything seems so convoluted."

Lluava listened to his voice as it intermingled with the clack of their steeds' hooves and the background shouts of brave merchants still hawking their wares. Varren had once admitted to her that his greatest fear was making a decision that would cost others' lives. Who would have guessed it would come to this?

"Now that I wear the crown, I have all the power and responsibility that come with it." Varren took off the polished headpiece and inspected it. "I cannot grant Alcove's request. The gates must stay closed at all costs."

For Lluava, hearing these words made the reality of their plight all the more grievous. Varren continued, "I cannot send out a rescue party. If they were discovered and found to be following my orders, I fear the result for Cronus and the rest of my people. Any knowledge I had of such an attempt would have similar devastating results, even if I did not give the orders."

Reaching over, Varren grabbed hold of Lluava's arm. "Do you understand me? I *cannot* know about any rescue operation, for I must have true deniability in case of discovery."

Lluava realized what Varren was telling her. "I understand," she replied.

"Good," noted her partner. "I want you by my side when this war ends."

Now, Lluava would have to enact two rescue missions without Varren's "knowledge." She would try her hardest to retrieve Derrick and the rest of his men, but first she needed to free Yamir. Tonight could not come soon enough.

***

Luka had warned her that they must do this alone. Even in the depths of Tartarus, too many people would draw unwanted attention. They needed to get in and out under the cover of darkness; no alarms must be sounded, no guards alerted. With Varren's edict still in place, Yamir was considered an enemy of Elysia, and anyone attempting to release him would be viewed similarly.

"My lord father would just love this," Luka said wickedly as he handed Lluava a braided belt and a pouch full of marbles. "Freeing someone who would threaten the king. Just the thought would make his stomach knot."

"Yamir would never harm Varren," Lluava asserted. "He is a good friend."

"Well, if good friends get tossed into the pit, I never want to be Varren's good friend. Being the dull brother-in-law is just fine by me."

Despite knowing that Luka was only making light of the situation, Lluava still wanted to defend Yamir. This was all Selene's doing, anyway, but saying that to Luka might make him change his mind. Lluava needed his help, so she bit her tongue.

"What else do we need?" she asked, after Luka had strapped on a gem-inlaid scabbard that sheathed a slingshot instead of a dagger.

"To get moving," he said with a smile. "Let's go; it will be dark soon."

As she followed the young man, Lluava inquired, "What do you want to do about the guards at the front entrance? What should our story be?"

"The guards are performing a just service," said Luka. "We should not even bother them. Let them continue as they are."

Lluava raised a dubious eyebrow, knowing that her friend was not about to give her a straight answer. He seemed to enjoy keeping her puzzled. If Luka weren't helping her, she would think all this a nuisance. Her sense of humor clearly did not match his.

Instead of making their way to the entrance to Tartarus, Luka headed off to another part of the castle, far from what Lluava had assumed would be their entry point.

"Did you know Cronus was built upon the ruins of another city?" he asked.

"No," admitted Lluava. The sudden history lesson was unexpected.

"King Merek chose this location for his future stronghold because it was originally the first, and one of the greatest, Theriomorph cities conquered in the Landon Wars. He wanted to devastate the Theriomorph people in a way that was more than physical. What could be better than building his future capital on top of one of the largest Theriomorph cities? Of course, he never saw the work to completion. It was his son, Hammond, who first lived in the completed castle."

"This sounds vaguely familiar," Lluava said, "though I don't understand why it is not better known."

"Think about it," said Luka as he opened a door to an unused chamber. "After King Thor decreed that Theriomorphs and humans should be viewed as equals, he may have thought that schooling future generations about the cruelty of human conquerors might work against unifying the two races."

"Yeah. I can see that. Still, the truth should not be forgotten," asserted Lluava. "Humans always seem to find ways to gloss over their historical indiscretions."

She watched Luka walk around the perimeter of the large room. One of Enya's remodeling projects, it reeked of new paint. The widowed queen did not have much to occupy her time. On the other hand, had she ever done anything of importance before Thor's death?

"Rhadamanthus, the original city, was supposedly far vaster than Cronus. Most of the buildings were constructed of wood and clay. They were easily torn down and forgotten." Luka moved to the old fireplace, large enough that several people could stand inside it. "But the temple and a few other buildings were of stronger stuff. King Merek converted the Theriomorph temple into the human's church. Everything else was torn down; the stones became cornerstones of this castle."

Luka felt the walls of the fireplace the way the blind use their hands to see. "Interestingly enough, Merek left the underground intact. This underground's network of tunnels and cavernous spaces became Tartarus. Yet this subterranean maze extends far beyond Tartarus itself. It seemed that the humans gave up trying to explore it all and sealed up the areas they decided not to use."

"How do you know all this?" she asked.

"I read," replied Luka as he shoved a brick. "A lot."

There was a clanking sound. Suddenly the hearth seemed to tip downward. Luka waved Lluava over just as the stone slide locked into place. Whispering into her ear, he added, "Some of the seals are more permanent than others."

Luka led the way and carefully slid down into the tunnel. Lluava followed. When her feet touched the flat surface, the cranking noise began again and the trapdoor rose.

"The door!" she gasped, but Luka held her back.

"That was me," he said soothingly. "We're fine."

Once the light from above had disappeared, Lluava turned and realized her eyes were adjusting to the dark space. "I can see!" she exclaimed. "How? Even Theriomorphs can't see in total blackness."

Beside her, Luka smirked. In the gloom, his face took on a wicked look. "See the moss that coats the walls and ceiling? Whatever it is, it emits a low glow. It's luminescent. Not enough for humans to see by without their torches and lanterns, but for Theriomorphs, the way is lit."

"That's amazing," said Lluava as she touched the moss. It felt slimy. The goo made her fingertips glow briefly.

"Come on." Luka waved at her. "We need to get your friend out of here while it is still night."

Lluava followed Luka's lead as they climbed down stairwells, crossed bridges, and crept through narrow corridors. Sometimes Luka would pause and retrace his steps for a moment; at other times he told Lluava exactly where to step. Eventually, he stopped altogether and looked around a large inner room with at least a dozen doorways.

Sighing, Luka pulled out a crinkled parchment from his pocket. Lluava stood close enough to see what looked like a hodgepodge of scribbles with several scattered notes.

"Is that a map?" she asked, for the paper was clearly hand drawn.

"Of a sort." Taking a moment more to look over the parchment, he added, "Ah. This way." He steered Lluava to the left.

"How have you been able to explore so much? How did you discover it?"

As they made a sharp right turn followed by a left, her friend explained, "After we arrived at court, Selene had a short tryst with a young dungeon guard. To show off to her, he would sometimes lead her through Tartarus. Since Selene is a lady, I had to be her escort and thus accompanied them. That is, until they needed their privacy; then I would wander about alone. I began mapping the place for my own amusement."

The ceiling became significantly lower, and Luka cautioned Lluava to be careful. "I discovered that one of the sealed passageways that leads to the rest of the underground had collapsed. Humans are horrible builders, it seems. Anyway, my snooping resulted in finding that extremely useful opening into the castle. Since then, I occasionally spend my evenings wandering the corridors. They do seem to go on for eternity."

"Does Selene know about this?" questioned Lluava. Her neck was beginning to cramp at its odd angle.

"If she does, she doesn't seem interested. She has always had other sources of amusement."

"And what of the guard? What became of him?"

"He disappeared."

Had Selene had anything to do with his disappearance? Lluava wondered. If so, with how many others?

Slowing down, Luka warned, "Be careful. A narrow ledge is ahead."

Luka was not kidding. A few steps farther, the floor dropped away, leaving a huge, oblong hole the size of Lluava's quarters. Even with the subtle glow from the moss, Lluava could not see how deep it was.

Removing his belt, Luka asked Lluava to do the same. When he unbraided the two belts, a respectable length of thin rope lay coiled at his feet. Tying the two cords together, he affixed one end to a stone loop carved into the wall. He dropped the other end over the side of the pit.

"We need to climb down—for a good while. There, we will find another opening like this one. I'll go first," said Luka as he began his descent.

Lluava watched warily as her companion was swallowed up by the darkness.

Taking a breath, the young woman followed. She had trained on climbing ropes in the camps. Unfortunately, this cord was more frayed, and its strands cut into her hands. Slowly inching downward, she tried to guess how far they had gone.

Knowing that she should be getting close, Lluava looked down. No bottom was in sight, and she suddenly felt dizzy. Gripping the rope tighter, she continued her descent and finally arrived at a platform, where Luka waited.

"That wasn't so bad, was it?" piped Luka as he waved her forward. They resumed their journey.

"What the heck kind of rope is that?"

"Endun comes in many forms."

"And you discovered all this on your own?" Lluava could not decide whether she was doubtful or awestruck.

Luka grinned. After checking his map several more times, he finally said, "We are almost there. Being quiet from now on is essential."

Turning the corner, they crawled through a hole in a crumbling wall and entered one of the corridors, which contained rows of cells. Lluava knew they were close. Soon they would reach Yamir.

Then they heard the voices. Rosalyn must be visiting their friend again.

Lluava grimaced in annoyance. Rosalyn meant well, but if she or her escorting guard caught sight of either of them, their mission would be a failure.

"Don't give up." someone said.

Horseshit, thought Lluava, Talos is there, too. Go away! Get lost!

A few minutes later, the flicker of lit torches approached. Luka pulled Lluava into an open cell and shut the door far enough for it to look secure. Then, pressing their bodies against each other near the back, they watched as Talos, Rosalyn, and Byron walked past, escorted by a pair of royal guards.

Lluava could hear Luka's heart racing. He smelled of clean linens and something canine that was not unappealing. Luka looked down at her. His eyes seemed to ask the question, Ready? She nodded, and the pair slipped out of the cell and down the hall.

"Yamir," Lluava whispered as she peered into the cell. The coppery-skinned youth moved forward.

"Lluava! What are you doing here?" he asked, as Luka and Lluava tried to shush him.

While Luka unpinned a decorative brooch he wore, Lluava explained, "We are getting you out of here."

"'Bout time," Yamir whispered wearily. "The way Talos and the others were acting, I wasn't sure you would."

"They don't know," Lluava told him. She eyed Luka as he began to work the lock with the pin of his brooch. "Small parties get better results. You know that."

There was a click, and the door edged open.

"That was fast," noted Yamir as he slid out and closed the gate behind him.

"It's a talent," acknowledged Luka as he refastened his brooch. "Shall we?"

They had been retracing their steps for a while when Yamir asked, "Are we still in the dungeons?"

"No," explained Lluava eagerly. "We are in part of the ancient Theriomorph city that Cronus was built upon. This part is not used by anyone anymore. And look at the moss!" She pointed it out. "It glows just enough for us to see by."

"A forgotten city buried by time." Excitement returned to Yamir's eyes. "But...where is Luka?"

Looking around, Lluava realized they had somehow lost their subterranean guide. "Luka?" she called out. "Luka, where are you?"

Hurrying forward, the pair saw that the corridor branched. Sniffing the air, Lluava said, "I think he went this way."

There was a bridge up ahead. She had crossed several bridges on their journey; surely this was one of them. They moved forward.

"I don't smell Luka anymore," commented Yamir when they were a third of the way across the bridge.

Pausing, Lluava realized he was right. Had the scent already dissipated, or had she gone the wrong way?

"Lluava," Yamir said, "I think we should head back now." He pointed above them, where several rigged stone blocks hung. "Are those booby traps?"

Glancing up, she said, "I think you're right." As she stepped back, there was a clinking sound.

"Run!"

The stone blocks plummeted.

Chapter 32

Freedom Falling

There was a thunderous boom.

The once-solid ground underneath their feet began to fragment rapidly, which caused both Yamir and Lluava to stumble as they ran. Yamir was ahead of her. He leaped back into the dim tunnel and skidded down the corridor.

Lluava was almost there when the bridge collapsed. In a split second, she remembered last summer, when a suspension bridge had broken; she had survived by transforming and digging her claws into the wooden planks. But there was no wood here, just tumbling stone and crumbling debris.

Reaching up, Lluava groped for some source of salvation. Abruptly, her body jerked into place, though not by her own accord. Luka had grabbed her wrist. He was not strong enough to hoist her up, but he did not let go. Behind him, Yamir, his forehead bleeding, came to assist. The two young men pulled Lluava up and hauled her into the tunnel.

"That was," breathed out Luka, "intense."

"That shouldn't have happened," griped Yamir as he glared at Luka. "Where were you?"

"Where was I?" repeated Luka. "Where were *you*? I turned around, and you both had vanished."

"That was my fault," admitted Lluava. Her heart still raced from coming so close to a seemingly endless drop.

"Regardless," Luka said, looking disheartened, "we have to stick together now more than ever if we want to get out of here."

"What do you mean?" Lluava wanted to know.

"You and I must put our minds together and retrace our original steps."

"What about the map?"

Luka turned and nodded at the cavernous opening. "I dropped it when I reached for you."

Carefully peering over the side, Lluava knew the map was forever lost. "We can do this," she said as she tried to convince herself. "We can."

"I do hope you're right," acknowledged Luka. "I don't want to live the rest of my life down here. I'm too good-looking to be kept in the dark." Yamir rolled his eyes while Luka stood up and brushed himself off. "Let's get us out of here."

Heading back down the tunnel, Luka steered them on what they all hoped was the right path. Trying her best to remember, Lluava had to place her trust in Luka's decisions. For the most part, they seemed fine, although after a while even Luka appeared to be questioning himself.

Could they be lost in these tunnels forever? They could wander around in hope of stumbling upon a way out, but for how long? They could starve or die of thirst before then. And what about the booby traps? Lluava asked Luka what he knew about them.

"I don't know why they rigged so many," he admitted. "There is a nice assortment of those nasty buggers scattered about."

"So, you did know about them! Why didn't you tell us?" Lluava was none too happy.

"I didn't think it was necessary. If we had been able to follow my map, all would have been fine." Luka didn't appear angry, although a tinge of fear had crept into his voice. What other dreadful devices were hiding in the dark?

As they continued down the corridor, Lluava heard Luka sigh in relief. Up ahead was the opening with the rope. He turned to them and asked, "Ready to climb?"

Although not a trained climber, Luka scaled the cliff face rather easily. Yamir followed, and Lluava was last. "We have to hurry," said Luka as he quickly rewound the rope. "Sunrise cannot be too far away."

Had they been down there all night? Lluava was filled with nervous energy from her near-death incident and felt sprightly as ever. Moving faster now, Luka seemed more certain of which way to go.

Suddenly he stopped. They were in a tunnel that had no others intersecting it. In the dull glow of the moss, the corridor seemed to stretch endlessly in both directions.

"Nobody move," Luka ordered as he scanned the entire area.

Yamir asked, "Did you hear something?"

"No," snarled Luka. "Just don't move."

"What are you looking for?" Lluava asked impatiently.

"Markers," answered Luka. "Hand me my marbles."

Lluava passed the corded pouch forward, and Luka pulled a marble out. "There are traps here; I remember. What I can't be certain of is the particular pattern. Everyone step exactly where I do."

Slowly they moved forward. Lluava tried to detect whatever sign Luka was looking for, but all the stone tiles and rock slabs appeared the same.

Luka froze again. His skin seemed to grow almost as pale as Rosalyn's. Then a creaking and groaning began from above. Looking up, Lluava observed a strange design in the ceiling, which consisted of stone gears that had begun to rotate.

"Go! Go!" shouted Luka as he waved them past him. "Get to the end of the hall!"

Yamir's voice cracked as he ran. "The walls are moving in!"

He was right; both walls were pressing together. The end of this tunnel was too far away to reach in time. Realizing that it was a lost cause, Lluava glanced back and saw that Luka had stopped to arm his slingshot.

"What are you doing?" she called to him, slowing.

Taking aim, Luka let loose a marble. It flew into a crevice of the ceiling. The gears groaned to a halt. Luka ran after his friends. "Keep moving!" he cried. "It won't hold long."

There was a crackling sound. The gears shifted slightly, which caused the walls to lurch. When the second crunch came, the walls and gears were back in motion. With only seconds to spare, they squeezed out of the death trap.

Panting, Yamir asked, "How did you know that would work?"

From the look on Luka's face, it was clear he hadn't.

Fortunately, the rest of the journey was far smoother. At the entrance to the tunnels, Luka pulled the lever, and the slide dropped down.

Once all three were inside the castle, Luka said, "Yamir can stay in my room for now, but he must leave by the end of the day. They will be searching for him, but I doubt they will check my rooms first."

"Thanks, Luka," Lluava said, "but I need to get Yamir far away from here."

"Then, my friend," responded Luka, "I think our adventure is over. I myself will be turning in for some much-needed beauty rest."

"We are forever grateful," admitted Lluava as she gave Luka a large hug. Returning her squeeze, he whispered in her ear, "What are fellow Incarns for?"

***

Having instructed June to take the day off, Lluava smuggled Yamir into her quarters. She took only a few minutes to make sure he was comfortable before heading to the training yard.

Entering the yard, she saw Vidrick approaching the castle, his face downcast. She did not have to ask what was wrong. The young, red-headed lieutenant said, "They beheaded a second one."

"Was it—"

"No. It wasn't Derrick. General Domar and his men are on watch now."

Allowing the weary commander to slip past, Lluava knew it was time to act. Her own exhaustion would have to wait. Why should she sleep when,

216

with each passing hour, another Elysian soldier was brought closer to death?

Lluava found Talos and Byron enjoying their morning meal. "You want to do something completely illegal? Something that could cost our lives and tarnish our names for generations to come if we get caught?"

"Sounds like just what we've been waiting for," retorted Byron, still chewing a biscuit.

"We would be disobeying the king's order," admitted Lluava. She wanted to be completely honest with them.

"Let me get my sword." Talos stood up, as did Byron.

Lluava nodded. "Meet me in my room when you're ready."

As she headed to her room, Lluava passed Apex's quarters. She had not talked with him since his ludicrous statements in the library. Should she leave him out of this? She hesitated a moment before his door, then entered.

Apex was looking out his window at something she could not see. He waved her over. "Look at the sky. The carrion-eaters know doom is afoot."

He was right. The sky was peppered with crows, vultures, and ravens. They were waiting hopefully for the bloodshed to begin. Lluava wondered if their first meals had been some of Derrick's men. The thought was quite disturbing.

"Apex," Lluava began awkwardly. She wanted to say something about the other day, but instead said, "I am leading a small party of people outside Cronus for a rescue mission. I'm hoping to free Derrick and his men, who are currently held prisoner by the Raiders. Since we are disobeying the king's orders, we will be entirely on our own. I—"

"I'm coming." Turning to look at her, Apex explained, "I hate this place. It's cold and suffocating. I should never have come." There was a heavy silence, and Lluava's words somehow got caught in her throat. The huntsman added, "I need to be outside these walls."

"Are we okay?" Lluava had to ask. Without Varren at her side, she needed someone who could watch her back. The only one as good as her partner was Apex.

"I will help you save the wolf."

Lluava was relieved. She knew she could rely on Apex if the plan went awry. But she also knew something had changed between them, and this made her sad.

Apex accompanied her to her room, where Byron and Talos were already waiting. They looked only mildly surprised at the huntsman's presence.

Once inside, Lluava said, "You can come out now."

Yamir appeared from the bedroom, to the astonishment of everyone else.

"How did you do it?" Talos asked Lluava. "We would have helped you."

Byron asked, "*When* did you do it? We just saw him last night."

"I know," she said. "You almost saw me hiding down there."

"You couldn't have freed him alone," noted Apex, who was scrutinizing Yamir's head wound with his harsh gaze. "Who helped you, if it was none of us? Surely not the king."

"No," admitted Lluava sullenly. Before Yamir could answer, the young woman said, "The person who helped will remain anonymous, for his own safety."

"Fair enough," said Talos as he brushed his golden locks away from his eyes. "What now?"

"Now we have to figure out how to leave Cronus unnoticed," she stated. From the way the others looked at her, they seemed to expect that she had some sort of plan. "This is where you come in. I don't know how to get past the walls. Where is Rosalyn?"

Lluava had assumed that Talos would bring her.

Talos explained, "She was not feeling well this morning. She told me that whatever we planned to do, she would support us, though she will not risk hurting our chances with her sudden ailment."

"So, how should we deal with the main gates?" questioned Byron once his partner finished.

Lluava shook her head. As everyone quieted, Apex asked, "Why are they called the 'main gates'? That implies there are others."

"True," acknowledged Talos. Raised by a noble Theriomorph family, he had spent time at court and knew the city better than any of them. "Other entry points were originally constructed. They were more like regular doors than gates. Their only purpose was to allow supplies to enter from all four sides while the castle was being built. They were sealed afterward. Cronus was designed to be a fortress, able to withstand any attack."

"Let's hope that holds true," noted Byron. "But we still need a secondary way out."

"What of the foundation?" questioned Yamir as he prepped his pouch of porcupine quills he used as weapons. He certainly did not waste his time. "Could we dig out?"

"From what I was told, the wall's structures go deep into the earth and thus hinder that approach," Talos responded.

Apex was gazing out Lluava's window overlooking the city. "How are supplies from the port city of Pern brought in?" he asked. "Certainly the northern ports use the Okeanos River to send shipments down to Cronus and back. Are you telling me these shipments are hauled from the docks all the way around to the main gates of Cronus?"

"No," admitted Talos. "They use a lift that takes the supplies up and over the wall and deposits them inside Cronus. That is the reason many markets are located on the eastern side of the city. If you are thinking about using those contraptions, consider that there are guards constantly patrolling the entire wall. We will be at great risk using those lifts."

"Do we have another choice?" questioned Yamir.

"No," admitted Byron.

"We should go now," stated Talos decisively. "At night, in the dark, the guards will be on high alert for any strange movement. With the sun high in the sky, illuminating everything, they will be looking beyond the walls. Also, they will not expect anyone to want to leave the city. We should do it today."

"Stay with Rosalyn," Lluava ordered him. "You've just returned to her. The patrols will certainly pull up the lift, and if we can't make it back, we might be forced to flee south."

Talos looked forlorn. "I know, but Derrick and his men have helped us in the past. I doubt that any of us would be here without them. We owe it to him to try to save them."

Byron's stern look told Lluava that he, too, agreed with his partner.

After double-checking that everyone had brought their weapons, Lluava said, "Let's go, then."

The trickiest part, getting Yamir out of the castle, proved easy enough. None of the posted guards had been on duty the day he was arrested, so they did not recognize him. The spiky-haired clansman donned some of Talos's upper-class garb, loose as it was on his thin form; removed several of his piercings, combed his hair, and passed as a young lord.

Yamir left with Byron and Talos. Apex and Lluava waited a while before heading out. Once in the city, Byron approached them and led his four followers through alleys, around buildings, and down infrequently used passageways.

To Lluava, Byron looked far more comfortable in this role as guide than when he had tried to track the Raiders through the Yorrick Forest. Without Apex's aid, they would have been lost. Now, Byron was in control, and it suited him. This was good news to Lluava.

Lead the way, she thought. Once they had escaped from Cronus, they would hopefully rescue some of their fellow comrades, and Yamir would be free to flee.

The buildings around them cast long shadows in the morning's light, making the chill in the air seem far worse. A shiver was rolling down Lluava's spine by the time they reached the wall. That stone guardian stood rigidly before them, cold and unyielding.

"Over here," Byron directed with a wave, as he entered one of the wall's towers. They ascended a circular staircase, its narrow stone steps worn down from the passage of generations of feet.

At the top, Lluava peered through one of the crenellations toward the snow-whitened landscape. The forest lay beyond a slight clearing and an unused roadway that was fast disappearing under a fresh snowfall. In the distance, Lluava could make out the Okeanos River.

Byron led them off to the right. The wind came in strong gusts, and Lluava hunched over to prevent herself from veering sideways.

Ahead of them stood an impressive contraption. Freight could be secured to an outer platform, which was then hoisted to a height above the castle wall, slowly swung 180 degrees, then lowered to the ground on the other side. This normally bustling market focused on lumber and mined goods. Due to the war, however, the buildings were vacant and eerily quiet.

"Who goes there?" an armed guard barked at the approaching group.

"I, Corporal Lluava Kargen, daughter to Haliden Kargen, military partner to King Varren, have come to inspect the security of the wall and all stationed soldiers." Forcing herself to look directly at the inquiring guard, Lluava hoped that he would not ask too many questions.

"I was not informed of an inspection."

"In these times, one can never have too many," she asserted. Knowing that she needed to acknowledge her comrades, she added, "I have brought with me fellow soldiers to help with my task. The more eyes, the better to spot any potential weak points."

"Very well," the guard said after pulling his eyes away from Yamir's bedraggled appearance. "Follow me. I will review our orders once more."

Lluava motioned for Talos and Byron to walk right behind their begrudging guide. She whispered into Byron's ear, "Distract him."

As they passed the lift, Lluava nodded to Yamir. He slipped behind the others and clambered onto the lift's large platform. Apex followed suit, along with Lluava.

"Get off there!" shouted their guide when he saw the trio on the lift. "That's out of commission."

Byron reached for Phin, his longsword. Lluava knew that he and Talos would do whatever was necessary to prevent the guard from taking action. They would become enemies of Elysia for disobeying the king's orders. Their new titles would be revoked. Though neither one would care, Lluava had to consider that once they left Cronus's protection, they would not be allowed back inside. Rosalyn and Talos had just been reunited a few days ago. What would this action mean for them?

Turning to Talos, she shouted, "Forgive me!" Then she pulled the lever.

The entire lift began to drop. She saw the shocked faces of her friends peering over the parapets while the guard tried to immobilize the crank.

The entire platform jolted to a standstill.

"Hold on," Lluava yelled over her shoulder. She began to slice through the rope above them.

"Stop, Lluava! We are too high!" Yamir cried out. At the same time, Apex pulled her backward.

Regardless, the rope snapped, and the platform plummeted into the blanket of snow below.

Chapter 33

Caged Beasts

Every inhalation felt like a dagger thrusting into her lungs. Flailing about to right herself in the white that surrounded her, Lluava clawed her way out of the pile of snow. As she did, she noticed shards of wood scattered about. Apex lay awkwardly off to one side, half-buried in the snowdrift.

"Apex," Lluava whispered, as harshly as she dared. Thinking, please don't be dead.

Stumbling to the huntsman on wobbly legs, she knelt at his side and felt his rigid face. He was warm to the touch. Placing her fingers on his neck, she felt a subtle pulse. "Apex, wake up."

"You're trembling," muttered the huntsman with his eyes still closed. He grunted, then pushed himself up on one elbow. "What were you thinking?"

Someone else approached. Yamir staggered over broken beams of wood and piles of snow. He was holding a two-pronged dagger loosely in one hand.

"Where did you get that?" questioned Lluava.

Yamir glanced down at the pointed object. "I removed it from the guard's person. I needed something."

Men ran about on top of the wall like bees buzzing around a hive. Why were they not sounding an alarm? Were they trying to avoid alerting the enemy?

"Head for the woods. We need to get out of sight," snapped Apex as he dug both Fangs out of the snowdrift.

Plodding ahead, Yamir grumbled, "You left Talos and Byron. How could you do that?"

"They are safer behind the walls. You needed to escape."

Rather than continue to be chastised for her sudden indiscretions, Lluava countered, "We made it outside the walls. Let's go save our comrades."

221

Yamir was clearly upset.

"The enemy's camp is in that direction," gestured the huntsman as he began to change his course.

Partially stumbling, the small group trudged through the snow as flakes began to fall again. Lluava shivered under her cloak. She had dressed warmly, but the cold still found its way through. One day, she would return south to her hometown and its milder winters, and this would all be a horrid memory. At least, that was what she hoped.

When they had gotten as close to the enemy camp as they dared, Apex gave a signal and they halted. He pointed to the trees, and Yamir instantly began climbing. Lluava and Apex remained on the ground and waited for him to bring them news from above.

"About the other night—" Lluava began, just as Apex said, "After this rescue, I'm leaving Elysia."

"And going where?" Lluava was shocked. "Back to Leucrocotta?"

"Possibly. If they will have me."

"You mean if Yena will have you. You don't know what she expects of you."

"And you do?"

Yamir dropped to the ground. "You might want to take a look for yourselves."

Lluava gave Apex a questioning glance before she headed to a tree.

Once she had reached the highest limb she dared, Lluava actually felt exhilarated. Scooting around to face the right direction, she saw the Raider's vast camp and shivered again. Through the partial shield formed by the trees, she observed the seemingly endless rows of tents. Farther back, trees were being cut down to build siege weapons. Several clearings had already been made. One held a rough corral for horses; another, several barred wagons.

Cages, Lluava thought. I bet I know what sort of beast they contain.

Figures moved in a trained fashion around the perimeter. She did not see any Berserkers among the Raiders; maybe the gods were with the them after all. Or could the Berserkers have their own camp elsewhere? She tried to count the active guards. From her perspective, she could not see very well. Hopefully Apex and Yamir would have better luck. She shimmied down the tree trunk.

Nearby, Yamir was doing the same, his face slashed with determination. Leaping to the ground, the coppery-skinned youth announced, "The prisoners are rather centralized. We'd best wait until dark to have any chance to infiltrate their network of guards."

"How many? Lluava asked. "I did not have the best vantage point."

"Too many."

Lluava studied her companions. Apex looked like he might charge right into the camp. Yamir, not as suicidal as the huntsman, might have a better solution. Yet, what if Apex acted rashly? He would not only ruin their one chance at rescue but also get himself killed.

Anyway, what did she care? She did not love him. She didn't even like him.

Yet hadn't she felt a sudden fear when she saw Apex lying so still in the snow?

This was nonsense. The huntsman had been her companion for so long that she had developed an affinity for him. How could she not? But affinity was not love, nor was the desire for him to be by her side in this upcoming raid. They needed to work together in order to help her friends. When she touched Apex's arm lightly, the battle thirst seemed to dim in the huntsman's red-flecked eyes.

Moving deeper into the woods, the group hunkered down as the daylight began to dwindle. In low voices, they bickered over specific plans of action. Yamir, attempting to re-spike his hair, noted somewhat hopefully, "This time there are no walls, no set structures."

"Last time," Lluava reminded him, "we used disguises, and the Raiders felt somewhat secure in their hidden encampment. Here, out in the open, they will be on full alert."

Apex added, "They will have too many sentinels in position for us to attack straight on without an army of our own."

Yamir agreed. "We are few as it is. We have to stick together. We are three Theriomorphs. What can we do against an army of those sea brutes? If what they told us was true, the rest of the Berserker Legion is residing within those snow-covered tents."

"So, are you saying this is all futile?" Lluava demanded. "That we made it this far just to give up?"

"In the past, it seemed that some god or gods were on our side," Yamir said resolutely. "Maybe they still are. This mission, as you see it, is impossible for three Theriomorphs to undertake. But maybe two gods can.

"Lluava, the Guardians call you and Apex Incarn and believe you have a connection with the gods. Mortals might not be able to achieve this task, but you are each linked with an immortal."

Apex muttered, "Then let Ullr and Theri use us to free our comrades." He seemed to like the idea instead of worrying that their secret was out.

Lluava had a different opinion. "When did you start believing in the gods?"

"I always have, Lluava," noted Yamir kindly. "Maybe it's time for you to do the same."

Lluava had not realized how pious some of her friends were. This realization made her uncomfortable. "What will you do while we are rescuing Derrick?"

"I will find the Cloven-Hoofed Clan. They will protect me, since I am now the best-looking outlaw in Elysia," Yamir answered with a smile. He had finished touching up his hair and was pulling threads out of his cuffs to fray the edges. "You can come, too."

"I would have to think about the Clans," stated Lluava, glancing back in the direction of Cronus's walls. "So this is goodbye?"

"For now. It is up to you both to save our friend," said Yamir as he looked about in the gloom of dusk. "We see better in the dark than the Raiders do. Be off with you." Apex gave Yamir a strong handshake, but

Lluava could not bear to say goodbye. For once, the thought that she might not return created a knot in her chest.

She stood off to one side and quietly resolved to push her exhaustion aside for a little longer. She would do this, without the help of that dark beast within her. She was Lluava, soldier for Elysia—not Issaura, warrior of the gods.

As she turned toward the Raiders' encampment, she felt a subtle fire ignite inside her, burning away her fear of death. She had waited too long for a fight. This night was truly hers.

Torches flickered around the perimeter of the camp. This was not good; they needed darkness. But where the night lights glimmered, dark shadows also presided. Apex and Lluava crept as close as possible and watched the guards patrolling, their steady rhythm like the ebb and flow of the ocean. If they timed it perfectly, the pair had but a moment to slip past the perimeter firelight.

When a murder of crows took wing nearby, the patrolling Raiders turned to investigate. This was their chance. The huntsman went first, barely making it to the trunk of a nearby tree before one of the patrol returned. Lluava waited through several more laps to make sure her count was right, then dove past the torches into the trees beyond.

There was a rustle as one Raider left his post and approached. Lluava could hear his footsteps and his wheezing breath. Just as the tip of his nose poked past the tree trunk that served as Lluava's refuge, he did an about-face and returned to his steady walk.

They had made it into the nest of vipers. Now the trick was to tread lightly so that none would strike. Slowly, Apex and Lluava penetrated farther into the camp, moving from shadow to shadow, hoping not to draw an unwanted eye. Lluava wondered if this was what it was like to be an Obsidian Guard like Holly, eternally lurking in the gloom, always on guard.

Every so often, one of the Raiders meandering amid the snow-laden tents would glance in their direction, but no action was ever taken. Apex was wide of shoulder and chest; his silhouette could easily be mistaken for one of the Raiders'. Lluava's, on the other hand, would stand out like a thistle in a rose garden. If seen, she would raise not merely suspicion but alarm. She must be extremely cautious.

In an attempt to evade the largest group of dicing and drinking Raiders, Apex led Lluava by way of a longer path, which passed close to one of the clearings. The clearing, though small, sported half a dozen metal sculptures, all cast to look like the winged lizards carved on the bows of the Raiders' wooden longships. Under each was a fire, and through their nostrils white steam escaped, making moaning sounds.

She had seen them before, yet they still provoked in her a foul unease. In the distance, beyond the metallic wings, were the silhouettes of partially constructed siege weapons. Should they destroy those machines? If they did, they would never be able to free the prisoners.

Moving away from the large, dark lizard forms, the two approached an area thick with the sea brutes. Skirting them, Apex whispered, "There is no good entry point. It's time."

What if Yamir were wrong, and the pair of them were not strong enough to accomplish this? With so many armed enemies, how could they even expect to survive without grievous wounds? Yet Lluava felt no fear. She knew her life could be cut short by any one of the terrible weapons about her, but all she felt was a calm confidence that seemed to radiate from her innermost core.

Shifting, Apex became the enormous bronze wolverine. Where the Fangs reformed, his muzzle glinted metallic. Lluava, following suit, transformed into the white tigress with golden claws. The two beasts, like monstrous entities wrought from the seven hells, erupted into the throng of Raiders.

Devastation ensued.

Burly men grabbed for any sort of defensive weapon to hold off the savage animals that had appeared from nowhere. Slicing, biting, tearing her way through, Lluava felt warm blood splatter her face and coat her paws. She yowled when a blade grazed her hindquarters. Turning, she grappled with her attacker. The man stumbled back to run. He had no chance.

Nearby, Apex ripped out a Raider's jugular as the man attempted to blow a war horn in warning. They had to hurry lest someone else do the same.

Surprisingly, most of the men ran off, perhaps to retrieve weapons from their tents. Others held their ground. Their demise came soon enough. They were not Berserkers, nor was there any odor of sour smoke to alert the two Incarn of oncoming behemoths.

Ahead, Lluava spotted the barred wagons. The captives were waving, beckoning and cheering them on.

Now, helmeted Raiders began to appear, wielding war axes and thin, lightning-quick swords. Somehow, Lluava and Apex knew what to do. Without a word or glance at one another, they battled as a team, one always blocking the other's blind spots. It was instinctual. As though they shared an untaught mental link, each knew what the other needed.

Ducking under a throwing axe, Lluava spotted Apex shifting in order to return the discarded weapon to the forehead of its original thrower. She, in turn, severed the spine of a man loading his crossbow.

Oddly, Lluava took comfort whenever she caught sight of Apex—a trust she had not experienced with any fellow soldier other than Varren. With each life she took, Lluava's confidence grew, as did her strength. Her inner heat felt scorching. Was that elation she felt? The darkness within her stirred.

A new thought occurred to her. Should she allow that inner darkness to take over? Would she be able to differentiate friend from foe? If not, she would be no better than the bloodthirsty Berserkers. Lluava struggled to keep herself under control. She glanced at Apex and was reassured that he had not given in, at least not yet.

A rogue arrow tore through the air and grazed Apex's shoulder. The wolverine snarled angrily. "Keep moving," he snapped at Lluava as more Raiders closed in on the clearing.

In several bounds, Lluava came to the first wagon. The thick metal bars were welded into the base, the door bolted. Where were the keys? Several corpses were scattered about. Could one of them be the jailer? Or had he run off at her initial approach?

Hurrying over to the first figure, Lluava shifted back and began to quickly search his pockets and flaps for the keys. Moving to the next body, she futilely searched anew.

Standing up just in time, she parried the swing of an enemy's sword. Though handsome for a Raider, the hatred in this man's eyes was clear enough. He wanted to mount her head on a pike.

"Apex," she cried out. "I need you to break the locks!"

Quickly driving one of the Claws deep into the man's torso, Lluava shifted back before the next attack. Behind her, the clanging of the Fangs against metal bars reverberated. She needed to keep any approaching Raiders at bay.

A war horn sounded, followed by the resounding echoes of drums.

Soon the entire camp would converge on Lluava and Apex.

Taking down another pair of men, she was glad to see Apex working on the last of the three full cages. With a clang, the final bolt came free. The captives poured from the wagons. Some grabbed discarded weapons; others shifted immediately.

Lluava felt herself bowled over and heard the thump of a hammer colliding with the frozen earth. A large black wolf jumped off her and leaped at her would-be killer. The victim's screams were muffled by a second blast of the war horn.

"Everyone, to Cronus!" barked Apex as he led the wolfpack behind him.

A line of Raiders blocked their return. Lluava saw Alcove give the command; the marauders charged the trapped beasts. The Ambassador disappeared from sight as humans and animals rent each other's flesh and fur. She saw crimson droplets explode from Apex's fur as another arrow bit into his haunch.

Snow turned red and then, atypically, grew vibrant, as if it glowed. Colors grayed and left a blue-green cast on everything else. When she felt the bite of the sword, Lluava acquiesced and let the darkness overpower her.

Now and again, glimpses of the battle registered: the taste of hot blood filling her throat; the shrill screaming of someone in unimaginable pain; the stench of that vile, tainted smoke; bearded figures crusted with snow and blood.

Suddenly, she heard the familiar voice of Ambassador Alcove resonate through her own darkness, as if he called out directly to her.

"Run!"

Chapter 34

The Hot Box

Alcove's voice carved through the darkness—the voice of the enemy she needed to kill. Slicing Issaura's Claws out before her, Lluava began to regain control of herself. When had she shifted back?

A man cried out. Ripping the Claw out of his leather-encased sternum, the Raider collapsed before her. Was it Alcove? No. This man had silver hair.

Colors locked back into place, although her surroundings retained the gray gloom of darkness. Raiders were all about her. Several on horseback galloped after ragged wolves. The bodies of those who had unsuccessfully tried to escape the encampment were scattered in a jagged line. Nearby, a wolf's corpse shifted back into its human form. Its killer, bleeding from a gaping bite wound in his stocky neck, was dying at his victim's side.

Turning about, Lluava scanned the chaos for the ambassador. With so many forms moving among the trees, she could not tell which way he had gone—if he had really been there at all.

There was a yelp.

One ruddy wolf had been knocked sideways by a war hammer. The poor creature struggled to regain its footing. Lluava ran to its aid and sliced through its attacker's meaty back. She could feel his spine crack as he dropped his weapon; the wolf hobbled off.

Far ahead of her, Derrick's solemn howl rang out. At least some were getting away. Not all had been so fortunate.

Suddenly, a heavy net with cords as big as a man's forearm dropped down over Lluava, its weight alone thrusting her to the ground. Quickly trying to untangle her weapons, she had no chance to cut through the rope before she was surrounded by a half dozen of the enemy. One grunted, and all of them grabbed her. Issaura's Claws were violently torn free as they lifted her kicking form into the air.

"Apex!" she cried, but she could not be heard amid the din. Lluava knew that if she shifted, her captors would not hesitate to slay the tigress. She was stuck for now.

Roughly she was carried off, and the Raiders deposited her somewhere deep in the encampment where cruel faces stared at her. She was forcefully bound and, with the tips of several spears at the back of her head, commanded to sit still.

Before her stood two men. One was Alcove, who had donned his wolf-headed cloak. Did he look sorry, or was he disappointed? Beside him was a man, far more muscular than the ambassador. A redhead, this one wore his long beard split into two braids.

"This be the she-tiger?" asked the redhead. "Looks more like a cub to me. Move 'er into the light."

Two men forcefully pulled Lluava into the torchlight.

"'Er face makes up where else she lacks," he said, nodding at her small breasts and pressing his thin lips into a wan smile. "A warrior, she is? She looks like a boy in his first year of training. Meh." The man turned away from her to face the ambassador. "You must want your payment now."

One of the Raiders handed Alcove Issaura's Claws. The ambassador handled them like one who knew their true worth. "And the girl?" he finally asked, after inspecting the golden weapons.

"Not her!" barked the redbeard.

"Sweyn, you must not understand—" Alcove began but was cut off.

"Orders must be followed," Sweyn stated. "You were summoned."

"By whom?"

"By Ivar Níðingr, himself."

A realization seemed to overwhelm Alcove. His features took on a dreary appearance. "I have no need for a broken set." He tossed the weapons on the ground before Lluava. "Let the cat have her claws." Then he strode off with two armed men in tow.

Once Alcove had left, everyone turned back to Lluava.

"Box 'er up," commanded Sweyn. "'Er weapons, too. Let's see 'ow she likes 'em permanently affixed to 'er."

Men swarmed about Lluava, seizing her arms and legs and lifting her like a sack of flour. At first she squirmed, hoping to loosen a limb, but with firm hands squeezing she realized that even if she escaped, there was nowhere for her to go. If she fought, she would be killed.

"Where are you taking me?" Lluava was compelled to ask, even though she knew she would receive no response. "What are you going to do?"

The men carried her to the clearing where the giant lizard statues stood. The metal monsters with the fires beneath them emitted unearthly sounds as steam spewed from their nostrils. Suddenly, Lluava wondered if the clearing could be an area for ceremony. Or maybe sacrifice.

They tossed her to the ground. Her head struck the hard earth, making her ears ring. Several men moved to an unlit statue. Reaching under one folded wing, they unfastened a latch, then pushed up the batlike appendage to expose a large opening in the hollow form. Issaura's Claws were tossed inside while other men picked her up and carried her toward the statue.

She was about to be thrust into a windowless cage. Her all-but-forgotten fear of being trapped resurfaced.

"No!" she screamed. "No!"

Lluava had only begun to shift when she was roughly deposited inside the belly of the lizard. Its hollow space was far too small for a fully formed tiger. She tried to leap out of the hole, but the wing swung down and the hatch was sealed.

She screamed and beat on the door, but her cries were unanswered. Putting on the Claws, she sliced at the metal, sending angry sparks into the air around her. At first, everything was black. Then she perceived that two meager beams of milky light dimly illuminated the metallic prison. On her hands and knees, Lluava could not see the light's source, for it seemed to emanate from a small hollow that bent in an upward arc. The lizard's neck, she soon realized. Her light source—and possibly her only air supply—were the lizard's metal nostrils.

Panic seized her. Yelling, she flailed about, beating the walls with her elbows and hands and kicking them with her feet. In fact, the air coming through the hollow was enough; but then why couldn't she breathe? She was going to suffocate before help could arrive. She remembered being buried alive by the avalanche and how she had been left to die in the prison of the fort. Both times, she had been left utterly alone in blackness.

The metal was so cold it burned her flesh like ice. She shivered as she gasped for air. She had felt the same way in the snows in the mountains. The avalanche had been her undoing. Then she remembered arms digging through the snow, pulling her out, saving her life.

"Apex," she uttered, and air seemed to flow back into her lungs. Picturing his scraggly face, Lluava found that she could breathe again. This metal case would not entomb her after all.

Lluava screamed up through the hollow neck, hoping one of her comrades would hear her. They could not all have abandoned her, especially not after she had rescued them. Apex would not abandon her. He would come back. He would.

"Help me!" she cried. "Apex, I'm in here!"

Lluava's screams reverberated so loudly that her ears began to throb. She had to be making a ruckus. Where was her rescuer?

Another thought occurred to her. The sounds the statues made, those low grunts and moans, were neither the result of metal expanding from the fire's heat nor the whistle of steam through nostrils. They were the cries of prisoners.

Then she thought about the steam itself, the white-hot air from the fires built underneath. She touched the bottom of the hollow, feeling the metal. Was it warm, or was this, too, her imagination? She had been sitting there; maybe it was just her body heat.

"Somebody help me!" she screamed again. "Get me out of here!"

She felt her way around the seam to the opening, but the entire door proved to be secured. Using all the strength she could muster, Lluava lay on her back and started kicking the precise spot where the latch should be, hoping to weaken it.

She stopped when her entire back seemed to heat up. The floor began to burn her skin. Lluava kicked with a fierce passion. The Raiders had lit a fire underneath her. They were going to cook her alive!

Sweat beaded Lluava's forehead as the heat from the fire forced her to shift position. She moved back onto her hands and knees, but anything that touched the floor was burned.

"No!" she cried out again as she struggled to position herself in a squat. At least the soles of her shoes would prevent the searing pain. For now.

Lluava's attempt to pry the door open using a blade of one of the Claws resulted only in getting the blade stuck in the crack. Jerking it free, she could feel that the warmth had spread up the walls. The floor was now too hot to touch barehanded. Her feet had begun to feel the heat even through her soles. Only Issaura's Claws remained cool to the touch, but that would not be enough to save her.

At a loss, Lluava yelled out anew. At first she yelled words or short sentences but was soon reduced to unintelligible screams. The entire hollow space radiated heat. Even the air seemed to boil. Lluava's feet began to burn, and she was compelled to move; but any part of her body that touched the floor or walls was seared. She began to squirm, hoping that if she moved quickly enough no one part of her would be burned. But as the space continued to heat up, this proved useless. The air seemed to ripple with steam. Her skin began to boil and blister. Tears ran sizzling down her face. The pain was excruciating.

Lluava did not know how long she could last under these conditions. Maybe this was the end—yet she could not will herself to die. She shut her eyes and tried anyway.

Cold. Piercing cold. Something groped at her burned flesh, and Lluava cried out. She felt herself being pulled up and out, then tossed onto packed snow. The icy fluff burned her skin even more than had the metal of her broken tomb. She was crying so hard that she could not see, not daring to move for fear of worsening her pain.

Slowly, her mind began to function again. She was out of the metal lizard. She was out. Out.

Through her veil of tears, she saw a figure kneeling near her.

"Lluava, you're going to be okay."

She knew this voice. The figure got up and left. He was leaving her.

"Apex!" Lluava cried out. "Apex! Apex!"

"Quiet, now," Apex said as he ran back to her side. "I have you. But you must be quiet."

He wiped her eyes, and she could see his determination, blighted though it was by fear. Apex went to another statue. He broke the latch with one of the Fangs and pulled out a blackened body. Leaving the dead man in the snow, he moved to another metal lizard.

Out of the corners of her eyes, Lluava saw the corpses of several Raiders as well as some scorched men. More Raiders would come.

"Apex," Lluava seemed to form his name over all other words. She wanted to tell him they had to run. They had to get away. More tears bubbled up, blurring her sight.

"Apex," she murmured even louder.

Raiders were approaching.

Lluava cried out, "Apex! Hurry!"

The huntsman was running back to her with someone else limping painfully at his side. As they neared, she saw that the person's features were scarred with burns both old and new. His hair was all but gone, only a few measly tufts sticking out of charred skin. What scraps of clothing he had left were permanently burned into his flesh, along with hardened tar and clumps of feathers.

Bending down, Apex said to her, "I'm going to pick you up. Don't yell."

Lluava had not moved from the position he had left her in. As soon as Apex touched her, she gasped in pain and tried desperately to choke back the louder cries that rose in her throat. Once the huntsman had her in his arms, he and the other victim hurriedly moved away from the foul torture devices and into the shadows of the main camp.

Lluava could not stop crying. Every movement aggravated her burns, which in turn bound her thoughts to the metal prison in which she had been confined. The distance Apex carried her without being caught should have caused her to take notice, yet it did not. All she wanted was to be whisked away from death, from the darkness, from the scorching metal.

"Shift," their new companion gargled out of disfigured lips.

Apex had halted. Why was he not running? They were still in the camp. Lluava wanted to scream in panic but could managed no more than a whimper.

"She won't make it," snarled Apex as he adjusted his grip on Lluava. She cried out anew.

Raiders were charging them.

With surprising gentleness, Apex quickly set Lluava on the ground and drew Ullr's Fangs. Clanging sounds followed.

Look around, Lluava thought. Turn and see.

Though her neck remained unburned, Lluava feared the pain that could occur from any movement. Curled on the slushy ground, the injured teen watched as fur-trimmed boots plodded past; then the tarred feet of their new friend hobbled away.

Someone approached.

Just as Lluava felt herself jerked upward, their tortured companion shoved a rapier through the Raider's neck. Spitting blood, the brute released her, and she tumbled back into the muddy snow. Should she revert into the darkness? Would the thing inside her come alive? Could it shield her from the pain?

A pair of golden eyes stared into hers, somehow familiar. The tortured man squatted next to her. "Warn the king," he wheezed. "He is no friend."

A roar reverberated around them. The tarred man grabbed Lluava and pulled her to her feet once more. This time, she was assisted onto the Yorrick wolverine's back. The man was about to follow when he abruptly stumbled backward. He waved them away, and then he turned to face the Raider whose dagger was now planted in his back.

Before Lluava could cry out again, she felt Apex take off. Fresh pain coursed through her body. Gripping the wolverine's fur as tightly as her blistered fingers would allow, she finally lost consciousness.

She was aware of the passage of time. The steady movement of the lumbering beast occasionally awakened her. Soon the dim light of the approaching sun evaporated the darkness.

They were somewhere in the forest. Apex, exhausted, had finally slowed down. Finding a natural lean-to made by a steeply listing oak, the huntsman collapsed. Lluava was surprisingly alert. She must have slept as they traveled.

When Apex finally awoke, he returned to his human form and went out to scout. Upon his return, he bore a foul-smelling poultice, which he placed over every major burn on Lluava's body. They both rested for the remainder of the day.

Lluava's thoughts kept turning to the poor burned man and what he had said. In the middle of the night, she awoke with a jolt. "I knew him!" she exclaimed in dismay.

Chapter 35

Cured

"Calm down," griped Apex. He grabbed Lluava before she made a maddened dash for the forest. "Who'd you know?"

"The man," Lluava began. "The one who was with us. I knew him. I fought with him. I trained with him. His name was Horus. I thought...we thought he was killed last summer. His partner was a childhood friend of the king. We just left him back there."

Instead of saying everything was all right, that Horus might have survived, that they could save him, Apex merely said, "He is dead."

"What if—"

"You saw his wound as well as I. No one could survive that."

"He was alive," Lluava said, more to herself than the huntsman. "Maybe Thad is, too."

"His partner?" questioned Apex. "Pray that he is not. Think of what pain and suffering they would have put a human through for working alongside one of us. I would not wish that on my worst enemy."

"Even an enemy who is capable of that?" questioned Lluava darkly. If her whole body weren't aching, she would love to dig Issaura's Claws into the first Raider she could find.

"No." Apex looked out at the snow-laden woods. "There is no honor in that. Men should die from tooth and blade, should have a chance to fight back. Those devices, those *methods*, are cowards' work. The Raiders will die, all of them, but not by those means."

"I want them to feel it. The heat, the fire, the smell... the charring." Suddenly Lluava was sobbing again, her entire body shaking. "All alone...in the blackness... the pain...just alone."

233

"You're not alone." Apex's voice was assertive yet gentle. "You're safe. I have you. You're safe."

And there in his arms she stayed until she was able to fall asleep again.

When she woke, Apex was gone, and the deep feeling of loneliness returned. Where had he gone? What if he was looking for help, for some sign of the others, and got captured, or worse? The thought of him gone forever almost caused her to cry out. She realized she wanted Apex in her life, whatever he was to her.

She turned her attention to her wounds. As she slowly peeled away the poultices, Lluava found that much of her blistered skin did not hurt anymore; instead, it was numb. She could move slowly. Rising to her feet, she shuffled into the snow.

"I'm glad you're moving." Apex's voice came as a relief to her. "We should change our camp so as not to be found. There is an old—what is it?"

Lluava realized that she must have been looking at the huntsman strangely. Somehow, she felt that she needed him with her.

Before she could explain, Apex raised a finger to his lips and peered about warily. "We should go now," was all he said.

Assisting her as they went, Apex led Lluava to an abandoned chicken coop. The shack was small but could shelter the pair for the moment. The nearby homestead and barn had been torched, probably by the Raiders as they passed through.

"Here." Apex handed her a dead rabbit. He must have stashed it earlier that morning. "You'll have to eat it raw. It's the best we can do so close to *them*."

Caring little about the raw meat she slowly gnawed or the cold wind picking up outside, Lluava felt as if she were seeing the huntsman for the first time. She liked how his hair took on a bronze hue when he walked through the beams of sunlight that came through the holes in the roof. As powerful as his strong back, shoulders and arms were, his hands could nimbly manipulate his prey, using only one small cut to skin the animal whole. This was beneficial to his trade, for unmarred hides brought in a better price. Yet those large hands could also be gentle when adding a new layer of poultices to Lluava's burns.

Now, when he touched her, a new sensation manifested. A hyperawareness, a sort of tingling that made her heart race. Something in her began to yearn for more of his touch, for his rough fingers to brush her neck and face. She wondered if Apex could hear each thump of her heart.

Quickly jerking backward, Lluava physically shook the sensations away. Apex, in turn, moved away from her. Refusing to explain, Lluava stared at the closed door. For once, she would not focus on herself. They were in danger as long as they stayed so near the capital. She had to come up with a plan. Apex's proximity was clouding her thoughts, just as it had in Leucrocotta.

They had to get away, that was clear. But when, where, and how?

Movement was still painful. She could barely force herself to walk steadily. Yet movement…

Was outside the coop.

Apex already had the Fangs in hand. Lluava shuffled over to Issaura's Claws, which had been placed nearby. The door of the coop was kicked in. Apex charged. The intruders called out. Everyone halted.

With blades at each other's throats, Apex and Talos stared at each other, their faces mirroring each other's shock.

Behind them, Byron said, "See, I knew they were still around."

"I thought you were Raiders," Talos said as he lowered his sword.

"As I did you."

"Why did you not follow the others? From our vantage point on the wall, we saw them fleeing."

Apex stepped aside to allow the young men a better glimpse of Lluava. Both looked dismayed.

"What happened?" Talos demanded. Then, glancing about, he asked, "Can she travel?"

There was not enough space inside the coop for the four of them. Lluava realized that Talos intended to take her elsewhere. She nodded and stood shakily. Several of the poultices sloughed off, exposing her blistered flesh.

"Gods!" breathed Talos.

Apex was far less concerned. "The wounds will scar, but she will survive. She needs time to heal."

"She can take all the time she needs once she is inside the walls," responded Talos, and Byron added, "We really need to get moving."

"Inside the walls?" questioned Lluava as Apex helped her to the doorway. "I thought they were sealed shut permanently."

Byron spoke directly to Talos. "Tell her."

"Tell me what?"

Talos began in a hushed voice as he led them back into the woods. "It is strange. Varren woke up the other night *cured*. He admitted that most of the past few months had been hazy, although he thinks he remembers some of it. He said it was like waking from a prolonged dream. The first thing he did was command the gates to be opened so he could come find you. He knew you had left Cronus."

"Where is he, then?" inquired Lluava skeptically.

"Along with the High Council, I implored Varren not to put himself at risk by trying to find you. Byron and I volunteered to bring you back if— when—we found you." Talos assisted Lluava around a fallen tree limb before adding, "Varren awaits you in the castle."

"By opening the gates, he risks the Raiders entering Cronus," stated Apex.

"I know. Several councilmen, including your old friend Themis, tried to persuade Varren to leave the gates sealed. But he was adamant that someone would be leaving to retrieve you." Byron's eyes seemed to smile. "Lluava, he is truly back."

But for how long? wondered Lluava. And why now? What was Selene up to? Could she be trusted not to interfere again? The only answers were back in Cronus, and she was determined to find them.

"Here's where things are going to get tricky," admitted Talos. "After your little caper, Ambassador Alcove applauded your effort but warned that Varren's time frame had been shortened considerably. This means we need to get back inside the gates, and fast. I would be surprised if the Raiders were not keeping watch near the doors. If they are, we will have to slip past them until we are in range of our own archers. They will help protect us as we move toward the gates."

"I can handle a few Raiders," growled Apex.

"That may be, but what about the rest of us?" Talos looked at Lluava. "Can you fight? Be honest with me."

Gripping the Claws, she could barely force her fingers to close around them. Lluava shook her head. "No."

"I can keep up with you despite my limp," admitted Byron, "but I won't be much help otherwise."

"Apex," Talos began, "you and I will be responsible for getting Lluava and Byron back into the safe zone. I need to know if you will work with me if anything goes awry."

"Of course."

As Talos began walking in front of her, Lluava felt compelled to say, "I was only trying to make the best choice, back there at the lift."

Breeze and snow played with Talos's golden locks as he paused for a moment. "How could you know what was best?"

"You had both been fighting out here for so long...." Lluava stopped, then continued, "I just... I just thought you did not deserve to return to the war front so soon."

"We may be standing in the war front now," added Byron, whose darker blond hair was too short to be wind tossed, "but Cronus is part of the war front, too."

"I made the best choice I could," sulked Lluava. She could feel patches of her flesh crack and ooze as she moved.

Talos's look toward her was, for once, unkind. "For whom?"

How could the pair of them not see that for once she was not being selfish? How could Talos not understand that she had given them the opportunity to stay safe, particularly for him to stay with Rosalyn?

"The only people," Talos began anew, "who can make a decision for me without my knowledge are my wife and Byron."

Biting her tongue, Lluava continued to shuffle along. She had given him the opportunity to be near Rosalyn, yet Talos and Byron both threw that away when they came out here. They were the foolish ones.

Their pace back to Cronus was painfully slow. Lluava silently cursed her aching body for causing the delay. When they finally neared the castle, everyone went on high alert. Using the woods for cover, they headed toward the eastern side of the fortification. If they could reach the wall, the archers on the parapets would be able to protect them from an attack while they navigated the perimeter and reached the main gates. Luckily, no Raiders were in sight.

"So far, so good," mumbled Byron.

They were nearing the edge of the forest. The clearing beyond was twice as wide as an arrow could be shot. They only had to make it into the protective range of the archers, and all would be well.

Talos sniffed the air. "Do you smell that?"

"Yes," snarled Apex. Lluava could only smell the taint of her marred flesh, and Byron— well, he was only human. What was out there?

Suddenly, Talos flashed the whites of his eyes. "Byron, take Lluava. Get her to the castle. Run!"

A sapling came crashing down in front of Apex's boots. Then, out of the shadows of the understory loomed a Berserker. He was over seven feet tall with a muscular body to match. Crowned with a horned helmet, the brute dragged an extraordinarily large maul.

If Apex and Talos could smell the smoke, then this Berserker was already drugged. The enormous man would not stop unless he lost too much blood or was decapitated. In the past, when dealing with these sorts of men— creatures—it had taken two, often three Elysian soldiers to kill one Berserker.

Byron grabbed Lluava. Before she knew it, he was pulling her along with him as he dashed toward the clearing. Even though she knew that she would be of no help against the giant Raider, she felt compelled to stay and fight. Byron, however, would not let her.

All she could do was catch a glimpse over her shoulder. Talos shifted into his stag form as Apex desperately tried to parry the blow from the maul.

"Come on! We are almost there!" shouted Byron as, limping, he half dragged Lluava with him.

An arrow was fired from the wall. Its tip bit into the earth several feet in front of them. Didn't the archers know they were friends? When no other arrows followed, she realized that the single arrow had been only a signal indicating where the safe zone began.

After they had passed the marker, Byron finally allowed Lluava to collapse on the ground. She felt as if her skin would tear apart. Looking back toward the forest, Lluava saw that the Berserker had Talos by the horns. The monster had forced the buck to the ground and now had the heel of his boot pressing firmly on Talos's ribs. He was going to snap the buck's neck.

An enormous wolverine clambered onto the Berserker's back and ripped off the horned helmet. The Raider tightened his grip on the horns and then jerked his arms upward. There was a loud crack. The Berserker held up a pair of bloody antlers, new weapons with which to skewer the wolverine. The buck's head was drenched in red; its body lay still on the ground.

Byron turned away from the sight and scanned the trees. "To your right!" he shouted to Lluava. His voice held a note of hysteria.

Out of the forest charged another Berserker, taller than the first one and bearing a spiked club the size of a small tree trunk. His sole focus was the pair of injured Elysians hobbling toward the gates.

That's right, thought Lluava. They always travel in threes.

There was a sound like a flock of birds in flight as countless arrows arced overhead, many finding their targets. Thick shafts, several feet long, dug deep into biceps and quads, dented the metal helmet; yet none stopped the charge of the Berserker.

"Head for the gates," ordered Byron as he pulled out Phin, his sword. He looked about to make some last stand.

"Come with me," implored Lluava as she struggled to her feet.

"Together we would be too slow. Off with you!"

Lluava turned, stumbled, and shifted. With four limbs on the ground, she was able to move faster. Her skin took on the odor of charred hair where patches of boiled flesh hindered some of her fur from sprouting. The tigress was almost at the gate when she halted. What was she doing? Wasn't she supposed to be the embodiment of the Goddess of War? Why was she turning tail and running?

Turning around, Lluava loped toward Byron just as the pincushion-like Berserker reached him. Byron sliced at the large Raider. Blood spattered the air. He must have damaged the brute's left arm, for it hung limply. Despite his wounds, the behemoth raised his weapon and knocked Byron off his already poor balance. Or had Byron fallen on his own?

The Raider toppled forward. The weight of his body forced many of the quarrels, the square-headed bolts from the Elysian's confiscated crossbows, through his torso. Suddenly, the enormous form was rapidly dragged backward by the wolverine. The animal's metallic mouth was coated in a crimson film, its eyes black and soulless. Apex had succumbed to the darkness within. The wolverine dragged its still-moving prey into the depths of the forest and disappeared from sight.

Byron regained his footing and, with Lluava by his side, headed for the gates. A new round of arrows flew through the air. Either the third Berserker had appeared, or one of the first two had survived—which would mean Apex had not.

The gates of the capital groaned open just far enough for a man to slide through sideways. Byron went first while Lluava shifted back. She was partway through the opening when she heard footsteps right behind her.

Turning her head, she saw the blood-drenched body of Talos. He was alive!

Beyond him, the third Berserker was almost at the gates. As soon as Talos was inside, the doors heaved shut, leaving the Berserker to be shot with yet more quarrels.

Talos stumbled and collapsed. Byron caught him mid-fall. Rosalyn and several others ran up to them. In the flurry of movement, Lluava did not see Varren approach. He gently swept her up in his arms as carefully as he could and helped her into his carriage.

As they headed to the castle, Lluava could see the intense worry in her partner's gaze as he observed her injuries. Although Varren appeared disheveled and exhausted, he was lucid. Not a trace of Selene's influence appeared in his cool blue eyes.

"I am so sorry—" he began just as a horn blasted out.

"What was that?" questioned Lluava, wishing she could see past the curtains at the carriage window.

"They have released the Berserker Legion upon us."

Chapter 36

Vial Thoughts

The entire legion?" Lluava was aghast. Thousands of Berserkers had already died in the Borren Mountain avalanche. How many of these brutal killers remained?

The look on Varren's face was grim. "I ordered the gates to be resealed. If the Berserkers get through...all these people...they *cannot* be slaughtered, Lluava. I will do whatever it takes to prevent that."

"Will the gates hold?"

"Pray that they do."

The steady clacking of the horses' hooves on the cobblestones was the only sound that could be heard. The entire city seemed to freeze, as if everyone were holding their breath. Another war horn trumpeted; the thrum of drums quickly followed.

"Apex is out there with all those Berserkers," Lluava said.

"I know. I am concerned about that, too. He has been a good friend to you," Varren reached over consolingly to touch the top of her hand. "If I could have kept the doors open longer—"

"We both know you had no choice," she quickly responded, although she felt resentful toward the prince nonetheless.

"Apex is extraordinary in the forest. He might be able to evade them and catch up with Derrick's men."

"Yeah. Maybe."

Shakily Varren added, "At least I have you back." He tenderly kissed her forehead, one of the few places not marred by burns or blisters. "I will send the royal healer to your quarters immediately. Knowing you, you will want to return to the fight far sooner than I would like, but please promise me that you will allow yourself time to mend."

"What about Talos? He was covered in blood."

"He has Rosalyn. You know she is an excellent healer."

They continued a little farther in silence before Lluava spoke. "I was told that you remember things."

Varren nodded, avoiding her eyes

"The council? Your wedding? Yamir?"

"Yes. Yes. *Yes*. I ordered Yamir to be released but was told that he was already gone. I am afraid that he could be lost in Tartarus. That is my fault. Everything is my fault. Maybe my grandfather's ailment is also mine." His voice betrayed his inner anguish.

Lluava could have told him the truth. She knew she could alleviate his grief with an explanation but chose to remain silent. Varren had not made those decisions on his own, yet he was still part of it. He had given the commands, changed the laws, made the announcements. He was not unblemished in this.

Lluava realized that she was very angry, that she wanted him to feel the pain he had caused her, at least a little longer.

The first thunderous boom rang out as they arrived at the castle. By the time Lluava reached her quarters, she had heard the booming several more times. She hoped many Berserkers would die at the gates while using their battering rams. How many arrows did it take to kill just one? How many Berserkers did it take to wield those heinous devices? Certainly fewer than the number of normal men.

Another boom thundered out, then everything grew quiet. The silence was far more terrifying. What were the Raiders up to now? What was their strategy? Lluava warily approached the balcony and scrutinized the city below, half expecting to see the main gates implode from another strike. But the battering rams were silent.

On his perch, Onyx stared outside as well. He did not seem to notice Lluava when she entered. Stupid bird. Such a useless creature. Lluava found it hard to understand why little June liked him so much.

Tired and sore, all she wanted to do was sleep for days. Now that the booming had ceased, maybe she could. Should she bathe first? The baths were so far away, and every movement was excruciating.

Varren called from the doorway, "I have Nicolas Albidum, my family's healer, here to see you."

"Come in," replied Lluava as she slowly shuffled to her chaise.

The royal healer was younger than Lluava had expected, only about forty years old. To have reached his current position, Albidum must be extremely knowledgeable. Maybe he could help, but she knew her full recovery was doubtful.

"Oh my." Albidum's words confirmed Lluava's suspicions. He carefully inspected her limbs and pulled up her shirt to examine her back. "I will give you an ointment for this, but there will be scarring. How bad it will be, I cannot be certain."

Lluava sensed his reluctance to inform her of the dreary truth at this time. Albidum handed her a bottle, along with a serum to help ease the pain. Lluava thanked him, and he and Varren left her to her rest. Time alone would be the best healer. But how much time did she have?

She had barely slipped under the covers when she heard a knock at her door. "Come in!" Lluava shouted, unwilling to leave her bed.

"I'm only going to stay a moment," said Luka, approaching. Then he hesitated. How bad must she look? Lluava wondered. Or maybe it was the smell of her burned flesh.

"I..." Luka began again. "I am glad you made it back."

Cracking a smile, Lluava added, "As am I. Luka—" she called out before her friend could leave, "I know that your sister released Varren—really released him. Why?"

"She had her reasons. Anyway, I'll visit you again soon."

***

Onyx was mumbling by her ear when Lluava finally forced her eyes open. She wasn't sure how long she had slept, but the sun was still up.

"What do you want, bird?" griped Lluava as she pushed the feathered creature away from her face.

The raven hopped back to her side and resumed his mumbling. Knowing that sleep was hopeless now, Lluava sat up.

"What?" She glared at the bird. Onyx cocked his good eye up at her and continued to mutter.

"What?" Lluava asked again. "Is the door shut? Do you want to go out?"

Slowly standing up, Lluava shuffled into the main chamber. The balcony door was still open, and frigid air chilled the room. Onyx alighted on her shoulder and tugged at her hair.

"Don't you know how much pain I'm already in?" she asked him.

If a bird could look amused, Onyx did.

"You're evil, you know that?"

Lluava walked out onto the balcony. Onyx began to caw and flap his wings, batting his feathers in her face before he flew back inside.

"What in the seven hells?" snarled Lluava. In the distance, she saw massing flocks of birds. They were too far away for her to see what sort they were. She shivered and stepped inside, shutting the door behind her.

"Too cold to be out there anyway," she grumbled, although the cold air had felt pleasant on her skin.

There was a clatter of dishes on a tray. June struggled to rebalance her load as she stared wide-eyed at Lluava.

I must look like a monster, thought Lluava sourly. "I'm fine," she stated.

As soon as June had set the tray down on the table, she ran over and gave Lluava a large squeeze. Tears streamed into Lluava's eyes from the pain, but she had no heart to tell the little girl that the hug was hurting her.

Stepping back, June asked, "Is there anything I can get you?"

Knowing that her handmaiden must have been instructed not to ask about the war, Lluava felt somewhat relieved. She did not care to explain her injuries. Better to let the girl wonder rather than give her nightmares.

"No. Thank you."

"Oh," June began as she reached into one of her dress's hidden pockets. "Someone left you these."

In her small hands were four vials of liquid.

"Who?" Lluava asked as she opened one vial and ran her finger around the rim. She sniffed the contents and then licked her finger. The smell was as putrid as its taste. Lluava quickly realized what it was.

"I don't know. They were left here with a note with your name on it."

"Do you have the note? Let me see it."

June fumbled in her pockets, then pulled out a crumpled piece of parchment. Lluava's name was written in a flowing script. Underneath, her name was spelled out in runes as well.

"Thank you, June. That will be all for now."

Once her handmaiden had left, Lluava downed one of the vials of liquid, gagging on the taste. Idun was the only medicine that could help her heal quickly. Had Yena delivered this? If so, where was she? Had the high priestess decided not to bring her army? Maybe this was supposed to be consolation for not keeping her end of the bargain. Then again, Lluava had evaded hers.

With three vials remaining, Lluava went in search of Talos. She found him, along with Rosalyn and Byron. His head was bandaged, but he was smiling and talking.

"How bad?" Lluava asked as she approached Talos's bedside.

"I'll be fine once this headache goes away."

"But your antlers…"

"It was time for me to shed them anyway," laughed Talos. "I just wish it had not been so wrenching."

"You are lucky that you are a stag," added Byron.

Rosalyn was glowing. She seemed relieved that the wounds were not severe. "Head wounds bleed a lot, but they usually look worse than they are."

"Well, here." Lluava handed Talos and Byron two of the vials. Holding the third, Lluava wondered if she should save it for Varren. Then she passed it to Rosalyn. "Use these at your discretion. There is not much in them, so I doubt they can perform miracles, but they should help."

"What are they?" questioned Byron.

Lluava realized that she must have sounded quite mysterious. "This is Idun, the stuff they use in Leucrocotta to heal."

Byron's eyes sparkled.

"I just took mine," noted Lluava. "I don't know how much such a small dose will help, but anything is better than nothing."

"Why don't you take mine?" Rosalyn tried to pass the vial back.

"No. Keep it. You might need it in the future." Turning to Byron, Lluava said, "I don't know if it will help your leg. Be forewarned: this stuff is disgusting. It will make you want to vomit."

"Tell me how you came by these?" Talos asked as he placed his vial on the bedside table.

"They were left for me. That's all I know."

"Well, I'm grateful," Byron said with a grin.

Lluava excused herself, explaining that she needed to rest. The hallway outside Talos's room was dim, and her footfalls echoed softly on the floor.

"Something has to be done." Voices trailed from around a corner. Lluava recognized the Queen Enya's syrupy sweet trill.

"I know, Your Highness. We are doing the best we can."

Themis. The little queen was bickering with the head councilman.

"Do better. The noise must stop!"

"Yes, Your Highness."

Lluava stepped into their view. She was not surprised that neither one seemed to care for the sight of her.

Enya had the nerve to say, "Tsk, tsk. You used to be almost pretty."

"Your Highness. Head Councilman," Lluava acknowledged as she shuffled past.

Boom.

"See!" Enya squawked. "There it is again!"

The Raiders were back at the gates. This only increased Lluava's distress. Once in her bed, she snatched what sleep she could in the intervals between the thumps of the battering rams.

***

When morning arrived, Lluava felt a good deal better. Her blisters were gone, and much of the pain from the burns had subsided. There were still reddened patches and sensitive areas of skin, but even the most severe were merely aggravating, not debilitating. She could move without the desire to cry out.

"Lady Lluava!" gasped June, who had been waiting for her to rise. "You look so much better!"

"I really want a bath."

The little maid scurried to help.

Once clean, Lluava returned to her room and hungrily ate enough breakfast for two. As she left her quarters to find the king, she encountered Varren, Byron, and Talos, who had come to fetch her.

"They are inside the walls," her partner informed her hastily.

"The Berserkers? How?"

"Siege ladders. Early this morning, several breached the walls. Guards are currently preventing others from doing the same, but Berserkers are rampaging through Cronus." Varren inspected her. "I've never seen ointment work so quickly."

Talos had not told Varren about the vials. There was much to explain, but this was not the time.

"It is amazing," agreed Lluava, "but what are we waiting for?"

Varren clearly did not like the idea of Lluava returning to battle. But with no obvious physical hindrances, he could find nothing to say against it. "Go get Issaura's Claws. We will fight together this time."

Once, those words would have thrilled her, but now she only wondered what had happened to Apex. He was out there among the Berserkers, possibly fighting for his life. As they left the castle, Lluava's mood darkened further as the screams of victims reached them.

Chapter 37

Growing Fissures

Screams emanated from multiple locations around the city. Despite her keen sense of hearing, Lluava wondered how many more dying people were just out of earshot.

"Who else is out there? Soldiers? Guards?" She needed to better understand what they were up against.

"General Domar headed to the infiltration point on the western side of the capital with a score of men. Lieutenant Bern took another score to the south," replied Varren. He was more in control of the situation than Lluava had thought. "We will head to the northern quadrant."

"Just us?" No matter how many Berserkers had gotten through, the four of them would hardly be enough in this labyrinthine city.

"They are coming, too," Varren said, nodding toward Daniel and a small group of familiar-looking men. Lluava assumed they had been training in the yards when the breach occurred.

Somewhat more confident now, Lluava said, "Lead the way."

At first they jogged together in a rectangular formation, squeezing four to a row, though in the smaller lanes this number shrank to two and then one. As they wound through the maze of passageways, their knowledge of the city was an advantage.

Lluava did not have to wonder where the enemy was. The Berserkers were not at all concerned with stealth. Sounds of splintering wood and breaking glass were easily heard above the shouts of the common people. Seeking protection, locals ran past the soldiers. Even without seeing the Raiders, Lluava knew they were rampaging through households and shops and causing horrendous devastation.

"You ready for this?" Lluava questioned Byron as they neared the chaos.

"More than I have been in a while."

"The Idun?

"My leg is not perfectly healed, but it no longer hurts," he said as he nodded toward the injured limb.

Talos's forehead was still bandaged. Lluava realized he had not taken the Idun, but she did not have time to ask him why.

"Here they come!" he shouted as the soldiers formed lines.

One Berserker with a war hammer lumbered toward them. His left foot seemed twisted at an odd angle. Lluava wondered if he had injured it in climbing over the wall or if some brave victim had chosen his last moments to be heroic.

Tightening her grip on the Claws, Lluava followed Varren as he charged the behemoth. The war hammer swung down, and Varren sprang away. Shards of cobblestone flew up. One pierced Lluava's lip. She tasted the warmth of her blood and felt a stirring inside as her core began to heat up. As she aimed for the man's torso, the Berserker turned and prepared to slam his weapon into her. Using this moment to his advantage, Varren thrust his sword into the brute's back.

A second Berserker appeared. "Varren!" Lluava shouted. "Look out behind you!" Fortunately, Talos and Byron were in combat positions and moved to protect their king. With a jerk, Varren freed his sword and turned to face the new attacker.

Despite his wound, the first Raider was undeterred. He focused on Lluava, and now it was her turn to dodge the swing of the massive war hammer. One near miss later, she was forced to retreat and ducked around the corner of a building.

Farther down the street, several soldiers ran into a home where the third Berserker was wreaking havoc. Members of the household were trapped inside with this monster. The window of the upper story shattered, spilling glass onto the street and the soldiers below.

The wounded Berserker attacked Varren. As the Raider prepared to strike the young king, Lluava saw her chance. She allowed her inner heat to envelop her as she shifted in mid leap. Seizing the man's arms, Lluava bit into the knuckles of a hand. Bones and flesh tore in her sharp teeth. As she was flung off by the enraged attacker, Lluava saw a small figure fall—no, jump—from the shattered window of the house down the street.

Landing on her side, Lluava spat out fingertips and blood. A few feet away, Daniel placed a little girl on the ground and then turned to catch a swaddled baby dropped by the mother from a window.

Regaining her footing, Lluava saw that Varren had positioned himself between the discarded hammer and the bleeding Berserker. With his good hand, the giant man pulled out a dagger the size of anyone else's short sword.

Then metal met metal.

A woman screamed.

Men shouted.

Several soldiers came to Varren's aid. With the help of two other men, Talos and Byron had cornered their foe. Lluava raced toward the children. The young girl sobbed hysterically as she rocked her baby brother. For a moment, Lluava saw the faces of her own siblings in this pair.

"I'll get them somewhere safe," Lluava said. Daniel nodded and helped the girl, with the baby held tightly in her arms, onto the tiger's back. He made a move for the door of the house but was halted by an attack from another Berserker. The girl sobbed harder, and Lluava felt her slip.

"Listen to me," Lluava said firmly. "I need you to be brave for your brother. He is scared as well. Can you be brave for him? Can you let him know you are here for him?"

"Yes," a meek voice answered from above. The girl's sobs lessened.

"Okay," soothed Lluava. "I need you to hold on real tight. I'm going to take you away from here."

"Mama…" the girl coughed out between heaving breaths.

Inside the house, more crashing sounds were heard. Behind them, Daniel swung the abandoned war hammer in a huge circle and then released the weapon. The hammer smashed into the crippled leg of the Berserker, cracking a bone in two.

"You'll have to hold your brother and hang onto me," Lluava continued. "Keep your eyes on him. He needs you to be strong."

Lluava began to run. The way she had originally come was now blocked by the skirmishing combatants. She tried several alternate routes. Darting around corners and skidding around abandoned carts, she somehow found a roundabout route to the castle. It was the only place in the city that Lluava knew was safe. With Berserkers inside the walls of Cronus, very few households, if any, could defend themselves against these gigantic terrorizing monstrosities.

Even in the cold, Lluava felt feverish as she ran. Had she been in human form, she would have been sweating profusely. Panting heavily, she finally bounded up to the castle. Several bodies lay scattered about the gates of the curtain wall. The gates were ajar.

No! Lluava thought fearfully. A Berserker had gotten through. How? Although Lluava yearned to charge through the doors, she could not do so with the young girl still clinging desperately to her back. Instead, the tigress entered the castle cautiously, stepping over the corpse of a minor steward. She looked left and right but could not tell which way the brute might have gone.

Someone was running toward the doors. It was Howard, the head steward.

"Lady Lluava?" he called out in a cracking voice. "He's inside. Upstairs."

"How many?"

"Only one."

"Take the children," snarled Lluava. She paused only long enough for the man to pick up the girl and the baby. As she ran toward the main stairs, she shouted back, "The doors and gates must be sealed! At once!"

How could she find the brute in such a large castle? She hoped to hear his lumbering footsteps, or maybe... Lluava sniffed the air. There it was: the subtle trace of the potent smoke.

As the tiger bounded upstairs, raced down corridors, and searched rooms, she spotted other victims. The odor of smoke grew stronger as she passed a serving man slumped in a doorway, spitting up blood.

Skidding to a stop, Lluava shifted and approached to see if she could help, but the man's wounds were beyond her abilities. He was bleeding internally and needed a healer.

The man looked at her with wild eyes. "Help me," he cried out. "Please, I need your help."

"I'll send someone," she lied, knowing that first she had to find the Berserker before more people died. She turned away.

The man screamed, "Don't leave me! Don't leave me!"

What could she do? If she stayed, she still would not be able to save him, and the enemy would continue to kill others in the castle. Her best hope was that she might cross paths with someone who could offer assistance. Lluava kept hearing his voice as he called after her.

On the next floor, she heard the sound of a door breaking. She recognized Selene's quarters just as the large form of a Berserker slipped inside. For a moment, she hesitated. Then she heard Selene cry out.

The young woman cowered at the end of the canopied bed. Why wasn't she running? Or shifting? Where was her will to fight or, at the very least, to flee? But Selene just sat there, knees pulled up to her chest. Tears streamed down her lovely sepia face.

The maddened attacker was focused on Selene. Lluava grabbed a vase from a table and threw it at the exposed skin on the back of his neck. The vase shattered, yet the Berserker took no notice. She clenched her fists and the Claws sprang up. Running at full force toward him, she drove the Claws through the boiled-leather hides and into the brute's flesh. His only response was to swat at her as if she were a pesky mosquito.

"Run, you fool!" Lluava called out to Selene.

Unable to see around the massive form, Lluava jerked the Claws out as violently as she could and shifted once more. This time, with a tigress clambering on his back, the Berserker took notice. The man grabbed tufts of Lluava's fur and attempted to pull her off. She tried to rip through his layers of protective leathers and hides. In her struggle, Lluava knocked off the crossbow strapped to the Raider's back; it skidded across the room.

"The weapon," Lluava growled out. "Selene, use the weapon."

The Berserker's large fingers closed around Lluava's pointed ear and peeled her off his back. She released a piercing scream as he swung her down and around. He pulled her massive form against himself, her back to his chest, and proceeded to squeeze the air out of her with his enormous arms.

The tigress gasped for breath and desperately clawed up at the man's face, slashing nose and lips. His blood poured down her white fur, but the Berserker's grip only tightened. Lluava wondered if her ribs would crack. Her strength began to wane. Her form was so large that her rear paws still touched the ground, but this provided scant help now.

There was a thrum and a sharp pain near Lluava's spine like the thin blade of a knife pressing hard against her. Another thrum, and Lluava was released; both she and the Raider toppled to the floor. The man's body overpowered her own, and she was half crushed beneath him.

A ring-laden hand reached down to her. Shifting to human form, Lluava seized it and was slowly pulled from under the bleeding corpse. Once she was able to turn, she saw two bolts, one embedded in the Raider's back and one lodged at the base of his skull. Selene stood holding the crossbow.

"For a moment there, I thought you weren't going to move," huffed Lluava as she caught her breath.

"For a moment, I wasn't sure I could," Selene admitted. Her hair, always perfectly coiffed, was now disheveled, as was her makeup. Her eyes looked puffy and sad.

Lluava found it hard to sympathize. "Next time, just act. Don't think too much. Hesitation can cost your life or someone else's."

"What life?" Selene appeared totally confused. "There is no point to any of this, is there?"

Selene clearly wasn't herself. Was she sick? What was she mumbling about? Did she mean the war? Lluava did not have time to question her.

"He doesn't love me," said Selene sadly.

Lluava did not know what to make of that last statement. Was this what Selene had been worrying about when the Berserker broke in?

Selene wiped the tear trails off her cheeks. "He never did. It was all a lie. What is left without love or security?" She looked on the verge of crying again. As she began to wander aimlessly around her room, she asked, "H…h…have you seen my necklace? The…the silver pendant?"

"No."

"It seems that I am losing everything…"

"You have your brother," Lluava responded. What else could she say? Why should she care? Selene had to come to terms with the fact that she could not manipulate others. She had gotten herself into this situation. Yet, was the woman actually shaking? She should be. She had been nearly strangled by the enemy.

"Luka is all I have," Selene acknowledged as she struggled not to cry.

Reaching out, Lluava gently touched the young woman's slender shoulder. "You have me as well."

Lluava did not know why she'd said that. She was still very angry at her former friend. But Lluava also realized that Selene had been so distraught she had almost let herself be killed, and this awareness allowed Lluava to dredge up some kindness, however hollow it sounded.

"Thank you," sniffled Selene.

"Now, let's get out of here," replied Lluava. She needed to get Selene away from the corpse. "Let me take that." Lluava grabbed the arrowless crossbow from Selene's hands and placed it on the ground.

In the large foyer at the front of the castle, Lluava spotted Howard, along with Enya and her handmaidens. The queen looked angry and pursed her already tight lips even tighter.

"They are not allowed inside. Do you hear me? The king can play his game outside, but not in here. Do you realize what has happened to my new tea room? Everything smashed to bits!"

Knowing better than to argue with the child Queen, the steward bowed down and said, "Yes, Your Highness."

The spoiled brat finally took note of the pair. "Lady Selene," Enya said, purposefully snubbing Lluava, "have you heard the dreary news? Why…what has happened to you? Your hair! That will never do. Come with me at once—and Marge," Enya nodded toward a slightly built girl among her entourage, "will fix you up. Then we can play Kings and Crowns."

"Of course, Your Highness," responded Selene sweetly.

The queen risked what might have been a smile before she turned abruptly and strode off. Selene gave Lluava a quick grimace, and both of them swallowed a laugh. As the young woman followed Enya's flock, Lluava called out, "Goodbye, Your Highness!"

Enya ignored her completely.

Turning to the steward, Lluava said, "The intruder was killed in Selene's quarters; he needs to be removed. There is also an injured man somewhere on the fourth floor." Lluava hoped he could be saved. She added, "It is time for me to play King's War outside."

Several soldiers in moss-green uniforms trooped past her. "Where are you headed?" she inquired.

"The gates," one shouted back. "They are giving way!"

Instinctively, she knew that Varren was safe with their friends at his side. If the Berserkers broke through the main gate, she would be needed there. She turned and followed the men. If the doors did not hold, the enemy would flood into the city.

The majority of fighting men were stationed outside the beleaguered wooden gates. With each boom, the enormous doors shivered and groaned.

"Lluava!" she heard Talos shout from a group of men. "Over here!"

Trotting up to them, Lluava said, "Did you kill them? I went off to—"

"I saw what you did. I would have done the same," Talos reassured her. "Those three were finally killed, as were the others that entered the city. Cronus has been cleared of the enemy. Lieutenant Bern and General Domar are with Varren at the top of the gates. You should join them there."

As Lluava took the stairs two at a time, one enormous blow caused the steps to shake dangerously. From the parapet, the archers still fired on the Berserkers below. The sorry state of their quivers told her that ammunition was becoming sparse. Nearby, grim faced, the military commanders were conferring.

"Again!" ordered Domar, and several men carrying a bucket of pitch poured the steaming liquid over the parapet.

Looking over one of the embrasures, Lluava was horrified to see that several Berserkers still struggled to lift the battering ram, although their skin had apparently melted off. Others arrived, treading on their dead or dying comrades to continue breaking down the gates.

Large fissures split the thick wood of the doors. The Raiders struck the wood again. Huge splinters flew off.

Lluava sensed Varren's approach. "What now?" she asked.

"Fight for everything we love," was the young king's response.

Part of her wanted to give Varren's hand a comforting squeeze, but she held back. Then, weapons at the ready, the partners watched as the Berserkers rammed the wood with tremendous force, creating a gaping hole in the gates.

Chapter 38

Feathered Rain

Down below, the clattering of weapons competed with the grunts and groans of men. Archers fired as rapidly as they could while still hitting their targets. Other soldiers poured more pitch over the wall. The hot liquid hissed on its way down. War drums boomed from the approaching enemy horde, while loathsome horns rang out. The Raiders rushed forward like a disturbed nest of hornets ready to sting.

"Bottleneck them at the gates!" General Domar shouted as he made his way down toward the pandemonium below.

"Watch out!"

Vidrick bowled into Varren and nearly knocked the king off the wall. A javelin hurtled by, impaling an archer who, in turn, let loose his arrow in the wrong direction. Helping his ruler up, the lieutenant said, "You should return to the castle."

Varren retorted, "I will fight with you here at the gates. We are all needed down on the ground."

"Wait," Lluava hissed as her ears perked up. "Did you hear that?"

"The fighting, or the dying? I hear both," Vidrick responded wearily.

"No, no." Lluava scanned the torched earth beyond Cronus. "I hear howling. Wolves."

Another lonesome wail pierced the cacophony.

"Derrick!" Lluava could not hide her dismay. "He has returned."

"There will be no helping him if he fights out there," Varren added sorrowfully. Below, the only way out of Cronus was clogged with Berserkers.

"There will be no helping *us* if more of those monsters enter our city," pointed out Vidrick as he headed toward the stairs.

"Why didn't Derrick leave?" Lluava couldn't understand the suicidal decision her friend had made. Had she fought so hard to save him, only to watch him die a few days later?

"You idiot!" she screamed, though her cry was drowned out by the noise.

Above her, a cawing was heard. Lluava looked up, half expecting to see Onyx inspecting the chaos. However, it was not her raven but a multitude of every flying thing she had ever seen. The flock consisted of numerous species of birds and insects; even several bats flittered past. The swarm flew over them and toward the Raiders' encampment. Above the skyline, several other flocks converged over the enemy lines.

Without warning, the flying creatures fell upon the Raiders. Though the Berserkers took no notice, the other Raiders stopped in their tracks. Then the flying swarm began to shift. They were all Theriomorphs!

Shifting between human and animal form, they began breaking up the marching mass. Those who were able to retrieve weapons from the enemy fought on the ground. Others caused havoc from above.

"That's impossible," uttered Varren. "Are there that many Theriomorphs in Elysia?"

"No," replied Lluava breathlessly, who finally realized what she was seeing. "I summoned them."

Her partner stared at her as if she were half-crazed. Lluava could not look away from the mythic scene unfolding before them. But she owed Varren an explanation.

"They are Outlanders. I met their leaders while I was traveling beyond Elysia. I asked them for assistance in our war. I wasn't sure if they would come."

"Whatever you said to them," Varren began, "I cannot thank you enough." He turned her toward him. "Lluava, you may have saved us."

As Varren pulled her into his embrace, all she could think about was Apex. Could he be out there with Derrick? She hoped he was still alive. Wriggling out of the king's grip, Lluava said, "We can't just stand around. Berserkers are still pushing through the gates."

"You are right," acknowledged her partner.

"They. *Are*. Monstrous."

A familiar voice permeated the air above them, and the sarus crane alighted on the walkway right in front of the pair. "I never imagined them so *overgrown*." Thoth shifted into his human form.

Lluava hastily introduced Varren to the ruire. Both men inclined their heads to one another. Varren added, "I am so grateful that you have come to help us in our time of need."

"Wait until we have this rubbish under control," Thoth cautioned. Turning toward Lluava, he added, "The high priestess sends her regards." To the king, he explained, "The bulk of our army is on its way. Since those of us who can fly could travel much faster, we were sent ahead. The rest will be here in a few days. Until they arrive, how can we be of service?" The ruire was under no obligation to ask but had done so out of courtesy. Lluava was both grateful and impressed.

Varren began, "Our highest priority is to secure the gates and slay any Raider that has passed through them. After that, our goal will be to force the enemy back to their ships."

"You are a merciful ruler," noted Thoth. "I would tear the eyes out of each one myself before ripping their souls from their chests. But this is where we clearly differ." He shifted abruptly and flew off to give commands to the winged army.

All around them, the symphony of war was played. Over the din, Varren's voice was urgent. "Lluava, we must help secure the gates."

He was right. As it currently stood, more than a score of Berserkers had muscled their way inside, slaughtering anyone in their way. From where they stood on the wall, Lluava spotted a helmetless Berserker. Instead of taking the stairs, she vaulted from the wall, shifted midair, and snapped the man's neck as she crashed down upon him. Lucky not to have been impaled by the behemoth's sword, she charged at yet another invader, who was shaking entrails off his double-bladed axe.

Within moments Varren arrived to assist her. She should have been glad to have him back at her side. There was no need for verbal communication; each knew what the other would do, where their partner should be. Despite the danger, each time Lluava looked at Varren's face, she envisioned Selene touching him, kissing him. Somehow that thought disgusted her, and she yearned for Apex's presence.

As the day progressed, the aerial army relentlessly attacked the Raiders outside the walls and managed to prevent most from entering through the damaged doors. Inside Cronus, every attacker that intruded into the city was eradicated, although the Elysians' losses were far greater than anticipated. However, with the help of Thoth and his warriors, there were still men to fight in the morning. The damaged gates were patched and the discarded battering rams burned. As the sun began to set and the smoke-induced rage abated, Berserkers and Raiders alike were forced back to their encampment.

Thoth's numbers had also diminished, although not as dramatically as the Elysians. His troops flew over the walls to find rest in the city. At dusk, a number of owl and bat Theriomorphs were stationed to keep eyes on the enemy's movements. Thoth, in his human form, trudged with Lluava and the king back toward the castle.

"We need weapons," the ruire stated frankly. "In order to fly in our dual forms, we had to leave our own weapons behind. Come morning, my men will need to protect themselves. Surely you have an armory of sorts. Today was one thing, but I will not send them back out without protection of their own. When High Priestess Yena arrives with the rest of our army, she will bring weapons, and we will return what is not ours. Until then, I ask you to lend us what we need if you want our assistance in the coming days."

"Of course," said Varren. "Whatever you need will be yours, for without you my people would not have survived. Come." He gestured to Thoth to follow them inside the curtain wall. "Let me give you a place to rest for the night. In the morning, your troops may choose whatever weapons they desire."

Thoth, Lluava, and Varren entered the castle, where several stewards rushed toward them offering service.

"Hot food and strong drink," requested the exhausted king, who then led the other two into the banquet hall. Thoth's face showed a dignified awe as he looked around the magnificent room. The castle was unlike any structure in Leucrocotta. Lluava wondered what he thought.

The hall was strangely empty. Choosing to sit at the common tables, Varren, Lluava and Thoth began to eat as soon as platters were placed before them. Just as Lluava raised her cup of mulled wine to her lips, Themis, along with half the council, strode through the doors.

"What am I hearing about Outlanders in our streets?" boomed Themis's voice as he approached the trio.

"Head Councilman Themis," Varren said, rising from the long bench. "May I introduce to you Ruire Thoth, the leader of our salvation. Without his aid, we might not have withstood the attack today."

Themis pursed his lips as others behind him whispered among themselves. Lluava did not see Hyrax. Had he been informed? Not one of the Theriomorph councilmen was present.

Thoth silently went on eating his meal.

Finally, the head councilman said, "There are rumors that you will be emptying our armory."

"In order to help assist us in a timely manner, the ruire and his men were not able to travel with their own weapons. We will supplement them until theirs arrive."

"More are coming?" another councilman questioned.

"With all due respect, Your Majesty," Themis began, "we do not know these *people*. How are you so sure that we can trust them? You are willing to hand over the keys to our defense. I must point out how unwise that seems."

How did Themis know this? He truly did have ears everywhere. Yet, what he was saying was in fact true; they did not know the Leucrocottans.

But Lluava did. "I will vouch for them," she said.

Themis did not bother to hide the scowl he gave her.

"It was I who asked for their assistance. We needed help to win this war."

"Might I ask if you will take responsibility for whatever comes of this?" The head councilman's words were laced with contempt.

"When we win this war, I will personally thank them," she responded.

"Enough," asserted Varren. "The decision has been made. Ruire Thoth will receive all the accommodations and provisions he needs. I trust Lluava and therefore these people. I do understand your concern, Councilmen, but my mind is made up. I wish you all a good night, for I am about to take my rest. I suggest you do the same."

"As you wish." Themis bowed briefly, then led the council from the room.

"I apologize for my council's rude welcome," said Varren as he returned to his seat.

"Don't," noted Thoth. "They are doing what they are supposed to do. They are questioning everything."

"Thank you for your gifts," Lluava said between bites, remembering the vials that had been mysteriously delivered to her.

Thoth smiled. "They were sent by command of the high priestess herself."

Varren looked questioningly from one to the other as the doors to the hall opened again. This time, the voices were of laughing men. Soldiers from both armies began trickling in while serving women hurried about carrying steaming platters of food and filling cups with wine and mead.

"This guy thinks he is some kind of hero," Byron declared as he and Talos arrived, supporting Vidrick between them. "He was nearly cut in two trying to protect those unable to defend themselves."

Lluava noted that Vidrick's torso was wrapped in bindings. "How bad?"

"Well, it's…it is feeling better since Talos gave me some foul medicine."

Realizing what her friend had done, Lluava helped Vidrick to a seat. "Did you see Apex out there?"

"If he is out there," said Vidrick, "I did not see him."

"He did not enter through the gates," added Talos. "I am sorry."

"For what?" Lluava forced herself to smile. "He wanted to be rid of this place. He just found his chance."

***

The following days were difficult, but the gates held. With Thoth's men conducting hundreds of skirmishes beyond the gates, the Elysians concentrated on repairing the doors and securing the perimeter of the city.

During odd moments of free time, Lluava felt hollow and distant from the rest of her comrades, especially Varren. Shouldn't she be reconnecting with him? Hadn't she wanted to open up? Why did she hold back the truth about Selene? She had shared nothing of her journey since they parted ways. He knew nothing of the prophecy or even the Incarn; she had been purposely vague about their Theriomorph aid.

In a last-ditch attempt to reestablish their bond, Lluava invited Varren to her quarters. He was still her military partner and her king; he should know everything. But as soon as he looked at her, she knew that Varren realized this visit was not for pleasure.

"I want you to know what happened to me in the Outlands with Apex." Lluava paused while she tried to decide whether to start with her departure from the Alcazar Castle or just lead into the more pertinent topics.

Though he tried to wait patiently, Varren seemed discomforted and soon replied, "I am just glad that you made it back safely to me."

Tentatively, he bent over to kiss her, but Lluava quickly said, "There is something you should be aware of." Varren would want to know about Horus.

"What is that?"

Someone was banging on the door to Lluava's quarters. Onyx flew angrily into Lluava's bedroom recess to escape the noise. The bird, having made himself scarce for several days, had shown up earlier that day.

Sighing, Varren admitted their unwelcome guest. Vidrick looked far better than he had previously. "Sorry for the interruption, Your Majesty. A report was passed to me that the rest of the Theriomorph army has been spotted approaching from the west. A number of Berserkers have been sent out to attack them. The Outlanders will require assistance to enter Cronus's gates."

"They shall receive an escort at once," pronounced the king.

The thought that she would actually have a chance to search for Apex beyond the walls suddenly filled Lluava with an energy that she had not felt for quite some time. Vidrick looked as if he were going to speak.

"Do not say anything," said Varren. "I will not leave these walls."

Lluava's hopes dimmed. As she was bound to her military partner by Elysian law, she would have to keep watch from the castle's high towers.

The king continued, "I will not put my life at undue risk. I understand that if I were killed, Elysia would be placed in great peril." Turning to his partner, he said, "Lluava, you have served as my eyes before in times such as this. I want you to go and bring back this high priestess who has traveled so far to offer us assistance."

"Come with me then, Corporal Kargen," barked out Vidrick as he strode off.

Before she could follow, Varren added, "Be careful out there."

Lluava nodded, then left.

At the main gates, Colonel Ojewa approached her. "Let me come with you."

"Yena tried to have you killed," said Lluava, rather shocked.

"That was the law. But Yena was my mate for some years. I wish her no ill will." Ojewa's dark eyes gleamed.

"Well, I am one partner short," noted Lluava. Ojewa inclined his head toward her; then they both headed out the gates to the front lines.

They were a mere cart's length away from the doors when a Berserker charged the crowd. Ojewa threw his spear into the Raider's shoulder and shifted into his black panther form. Lluava tried to assist but found herself lifted off the ground by her platinum braid.

A blond-bearded Berserker held her firmly in his grip, his sword pointed at her navel.

Chapter 39

Returning to Refuge

"Theri," grunted the Berserker as he pressed the tip of the blade into her torso.

Using one of the Claws, Lluava forced the sword to one side, which tore her shirt. With her other hand, she severed her braid. She landed on her feet as the platinum-blond hair unwound right above her shoulders.

Somersaulting to the left, Lluava evaded the angry blade and its merciless wielder. The giant brute continued to pummel her with strike after strike. Lluava could feel her arms tiring. She could not combat this monster by herself.

Fortunately, she did not have to.

Vidrick appeared, and in a whirl of movement, he and the Berserker attacked one another. In another moment, Lluava had shifted; she bit a huge chunk of flesh from the enemy's thigh. The only response she received for her bloody work was an annoyed grumble.

The Raider would have decapitated Vidrick, but luckily the redheaded lieutenant misstepped and fell backward. Lluava grappled with the Berserker's torso while a dark form leapt onto the Raider's bulky shoulders. With the black panther tearing bits of cheek and Lluava restraining the attacker's movement, Vidrick was able to stab the man through his heart.

Although this Berserker was vanquished, he was but one of many. Ojewa panted, "We must push forward."

Their progress around Cronus's walls was painstakingly slow. The small band of soldiers was repeatedly attacked by trios of Berserkers or small bands of regular Raiders. Lluava was worried that they might lose too many men before ever reaching Yena.

Another concern was Talos. During one skirmish, he clearly was not paying attention when a small party of Raiders attacked them in the forest. He nearly allowed one sea brute to impale him with a spear; Byron had had to shove his partner aside to deflect the tip. This was not the only time Lluava had glanced over and seen Talos looking distracted.

After the skirmish was over, Lluava shifted and went over to her blond friend. "Whatever is on your mind today, put it aside. Get a grip on yourself before you get yourself or Byron killed. What good would that do?"

She had not meant to sound so harsh. Looking ashamed, Talos nodded. As strange as his behavior was to Lluava, Byron too seemed at a loss. He just looked at her and shrugged.

Returning to Lluava's side, Ojewa informed her, "We should be nearing Yena's army." This also was quite unusual. The man who had once instructed her in warfare now looked to her as his leader. A colonel, Ojewa was several ranks above her in military command. Moreover, Lluava could not match his years of experience. Yet he seemed to be waiting for her to take command.

Lieutenant Vidrick, however, still looked to Ojewa for orders: "How do you recommend we proceed from here?"

With General Domar stationed at the castle gates, Ojewa was the highest-ranking officer present. "Lluava," the colonel replied, "I want you to scout ahead. Knowing the high priestess, she will have her men on high alert for an attack. I do not want anyone injured or killed due to mistaken identity. Since she will recognize you, you can prepare her army for our arrival. We will then proceed to escort our travel-weary companions to Cronus."

Not wishing to question the tall man, Lluava replied, "Yes, sir."

Byron asked, "Would you like us to come with you?"

"No. Keep an eye on him," she nodded at Talos, who was standing nearby, deep in thought.

"Of course."

***

It was strange to be alone. Thinking back, Lluava could not remember when she had last traveled solo. Had she *ever* done so? During all her missions, she had always relied on either Varren or, more recently, Apex to be by her side. Even when training in Durog, she had been taught to fight as one of a pair. Shivering, Lluava tried to shake off the unsettled feeling that being on her own gave her.

Though evening had not arrived, it seemed to have already permeated the understory of the forest. A lone owl hooted above her. Lluava sensed that it was not Theriomorph, so she continued. Then the hairs on the back of her neck stood on end as the nocturnal raptor flew by in almost dead silence.

Taking a shaky breath, Lluava tried to calm her nerves. What was she so afraid of? A surprise attack from the enemy? She was half expecting them to appear around the next tree trunk. Was it coming face-to-face with Yena once more? Thoth had said that Yena had come to help. Surely the priestess held no grudge against her. So why was she so on edge?

The forest was alive with wildlife. Birds flitted among branches in the trees. A rabbit bounded out of sight. Tracks crisscrossed everywhere over the new-laid snow. Oddly enough, the peaceful atmosphere only added to Lluava's worry. She shivered again.

Shifting into her dual form, Lluava continued on four paws. At least now she had natural camouflage to hide her in the forest. Her winter coat was still growing out after she had shed much of it in the heat of Leucrocotta. Yet it was far warmer than Endun, a thin material.

The sound of cracking wood came to her pointed ears. Turning to the noise, Lluava saw a large, dead pine give way from the weight of snow on its boughs. The ancient tree began to topple in her direction, taking down smaller trees in its shadow. Lluava scooted backward to evade the splintering limbs. Just as she did, another pine fell behind her. Clambering over the rough trunk of the first one, she had to leap away. Then a third pine did the same.

This was no coincidence. These trees had been rigged to fall.

A fourth tree pinned her to the snow-laden earth. She struggled to claw her way out from underneath its suffocating weight. Then silhouettes of horned Raiders appeared. Lluava took no time to count them but frantically fought to free herself. Shifting to human form, she hoped to slide out from underneath the tree. Instead, the trunk pressed down more heavily on her thighs.

Oddly, with several pairs of fur-trimmed boots before her, Lluava considered how diminished these men seemed now that she had combated their larger comrades. Trying to turn and strike out, Lluava knew she had made herself an easy kill.

Yena, she thought solemnly. Please help Varren slay every last one of these sea brutes. They deserve no mercy.

Refusing to give up, Lluava kept trying to claw at the Raiders. Several laughed at her pathetic attempts. She released an ear-piercing scream—but the sound ended in a deafening roar. One that was not her own.

"Apex!" she cried out, just as the man about to behead her was bowled over by a massive bronze wolverine.

Raiders scattered and ran. The Yorrick wolverine charged past her. From the obstructed viewpoint behind the pine limbs, Lluava could only glimpse the skirmish as she struggled to dig herself out. The earth was far too frozen and, even with the Claws, her attempt was all but useless. Lluava tried to turn and lift the tree, but she was pinned on her stomach and could not reach far enough around.

Come on! she chastised herself. You can do this!

Someone approached. If she could not escape in the next few moments, she was as good as dead. Issaura's Claws finally caught the rough bark, but it just sloughed off.

Something wet dripped on the back of her head. Another drop spattered the white snow with red. Before Lluava could turn toward the intruder, she felt the trunk being lifted off her. Rolling out from under it, she watched as Apex, in human form, dropped the pine. Red-tinged sweat dripped from his face. His beard was coated with blood.

The huntsman was already helping Lluava to her feet when she finally said his name aloud. She was shaking, but not from her close brush with death. Apex was alive, here, with her.

The huntsman inquired worriedly, "Can you walk?"

Though greatly bruised and scraped, Lluava could still move about. Adrenaline made her feel far less pain than she should. She nodded. Her voice seemed to be caught in her throat.

"This way," Apex said as he helped over several trees and corpses.

"Apex, I…" Lluava began as they navigated the forest. What should she say? The red flecks in Apex's eyes seemed to glimmer at her as he studied her. Was he wondering about her miraculous recovery from her burns? Or was he looking at her that way because it was her?

"…I'm glad you are all right."

"As am I."

Lluava recognized the husky voice of the high priestess. Yena approached them, garbed entirely in silvery material that allowed only her hands and eyes to be seen. Behind her, the woods teemed with animals. This time, they were Theriomorphs. From the look on his face, Apex had expected to see the priestess. Lluava could only be relieved at that.

She addressed the silver-clad figure. "I have come to inform you that a band of soldiers has been sent to escort you to the capital. We were not sure what state you would be in upon arrival and wanted to make sure that you could rest before facing our enemy."

"How kind of you." Yena smiled in a way that made it appear she had expected as much. Had she been scrying during her journey? Had she watched all that had occurred? Or had she seen this happen days before? Was that the reason Apex had been there for Lluava when the Raiders attacked?

Several other figures stood about in their human forms. Lluava recognized Ammit and Master Hon. She wondered if Maruny was somewhere in the ranks of the Warrior Caste. The girl had been so angry at her when they last met.

"Lead us, Lluava," commanded the priestess.

The Theriomorphs had several wagons, which hauled weapons and other valued items. These were the largest hindrances, for they could become stuck in the snow or be overturned in an attack. Lluava retraced her steps cautiously. She was especially careful around the fallen trees.

Not far away, the Elysian troops awaited them.

***

Upon arrival, Colonel Ojewa formally introduced Lieutenant Vidrick, as well as Talos and Byron, to the high priestess. The enormous menagerie of animals was an impressive sight, especially for those who had not seen the might of Leucrocotta. Even Talos and Byron seemed awestruck.

The Elysian escorts traveled alongside the Theriomorph army as they began the last leg of their journey. Cronus's gates were not so far away. Seeing no Raiders during their return, the small army continued without fear of a threat.

Lluava kept glancing over at Apex. Once he seemed satisfied that she had truly found her footing, he stayed away from her. Lluava knew that the next time she had a chance she would talk with him. He needed to know where things stood between them, how things had changed, and what he meant to her.

If Apex noticed Lluava's repeated looks, he pretended not to. Instead, he rapidly scanned the forest as if on high alert. The Theriomorphs were first to discern the odor, followed by the humans—the odor of pungent, sour smoke.

Ojewa shouted, "Weapons ready!"

There was no further need for silence. They had been discovered. All at once, several dozen Berserkers appeared.

"I thought they only traveled in threes," said a man who had trained recently in Cronus.

"Yeah," noted someone next to him. "But that don't mean there can only be one trio at a time."

There was no more time for speculation. The monstrous men moved in for the kill. Beasts and beings collided. Bellows and roars combated screams and shouts as the ruckus began.

Never having fought together, Yena's men and Ojewa's seemed out of sync. They either tried to slay the enormous Raiders on their own, or they got in each other's way.

A fearsome snap jolted Lluava's ears. At her side, she recognized Yena, who had discarded her robes and was now fighting with Crocotta's Hackles. The long-corded weapon whipped the air and wrapped about a Berserker's longsword. A moment later, she had effortlessly disarmed the sea brute.

There was a splintering sound as a Berserker shouldered one of the wagons onto its side. Large casks rolled away; others were trampled in the fray. Lluava was assisting in the takedown of another giant Raider. Ammit had shifted into his crocodilian form. Though she knew that in this battle he was on her side, the crunching sound of the reptilian's jaws closing on the enemy's leg made Lluava's insides churn.

Ojewa was protecting her back when another marauder appeared. Shifting, Lluava joined the colonel in their felid forms and assisted in bringing down the rage-induced Raider.

Yena loped up beside Lluava in her silvery hyena form as this particular fight drew to a bloody close. "I will admit I had not expected creatures such as these. Human, they are, but so much more. I will have to ask Crocotta what path to take toward victory."

Ignoring the comment about the goddess, Lluava said, "This is why I needed your help."

Their conversation was cut short when Master Hon, in his dual form of a rhinoceros, announced, "A new wave of those monstrosities is approaching. They intend to cut us off from the city."

"I didn't know they were capable of so much intelligent thought," sneered Lluava. "Their drug reverts them to the most bestial essence."

"Never underestimate one's enemy," purred Ojewa before ordering his fractured troops, "Make a push for the gates!"

Moments later, everyone was thrust back into battle. In the blur of defensive movements and offensive attacks, Lluava glimpsed the familiar red-bearded Raider Sweyn. She remembered him clearly; he had ordered her to die in the hot box. A cry of hatred escaped her whiskered lips.

"We must kill that man," she said to Ojewa, who was still at her side. "He tried to have me burned alive."

Looking at Sweyn, Lluava was blocked by another Berserker who separated her from her prey. "Colonel Ojewa," Lluava begged, "kill the redbeard."

Somewhere behind the behemoth, Ojewa asserted, "One never leaves one's military partner."

She had heard these words countless times before, but now she hated them. Lluava wanted to scream again but had to evade a blood-encrusted blade.

"I have her," Apex's rough voice barked out to the officer. "Go!"

Moving next to Lluava, the massive wolverine lunged at the enemy before them. With Apex assisting her, an odd calm washed over Lluava. Together they brought down the Raider, working as a unit as partners should.

Looking around, Lluava suddenly recognized new faces. General Domar's men must have joined the battle. Not far off, the grand master chief, with his son at his side, was severing the head of a Berserker.

"Lluava!"

Byron shouted her name. He and Talos were struggling with a Raider of their own. As Vidrick helped usher the Theriomorphs toward the opened gates, Lluava—along with Apex—moved to assist her friends.

When they finally defeated the brute, she was happy to see that the majority of the Theriomorph army had reached the doors. They all pressed into the small entry area designed to protect Cronus from attack. General Domar kept watch for stragglers.

"Everyone inside," he ordered. Lluava knew he would not leave a single soldier behind if he could help it.

Moving over to an injured Cronian, Apex shifted and lifted the man onto Lluava's back. Very weak and dripping blood, the man lay draped over her form listlessly. Before she could head for the door, Lluava saw Domar heading their way.

Behind him rose a corpse.

Chapter 40

Blood on the Lips

N o.

Not a corpse—a Berserker, grievously wounded but alive. The massive, disemboweled Raider lifted his war hammer and struck Domar. The general stumbled to the ground. Behind him, the Berserker collapsed in his own pooling blood.

Lluava desperately wanted to help the general. She felt the man on her back slip to the side. He needed medical attention immediately, but what about Domar? The soldier she carried was just a recent volunteer, but the general had a voice in the army; his knowledge and experience were invaluable. Wasn't Domar's life more important? Did she have the right to make such a choice?

"Inside!" Lluava heard Vidrick shouting in the distance.

What should she do?

In a bronze blur, Apex charged. The Yorrick wolverine shifted and, in one large heave, flung the incapacitated general over his own broad shoulders. With the decision made for her, Lluava, still carrying the man, ran past the closing gates. There was just enough time for them to slip through before the doors groaned shut.

Cronus seemed about to burst with the influx of people, Elysian refugees as well as Leucrocottan soldiers. Lluava made her way to one of the buildings now designated for medical care. After depositing her ward, she looked for Apex, but he had disappeared. Instead, she found the high priestess conversing with Thoth, who had recently returned from the war front. After checking that the injured general was being treated, Lluava led the visitors to the castle.

For the first time in a long while, the entire High Council had assembled in the Grand Hall, along with the nobles. As protocol dictated, formal introductions were made. Lluava was surprised how tedious that was. Her thoughts kept returning to Apex. She wanted to find him, to look at him, to talk with him. Instead she was trapped by this dull procedure.

After all the flourishes were made and titles given, King Varren inquired of their guests, "May we invite you to have supper with us? I assume you are weary."

Seated next to Varren, little Enya looked as if her nose had just picked up a foul smell. She pursed her brilliant red lips in a prominent pout. On the other side of the table, Themis, though blank of face, must have been dealing with the same train of thought as the queen.

Yena, who had re-robed upon entering Cronus, inclined her veiled head. "If it please you, I have traveled far to assist your kingdom in its time of need. Let us not stall longer. A strategy to combat this mighty foe must be solidified."

Nodding in agreement, Varren said, "Let us adjourn to the Lesser Hall to discuss the matter further."

Rising, Varren and Enya, followed by Head Councilman Themis, Lluava, and the rest of the council, filed out of the hall. The nobles, who were clustered about the room, moved aside. As the procession approached the high priestess, Varren, in a gesture of hospitality and good faith, offered his arm to Yena to walk beside him. Lluava wondered what Themis thought of all this.

Inside the smaller meeting room, Varren asked the head councilman to move down a seat to allow the high priestess a place next to the king. Themis shifted position without complaint, although Lluava could see the burning hatred in his eyes.

"Who may he be?" questioned Yena after taking her seat.

For a moment, everyone seemed confused before Varren figured out whom the priestess was referring to. At the king's signal, Regin, in his skin-tight black garb, stepped out of the shadows. The leader of the Obsidian Guard took a position behind Varren's high-backed chair in silence.

As Varren introduced Regin, Lluava wondered how Yena had sensed him. Even with her own hyperactive senses, she could not smell him. He was a shadow in human form. Was this one of Yena's abilities as Crocotta's Incarn?

The conversation turned to the war. During the detailed recap of what had occurred around Cronus, Varren inquired of his military partner, "Lluava, where are the rest of the officers? They should have arrived by now."

"Lieutenant Vidrick Bern is at the gates. I assume he is regrouping his regiment. Corporals Talos Cremwell and Byron Larson are with him." Varren seemed to understand that remark. Lluava continued grimly, "Grand Master Chief Domar sustained a grievous injury. He was brought inside the gates, but I do not know what his status is."

Lluava gave a respectful pause. She had grown fond of the general.

"If it please Your Majesty," Themis began, "with the commanding general down, who is next in command? He should be informed immediately."

"That would be Colonel Ojewa. Where is the colonel?"

Suddenly, Lluava felt nauseous. "I last saw the major in pursuit of a Berserker officer." She purposely omitted the fact that she had sent him on that task. Had he returned? Was he still outside the gates? Was he even alive?

"An officer?" questioned a pensive-looking councilman.

Varren motioned for a steward. "Find out if the colonel returned before the gates were closed."

The steward disappeared.

"I must say," began Yena, her voice seeming to fill every corner of the room, "I was not expecting those humans to be so *inhuman*."

"Yes," answered the young king. "The Berserker Legion is an extraordinary enemy. They are a bit weaker if attacked prior to smoking that substance they brought with them over the ocean."

"Would it be possible to destroy their drug?" questioned the shortest councilman at the table.

"How do you suggest we do that?" Lluava asked contemptuously. She was furious that these men, who had not set foot on the field of battle and had no knowledge of the cruel truth of what lay beyond the capital, dared to offer suggestions. "Have you stood in front of one of those men? Have you seen their soulless eyes? Do you think someone can just steal all the drugs away from an army of giants? What you are suggesting is suicide. Are *you* going to volunteer for that mission?"

The small councilman shrank down in his chair. Good riddance, she thought. He had never felt the bite of a blade, or the searing pain of flesh on metal.

"If I am not mistaken," interjected Hyrax from the far end of the table, "you and the one called Apex recently undertook a similar mission. Both of you returned alive."

Lluava had half a mind to climb over the table and throttle Hyrax. Why was he encouraging this line of discussion? Was this one of his manipulations as a Guardian, to force her to assume the role of an Incarn?

"I will admit," Lluava growled, "that plan was poorly thought out. An attempt like that should not be made again." Suddenly Lluava realized she had been running her fingers over the parts of her body that had been the most severely burned. She shivered. The air in the room must be cold.

Thoth spoke up, "Allow me to command the army in your officer's absence. With my aerial Theriomorphs, I may be able to come up with a far more reasonable solution."

"I beg your pardon," boomed Themis. "You are a welcome aid, but many of us know little about you. Do not presume that you will be handed authority over our troops. We have other officers who can take the command."

With half the table taking up the argument, Lluava placed her head in her hands. Her temples throbbed with every voice that reverberated around the stone walls. Her queasiness increased. Suddenly she jumped to her feet.

"I need to be excused," she said, then hurried from the room.

She was only partway down the hall when she heaved up the few remnants in her stomach. Bits of half-digested food and bile splattered onto the hall floor and wall. Walking away from the mess, she found her way to her room and rinsed her mouth out with water.

Onyx flapped over to her and perched on the lip of the washbasin. The bird cawed testily and tugged at her hair.

"Leave me," snapped Lluava, but the raven continued to bid for her attention. When she splashed water over her face, Onyx had the nerve to peck her hand as she reached for the wash towel. Lluava angrily batted the bird away from her, and he screeched all the way over to his perch.

"Stupid bird," snarled Lluava. Not finding any solace there, she headed out of her chambers, leaving Onyx to squawk angrily alone.

She headed to Apex's room. Why she chose to go there, Lluava did not know. The door was unlatched, but his room was empty. She curled up in his wing chair and promptly fell asleep.

Movement inside the room awoke her. Apex had returned and was lighting a fire in the hearth. Lluava cleared her throat so as not to startle him. Without glancing at her, he said, "The general has yet to awaken."

Sparks jumped from his flint and found refuge in the pile of wood. A warm glow took hold. Lluava could now see the blood that stained Apex's tattered clothes. He stood up, and before she could ask, he said, "Most is not mine."

Lluava watched him struggle to peel off his damp shirt. She moved to help him. "I thought you left after the gates were shut. I thought you wanted to be rid of the capital."

A large bruise had bloomed on Apex's right shoulder and spread down his ribcage. He winced as Lluava accidentally touched it. "I could have. I wanted to."

Blood was caked on the back of his neck and around his left ear. "Sit down," Lluava ordered as she dipped a cloth in his washbowl. "Let me help."

Apex stared at the flames in the hearth, then took a seat on the footstool. Slowly Lluava cleaned the huntsman's wounds. The water in the bowl darkened dramatically.

"Why didn't you go?" Lluava could feel him stiffen under her touch.

"There was something I couldn't leave behind."

Discarding the soiled cloth, Lluava picked up a dry one. Gently wiping down his neck once more, Lluava said, "I was afraid I wouldn't see you again."

The huntsman remained silent.

"There is something I want to give you," breathed Lluava. Her voice had shrunk down to a whisper.

He turned his head to her and looked up into her eyes. She bent down and kissed him. His beard prickled her face, though far less than she had imagined it would. Breathing in his sweat, she found it bearable. More than bearable—she actually liked his odor. She was about to pull away when his lips parted, and Lluava explored them a moment longer.

In a heart-racing flurry of movement, Apex's arms wrapped around her and pulled her close. His kisses were hard, filled with a yearning she had not expected. She met his need with the same passion. As her fingers played with his hair and traced old scars down his back, he tore off her top.

Lluava tasted the saltiness that coated his skin, the flavor that was truly his own. His lips moved down her neck and traced the outline of the undergarment that covered her small breasts. She suddenly wanted him to remove that as well, but her voice was lost in their hungered movements. The fervor of Apex's kisses intensified into nips and bites. He growled throatily. Or was that her? Heartbeats seemed to thrum in a matched rhythm.

In one motion, Apex lifted her up. She wrapped her legs around his waist. He swung her about, causing a vase to clatter to the floor. She nipped his ear. The huntsman grunted and shoved her back against a wall. She gasped when the unforgiving stone hit her spine, yet she would not ask him to stop. Instead, she tugged his shaggy hair, and his lips caught hers in an ardent kiss. Pulling his head back, she saw that his lip was bleeding.

Lluava felt herself purr and kissed him anew. Apex carried her over to his bed. As soon as she felt the sheets, her pupils narrowed like a cat's. Chuffing, she watched as he hastily kicked off his shoes.

He moved on top of her, not crushing her but holding her so that she could not get away. Lluava could not even think of resisting. She thirsted for his kisses, craved his touch, the feel of his chest hair moving over her breasts and belly.

Pinning her arms above her head, he moved his lips over her collarbone, between her breasts, and down to her navel. She shivered in excitement. His free hand played with her corded belt, and she closed her eyes.

Apex paused. Lluava's desire grew tenfold in that moment. "What?" she whispered huskily.

Apex looked down into her eyes. "What of Varren?"

"Varren?" The name seemed almost foreign to her. Lluava's heart thumped so loudly she could barely concentrate. She looked longingly at Apex. "Do you care?"

"Are you over him? Completely?"

Apex gripped her wrists, and Lluava strained to reach up to kiss the huntsman's lips. He did not give her the opportunity. "Tell me you have no more feelings for him."

"What does it matter?" she purred.

"It matters."

At the harshness of his voice, Lluava grew serious at last. She tried to say what he wanted to hear, but the words did not come. "You have had plenty of women. Why not have me?"

"I will." Apex let her go. "When you are ready."

"I'm ready!" demanded Lluava. She felt the heat in her cheeks.

"No. You're not," declared the huntsman as he backed away from her. As he handed her one of his own spare shirts, he said, "Until Varren is completely out of your heart, you are not ready. You need to leave."

Lluava lay on the bed open mouthed. Apex had desired her all this time, yet he was turning her down. He should be thrilled that she had come to him. Did he understand that this was a privilege? He might not have a second opportunity.

Apex lifted Lluava to her feet and walked her to the door. He pushed her into the hall and closed the door behind her.

How dare he? She wasn't some harlot. How could he have the nerve to say no? Lluava beat her fists on the wooden door.

"This was your chance," she shouted, "and you ruined it!"

Voices drifted down the hall. Tossing the oversized shirt over her head, she strode back to her quarters, fighting the tears brimming in her eyes. Apex was a fool. Why had she ever thought otherwise? How could she have let him convince her that he meant anything to her?

Lluava had barely slammed the door behind her when there was a soft knock.

"What now?" she complained. She had half a mind to ignore the knock but flung the door open anyway, revealing Rosalyn, who looked nearly as distraught as Lluava.

"Has something happened to Talos?" Lluava asked quickly. Her own anger momentarily subsided.

"No," Rosalyn said. Her voice wavered, and her enlarged eyes darted about the room. "Are we alone?"

"June?" Lluava called out, but the little girl did not appear. "I think so. What's wrong? What happened?"

"I have a bad feeling about the upcoming battle."

Resting a hand on Rosalyn's shoulder, Lluava consoled her. "Everyone should. It's war. That's to be expected."

"But suddenly everything seems to have changed. There is too much at stake now. I feel as if I cannot take any more of this turmoil. I feel a pressure on my chest, like I cannot breathe."

Rosalyn looked about to hyperventilate.

"Come on. Breathe. We're going to be all right. Help is here. The people I escorted back to Cronus, that Talos helped inside the gates, are Theriomorphs from the Outlands come to assist us. With their help, we can win."

Rosalyn shook her head. Her skin seemed to glisten.

"Are you still ill?" Lluava felt Rosalyn's brow. She was not sweating, although she was warm to the touch. "Do you have a fever?"

Rosalyn began to cry.

"Oh no," Lluava tucked back a loose strand of her friend's black hair. "We're going to be all right."

Between her sobs, Rosalyn whispered, "I'm pregnant."

Chapter 41

Bargaining Chip

"You sure?" Lluava questioned.

"Yes," replied Rosalyn. "I can sense my body changing. Humans might not recognize the minute alterations until the signs are all too obvious, but Theriomorphs can. My mother told me that you know almost immediately. I am with child."

How should she react? wondered Lluava as her raven-haired friend began to cry again. "This is wonderful news. You should not be sad."

"It is the last thing I wanted." Rosalyn wiped her deep blue eyes with the cuffs of her dress. "We are in the middle of a war which, of late, we have not been winning. How can I ever hope to have my child grow up safely when the enemy is just outside our doors? What future, if any, could I provide? What of my husband? If he is killed, our child will have no father."

"Oh…" Lluava began to understand. "You've told Talos." This explained his strange, abstracted behavior on the battlefield.

Sniffing, Rosalyn nodded. "After I was certain. I had hoped we would one day have a family of our own. But not like this. Not now."

Firmly gripping her friend's slender hands, Lluava affirmed, "We are going to win this war." Her words sounded hollow to herself, yet she would not allow Rosalyn to sense that. "Your child will grow up learning about this only from schoolbooks and your stories."

Rosalyn nodded. Her eyes glistened again. Standing up, she moved toward the door. "I needed to talk to someone. No one else should know."

"Of course."

As she was about to step through the doorway, Rosalyn turned back. "I am the worst friend. I have not even inquired how you are doing."

Lluava knew she must look horrendous with her hacked-off hair, Apex's oversized shirt draped over her, and her own puffy eyes. "I am better now that I know about the joy that is to come."

Smiling ever so slightly, Rosalyn left.

"I thought we would never be alone."

Startled, Lluava spun around, fists at the ready. A smaller figure emerged, dressed entirely in black save for green eyes.

"Holly," Lluava breathed out in relief. "You can use the door, you know."

"I did. Before you arrived." The woman smiled as she pulled off her skin-tight head garb, allowing her thick, curly red locks to tumble down over her shoulders.

"To what do I owe the pleasure?" asked Lluava as she motioned Holly to take a seat. But Holly remained standing. So, instead, Lluava plopped down on her couch and looked at her uninvited guest.

"The Outlanders inside the castle…" began Holly. Her face was as stern as her voice. "You brought them here. Now ask them to leave."

"What? No," countered Lluava. "They are here to help Elysia."

"Then they can help from outside Cronus's walls. That is where they will be of most use."

Onyx cawed from his perch.

"I will not ask them to stay outside with the enemy. They are our allies and my friends."

"They are not friends of the Obsidian Guard or of the king," retorted the Shadow. "Outlanders have opposed Elysia since this kingdom's founding. *You* have invited them through our capital's gates. I cannot allow this."

"Outlanders," began Lluava calmly, "were never our enemy. Our ancestors drew up the boundaries for the kingdom. There was and is no choice about which side of that invisible line you are born on. These people have never invaded our kingdom. We did not know of their history and culture. You have been taught to feel this way, to believe these lies. This enmity should never have been validated in the first place. Your so-called Outlanders are the key to helping us win this war. Just wait and see."

"Ask them to be allies *outside* Cronus."

"I will not." It was disheartening to discover that Holly was so prejudiced. Lluava understood that the secret group of human assassins known as the Obsidian Guard was committed to protecting the king and associated only with him. Somehow, though, she had hoped Holly was different.

The Shadow stated bluntly, "I will kill anyone who wishes to harm Varren, even if it is you. Know this. I have sworn to protect his royal highness's life and his alone."

"I thought we were friends," said Lluava icily.

"I don't have the luxury of friends."

The door swung open, and June hurried inside, crying, "Don't go back,

Lluava! You're all I have."

The little girl stopped short and stared wide-eyed at Holly, who had reflexively pulled out her sai from their holster around her waist. Holly froze under the small girl's gaze.

"You're a Sh…Sh…Shadow," June gasped out. "You're so *pretty*."

Holly realized that her mask was off, for her cheeks flushed almost as vibrant a shade as her red hair.

"Can I get you something? Are you thirsty? What's it like to be one of the Guard?" June's string of questions was cut short when Lluava called her name.

"Lady Lluava?" June blinked at her. "Did you see—"

June turned back to the redheaded woman, but Holly had vanished. "How did she do that?" The small handmaiden gaped at the empty space.

"She's a Shadow," said Lluava.

After a moment, June seemed to remember why she had come. "I heard you were back but that they were sending you out again. I know it. Please don't go. Some of the men who went did not return."

"You know I am a soldier," Lluava said gently. "I am supposed to fight."

"But you're like a sister to me. I want you to come back."

"I will."

Pulling June down on the seat next to her, Lluava hugged the sweet girl and brushed her dark auburn hair away from her eyes. As Lluava sat there lost in thought, Onyx flew onto her shoulder and began muttering in her ear. Though most of the bird's vocalizations were purely animal sounds, some sounded like actual words. Maybe it was her brain trying to make sense of the avian's speech, but she thought she heard him crackle out the word "war" several times.

The war must come to an end before it was too late for Lluava's friends—and for her own family, still safe for now in the South. How much longer would it be before Raiders ransacked Rivendale, burning her home and killing her siblings and her mother? The war *must* be brought to an end. The only way to do so was to allow Yena's army to fight alongside the Elysians.

Tearing herself away from June, Lluava changed her clothes and hurried back to the Lesser Hall.

By the time she arrived, the council room was vacant. Had they come to terms? What strategy, if any, had they decided upon? Why had she left so quickly? She was a warrior, and now an officer in the army; she should have helped with the decision-making process. Her own selfish concerns had interfered with what she was truly meant to do: end the war.

Lluava considered what she must do in order to succeed. She should disregard nothing, even if it involved the so-called Incarn. If the Incarn did have abilities, maybe they could be used to save the kingdom.

***

She rapped on Luka's door, and the lanky man greeted her with a raised eyebrow. Behind him, his sister reclined on a couch.

"Come with me," Lluava ordered. "Both of you."

The twins shared a puzzled look before following her down the dimly lit corridor.

"What, may I ask, are we doing?" inquired Luka, whose long legs easily kept up with Lluava's swift pace.

"Do you know what's been going on recently?" she countered.

"If you are referring to what's been happening outside, such business is not my interest. Since the Open Council was disbanded, puttering around in the Grand Hall has become less than amusing. Anyway, what better entertainment could I ask for than my sweet sister?"

Selene was quiet. Was she still "mourning" the loss of the king's affection?

"Do you know about the army of Theriomorphs that has arrived to aid us?"

Luka raised his eyebrow again. "Rumors, mainly."

Arriving at their destination, Lluava knocked on a door. She hoped this was the correct room.

"Come inside," invited Yena's husky voice.

These quarters were larger than Lluava's; however, the furniture had been pushed aside and replaced with a layer of pillows and blankets. Yena, still in her silver garb, was seated in the center of the floor.

"High Priestess Yena," Lluava began, "may I introduce Luka and Selene Fárbauti, Incarn of the Twins?" Turning to the young pair, Lluava indicated the priestess. "This is High Priestess Yena, Crocotta's Incarn."

For once, Yena looked surprisingly pleased. "Come, children. Take a seat near me. I want to learn all about you both."

Almost dreamily, Selene moved to Yena's side, and the pair began to converse like friends who have not seen one another in ages. Luka chuckled to himself as he observed Selene happily lost in conversation with the priestess.

"Look what you have done," he said to Lluava. "I can tell you now that those two are going to be trouble."

"For the enemy, I hope," said Lluava as she followed Luka to the cushions.

"For the *enemy*," agreed Luka.

***

When a page finally located her in Yena's quarter's, Lluava at last had a reason to leave the odd reunion. As interested as she was in hearing the historical tales Yena shared, she had to respond to the summons. The king was looking for her. She must comply.

Armed guards were everywhere in the lower section of the castle, but the page ignored her questions about what had happened. She was glad to spot Varren standing next to Themis and Hyrax; they would have answers. The head councilman was looking a bit pale. Perhaps he, too, was sick.

"Your Majesty," Lluava greeted her partner. "Councilmen."

"Watch out," Varren said as he pulled Lluava close. A throng of soldiers pushed past them unceremoniously.

Lluava recognized the faces of several Leucrocottans scattered among the Elysian uniforms. Ammit and Master Hon were there, as was Maruny. When Lluava caught her eye, Maruny merely gave Lluava a gloomy stare before returning to the focus of their attention. Trapped at the center of the group of soldiers was a Berserker, bound tightly, with a sack covering his head.

Limping up to Varren, Colonel Ojewa knelt. "I bring you a prisoner of rank. His authority supersedes that of many."

Lluava could not look away from the large, moist stain on the major's black shirt. "You're hurt!" she exclaimed.

"A flesh wound at most," replied Ojewa, his head still bowed.

"Colonel Ojewa," Varren began, "you have provided a great service. This deed will not be forgotten. Go receive medical attention. You have my blessing."

"I will see that he has everything he needs," put in Hyrax graciously.

Positioning the prisoner in clear sight of Varren, Ammit lifted the sack to reveal Sweyn.

"They've captured one of the lead Berserkers," gasped Lluava. "He was the one who had me burned!"

Varren, who still had his hands on Lluava, ordered harshly, "Execute him. Return his corpse to his men come sunrise."

"Ya be their ruler?" Sweyn shouted over the heads of the others as they began to drag him away, their weapons at the ready.

"I am King Varren Mandrun, rightful ruler of Elysia."

"I wouldn't be so hasty if I be th' king."

"Halt!" Varren commanded, releasing Lluava.

Themis stepped between them. "Do not let that barbarian speak. He will only cloud your judgment. It is a pathetic attempt to save his own life."

For once, Lluava agreed with the head councilman. "He must die, Varren."

"If I die, Mandrun," the Berserker boomed, "ya'll have no bargaining chip. Such is ya loss."

Varren stepped closer to the prisoner. "And why would I need a bargaining chip? Unless your people will leave my shores upon your safe return, there is nothing to trade."

"Oh, but there be."

"Don't listen to him, Varren," implored Lluava.

"He is just stalling," added Themis.

Varren motioned for silence. "And what do you have that is so valuable?"

Sweyn furrowed his wide brow. "Oh...what's 'is name?"

"He is only trying to make you question him longer," pointed out Themis. "Send him on his way."

Varren, looking grim, ordered, "Be off with him!"

Sweyn suddenly grinned, exposing teeth stained yellow.

"Thadius! His name is Thadius!"

Chapter 42

Gain and Loss

Varren froze, as if the name held a strange power over him.

"That's impossible. You are lying!" Lluava affirmed. "Thad died during the summer."

"He be alive," huffed Sweyn.

By the look on the young king's gentle face, a hope sparked in his eyes for the childhood friend he thought he had lost.

"Varren, look at me," Lluava said. Her partner's gaze found hers. "Thad was killed at Fort Brinsdale. You know this. Don't let that man trick you into believing otherwise."

"Naw," smirked the Berserker. "He was kept alive. He was valuable, we was told. He be close to the false prince, we was told." Sweyn loomed over the soldiers' heads. "A trade can be made. Him fa' me. Ya' want that trade, Son of Mandrun?"

Lluava could tell Varren's hope was causing him to believe this rubbish. "He's lying, Varren!" she said more emphatically.

"But how can you be certain?" Varren's question only confirmed Lluava's fears.

"Because I saw Horus when I was in their encampment. He told me not to trust him." She pointed to Sweyn.

"Thad's partner was alive?" gasped Varren angrily. "Why did you not tell me this? If he is alive, Thad could be also."

"Horus is dead. Just like Thad. They killed them," countered Lluava defensively. "I didn't tell you because I didn't want you to make a rash decision and do something stupid. Just as you are about to do now."

"You should have told me, Lluava," stated Varren icily. "You had no right to keep that a secret. No more secrets, you said. Yet you keep lying to me. I do not want you near me until you have ended your deceit."

"Varren—" Lluava reached out, but the king stepped away.

"A trade will be made," Varren said to Sweyn. The Berserker's confident grin grew wider.

Themis broke in, "Your Majesty, you cannot possibly agree to this trade. This creature could be lying."

"Or he could be telling the truth."

The head councilman tried to reason with the king. "Thadius was a wonderful young man, but he would not want you to work with the enemy for the sake of his life."

"A trade *will* be made!" ordered Varren. His words echoed off the vaulted ceiling.

Sweyn grunted, "Ya want me alive. Come sunup, this trade 'll be offered. Wait 'n' see."

"Take him to Tartarus for safekeeping," instructed Varren. "Make sure he is held until morning." Varren strode away as Sweyn was marched off to the dungeons.

"This is bad," Lluava said.

Themis replied, "I think you have chosen far too mild a word."

***

Before sunrise the following morning, Lluava found the high priestess at odds with the king in the Grand Hall.

"You captured one of their leaders, and you are returning him! Your youth has never been more apparent."

"I do not have to explain myself to you," stated Varren loftily.

"If you return him, much pain will follow. I have seen it," warned Yena. Her eyes seared like a pair of branding irons. "That loathsome being should not be treated with any compassion. What a fool you are, human."

"If I were you, I would be careful what you say to me," replied Varren testily. Lluava could tell that her military partner had not slept. His exhaustion was not helping, nor were Yena's remarks.

"You are supposed to be a ruler. You cannot allow personal affections to influence your judgment."

Varren's look was grim. "You may be a guest under my roof, High Priestess, but do not presume you have any authority over my decision-making. My mind is made up."

Stepping away from the dais, Yena did not respond.

Vidrick was among those already in the hall. Varren asked him, "What news of Grand Master Chief Domar?"

"The general has not regained consciousness. The healers have done everything they can. We can only pray that he wakes up on his own."

Lluava, who had chosen not to take her seat on the dais, turned to

Rosalyn, who stood next to her. "Do you still have your vial of Idun? If so, Domar needs it."

"Lluava…" Rosalyn hesitated. "I cannot."

"You just heard about his condition. He needs help immediately."

"I am sorry, but I am saving that medicine for my baby. I have to think about my child's future," whispered Rosalyn.

"But I gave it to you."

"Yes. But one cannot simply ask for one's gift to be returned." Rosalyn stood defiantly. "Right now, Talos and our child are the two most important people to me. I must think about what is best for them."

Why was everyone being so narrow-minded? Lluava thought. There was a bigger picture at hand. Moving over to the offended priestess, Lluava asked, "May I have a word?"

Yena's eyes softened behind her veil. "Of course."

"General Domar is a good friend of mine and important to Elysia's military," Lluava began. "Do you have any Idun, so that he can recover?"

"Child," Yena said sweetly, "our wagon filled with Idun was damaged right before we arrived. Most of it was lost. What was saved is reserved for my people."

"Can't you spare a small vial? Anything that could help Domar?"

"I fear not. I brought my army here to help you, but the Idun is for my men, for *our* species. The human will live or die on his own. I am sorry. I gifted you several vials. Use one of them."

"I don't have them anymore," confessed Lluava bleakly.

Yena looked at her for a moment then said, "I will not give you Idun for the sake of the human, but I will for the savior of our race. You know what you must do to ensure our future."

"I tried," hissed Lluava through gritted teeth. The sudden reminder of the other evening's events caused her emotions to rise up. "He turned me down."

Yena touched Lluava's cheek with an ebony hand. "Try harder."

Around them, people began to stir. Lluava realized those of note were vacating the hall. The sun was rising, and Varren was heading out to hear whether or not the trade would be offered. Choosing not to walk at her partner's side, she followed at a distance. Yena and her men stayed behind. Lluava did not blame the priestess for not wanting to participate in this ludicrous endeavor.

Upon reaching the wall's walkway, Lluava noticed that Varren appeared worried and agitated. If Sweyn had lied, Varren's new hope would be crushed. It would be like hearing that Thad had died all over again. Maybe she should not have been so blunt the night before. Thad had been a special friend, and Varren had loved him like a brother.

Maybe she should have tried to be more sympathetic. The worry in her partner's eyes as he waited for any sort of communication from the enemy caused Lluava's heart to twinge. Varren was a good man. Yet, the truth still stood; releasing Sweyn was an irrational choice, no matter what was at stake. Part of Lluava hoped that Sweyn had lied. A quick death to the Berserker would be the best result.

A figure approached.

"The ambassador," breathed one of the councilmen. His cloak was frosted with snowflakes.

"No," corrected Lluava. "This is someone new."

A scrawny, elderly man stepped into the Elysians' view. His bear-furred cloak enveloped him. She wondered what had happened to Ambassador Alcove. Surely he had not been slain. Would the Raiders kill their own? If so, they were truly barbaric.

The unknown emissary announced, "I 'ave come t' offer a trade." Varren took a quick breath as the man continued, "We're offerin' to give back th' man called Thadius Sihia for Sweyn Surtur, which you 'ave captured. In so doing, no arrows will be shot, no man shall be killed during this interchange. Are ya' agreeable for this arrangement?" The slight figure had to shout the final words so they would reach the ears of the Elysians atop the wall.

"This trade shall be made!" shouted Varren resolutely. His grandfather's crown glimmered in the morning's light. "Our prisoner for yours when the sun reaches its peak."

"As ya' say, Son of Mandrun," responded the small man, who quickly backed out of the yeomen's range.

Before returning to the castle, Lluava offered one last bit of advice to Varren. "If they speak the truth, make sure they give you proof that Thadius lives before you send Sweyn out the gates."

"Of course."

When noon arrived, Lluava was back on the top of the wall. As she was military partner to the king, none could order her otherwise. She watched in pensive silence as a severely limping prisoner was led up to the gates. His downturned face and matted, dirty-blond hair distorted his features. Was that Thad? For all those on the wall could tell, this could be an impostor.

One of the prisoner's captors grabbed the tangled locks and jerked the man's face upward. Lluava's heart raced. The man was Thad. What horrors must he have endured during all this time?

Varren gave the signal, and the gates groaned open. A half-dozen Elysians led the bound Berserker out of Cronus as Thad was released to stumble toward the doors. There was a moment when the released prisoners passed one another. All archers held their weapons ready for any sort of foul play, but each moved on by, and both reached their designated sides.

As Sweyn moved out of shooting range, he spun around and shouted, his voice booming off the stone wall, "I speak for Ivar when I swear every skin-changer will be slaughtered, every human male killed, every woman raped! You are already defeated."

Several archers took aim, but Varren warned them, "Let him go." Below them, the gates creaked closed. Once they were secured, the young king hurried down to see his friend.

Thad was being hugged tightly by his sobbing wife, Emily. Varren joined the pair. Lluava watched at a distance and noted Thad's unfocused gaze and unnatural silence. He seemed more like a rag doll being jostled about than the jovial youth she had met in the camps.

After leaving the trio, Lluava went to the sick ward to which Domar had been brought. Rows of injured and afflicted soldiers lined every available wall. Heading up the stairs of the repurposed shop, Lluava glanced at the mostly unrecognizable faces.

She accosted a nurse and asked, "Where is the grand master chief? Has he been moved?"

"No, m'lady," chirped the woman as she wiped bloody hands on her already stained apron. She looked exhausted. "The general passed away several hours ago. I'm sorry."

Lluava blinked away sudden tears. "Where is his body?"

"His son just retrieved him." The nurse bowed her head and hurried off.

Lluava felt a numbness that was not due to the bitter cold. She would follow up with Daniel later to see if she could help with the burial arrangements, but for now she desired only to sit in front of her hearth and soak up the warmth.

***

That day was the first of several eerily quiet ones. The Berserkers did not attack and seemed to keep to their own encampment. The Elysians, in turn, reveled in their much-needed reprieve from battle. Thoth still led avian patrols, but the enemy showed no movement. Was this a thanks of sorts for the return of Sweyn? Lluava was doubtful; yet, if so, what status did the Berserker hold to elicit such a response?

During this time, Lluava kept to herself. The few occasions she crossed paths with Rosalyn, she couldn't help but stare angrily at her friend, whose selfish choice had cost the life of Domar. Varren was predominantly concerned with Thad's recovery. Fortunately, the young man was found to have no major physical injuries other than a poorly healed break in one leg. The king's anger toward Lluava seemed to have dissipated, but she gave him his space out of respect. To avoid Apex, Lluava decided her quarters were her best refuge. There, her main companions were June, Onyx, and occasionally Luka.

"You have ruined everything," Luka teased one day. "Ever since your introduction, Selene has barely left Yena's quarters. I don't know if she sees Yena as a mother figure or an older sister, but the pair are all but inseparable.

Where does that leave me? Cast aside just like that."

"I would never throw you out," said Lluava quietly as she handed Onyx several small cubes of meat. June was asleep on the couch.

Luka walked over to the double glass doors. Looking out beyond the balcony, he asked, "How long do you intend to hide in here?"

"As long as it takes," smiled Lluava.

"You're missing so much."

"That's why I have you, my informer."

Luka grinned wickedly. "Here's a tidbit for you. There is a rumor that Thadius's wife claims he is not Thadius."

"And what does Varren think?" questioned Lluava without interest. Onyx missed the meat and nipped her hand.

"Ouch!" she hissed.

Luka handed her his handkerchief to soak up the droplet of blood on her fingertip. "The healers claim that any strange behavior is due to the ordeal that he has been through. I believe the king hopes that his friend just needs time and rest."

Lluava handed back the handkerchief. "So, Selene has taken to Yena. What do they talk about?"

"Who knows?"

"Don't you ever visit them?" questioned Lluava as she put away Onyx's empty bowl. The raven grumbled.

"Do you?" countered Luka.

"You have me there." Lluava headed over to stoke the hearth.

"You must leave your room," chastised Luka playfully. "The few times I've joined them, much of the talk concerns the place where the priestess is from, how different everything is there. Better."

"What about the Incarn?"

"That comes up now and again. Destinies, prophecies, and such. Quite fanciful, I'd say. Nothing to get excited about."

Lluava rejoined Luka by the window. Together they watched one of the winter's last snowfalls. The small storm blurred much of their view.

Onyx began to caw wildly, causing June to blink awake.

"What's wrong with you?" asked Lluava testily. Recently she had had little patience with her temperamental bird.

Suddenly, warning trumpets rang from within Cronus.

"I think your wish is about to come true," Lluava said as she ran to grab Issaura's Claws. "It's time for me to leave my room."

Luka looked distressed. "Are we under attack again?"

"I don't know. Go find your sister and get to someplace safe."

"Where?" questioned Luka as he hurried to the door.

"Anywhere," replied Lluava. Then, turning to June, she ordered, "You stay here. Hide under the bed if you have to. Do not leave until I come to get you."

The little girl nodded her understanding, then scurried into Lluava's sleeping alcove. Lluava and Luka took off toward different areas of the castle.

As she hurried down the corridor, dagger in hand, Lluava nearly collided with Maruny, who took several quick steps backward. Her shocked eyes flickered to Lluava's weapons.

"Do you know what's going on?" Lluava demanded brusquely.

"Um…" began Maruny, regaining her sharp voice. "The Berserkers are entering Cronus in large numbers. You should head outside, where the battle is surely occurring."

"Outside. Yes," Lluava said as she weighed the information. "But first I need to find my partner."

Leaving Maruny, Lluava searched for Varren. Instinct told her that she needed him by her side. If this was the final fight, they needed to be together despite their disagreement.

Crack!

Something hard slammed against the back of Lluava's head and sent her sprawling onto the stone floor. Her vision spun as a figure approached. Her balance momentarily hindered, Lluava scooted backwards.

"Always in the way."

As Lluava's blurred vision began to clear, she saw Selene holding a heavy brass candlestick. The young woman, wearing a glimmering emerald dress, lifted her makeshift weapon as she spoke. "I should have known. Time to be rid of you."

Chapter 43

End of an Era

Tthere was a dull gleam of brass.

A wet warmth dripped down Lluava's neck.

Arms lifted in defense.

Then noise.

A clang of metal intermingled with a woman's scream and a prehistoric roar. The candlestick clattered to the ground as twin gladius blades pressed against Selene's neck and breasts.

"Are you all right?" Apex barked out his question without taking his eyes off Selene. Lluava carefully placed her hand on the back of her head. A sudden explosion of pain began to throb with each beat of her heart as blood oozed freely from the gash in the back of her skull. The wound, though small, felt as if it were on fire.

"The cut's not large," said Lluava, using the wall for support to get back to her feet. From this angle, she could see a droplet of blood beading on Selene's throat. "I don't know why I didn't sense her there. I guess I was in too much of a hurry."

Apex refocused on Selene, whose eyes had grown larger than Lluava had ever seen them. "Give me one reason why I shouldn't run you through," he snarled.

"You will want to talk to High Priestess Yena first," said Selene calmly and matter-of-factly.

"Why?" questioned Lluava. She felt lightheaded.

Selene replied, "She has answers."

"Take us to her, then." Apex slid one of Ullr's Fangs back into its sheath. With his free hand, he forcibly pulled Selene away from the wall. His other blade was pressed into her back. "Which way?"

Selene nodded to the left and tentatively took the lead; Apex kept her slender arm gripped in his fist. As they moved, Lluava pulled off one of the Claws and tucked it under her arm. Then she tore a section of cloth from her sleeve and pressed it to her head to stanch the bleeding.

"Where did you come from?" Lluava asked the huntsman.

"When I heard what was happening, I went in search of you," explained Apex. Then, jerking his prisoner, he added, "Just in time, I see."

"Thank you," Lluava said. Apex didn't respond.

Selene stopped in front of the Grand Hall's large double doors. "In there," she said.

Apex had her pull the door open. Inside, Yena was seated on Varren's throne. The sight caused a low rumble in Lluava's vocal cords.

Luka turned toward them, his eyes glinting with excitement. Thoth, too, waited at the bottom of the dais. From their expressions, they had expected to see Lluava and Apex arrive. What was happening?

"They are here," Selene spoke directly to Yena, "as you asked."

"Selene tried to kill me," Lluava growled.

"Selene," Yena began, her ivory irises seeming to bore into the young woman. "You have directly disobeyed my orders." Turning to the other pair, she added, "Selene will be reprimanded accordingly. You have my word. Now release her, Apex."

The huntsman obeyed. Selene hurried to her brother's side. He whispered something into her ear, and she stiffened.

Yena looked down upon them. The high priestess was far too comfortable in Varren's throne. This was all wrong. Dropping the bloodied strip of cloth, Lluava replaced Issaura's Claw. "I must ask you to step down from there," she said.

"The grandeur from this angle does give one a different perspective," mused the high priestess. "It illuminates much that would have been hidden otherwise."

Lluava stepped forward, but Apex held her back. In front of her, Thoth blocked her way, a hooked saber now in his hands.

"Where is Varren?" Lluava demanded.

"He should be here soon," replied the high priestess. She stood up and seemed to glide slowly down the tiered dais. "In the meantime, I wanted to talk to you. I have dreamed of this day, and now it has arrived. I could not have accomplished this without you. You are truly Theri's Incarn."

Stepping onto the floor, Yena motioned for Thoth to stand down. He obediently moved aside. "You have finally brought our people home. If you had not allowed us entry through these walls, we would still be hiding in the shadows. You have led us into the light. The time for Theriomorphs to reclaim what is rightfully theirs has arrived. We give you thanks."

Yena unwrapped her headdress and exposed her gently smiling face. "We owe you our thanks, Incarn of Theri."

"You're overthrowing the king?" Lluava gasped. She felt Apex's hand drop. He looked at Selene, who smiled back at him.

Yena spoke kindly. "I know this is not what you believe you want, but soon you will see it is the only way."

"You will be stopped," Lluava snarled.

"You are not the first to say so." Yena looked up.

Following the priestess's gaze, Lluava saw that many of the councilmen sat quietly in their seats, their stiffening bodies slumped, their eyes eternally gazing at the court over which they had so often presided.

"Casualties of the war," admitted the priestess. "That is to be expected."

The sound of the doors opening behind them startled Lluava. Apex swiftly pulled her out of the way of a stream of Theriomorphs, many of whom Lluava recognized from the Warrior Caste. She lost sight of Yena.

Pulling her close, Apex hissed, "Lower your weapons. There are too many to fight."

Lluava had taken a defensive position. "Berserkers in the capital. Now this?" She wanted to kill those who were destroying Elysia from within its very heart. Everyone around her was the enemy. Everyone but Apex.

"What Berserkers?" questioned the huntsman.

"The ones that everyone has gone to fight."

"There are no Berserkers, Lluava," Apex's steely voice sent a chill down Lluava's spine. "The capital is being attacked by Yena's men."

"No. I was told—" Lluava's voice was drowned out.

"Let go of me, you animal!" The shrill voice of Queen Enya was heard over the crowd.

Pushing her way through the throng of bodies, Lluava finally caught sight of Ammit, who was dragging the girl before the dais. Yena had returned to the throne.

"Release me!" ordered the child-queen. "How dare you even think of touching me! This treatment is heinous!"

"Big word for a little girl," grunted Ammit as he shoved her to the polished marble floor.

"I command everyone to leave or face punishment! I am the queen! You must listen to what I say!" Enya screamed. From her reddening face, she was about to pitch a fit. Her lavish dress nearly matched her new complexion.

Lluava heard Selene's melodious laughter. Lluava wanted to gut Selene first but could not see the beautiful teen.

"Child," Yena said in a motherly tone. For the first time, Enya seemed to notice the intruder seated on the throne. "I am ruler now."

There were far more sinister implications to the priestess's words. Gods, thought Lluava. Looking at Enya, she wanted to warn the blatant idiot to shut up, but the girl was already speaking again.

"You are not allowed on the throne. Get off at once. I am the queen." She pointed to the jeweled tiara atop her perfect, ink-black ringlets.

"Queen, is it?" questioned the priestess. "I am sorry to say, it is past time for you to retire your crown."

"My crown?" Enya looked furious. Then, seeing Ammit pull out his scythe, she blustered, "You cannot harm me. I am the queen. *I am* the queen!" Ammit stepped up to her, and the girl scooted away, her eyes growing wide. "You would not dare hurt Thor's child! I am pregnant with a new heir!"

Lluava had to give the thirteen-year-old credit for inventing such a story on the spot. Thor, alas, had been impotent. Burdensome as Enya was, the child was in dire trouble.

Although Lluava struggled to move closer to the girl, she was squeezed among too many of Yena's men. Nor could she see Apex.

"This is the problem," Yena explained in her authoritative tone. "There can be but one ruler of Elysia. You must understand that this heir of yours presents a difficulty, does it not?"

Several men grabbed the queen. Her face blanched, and then she screamed, "I am not pregnant! I was lying!"

Lluava shouted, "Let her go!"

As Lluava tried to push through the people in front of her, hands seized her. Turning, she stabbed a squat man in his paunch. Crimson sprayed the crowd. Everyone began to move about frantically. As she sliced an ear off another man, Lluava was tackled and brought to the ground by Master Hon. Her head began to drip anew; blood ran down the sides of her nose and pooled with a larger puddle spreading over the floor.

"What have you done?" Lluava growled as she struggled to retain the Claws. Enya's headless body lay not far from her, the tiara thrown off to one side. "What did you do? She was a child. A *child!*"

Above them, Yena's voice proclaimed, "Humans are no longer welcome on these shores. Slay any who cross your paths."

From Lluava's strange angle, she could see that several robed men had been forced to their knees. She tried to crane her neck to look at the captive councilmen, but her face was pressed into the puddle of blood. The thick red fluid seeped into her eyes, nose, and mouth. She tried hard not to swallow the coppery-tasting liquid.

Lluava realized that the three kneeling councilmen were Theriomorphs from the Elysian court. But not all of the court's Theriomorphs were accounted for; Hyrax was among the missing.

Yena spoke again. "You have a choice: renounce your beliefs and join in the new world order, or die. What say you?"

"Never!" shouted one; a second spat. Quickly, Ammit silenced them permanently. The third, rather large man blubbered, "I will join. I want to live."

"Before one can see the truth," Yena commented, "one must relinquish the sight of evil."

Thoth had shifted into the sarus crane. Lluava saw his spindly legs stride up to the third councilman. Closing her own eyes, the screams of the prisoner only confirmed his punishment. As the councilman was dragged away, Lluava now looked upon one brown eyeball that had rolled close to her.

"I may be harsh," began Yena, "but I am also merciful. Tell all Theriomorphs that if they choose to follow me, their lives will be spared."

Someone was trying to pull Issaura's Claws off her fists. Where was Apex? Why wasn't he fighting the Leucrocottans? Why had he not stopped any of these murders? He would never allow this. Lluava knew how appealing Leucrocotta had been to the huntsman, but he wasn't on their side. Was he?

"Now," Yena asked, "where is our guest of honor?"

"The king has yet to be located," grunted Hon as he continued to press Lluava's face into the ground.

Varren. They would kill him. In an explosion of white and black, Lluava shifted into her dual form and hurtled into the crowd. Most jumped to either side of the feline; a few were trampled under her large paws. As Lluava scrambled out of the Grand Hall, she heard Yena calmly order, "Bring her back." The priestess's ironic laughter reverberated throughout the chamber.

Running through the corridors, Lluava saw that havoc reigned in the castle. In the foyer, Obsidian Guards fought several Theriomorphs. One large kudu was brought down by several throwing stars. A lynx bled out in a corner, while a panther bit into the shoulder of a Shadow.

Leaping down on top of the panther, Lluava pulled the cat off the guard who, in turn, thrust a sai into the panther's head. The feline reverted to its human form as a last breath escaped its whiskered lips.

"The king?" she asked hurriedly, spitting out the splotchy fur that coated her rough tongue.

The Shadow only shrugged, and Lluava charged off. Other enemy Theriomorphs were emerging from the hall behind her. She had to make sure that she was not being followed before she could search for her partner. She would not be responsible for leading the enemy to the king.

Glancing back, Lluava saw a rhino burst into the foyer: Master Hon. The two Obsidian Guards were already entangled with a new set of Theriomorphs. With this area so well lit, they could not resort to their hallmark form of attack and disappear into the shadows.

Lluava would have helped them, but Master Hon had caught sight of her. She knew she had to run from the huge animal's horns. Beyond him, Ammit emerged, still in his human form, his serrated scythe hooked onto his cloth belt.

Behind her, the rhino stormed through the corridors. Lluava had to lose the raging beast. But how? Blood loss caused her head to swim, and her endurance was almost spent.

The castle was in chaos. There was little hope that Lluava would cross paths with any of her friends. She might have to face Master Hon alone. Did she have the strength? The massive beast filled much of the hallway; she would not be able to clamber over him to escape. And even if the hall widened, could she evade his horns? The larger one was nearly three feet long.

As she frantically searched for a solution, Lluava had to leap over several sprawled human corpses. Their dress marked them as some of those who had lived to gossip at court. Their frivolous talk was at an end, as humans were being eradicated inside the castle. Many would have no clue what was happening until too late.

Where was Varren? He must not have been in his quarters, for that was one of the first places they would have looked. Lluava hoped he had somehow been warned. Surely, some of the Obsidian Guards were protecting him.

Behind Lluava, the rhino snorted. He was closing in on her. Too bad the halls were large enough for Hon's dual form. Suddenly, Lluava emitted a pleased grumble as she realized a way out.

Leaping up a stairwell, she arrived on the floor where her own quarters were and burst through the first door she saw. The small bedroom contained an even smaller window. Lluava would be able to fit through it, but only in her human form.

Shifting back, she tossed a chair through the glass, then clambered out and onto a narrow decorative ledge. Pressing her back to the castle wall, she hoped that the wind would not blow her off. Carefully, she edged her way along the ledge until she reached her own quarters.

Behind her, Master Hon's face peered out the window. He struggled to fit his muscular human form through the opening but without success. Lluava turned her head to look at him. Hon did not move. From the look he gave her, it was unclear whether he was angry or impressed. Regardless, she had escaped. For now.

Lluava's hair blew about her face in the wind. With nothing to grasp, her sweaty hands seemed to slip over the stone behind her. Just let me make it to my balcony, she thought. Just let me get through this.

She had to sacrifice speed for safety. Her approach was maddeningly slow. Finally, she reached her quarters. Onyx cawed emphatically inside.

Leaping over her balustrade, Lluava cried, "June!"

Chapter 44

Transcendence

June was not safe. As a human, she was now prey to the invading Theriomorphs, and Lluava had left the little girl alone.

"June!" Lluava cried out again as she tried to open the double doors. They were locked from the inside. Breaking the glass with her elbow, Lluava reached inside and turned the knob.

Stepping over the shattered glass, Lluava hurriedly looked around her quarters. The little girl was not in sight. Was she still here? The front door had been tampered with. Shards of wood stuck out from the center, where some massive weapon had tried to break through. Or perhaps a horn?

Lluava hurried over to the bed and lifted the green bed skirt. "June? Are you here? Where are you?"

The chambermaid could not be found. Above Lluava, Onyx cawed and flapped in distressed circles. So haphazard was the bird's flight that he flew into furniture and collided with a window.

"June!" Lluava called out once more. Finally, the door to the wardrobe swung open, and the little auburn-haired girl clambered down.

Running to Lluava, June sobbed into her open arms, a small table knife clutched in her white-knuckled fist. She was trembling all over.

Brushing the matted curls out of June's face, Lluava said, "You need to come with me. Now."

Holding the girl's hand, Lluava crossed to the front door. Opening it slightly, she peered out. She could not sense anyone in the hall. They needed to make a break for the stairs immediately.

The next thing she knew, they were both running down the corridors, skidding around corners, doubling back whenever Lluava sensed another presence. Every so often, a scream rang out nearby, and Lluava abruptly changed course. Onyx flapped above them, although for once he was almost silent. Did he understand the direness of their situation?

The hall divided before them; flying down the right-hand corridor, Onyx disappeared. The second option was entirely dark, for the sconces had not been lit, or perhaps had been blown out.

"Come on," Lluava whispered to June, whose wide eyes scanned everything around them.

As they made their way down the corridor, Lluava heard Onyx returning. He had started to crow again. Stupid bird! Maybe she should have left him in her room. Behind the black shape, a small grey missile seemed to be plucking out the raven's tail feathers in midair.

As both birds flew past, the mockingbird alighted on the ground and shifted. Maruny positioned herself in the middle of the hall. Was she trying to stop them?

"Leave us, Maruny," Lluava said as calmly as she could. June tucked herself close into Lluava's side.

"I can't."

Lluava knew Maruny had no weapons on her. Since she had arrived as a bird, Maruny would not have been able to travel with such items. Once more, Lluava was thankful for Issaura's Claws and their ability to shift with her.

"I don't want to hurt you," admitted Lluava. "You were my friend once."

"We were never friends," replied Maruny. Her beady eyes surveyed Lluava's weapons warily. "Not truly."

Now Lluava heard footsteps coming from behind. Turning, she saw an antelope spring up to them.

"Really?" Lluava hissed sarcastically, and shifted. The antelope flared its nostrils; the whites of its eyes flashed. From the twitching of its flank, the antelope was struggling with the instinct to flee.

Then, stamping its small front hooves on the stone floor, the slender animal bounded toward Lluava, its horns pointed forward. Swiping her gilded claws in front of her, Lluava swatted at the antelope. The animal took a hit to its face and emitted an ear-piercing sound, then fled.

Turning again, Lluava saw that Maruny had pulled June in front of her, and both faced Lluava. The little knife that June had held was now pressed against the girl's throat.

"Let her go," Lluava implored as she shifted back.

Maruny squeezed June against her. "You have to come with me, Lluava." June's eyes brimmed with tears.

"Fine," Lluava replied. "Just don't hurt her."

The trio headed in the direction of the Grand Hall. June sniffled back tears, and Lluava wished she could somehow comfort the girl. Yet Maruny kept hold of June in such a way that Lluava did not dare try to free her.

"You there, halt!" a voice called from behind them.

"No!" Lluava screamed.

Maruny spun round in fright. Lluava saw the red spurt from June's throat. As the human soldier charged, Maruny shifted, and the knife clattered onto the stone. June swayed and collapsed to the floor. The mockingbird flew down the hall, and the soldier ran past Lluava, who in turn ran toward June.

"June," Lluava sobbed; she pulled the girl onto her lap. June's eyes had already dulled, and her head lolled limply on her shoulders. "June. Oh no...June!"

Several more Theriomorphs ran past her in their human forms. Behind them, Obsidian Guards threw their metal stars into the enemies' backs. One Theriomorph expired nearby. Yet Lluava did not move from the hall. Instead, her rage built through her horror and distress. The thing inside her awoke.

A coyote slunk down the corridor. Lluava's pupils narrowed, and she glared at the creature, daring it to approach her. Onyx dove at the animal's face. As the canine scurried past, another voice spoke in Lluava's ears. Spinning around, she almost slashed out at the Obsidian Guard standing over her. Holly.

"Let me take her," the Shadow said.

"No," sobbed Lluava, holding her handmaiden close.

"Lluava, let me take her." Lluava did not fight as Holly lifted little June from her. The Shadow gently readjusted the girl in her arms as a mother would a sleeping child, then said to Lluava. "Head to Tartarus. Hurry."

Nodding, tears ran down Lluava's face. Somehow, she knew Holly would take June's body somewhere safe. Then she ran.

As fast as she could, she tore through the castle, terrifying many as she flew past—a platinum-blond woman drenched in blood, golden weapons glinting on her fists.

Lluava was on the second floor when she heard Apex call her name. She stopped and spotted the huntsman jumping over upended furniture in a nearby room. Recently used, Ullr's Fangs were in his hands. She eyed him warily. Which side was he on?

"I've been looking for you," Apex said. Sniffing the air, he nodded at her blood-drenched clothes. "Human."

When Lluava did not respond, the huntsman waved her off to a side hall, "Varren is this way."

Could she trust him? He had done nothing to save Enya or the councilmen. Was he allied with Yena? Was he leading her into a trap?

"Lluava?" he questioned.

Lluava could do only one thing: trust her instinct. She followed Apex. There was a moment when she was unsure where they were headed; then she recognized the roundabout path to Tartarus. As they neared the dungeon's opening, they saw others in front of them approaching the same destination. Talos, Byron, and Themis stood there with several of the Obsidian Guard.

Hurrying to her friends, she hugged both young men tightly.

"I'm so glad you're here," Lluava whispered into Talos's chest. "How did you know to come to this place?"

"When the attacks began," Talos explained, "the Guard went in search of Varren. Byron and I tried to save any councilmen we could. Themis was the only one we found before the Grand Hall was taken."

Byron added, "They all headed to the Hall, not realizing it was a trap."

"These men saved my life," Themis acknowledged. He seemed genuinely grateful. Then his face darkened, and he turned to Lluava. "Which would not have been necessary had it not been for you. You let these savages inside our walls against my better judgment. You have ruined Elysia. You have destroyed our kingdom!"

Lluava did not know what to say. He was right. This was all her fault. She was the source of all this pain, this sorrow, this death.

"What is done is done," said Talos as he stepped between them. "We must think about the future."

"What future?" muttered Themis, still looking at Lluava darkly.

Lluava, trying to hide behind Talos, asked, "What now?"

Talos said, "Hope that the Guard brings the king here safely, and soon."

"There." Byron pointed.

Varren and Thad were following Regin. Varren was coated with blood, and Thad was barely functioning. When her partner saw Lluava, he asked, "Emily's?" He glanced worriedly at Thad.

"June's," she said in return.

Regin announced quickly, "We need to move to safety. Let's go." The Obsidian Guard headed off into the depths of Tartarus.

Talos turned back. "I must be with Rosalyn."

"I'll help you find her," said Byron. "We can catch up after."

"You know as well as I that we would never discover where the Obsidian Guard hides. Rosalyn and I will have to stay in the castle."

"What about your lives?" questioned Lluava, aghast. Byron, standing right behind her, also waited for the answer.

"We are Theriomorphs. We will be fine. Trust me."

"Then I will stay with you," Byron pronounced.

"No, Byron." Talos clasped his partner's broad shoulder. "You, being human, are not safe here. Go with the Guard. Keep Varren safe, for me."

The two men stared at each other for a long moment, then Byron moved toward the entry to Tartarus, where Varren had stopped.

The king was talking to the head of the Obsidian Guard. "Regin, I cannot abandon Cronus, not when my people need me the most."

"If you die here today," Regin countered, "your people will have no one to lead the rebellion when the time comes. They will rise together for you, but you must be alive for them to do so."

Varren looked at Lluava. She stoically replied, "The capital has fallen. None of us are safe here now."

As the Obsidian Guard slipped into the dungeons, Lluava wondered if she should stay at Cronus herself. She was the cause of this. She was at fault for the deaths of Enya, June, the High Council, and countless others. Shouldn't she be present to see the results of her indiscretion? Shouldn't she pay for the pain she had caused?

Lluava felt Varren touch her. "I need you with me. I cannot do this alone."

Following those in front of them, Varren and Lluava escaped into the underground labyrinth. Regin guided them into the dungeons and paused before the crumbling wall that led into the older section of the underground. He lifted the torch he carried to illuminate the way.

"What is this place?" Varren asked in awe, as they moved through the abandoned tunnels.

"Relics of an ancient city," noted Regin. "And our salvation."

Why was it so surprising that the Shadows had explored this dark place and discovered its secrets? Lluava knew she should have expected as much.

Even with the torchlight, the humans could not possibly have seen the magnificence of the ancient structures. Lluava was thankful that her hyperactive senses enhanced her appreciation. By the expression on Apex's face, he also seemed overwhelmed.

Behind them, the sound of stalactites dropping onto the floor reverberated through the tunnel. Someone had triggered one of the booby traps. They were being followed.

Several of the Obsidian Guard positioned themselves at the back of the group and prepared to attack the intruder. As Lluava continued, she saw the figure emerge into sight. It was Master Hon.

As the Guard moved to attack, Lluava shouted, "Wait! He's mine."

"Don't, Lluava," Varren implored as the other Shadows formed a human shield around him. Lluava did not care. Of all the Theriomorphs who had overrun the castle, Hon was not the first on her list to kill; yet he represented all those she hated, including Ammit, Thoth, Maruny, and of course Yena.

As Lluava approached the leader of the Warrior Caste, both she and Hon shifted into their dual forms. Apex kept the Guard from interrupting this ceremonial battle as Lluava and Hon attacked each other.

The rhino drove its horns toward Lluava like a double-tipped lance. Lluava quickly sprang to the side and ran up the curving tunnel's wall just far enough to spring off and land on the raging beast's back. She dug her claws into the rhino's thick hide, a task in and of itself.

Hon stopped abruptly, and Lluava flew forward, tumbling to the ground. She heard Varren's shouts of protest along with the rhino's snorts and grumbles. Above them, humans were being slaughtered. Beyond Cronus, a secondary enemy was afoot. All around her, an intangible presence was taking form: war. Lluava finally understood. She herself was War Incarnate.

Hon charged again. She watched as the horns drove forward, looming out of the tunnel's black depths. Then, at last, Lluava willed her inner darkness to take control. What color there was in the gloom dissipated, giving way to the blue-green tint. She felt herself lose control of her extremities, yet she still sensed them as she stood upright.

For the first time, she did not black out. Instead, a strange clarity of mind took hold. Suddenly, she knew exactly what to do to kill the rhino. Her body, as if with a mind of its own, moved in a pattern preset by some outside source. Yet Lluava remained calm. The fear of pain and death had left her. She was who she was always meant to be.

Lluava felt herself twist and veer, claw and bite, all the time knowing what she was about to do and when. Strangely, Lluava anticipated the rhino's actions several movements before it made them. She even knew the exact moment when the animal would take its last breath. And when he took it, Lluava's body was her own again.

Releasing the corpse, Lluava watched as Hon shifted back into his human form. Her anger was temporarily suppressed, and she felt at peace. Those about her gave her looks of respect, none more so than Apex. A moment later, they resumed their careful progression.

Soon the group encountered a subterranean bridge that spanned an enormous chasm. The bridge was so narrow they could only cross it single file. Regin led the way, with several Guards before and behind Varren, followed by Themis and Byron.

Lluava's ears perked up at a sound. Turning, she saw Apex already looking behind them. The Theriomorphs still followed.

"Regin, we are not alone," Lluava called as she held the Claws at the ready.

In front of her, Apex pulled out the Fangs. He took a position facing their followers. As she followed the huntsman, he growled, "Go with your king."

"Apex—" Lluava protested, but the huntsman replied, "I'll keep them at bay long enough for you to escape."

"We don't know how many there are. Don't be suicidal. Come with me."

"No time. I'll hold them off." A large number of Theriomorphs were now in sight, and more were coming. Apex barked, "Go! I'll be right behind you."

Then, clanging Ullr's Fangs together, Apex charged the Theriomorphs. Lluava ran toward the bridge. The rest of their group were at least halfway across. She increased her pace. The harrowing trek was made worse by the fact that the chasm seemed bottomless; her stomach churned uncomfortably. As she reached the far side, Lluava turned to see a pair of Theriomorphs running across the bridge in dual forms of a raccoon and a fox.

"Where's Apex?" questioned Varren.

Across the chasm, a glow radiated from the far opening. A torch of some kind? Lluava could see the giant silhouette of the Yorrick wolverine fending off a number of animals. An Obsidian Guard knocked the raccoon and the fox off the bridge with throwing stars, but still more Theriomorphs had slipped past Apex.

"Apex!" Lluava shouted. "Hurry!"

One of the stalactites fell, narrowly missing the bridge. She should go to him, help him before he was harmed!

More throwing stars whizzed past. Animals plummeted into the depths of the chasm. Apex shouted, "Lluava!" His cry transformed into a magnificent roar, overpowering all other senses.

The floors and walls in the tunnel and throughout the cavern vibrated with the noise. The ceiling began to fall. Lluava lurched toward the slender bridge, but Varren pulled her into a protective embrace, shielding her, as huge stalactites demolished the bridge. Other large stone fragments fell around them, and dust and debris blew out the torches. Darkness consumed Lluava and Varren as they were buried in a tomb of stone.

***

Muffled sounds, along with the lessening of pressure. Voices in distress; shifting stone. Her body was clamped in place as though in a vise; she was wrapped in some strange, corrupt evolution beyond pain. Then, suddenly, she was free. Free from the pressure, but not from the pain.

They had been calling her name: "Lluava! Lluava Kargen!" As soon as she was moved away from the rocky prison, the voices began shouting for the other victim.

"King Varren! Call out if you can hear!"

Nestled in veiled darkness, consciousness wavering along with the urge to live, fragments of garbled speech registered. "There's so much blood. Is it hers?" "She's slipping. Don't let her slip away." "Where is the king?"

Then the sounds of grating rocks and panting breath blended into a white noise that echoed in Lluava's mind until the darkness consumed her.

Epilogue

Encircled by torchlight, burly men wrapped in furs quickly responded to the one seated on a rough-hewn throne of gnarled alder. In the gloom of night, the helmetless man's dark auburn hair and beard had taken on the hue of blackening blood. The bite of frozen gales and the sting of sea salt had etched deep lines in his craggy face, but his eyes instilled fear. Cold and dead as lead now, in anger they blazed with a fire and intensity that could sear one's soul.

Two heavily cloaked guards shoved a badly beaten man to the ground in front of the leader. The victim coughed and spat up blood as he struggled to his feet.

"Strip him of his cloak."

The guards peeled the wolf-headed furs from the prisoner's shoulders. Although of normal stature, the man was far smaller than his captors and seemed to shrink even more without the bulky pelts. He shivered in the chill air.

Torchlight caught the white flashes of hair above the man's ears. His beard had grown ragged without the attentions of a blade; his strength had been sapped without food. Yet he stood proudly defiant in front of his accuser.

The seated man stroked a snarling head on his own wolfskin cloak. "You are no longer worthy to wear the Garb. You do not have a drop of our blood in your veins. The disgrace you have brought upon us has confirmed my suspicions. You are tainted by your affinity with those beasts. Your authority is hereby revoked."

No one contested the decision; the fate of the prisoner was understood. Words were irrelevant.

The man on the alder throne signaled the guards to remove the accused from his presence before summoning another figure, one far older and far more fearful than the one being marched away. Approaching submissively, the soothsayer knelt and pointed to the moonless sky. Both men gazed at the peculiar pattern of the planets.

The ancient seer murmured, "The omens favor us. Their fortress has indeed grown silent."

Waved off, the elder hobbled out of sight as quickly as possible.

A red-bearded man, who held the respect of all but the one seated, emerged from the shadows and strode up to the throne. Not waiting to be recognized, he spoke bluntly. "Th' boy's pets be many."

The seated figure rubbed the finger whose knuckle he had bitten off in his youth. The nub was cold to the touch. "If Mandrun thinks his monsters frighten us, he is wrong. We have *monsters* of our own."

His voice was as cold as a shard of ice.

"Release them."

APPENDICES

APPENDIX I

Diagram of the Theriomorph Pantheon

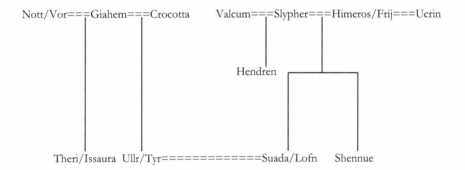

APPENDIX II

The Theriomorph Pantheon

Name	Sex	Divine Realm	Dual Form
Giahem	♂	King/ Husbands/ Fathers/ Heavens/ Males/ Sky	Gold Eagle
Crocotta	♀	Queen/Wives/Mothers/Prophecy/Mating Rights	Silver Hyena
Ullr/Tyr	♂	Young Men/ Inception of War/ Sun/ Courage	Bronze Wolverine
Nott/Vor	♀	Night/ Sleep/ Dreams/ Death/ Underworld	Black Raven
Theri/Issaura	♀	Young Women/ Cessation of War/ Moon/ Wisdom	White Tigress
Ucrin	♂	Ocean/ Water/ Wind	Blue Whale
Valcum	♂	Fire/ Volcanos/ Blacksmiths	Orange Orangutan
Slypher	♀	Earth/ Seasons/ Song/ Dance	Pink Parakeet
Frij/Himeros	♂♀	Love/ Beauty/ Hermaphrodites	Purple Peacock
Hendren	♂	Knowledge/ Virtue/ Health	Scarlet Panda
Suada/Lofn	♀	Lust/ Seduction/ Desire	Emerald Anaconda
Shennue	♂	Mischief/ Mayhem / Illusions	Black Jackal

APPENDIX III

Pronunciation Guide

Acrian	ACK-re-an
Albidum	AL-bee-dumb
Alcazar	AL-ca-czar
Alcove	AL-cove
Ammit	AH mit
Apex	A-pecks
Berserker	bur-ZERK-er
Borren	BOAR-en
Cronus	CROW-nus
Crocotta	crow COT ta
Domar	dough-MAR
Durog	DURE-og
Einherjar	ine-HAIR-ree-har
Endun	EN-dun
Elysia	ee-LAY-szuh
Fárbauti	far-BOUT-ee
Giahem	GUY-a-hem
Hyrax	HI-racks
Idun	EE-dun
Illia	ILL-ya
Incarn	IN-carn
Issaura	i-SAR-a
Ivar	EYE-var
Kani	CON-ee
Kargen	CARG-en
Karmasana	CAR-ma-SAW-naw
Kentril	KEN-trill
Leucrocotta	LEW-crow-COT-ta
Lluava	you-AA-va
Maruny	MAR-ou-nee
Mandrun	MAN-drun
Merek	MARE-ek

Mictla	MICKT-la
Nemorosus	NE-mo'ro-sus
Niflhel	NEEF-flell
Ojewa	OH-jay-wa
Okeanos	oak-EE-a-nos
Okran	O kran
Palal	PAL-al
Pardus	PAR-dus
Phin	FIN
Pra'un	PRAY-um
Regin	REEG-in
Rhadamanthus	RAD-a-MAN-thus
Rosalyn	ROZ-za-lin
Ruire	RUE
Selene	sa-LEAN
Shennu	SHEN-new
Sihia	sih-HIGH-uh
Sköll	SKOHL
Slypher	SLY-fer
Surtur	SUR-tur
Sweyn	SWAIN
Talos	TAL-ows
Themis	THEE-miss
Theri	TH'AIR-ee (like Carrie)
Therial	TH'AIR-ee-al
Theriomorph	TH'AIR-ee-OH-morph
Thoth	THAWTH
Thowcelemine	TH'OW-cell-e-mean
Tomius	TOE-my-us
Tucala	wo-CAL-a
Ullr	OU-yer
Valcum	VAL-come
Vidrick	VEE-drick
Vjeran	VEE'YAIR-en
Virisinu	VERE-i-SIN-ew
Vissa	VEE-sa
Yamir	YA-mear
Yena	YEN-ah
Yorrick	YOUR-ick

APPENDIX IV
Elysian Military Ranks

Terra Divisions
>   Private
>   Corporal
>   Sergeant
>   Warrant Officer
>   Lieutenant
>   Captain
>   Major
>   Colonel
>   General
>   Chief General
>   Master Chief (General)
>   Grand Master Chief (General)

Aerial Divisions
>   Private
>   Airman
>   Sergeant
>   Lieutenant
>   Captain
>   Major
>   Colonel
>   General
>   Chief General
>   Master Chief (General)
>   Grand Master Chief (General)

Marine Divisions
>   Private
>   Seaman
>   Petty Officer
>   Warrant Officer
>   Ensign
>   Lieutenant
>   Commander
>   Captain
>   Admiral
>   Chief Admiral
>   Master Chief (Admiral)
>   Grand Master Chief (Admiral)

Lluava's adventures will continue in Tome Four of The Incarn Saga

Giahem's Talons

Tome Four Prologue: Giahem's Talons

Darkness was their ally, like a vigilant brother always watching, always protecting. In the shadows, they lurked as silently as the ghosts they helped to create. Even when the thin eye of the moon was swallowed by the massing clouds, they could see as clearly as the giant night cats that lurked in these mountains. A decision was to be made, and soon.

At last, the one for whom they waited manifested out of the blackness. After a silent greeting, he observed the cargo in the middle of the clearing.

A low moan emerged. Too early, they all knew.

Another moan accompanied a few feeble movements.

One of the black-clad figures, taller than the rest, approached. A long needle was withdrawn from a hidden pouch; flesh was pierced in a move as quick as a viper's strike. The bound and blindfolded captive immediately went limp. Stepping back, the tall figure avoided the oozing liquid from the captive's reopened wounds. Blood might be smelled miles away. Caution must be taken.

A soft glimmer of starlight sifted through the ragged clouds as the sack covering the captive's head was removed. Long auburn locks streaked with blond tumbled over a face not yet marred by an abundance of years. Bare-chested, the prisoner's skin, which should have been pale, was deeply tinted and freckled by sunlight. His horsehide pants identified his origin.

"You were ordered to kill any that crossed the borders." This was the voice of authority.

"He is different from the rest," responded the tall one.

"He is human like the others. Same build, same look, same garb. Kill him, or I will." A glint of silver could be seen in the speaker's hands.

"No! Wait! He possessed something. Something you will want to see."

An item was brought forth, a bow that appeared to be made of gold but was far too light to be of that metal. Even the bowstring appeared to be formed from threads of spun gold. More extraordinary, the bow produced and disseminated warmth when touched. The weapon was unsurpassed in its strange, unnatural beauty. Each part of its workmanship vied for the observer's attention.

The clouds parted, and the silvery light above met the golden glow below. In the illuminating moonlight, the leader raised the bow so all could see the strange runes incised upon the weapon's handle.

The gleam of the runes was reflected in the black depths of their leader's eyes.

"Do you understand the meaning of this?" he demanded.

The others remained silent.

"The end of our age has arrived."

NOTE FROM THE AUTHOR

As an author, writing the story is just the beginning. Next come revising, editing, formatting, proofreading, and marketing. Surprisingly, marketing requires a huge amount of time. If you enjoy an author's work and want her or him to publish more in a shorter time span, you can help! Spread the word on social media and by word of mouth. Post reviews on Amazon, Goodreads and other websites. Believe me, I would much rather write a new book than spend time promoting the one I have just finished. So go ahead—pin, tweet, post, review, and like.

Thank you!

ABOUT THE AUTHOR

Katharine Wibell's lifelong interest in mythology includes epic poetry like the Odyssey, Ramayana, Beowulf, and the Nibelungenlied. In addition, she is interested in all things animal whether training dogs, apprenticing at a children's zoo, or caring for injured animals as a licensed wildlife rehabilitator. After receiving degrees from Mercer University in both art and psychology with an emphasis in animal behavior, Wibell moved to New Orleans with her dog, Alli, to kick start her career as an artist and a writer. Her first literary works blend her knowledge of the animal world with the world of high fantasy.

LEARN MORE

WWW.KATHARINEWIBELLBOOKS.COM

Made in the USA
Monee, IL
17 June 2021

71587480R00185